Until Tomorrow, Comrades

Also available from International Publishers
in its series of fictional works by
Manuel Tiago

Five Days, Five Nights
"devoid of the stilted political speechifying sometimes found
in political fiction, the novella manages to capture
the complexities, loneliness, and bravery of ordinary people"
(Monthly Review)

The Six-Pointed Star
"a breathtaking novel of heartbreaking vignettes"
(Culture Matters)

The 3rd Floor
"exciting and suspenseful...I could not put the
book down as I read the four stories, each in one
sitting. Each of them is a page-turner."
(People's World)

Border Crossings
"A work of unique concept and clever prose, richly translated.
It's both engaging and eye-opening."
(People's World)

The Slackers
"Gordon's faith and perspicacity in translating Cunhal/Tiago's sizable
obra into an eight-volume set of tales of war, peace, political struggle
and prison in plainspoken, absorbable English is a godsend for
armchair travelers—and great reading."
(People's World)

Eulalia's House
this is a must read for our times! *Eulalia's House* is a captivating
retelling of events that immerses the reader into the lives and
passions of partisan comrades waging an unconventional
struggle against the forces of fascism.
(Dan Wright)

A Line in the Sand
Tiago's powerful novella is both a work of history and a learning
experience for all who want to fight neofascism in America today.
(Norman Markowitz)

Until Tomorrow, Comrades

(Até amanhã, camaradas)

by Manuel Tiago

(Álvaro Cunhal)

Translated and with a Forword by

Eric A. Gordon

INTERNATIONAL PUBLISHERS, New York

Copyright © Editorial «Avante!», 2023

First English language edition, 2023 by International Publisher's Co., Inc. / NY by special arrangement with Editorial Avante!

Translated from the Portuguese by Eric Gordon © 2023

CIP data available from Library of Congress

ISBN 10: 0-7178-0938-2   ISBN-13 978-07178-0938-7
Typeset by Amnet Systems, Chennai, India

Publication of this book
is dedicated to the memory of our parents
Victor and Naomi Gordon.

The novel takes place in the early 1940s when, as the story reveals, the Portuguese people are suffering widespread hunger because the fascist régime is shipping so much of the country's food production to Nazi Germany to feed the Axis war machine.

In 1944, Victor, a young attorney with two children and another on the way, was drafted into the U.S. Army and sent to the European front of World War II. He was shivering in a trench at the Battle of the Bulge, his comrades being killed beside him, when Eric, the translator of this book, was born in early 1945. After serving in the Counter Intelligence Corps in Germany hunting down Nazis in the postwar months, it took until early 1946 before Victor was discharged and found his way back home to New Haven. Naomi was eagerly waiting for him, having bravely and fretfully held the family together on the home front. The youngest of their children came in 1952.

We surviving children of Victor and Naomi, along with our late sister Nina, would not be the people we are and became without their immeasurable sacrifices on behalf of democracy, freedom and simple human decency.

Frederic A. Gordon

Eric A. Gordon

Ilse Gordon

A Note About the Author

The typewritten original of the novel *Until Tomorrow, Comrades* was found, together with other original writings, in an archive formed over the years at the whimsy of incidents and accidents in the hectic life of people such as those types exemplified in the novel.

The author is unknown. The only copy that was found has no signature, except that on a small sheet of paper attached to it by paperclip, the hurriedly scrawled name of Manuel Tiago can be read, surely a pseudonym.

Various people were consulted who could have provided leads to an eventual identification, but without success. The author thus merits the label "a man without a name," just like the characters in his novel.[1]

1. Translator's note: On December 14, 1994, 20 years after the first publication of *Até amanhã, camaradas*, at the launch of the book *A estrela de seis pontas* (The Six-Pointed Star), Álvaro Cunhal admitted to his literary pseudonym Manuel Tiago, for reasons he publicly explained at the time. *The Six-Pointed Star*, a novel about the Portuguese fascist prison system, is available in English translation from International Publishers, along with all the others of Tiago's fictional works.

Table of Contents

Foreword

Eric A. Gordon

From the reader's perspective, now that *Until Tomorrow, Comrades* is appearing as the last entry in the International Publishers commitment to issue all of Manuel Tiago's fiction in English, it soon will hardly matter in which order these volumes came out. To me, as the translator of all of them, it made a huge difference, however.

This novel, by far the longest and most complex of the series, was written during the 1950s, thus being the earliest of Álvaro Cunhal's fictional efforts, alongside the novella *Five Days, Five Nights*, which he also wrote in a high-security prison. Cunhal left the novella behind when he escaped Peniche Fortress on January 3, 1960, but took with him the precious manuscript of *Até amanhã, camaradas*.

It's a kind of literary miracle. The manuscript must have run over a thousand pages (the printed Portuguese text has 539). Considering the precariousness of the underground existence and exile which would be the author's lot for the next 14 years, until Portugal's armed forces overthrew the almost 50-year-long fascist regime, this novel represents the last thing he wanted, and might have been able, to say to the world. Fortunately it, and its author, survived.

The story closely mirrors actual events and movements that the Communist Party promulgated in the early 1940s. Beginning in 1942, regional and general strikes with thousands of workers in the fields and the factories paralyzed the Portuguese economy, both in the capital and in the more rural areas, protesting hunger, unlivable wages, and the lack of foodstuffs (much of Portugal's produce was being sent to Nazi Germany). This bold strategy inevitably exposed numerous comrades, who suffered imprisonment, poor health and death, a risk leaders naturally assumed. But how else could the Portuguese people assert their demands and be heard?

In the novel, the general strike is specifically set for Monday, May 18. The only wartime year in which May 18 fell on a Monday was 1942, but we cannot take that too literally. In the first place, we are really not told exactly where, in what part of Portugal, these events took place, and it is clear that the succession of events telescoped into a few months for the author's literary purposes reflected a much longer time period, up to and including the biggest and most successful walkout in May of 1944.

These movements firmly established the PCP in the popular mind as the most dedicated force opposing the regime. Even while acknowledging that resistance could be severely punished, and individuals would suffer dearly, thousands of people continued to express their discontent by marching on May Day and participating in other mass actions to demonstrate their fearlessness.

This novel is not strictly autobiographical, though clearly it reflects Cunhal's lived experience. Much is made in the story of the importance of disseminating the underground press, and we know that Cunhal was in fact the editor-in-chief of the Party's newspaper *Avante!* during the years 1943-47, and again in 1948-49.

When the author returned to a free Portugal in 1974, the prison guards returned the abandoned manuscript to him of the novella that had been retained in his prisoner file. Thus it occurred that both these books were published soon after Portugal's liberation, under the pseudonym of Manuel Tiago. Clearly Cunhal, and the Portuguese Communist Party, intended these two fictional works to launch a new era in Portuguese literature and to ensure that the lessons learned in the decades-long struggle for democracy would be recorded, hopefully forever, in these fictional forms. They must have been concerned, too, that possibly democracy would not last, so immediate publication might be the only guarantee of these works' release to the world.

As the African-American novelist Walter Mosley has said, "If you want to be in the history of the culture, then you have to exist in the fiction. If you don't exist in the literature, your people don't exist."

Five Days, Five Nights was the first International Publishers issue, prompted by Edições Avante!, the Portuguese publisher, which felt that, given its continued popularity in Portugal and the fact that it had been turned into a feature film, that short work would be the most appropriate title to start interesting an English-reading public in the author's work.

I left *Until Tomorrow, Comrades* for last for two reasons: As a sort of grand finale to the project, and because, knowing how seminal a work this had become not just in Portuguese literature but in the entire cultural understanding of the fascist period, I wanted to become as practiced and fluent with Tiago's language and thought as I possibly could with the intervening eight other titles (seven in English because we combined one other novella into the collection *The 3rd Floor*).

Until Tomorrow, Comrades has enjoyed at least 12 printings, the most of any of his fictional works, I believe, testament to its continued popularity amongst the reading public in Portugal, for a total of more than 50,000 copies. Regarded as a literary classic, it has already seen publication in several other languages, namely, Russian, German, Bulgarian, Turkish, Spanish and French. And now English.

Not surprisingly, *Until Tomorrow, Comrades* was made into a six-episode miniseries in 2013, anchoring its significance as an Urtext of the long contested Portuguese democracy. Popular as that series was, nothing can replace the intense, tight focus on these few activists' lives that we find in the original print version. The terms "sprawling" and "granular" for a literary work were coined for exactly a book like this.

In that sense, it can be compared to works by such writers as Anna Seghers, Bertolt Brecht, Halldór Laxness, Henrik Ibsen, Jack London, Ernest Hemingway, George Orwell, Sinclair Lewis, Victor Serge, Maxim Gorky, Mikhail Alexandrovich Sholokhov and others who bring us an intimate portrait of ordinary people in the course of necessary rebellion against illegitimate authority, written, as Óscar Lopes says, in the "understated tones of everyday heroism," and with lessons that echo through time and across continents. Lopes references the French author Émile Zola in his "Reflections," and I feel it's fair to say that if there were any one author and novel that most served as Cunhal's inspiration, it would have been Zola's *Germinal*, which was also an in-depth portrait of a society in the throes of a massive strike—by miners in that story.

Written in the 1950s, about a time in the mid-1940s, this is not quite the book that might be written today. Readers will take note of the casually unexamined auxiliary roles given to women, for one thing—although Lopes reminds us how central the character of Maria is to almost all the others in the novel. The author's attention to his characters' complexions may also be a hallmark of the time: They are described as "white" or "dark"—in one case a young man has "Arabic" features, etc. Readers may also notice that the whole colonial question—which ultimately brought down the régime—is barely if ever broached or hinted at, not even the military draft or the enormous expense to the nation of keeping such a far-flung empire subdued under the metropolitan thumb. Readers will have to accept that these issues did not loom large on the historical agenda at the time, just as the colonial empires of France and Britain seldom surface in the works of those nations' most important writers, nor were they central to the platforms of the Communist and left parties there.

May I indulge the reader with one more personal observation? The latter half of my work on this translation took place in the wake of the Taliban victory in Afghanistan. The Afghani armed forces melted overnight after the president and other high officials fled the country in August 2021. Western aid, self-interested and misguided as it was from the outset, could not save Afghanistan from religious fanaticism and intolerance (which, to remind you, the U.S. bankrolled and armed in the earlier fight of the mujaheddin against the first flowering of socialism in the country in the late 1970s), much less secure permanent democratic norms for the country. Whatever becomes of Afghanistan, it seems destined, from my standpoint today, to suffer years of poverty, terror, forced ignorance, poor health and repression. The resistance will obviously take on its own contours and not exactly resemble that in any other time or place. But the passion for freedom, the thirst for knowledge, the yearning for equality—all that the resistance aspires to—can only be won by the same kind of patient, dedicated, self-sacrificing underground organizing, probably over the course of decades, that is illustrated so vividly in this book. Perhaps in Afghanistan it will be led by women.

Knowing that the struggle for a more just world is assuredly going to be a factor at least somewhere on the map for a long time into the future, *Until Tomorrow, Comrades* assumes a significance that transcends Portugal and its time, serving not as a blueprint but as a beacon to those who struggle everywhere.

Again I owe a profound debt of thanks to my "usual suspects," those dear friends, colleagues and comrades who read the manuscript of this book and offered their honest, helpful suggestions: Bill Gregory, Francisco Melo, Gary Bono, Janice Rothstein, John Mueter, José Oliveira and Rich Eisbrouch. And finally, once again, in this last entry in the Manuel Tiago series, I acknowledge the love for the language that my first Portuguese teacher, Malcolm Batchelor, instilled in me.

One technical comment: The reader will notice that occasionally Tiago leaps into the "historical present," that is, the use of the present tense in scenes that clearly took place in the past. This is a legitimate and widely used strategy for putting the reader right there in the room, and can be highly effective when adroitly used. My observation is that Tiago adopts this device only intermittently and inconsistently, which can be jarring. Another translator might have chosen to standardize the author's tenses, placing them all in the past—or perhaps employing the historical present even more generously than Tiago—and the reader would never have known the difference. But advisedly or not, I have left them as Tiago wrote them, hoping that at least some of his intentions come through.

Reflections on Reading *Until Tomorrow, Comrades* by Óscar Lopes

The first reflection that occurs to us, which in part leads to all those that follow, is this: How can we comprehend that a novel so widely read, and so important in many ways, has been so critically ignored? Certainly, critics and essayists who prior to the 25th of April 1974 Revolution had dedicated themselves to literature, even before that event had started ranging into rapidly expanding areas which provoked growing public interest, owing to a certain decompression of censorship and to the salience of great problems that up to then had been suppressed, relating to the economy, pedagogy, health care, etc. Also, clearly, many cultural workers were attracted to the means and arts of mass audiovisual communication, such as radio, film, television, theater, music and performances integrating several art forms. On the other hand, criticism and literary writing became a kind of second career for university scholars, an exercise in applying theories and methods of narrative or poetical textual analysis whose terminology rapidly became specialized, distancing itself from what a work can say to thousands of readers, above all readers of classes on the rise.

But more than anything else, familiarity with *Until Tomorrow, Comrades* was naturally suppressed by those who needed to forget (and needed to make others forget) all that which today's democracy owed, and still owes, in daily vigilance and struggle, to the main organized force in the resistance against fascism. Excuses are legion for those ill-inclined to examine the material this novel effectively brings to the discussion of the most obvious problems in the theory of literary text: How does the *social* subject of this text take shape? What is the *socially* subliminal movement that prompts its narrative milestones? How do its multiple meanings intersect and how are they organized? What is the subtextual interplay of voices that gives form (and what form?) to the novel? And so on.

We will attempt to answer these questions below in simple terms. But obviously it is safer and more inviting to discuss these things concerning texts produced in the most evolved capitalist societies, or concerning works inspired in a more transparent way by those texts, and addressed to the select Portuguese public that is already waiting for them. More difficult is to examine an experience that up to now has not had much presence in the novel form, described in its complex specificity—the long, dense experience of the Portuguese clandestine resistance—and to bring that experience to a public that is in the process of forming and becoming one. That public is rising to, among other things, the dignity of agency as a societal subject that already openly recognizes itself in literary fiction as though it were of its own authorship.

I don't know, for example, if one very important thing has been noted. This novel was probably conceived and the writing begun in the 1950s or '60s[1] perhaps as involuntary relief from the active social combat that gave rise to a global conceptualization and an evocation, in lively and typical imagery, of an exemplary episode taking place during World War II. The novel banishes the Zola-like emphasis on—and all the vague allegory of—hope for society, all the hidden games of allusions that, owing to internalized repression (and somewhat to the little pleasures in such games), hinder parts of the Neo-Realism of the 1940s and even later. A reader might not like all of it, or might, for example, advise a weeding out of brief explanatory lessons, or of certain traces of judgment—slender trunks, weak covers, right away on the first page—or of given moments of hesitant speech and even (but I happen to like this) the occasional, insidious sadness or fatigue that is projected onto the scene, but which a firm, infectious energy soon rescues from defeat in the understated tones of everyday heroism.

The general plotting of the action unfolds with great clarity. There's a flood, a high tide, an ebb, and a regrouping preceding the next tide. In a region with some important factory units, with various dispersed workshops, surrounded by a largely proletarianized rural zone, we are witness to the clandestine preparations for a general strike and a demonstration, to the progression of the big movement (with the ready support by party militants who face both unknown factors and weaknesses), to the repression and finally to the reconstitution of the broken organisms, achieved in great part by men and

---

1. Scholars have noted that Álvaro Cunhal wrote this book during his long imprisonment in the 1950s and took it with him when he escaped on January 3, 1960.

women, almost all of them young, who along the way stood out in the struggle. At issue are demands for salary increases, resistance to the arbitrary and destructive decimation of the smallest pine forests, and the spread of new tactics concerning rural labor markets and wage committees.

The extreme tension of work, privation, and rigid, defensive discipline to which those in the underground subject themselves intensifies feelings and problems, and defines the drama and the characters with incisive, palpable lines. There is an enormous need for emotional compensation which runs through the internal and external contacts of the clandestine group and neatly laces together the author's seven or eight principal human profiles through what they do, what they say and, above all, through what little by little transpires in their surprising little reactions.

It's impossible to sum up the extremely delicate web of feelings that the couple Vaz and Rosa weave, whose relationship would not appear to have an intimate history, immersed in their political work as they are, in cautiousness and conspiratorial hardships, and even in delicious little intrigues involving the collective townsfolk where they have installed themselves. One of the characters in the novel, Maria, is an intricate tangle of minor and major emotional dramas, with her aged father, an ex-anarchist and now an invalid, from whom she separates, by mutual accord, to dedicate herself to the struggle. And with (another instance of Maria's dramas) Afonso, who dives into clandestinity for her sake, a man of undefined vocation who, for not having found her in the party "machine," becomes demoralized and negligent, and later partially recovers. And with Ramos, almost fifty, healthy and exuberant, in some ways perfectly mature (and in other ways not), with bursts of the most unexpected humor and pluck. With António, the former student whose companion she was directed to become; and with Paulo, a militant who grows in our eyes and about whom, especially, we sense much more than what is explicitly said.

To these figures we add Gaspar, a jack-of-all-trades who wants to help out with everything and for that very reason makes a mess of so much. And Marques, a militant with so much proven experience, but who by the time we meet him is awkward and inconsistent, falling into error after error as he refuses to recognize his initial mistake. Various other figures are simultaneously "types" and "characters," to use the debatable opposites deriving from the classic manuals of fiction analysis. These are "types" to the extent that they highlight a political reflection about forms of behavior; and they are "characters" insofar as the novelist, in the end, judges no one in his role as the writer—and one could say that he shows his personal preference toward no one beyond the borders that separate political and moral practice from the other special practice which is that of intimate understanding filled with joy before the fact of human possibility, even just as people are, and even just as they couldn't help but be.

In the comportment of this group of underground militants we do not directly take stock of the psychological effects of the personal risks to which they expose themselves, risks which later will materialize in brutal acts, sadistic torture and cold-blooded assassination by the political police. What needs to be done is so exhaustive, and the sacrifices so extreme, that other things happen (perhaps contrary to expectation) with the perceptive acuity of someone who has little time and few opportunities to enjoy the simple things, the beautiful, fleeting little things most people ignore. Thus, the contacts with the outside world this highly organized central group makes abound in vivacity and the picturesque; and the precarious paupers' life they share together in various secret support houses possesses an exquisite refinement unimaginable to anyone who does not know such an experience.

Right in the first chapter, and certainly meant to demonstrate a typical pattern, we accompany Vaz through one day of moving about. He has eight encounters or meetings, involving many dozens of kilometers negotiated either on foot or by bicycle, some of it in the rain, with inadequate and infrequent meals, insufficient sleep—all of which is captured, to use a term in cinematography, by picturesquely "traveling" or "tracking" him treading over a great variety of environments (macadam and tar streets, local roads and woods, wading across a flooded stream). We also partake of many physical sensations of a tactile, muscular or olfactory nature, for example. And see him in various situations and with various people, in emotionally fluctuating moods that include anxiety, tenderness, and even what could be called a game or puzzle, giving an indication of the sense of humor of a man of the people.

Among the leaps of fantasy (or the need for dreaming which the author invokes at a given moment), there's one that comes up during a meager meal improvised for a meeting that Maria, almost without provisions, sees sadly going on longer than planned, but which Ramos compensates for with his expansive, contagious humor about the devices and contrivances required for fine dining, all accomplished using the most humble of means.

Elsewhere, many times, even the most sophisticated readers of the novel will find their mouths watering as they are, without asking for it, invited to share the appetite, or ravenousness, of healthy, enervated people who eat irregularly, when they can, and because of that can profoundly savor the simple satisfaction of boiled potatoes, a frugal meal of hot kale soup with a little salt pork, or calmly munching on some rosehips. The reader is constantly participating in such otherwise unremarkable intimate scenes, whether it's in a remote barn where a dozen day workers are discussing new concepts about day wages, or in the comfortable house of a sympathetic lawyer, where not even António, the former student and now underground activist and housemate of Maria unconsciously readapting to the social milieu of his own background, notices his friend's embarrassment amidst the polite bourgeois rituals of the salon and the dining table.

In sum, the rare opportunities to open up to the inexhaustibility of the life that surrounds them, and of their own personal lives, does not diminish the profound need for a plentiful life. To the contrary, they lend the greatest possible meaning to the apparently most insignificant experiences, as it appears to happen with the last vigil for a man condemned to death. In the end, we are all condemned to death, and each day may be our last; but only in the tensest, most extreme situations are we conscious of this, and can we take something positive from it.

To achieve such an outcome in a novel like this one, a keen understanding of how people really are is required, to gain awareness of that which such situations reveal even without the participants noticing, to dignify all of this with the proper consciousness, and to fully reconcile with that plentiful life that, at its core, we all have at our personal disposition. It's just that that disposition is generally small, unless we're speaking of someone who is entirely given over to the certainty that the Human Being is yet being born.

This explains the intense emotionality of the whole book. Not all readers will be able to appreciate its verbal dimension, such as all the diminutives and fond words such as "beloved" and "dear friend," because whoever has not had the experience of clandestine fraternity will spontaneously interpret such expressions in the context of a completely different kind of commercial writing. Yet this incomparable sweetness of tone in the mouths of women immersed in "freedom's underground,"[2] and this deep understanding of all the

---

2. The author alludes to *Os Subterrâneos da Liberdade* (*The Bowels of Liberty*), a 1954 trilogy by Jorge Amado focusing on the struggle of the Brazilian Communist Party during the dictatorship of Getúlio Vargas (known as the "New State" or *Estado Novo*, the same term for the Portuguese régime), which circulated surreptitiously in Portugal. The three novels are *Bitter Times, Agony of Night* and *Light at the End of the Tunnel*.

human weaknesses, can be counted as among the most rewarding experiences of those who had contact with the "illegals" of the fascist era. They—or the best among them—knew all the tricks and all the tics of weakness or simple fear, all the more because there is nothing less imaginative than reactions out of fear or out of the loss of character. Only this profound understanding—never to be separated from the most intransigent, unbending firmness as to the essential—can explain the "miracle" of that "machine" that the political police from time to time pronounced dismantled and dead, but that immediately rose up again out of the ashes like the mythological phoenix.

But this emotionality is not revealed only in dialogue: In certain episodes it is highly condensed for greater communicative effect, for example, in those episodes where children are babbling or running around, or where we see a mother unable to contain her pride in her baby. In one place Paulo saves a young child from a fire—but what touches us most is not the episode itself, but that we sense it in large part as the storyteller's strategy to allow the unexpressed tenderness of someone who protectively clutches that child to his breast to flow out. And there are so many of these earmarks of sympathy, of delicateness and many-sided dramas between men and women, where we find the most subtle and modern equivalents to the famous conflicts of honor and love in the work of classic French tragedian Pierre Corneille. Here they are described and resolved, implicitly but evidently, almost without words, in an ethic with no religious, chivalric or Puritan code, in a highly refined sensibility, or humanity, that is not explained—nor is it necessary—but is communicated.

No hovering sense of irony hangs over the novel, for I don't even feel it exists in repetitions such as the "intelligent eyes" of Marques, a man given to reciting theoretical solutions, a mercurial person who nevertheless was once outstanding and who, after a certain degradation, shows that he is capable of remaking himself in a limited but meaningful way. In any irony there's a pulsing sense of superiority and irresolution in the face of conflict. But this novel places itself at the level of the whole people, at least all the people who in one way or another are socially exploited.

That is where the richness of precise data comes from, which flow from the Dostoyevskian counterpoint of dialogue that speaks of things but indirectly refers to the meaning of things. Here, in sober notes about the locale and the picturesque, we get the ritualistic recipe for baking bread, rationing vouchers, or a detail such as the replacement of a headlight by a stearin candle protected from the wind, on a bicycle with a damaged generator.

Details like these serve no real function in the story (nor in all the intersecting stories). They don't obey the naturalist's demand for authentication, nor for a realistic effect in the context of all the arbitrary circumstances at the margins of the essential matter. They are the actual evidence—always very significant, at times inexplicably so—of that myriad of invisible ties that exist between human beings, and between humans and things. They are evidence that life is inexhaustible. Recapitulating Brazilian novelist João Guimarães Rosa, I would say that the lesson of the book is that to live (To Live, with capital letters) is dangerous. Those who dedicate themselves entirely to bettering it feel this. And they even help us to feel that much exists in the world without a name, waiting for courage. For out of courage, in large part, comes the capacity to understand, to feel deeply, and to do the right thing.

Until Tomorrow, Comrades

Chapter *I*

1

Sudden bursts of wind blew in from the South. With a clatter, a zinc plate coming from who knows where flew from one side of the road, made four grotesque pirouettes and curled up, silent and sad, in the gutter on the other side. Then a downpour swept the road. The men, already drenched by the drizzle that had been falling since dawn, sought shelter next to the slender trunks of the pine trees. Only two young boys were left crushing rocks, laughing at the men fleeing the rain. Cringing under the trees and pressed against them, the men shouted for them to take cover. Seeing themselves observed, the boys laughed some more, and one of them, still breaking up rocks, started sticking his long, gangling neck up high, showing the whites of his eyes and licking up the water running down his face. The other, blinking his eyes, looked at his friend, looked at the men and seemed to be saying, *We're funny, aren't we?*

"Look at those devils," said an old man, trying to wrap himself in a coat so small it seemed like a child's.

The thin little man to whom that was directed shrugged his shoulders. "The weather's not going to change today," he said with a soft, tired voice.

As if to give him confirmation, the wind blew even stronger, the air darkened, the sky reached the ground, the streams of water continued to swell. One by one, the men then left their weak covers. Some walking with determination, others in a quick run, and still others at a natural pace, as if they considered it undignified to be in a rush for such a little thing, they headed toward an isolated house a hundred or so meters away that seemed to be crouching under the rain. It was a tavern, and if not everyone was inclined to drink, at least they would have a roof overhead.

Seeing their friends going away, the two boys threw their sledgehammers to the ground. The one with the long neck flew off like an arrow, striking the puddles of water with his naked feet and waving his arms in big, disjointed gestures, possibly signaling that he was a great swimmer. The other followed, shaking with laughter. They got to the tavern before the others, but the comic, unable to wait there, went out into the rain calling the men with his arms, thereby claiming the privilege of discovering such a magnificent shelter.

They gathered in the small, dark saloon. Piled up at the door, they looked outside, intimating to the barkeeper that they were there only for a moment to protect themselves from the rain. Customers for his business were rare for the barkeeper, who quickly set to washing his already washed glasses, watching the men as if apologizing for the delay in serving them. Whether out of shame for refusing such a clear invitation, or because it seemed they couldn't just stay inside without spending a *tostão*,[1] or by the power of vice, three men with solemn expressions went forward for drinks. Then all the others felt at ease to settle in as they pleased, some sitting around the table, some stepping away from the portal, where the rain hammered away driven by the wind.

"The weather won't change," the thin man repeated.

"It was necessary, it was necessary," said the old man, who had not yet succeeded, and never would, in fitting the tiny coat around his shoulders.

All of those men were more peasants than workers. Some even had their own little plots of land and, since the dry spell had been so long, they felt tempted to forgive the soaking and the loss of an afternoon's work. Silent and drenched, they gazed through the open rectangle of the door onto the curtain of water that almost hid the other side of the road from view, harkening to the copious, deafening sound falling away in the depths of the pine forest, attesting to the weight of the rainstorm. Even the boys kept themselves quiet, and the funny one, with a sad face that would have seemed impossible just minutes before, was trying hard to contain the tremors of cold now turning his limbs purple.

At a moment when the rain was coming down hardest, a shadow rapidly passed across the doorway and, before anyone had seen who it was, the shadow appeared again and a man entered. He was curved forward, shaking his arms and head to jiggle off the water from his coat sleeves and cap. When he had completed his operation, he straightened up and, saying hello to everyone, presented his long,

---

1. The official Portuguese currency was the *escudo*, divided into 100 *centavos*. But people generally thought in terms of a *conto*, equivalent to 1000 *escudos*, and the *tostão* was 10 *centavos*.

angular face, with pale skin and a severe expression, his eyes standing out with their fixed gaze.

One of the boys, noticing the pants tucked into the socks, came to the door, looked out, said something to one of the men, who said to the unknown man, "Put your bike inside. There's plenty of room."

The unknown man appeared not to hear. He wiped his face and neck with a kerchief.

"Can any of you men tell me the way to Vale da Égua?" he asked.

The men looked at one another, some showing a barely disguised smile.

"To where?" a voice from the corner asked.

"Vale da Égua."

There was a brief silence, and again the men looked at one another.

"Nah, that's not around here," said another voice from the table.

"What did he say?"

"Vale da Égua."

He was definitely off-course, the old man with the little jacket informed him. He had been born there and had always lived in that place. He'd never heard of it. He was certainly off-course. The old man spoke and some smiled.

"This isn't the road to V—?" the unknown man asked.

"Yes, it is," one of the men responded. "Vvv...is just ahead. If it wasn't for so much rain, you could see the houses from here."

The stranger went to the door, looked out on the road, took off his cap and twisted it, coming back inside and slapping it on one of his hands, revealing his hair stuck to his head.

"So none of you men knows?"

"The road to where?" the barkeeper asked from the back of the room. He had heard perfectly well, but thought he should call the stranger's attention to the establishment he found himself in.

"Vale da Égua," one of the boys said.

The barkeeper stuck out his lower lip, which could have signaled that he didn't know of such a place as much as his displeasure because the stranger hadn't decided to buy anything.

"All right then, thank you!" said the unknown man. And adjusting his cap, pulling up the collar on his coat, he went to the door, looked at the sky, and headed out once again into the rain.

2

Right away he found the first houses, huddled side by side along the flooded street. Soaked in water, the large village looked deserted. Only in the heart of town did he find a fat man in shirt sleeves sheltered under a tile roof overhang, with his thumbs propped in the arm holes of his vest. In answer to the stranger, the man lightly signaled with his head for him to join him under the overhang. Keeping the same stance and position, he examined the stranger carefully, noting his modest suit now sodden with rain, his well-shaved face, and the leather briefcase hanging on the frame of the bicycle, which was now leaning against a wooden pole.

"Are you going there to sell something?" the man asked.

"No," the stranger replied, "I'm not selling anything," as once again he wiped his face and neck with his kerchief.

The fat man remained silent. Seemingly, he was hesitating to speak. With great interest he observed the kerchief with which the cyclist wiped himself down, then returned his gaze to the leather briefcase, to the drenched suit, to the flooded road and the falling rain.

"You're not from around here."

"No, I'm not." He stomped on the ground vigorously to ward off the chill, and added, "Who would have said yesterday we'd have a day like this?"

"It wasn't difficult," the fat man answered. "It rained all yesterday afternoon and it didn't stop all night."

The bicyclist understood this comment perfectly. The man meant: *If you don't want to say it, then don't tell me what forced you to go out in a storm like this. But don't take me for an idiot.* As he grasped the man's meaning, he thought it a poor decision to take shelter with him there.

"This much rain might ruin the crops."

"It's not going to ruin anything," the fat man answered irritably. "Worse is if it didn't rain. It's clear you don't work in farming. You must be a traveling salesman."

"No, I'm not a salesman," the stranger replied. "I'm freezing just standing here," he added, rubbing his hands and continuing to stamp his feet.

"Going out in this rain is surely not good for your health," the fat man said.

The bicyclist also understood these words correctly: *What you want is to go away and avoid conversation, but I understand you very well.*

"And the road to Vale da Égua? Does it go out from here?"

The fat man, still with his fingers in his vest arm holes, did not budge from his spot. His face seemed unchanging. But in his reddened eyes one could only guess at the profound irritation he felt from his unsatisfied curiosity.

"How should I know where that is?" he exclaimed as if the question itself were ridiculous.

Still stomping his feet on the ground, the stranger stopped rubbing his hands and suddenly turned his head to face the other man. The fat man instinctively took a step backward, as though he expected to be attacked. But the stranger, with slow movements, was already adjusting his socks outside his wet pants, pulling his hat over his head and his jacket collar up to his neck. He grabbed his bicycle and left for the street.

"Good day, then."

"Go with God!" came the irate voice of the fat man under the overhang.

The wind calmed down and the rain let up some, but on the flooded road full of potholes, the bicycle proceeded treacherously. The cyclist remembered what they had told him: *Get off at the station, ask there and then you'll be told.* It wouldn't work for him to take the train, but all the same he should have headed to the station. Thinking it would have to be seen from the road, he decided not to ask anything of anyone until he arrived there.

3

The station stood in front of a muddy lake drenching the square. Like the town itself, it appeared deserted. There was no one in the entrance hall, no one at the baggage counter, no one at the ticket window, no one on the platform. There was no sound of a voice nor of any kind of work, only the *plink-plink* of the rain and the gurgling of an unseen drain. After walking to the end of the platform, the stranger turned back, and suddenly saw an employee with thick denim pants and a woolen coat standing next to the clock and absently peering down the track.

He calmly responded to the question. "Zé Cavalinho should be around somewhere and he'll point it out to you soon. He's from those parts." And looking at the rain he added, "He's a funny guy, Zé Cavalinho."

He retrieved a tin of tobacco from his pocket, helped himself and offered, "Cigarette?"

The stranger wiped his hands and made a cigarette for himself. Meanwhile the railway worker slowly rolled his tobacco, licked the cigarette paper and hunted for a match in his pocket.

"He's a funny guy, Zé Cavalinho," he repeated languidly as he expelled his first puff. The stranger got the clear impression that before learning what he wanted, he'd have to listen to the other as long as the cigarette lasted.

"When he came to work here, no one knew him," he began. "Whatever his name was, or wasn't, we knew he was Zé. After a few days, one of our workers here, that we called Ruço because of his sandy-colored hair, asked him, 'Hey, partner, where are you from?' 'From Vale da Égua,' he answered—Valley of the Mare. Nothing unusual about that. But the guys found it funny—and you know what we did?"

The railwayman took another drag and went on, speaking relaxedly, and distractedly watching the rain, now falling harder, and exhaling smoke as he talked. "We started calling him Zé da Égua. And don't think he was annoyed by it, no, sir. You don't know him? He's a good fellow, but he has this kind of funny way of saying things. One day he told us, 'Listen up, boys! If I'm from "the mare," then I'm a horse, and since I'm a small guy, I'm a *cavalinho*—a little horse.' I can't imitate him or how he said it, and it doesn't matter anyway, but if you were there hearing and seeing him, you would have found it hilarious."

The rail worker took a few more puffs on his cigarette and slowly exhaled, then continued. "So that stuck and from then on he was Zé Cavalinho. We all called him that, even the boss, and he wasn't upset by it at all. *This is a solid guy*, we told ourselves. *At least he doesn't distrust us.* Until one day the mail came and left a letter for him. *What the hell*, I said to myself, *even the post office calls him Zé Cavalinho. It's not right to abuse a man like that, who's no child after all. Everyone has their name.* That's what I was thinking, and it seems I wasn't wrong. When I saw him next I told him like this: 'Listen, Mr. Zé. I've been thinking, and I don't feel good about the joke we've been making about you. There's a time for everything and sometimes it's not nice to kid around. What *is* your name?' 'My name?' he said. 'Yes, your name,' I said. 'Name of what?' he comes back at me. 'Your name, your real name,' I said. 'My name?' he said. 'But I am Zé Cavalinho.' 'Stop with the jokes, Mr. Zé, I'm asking you this seriously,' I said. 'But I'm talking seriously to you too,' he said, 'my name is José Cavalinho, José dos Santos Cavalinho.' At the time I thought he was still joking. But no. That really is his name: José dos Santos Cavalinho."

Taking one more drag, the railwayman kept watching the rain running off the roof, oblivious to the effect of his story. "All that time we were going around thinking we were amusing ourselves at his expense, and he was the trickster making fun of us."

He led the stranger to the station door. "The rain's letting up a little, so while you can, just follow along this wall and you'll come to the shed up ahead. He'll certainly be there and will tell you what you want to know."

4

This was some shed. Enormous, with an earthen floor and a simple tile roof, its inside retained all the humidity and discomfort of the open air. It even seemed the wind was stronger there. But it was out of the rain. A railway worker was talking with a bartender and a peasant. He was a short man, slender, with a white mustache and a cap pulled clumsily back over the nape of his neck. With a glass in hand, he was about to drink. When he saw the unknown man, he suspended his gesture, lowered his chin to his chest, and examined him from head to toe with shining eyes behind thin, graying eyebrows and kept repeating the last few words he was saying: "…at times when…at times when…at times when…."

This must be Zé Cavalinho, the stranger thought. And he said out loud, "Can any of you gentlemen show me the road to Vale da Égua?"

In an abrupt move, the railwayman placed his glass on the counter, pulled his cap even farther back, approached the unknown man and, quickly grabbing him by the arm, led him to the door.

"Come here, my friend. Go down there to the line and keep following it until you come to some houses. You can't go wrong because there aren't any others. When you get to the houses, cross the line and before you you'll see a pine forest. Go into the pine forest, keep going straight, you'll see the business card for the Guild"—and the railwayman winked an eye—"but continue straight all the way until you come to a road. Also here you can't go wrong because there's no other road. Cut to your left, the left is a good road"—and he winked his eye again—"and follow that road. You'll cross a stream over a chain of rocks, and then you can't go wrong. Keep on going, going, going, there's no roads to the right or the left, until you get to some water wheels. There you go right—. No, if I explain it to you now, you won't see the path. Ask at the mill and the woman who lives there will tell you right away. She's quite a piece of woman," he added, opening his eyes wide after a slight pause.

"How long will it take?"

"By foot, about an hour and half. With the bicycle, obviously, it'll take less."

"Let's see if I remember right," said the unknown man. "I follow the railway line to the houses, cross the line, go through the pine forest to the road and follow the road to the left to the water wheels. But I didn't understand that part about the business card for the Guild."

The railwayman's eyes lit up even more behind the gray hair and eyebrows. His eyes were those of a youthful pixie. "Now that's one very interesting story—" And he laughed hoarsely, almost coughing, as if to say, *Yes, sir, that's a very rich story, but I'm not going to tell it to you.*

"So, then, thank you."

The railwayman didn't answer. Without retreating from the rain, he kept his impish smile and nodded yes until the stranger disappeared from sight.

5

The stranger followed the line and was beginning to suspect he had passed the houses without seeing them when he made out two dark little buildings quite near the tracks, each one with its own door, so old and crumbling that they couldn't possibly keep out the rain. *Are these the houses?* he asked himself. But, remembering that Zé Cavalinho had told him they would be the only ones, he lifted his bicycle to his shoulder, crossed over the rail line, and entered a dark, sad pine forest with rutted terrain and ground covered by creeping undergrowth. When he got to a vast, devastated area cut clear with axes, he rested a little. Now the rain's freshness really struck him, and in the humidity of the air that he sucked in he tasted the heightened aroma of pine resin. When his heart calmed down, he continued his march. Once again he was ready to stop for a while when, after a sharp decline in the land, he found himself on a wide, sandy way. *Good, this is the road.* And he turned left. Just ahead, a stream crossed in front of him. It was a small rivulet, but the water was running in a muddy torrent barely allowing him to find the polished stones he needed to cross. *If I step on the stones, surely I'll fall,* he figured. And after looking from one side to the other, to the rain and to his own soaked suit, he told himself aloud, in a calm, serious tone, "Anyway, it won't make any difference," and stepped into the water.

He waded in up to his thighs. In just half a dozen cautious steps feeling the bottom, he got to the other side. A new and unpleasant surprise awaited him there. The road was a swamp stretching between the stream and a precipitous incline. He could either turn back or forge through. There was no other solution: He wrenched up his pants, rolled up the legs and pressed forward.

How long he sloshed about in the mud he'd never be able to tell. His shoes soon got stuck, and only by persistent effort did he manage to keep them on. He slipped and felt himself going under, paused out of exhaustion, then went on in despair only to stop again farther on, tempted to throw his bicycle into the quagmire to enable him to keep moving. At times the idea pursued him that he would lose his strength and wind up falling from fatigue. Finally, when the mud lessened and he could walk more securely, he placed his bike on the ground, supporting himself on the frame, and stood panting, his legs and arms trembling from overexertion, the sweat bathing his body and streaking from his temples down to his chin. Once recovered a little, now on a sandy path, he resumed his hike. But he walked uncertainly, not being able to ignore the mud that had reached well above his knees, nor the *splat-splat* of his shoes huffing like bellows. From time to time, the path devolved into flooded patches, and others of mud, but all that was nothing compared to the sea of mud he had already crossed.

He had left the rail station before eleven o'clock. Around two, at a curve in the road, he saw the black forms of the water wheels. As best as he could he cleaned the mud from his shoes, his socks and legs, unrolled his pant legs, wiped his face with his kerchief, adjusted his hat and approached the door. From inside he heard a baby's cries, muffled by the lapping waters on the wheel paddles. After knocking a few times, he heard the shuffle of slippers, and a woman appeared—formidable, dressed in black, with a dark kerchief framing her long brunette head with an immediately prominent bristle of hairs on her upper lip. *She's quite a piece of woman*, Zé Cavalinho had said.

"Good afternoon. Could you show me the way to Vale da Égua?"

"Did you come through the canebrakes?"

"I came from here," the stranger said, pointing to the road. Inside the house the child went on crying.

"Whoever showed you that road didn't have very good judgment," the woman said. "Oh my God, how did you get through? When the weather's like this, no one can pass that way. Oh my God. One time a man was lost there and the burro he was steering."

The crying stopped and, from the dark interior, a child's face appeared next to the woman's skirts. It was still wet with tears, and its upper lip was still trembling, but by its eyes wide open to the unknown man and the bicycle, it showed it had forgotten its unhappiness of a moment before. The woman glanced down at the child and stepped aside to give it room, allowing the stranger to see him, a boy naked from the waist down with a big belly red from the cold. Then she picked him up, kissed him quickly many times and, adjusting her kerchief that had fallen, smiled broadly at the unknown man.

"You can't go wrong," she explained. "See this grove of olive trees? Continue walking right alongside it until you get to a water hoist, go over to that side, and it's right there."

"I'd like to ask you one more favor," said the unknown man. "Could you give me a drop of water?"

"What?" the woman asked.

"A drop of water."

"Water?"

"Yes, to drink."

"But it is actually water that you want?"

"Yes, a drop of water to drink."

Only then did the woman seem to notice the man she had before her. She saw his suit and hat drenched from the rain, his shoes and pants all muddy, the bicycle useless on that path. She saw his face, dry, pale and grim. She looked into his quiet, staring eyes. She thought of nothing and made no judgment—what thought would she have and what judgment could she make?—but ran inside as though ashamed not to have remembered such a courtesy, and brought out an enormous mug of water. She wasn't surprised when the stranger raised it to his mouth and drank eagerly in huge, endless gulps. When he departed, trudging through the mud and shrugging his shoulders up as if to protect his neck from the rain, she embraced her son even closer to her breast, still without thought or judgment, but feeling full of tenderness and pity.

6

Vale da Água. A dozen small, dark houses spread out among the pines and olive trees. In the first house, a woman and a little girl, shoeless and bareheaded, appeared. The woman's face was pretty but troubled, and her body was thin and spent. She could just as easily have been twenty as forty. The girl looked like the woman, her hair well combed with her braids tied in an arc. She practically disappeared in the faded dress that was far too large for her.

"Can you tell me where Senhor Manuel Rato lives?"

"He lives here," the woman quickly replied, as her cheeks stood out in a shrunken face, "but he left and I don't know if he'll return today."

Saying this, the woman threw a rapid glance to the olive groves. Following her eyes, the stranger saw, at a certain distance and turned toward the house, a man whose head and shoulders were covered by a large burlap sack as a hood.

"What do you want of him?"

"I'm the shoemaker from Santarém," the unknown man responded.

"Isabel," the woman said to the girl, looking directly into her eyes, "go to my brother's house and see if your father is there. If he is, tell him the shoemaker from Santarém is here and wants to speak with him. Understand?"

The girl also glanced over to the olive grove, where the man with the sack had retreated. "Yes, mother."

The woman took her inside the house, and the girl shortly ran out with a dark bonnet on her head.

"Cover yourself," the woman said, withdrawing into the house.

After a few minutes, the girl reappeared, accompanied by the man with the sack. He had a dark face and a broad, closely clipped black mustache that gave him the look of a sergeant of the rural National Republican Guard, the GNR. He didn't seem to be in any hurry, standing outside the door in the rain, eyeing the unknown man. Finally he asked, "What did you want?"

"I'm looking for Senhor Manuel Rato."

"And what did you want of him?"

The unknown man looked at the woman as if to ask if he should respond, but only saw two eyes full of anxiety. "I'm the shoemaker from Santarém," he repeated.

"Did you bring the measurements?" the man with the sack asked.

"Yes, I did," said the stranger, and out of his pocket he pulled a paper outline of the sole of a shoe from which a corner was missing.

"Good," said the man with the sack. He entered the house, asked something of his wife in a low voice, and both disappeared inside. He returned instantly with a little piece of paper in his hand that he aligned with the place cut out from the paper sole the unknown man held out. The sole was complete.

"Good," the man said again. "Come in." And he himself lifted the bicycle inside.

7

It was an earthen room with a tile roof, without a single window. Its only furniture was a little stool in a corner next to two blackened bricks and the extinguished remains of a fire. Aside from the door to the road, there was only a flimsy interior door through which the wife and child had receded.

Like the woman at the water wheels, Manuel Rato was amazed by the route taken, and like her, he told the story of the man and his burro who one time got swallowed up by the mud. Given the impossibility of the stranger's returning by the same route where he had come from, Manuel Rato offered that he spend the night with them, promising that in the early morning he would lead him to a better trail.

When the new visitor told him how he had inquired in the tavern for directions, and then asked the fat man under the overhang without anyone knowing where to direct him, Manuel Rato turned thoughtful. "It's strange," he said. "I can hardly believe that among so many people no one knew."

"They didn't know the way," said the newcomer, "nor had even heard of Vale da Égua."

"Impossible!" Manuel Rato exclaimed.

The new arrival then related with greater detail the conversation he had had in the tavern and the response from the old man with the little jacket, saying that he had been born there and always lived there and had never heard anyone speak of such a place.

"Honestly, I don't understand," said Manuel Rato.

Asking his visitor to wait a bit, while he went to find a stool to sit on, he went to the interior door. "Comrade," the visitor called. "Can you get a drop of water to drink?"

Manuel Rato turned around and with a serious expression looked intently at the visitor, sopping wet from the rain and purple from the cold. Unlike the woman at the water wheels, he didn't ask questions. "Yes, I can" was all he said.

A whisper of voices came from the next room, and the head of the house reappeared with a little stool in one hand and a jug in the other. Right after him, his daughter came in with a pottery mug still dripping from the water she had just rinsed it in. She slightly tilted her well-coiffed head toward the stranger, and her face with its braided frame seemed to be saying, *Look, aren't I beautiful? I'm already a little woman, don't you think?* In fact, now she didn't seem like the child he had first seen at the door, vanishing into the faded, patched clothes too big for her. She was truly a little woman, and an enchanting one at that.

The visitor drank two mugs of water as the girl smiled in wonderment. Then the wife came in with half a big pan of corn bread. Manuel Rato had the visitor sit on one of the stools in the corner with the blackened walls near the ashes of a fire on the hearth.

"Want to hear something?" he asked his wife, taking a piece of corn bread that she held out. "Down there no one knew the way here and they said they'd never even heard of this place."

"No!"

"Seriously," Manuel Rato insisted. "I just don't understand it, but it's true."

The woman remained silent for a moment. Then her black eyes brightened, her worried face turned emotional as she almost shouted, "The Guild!"

Clearly, read the pleased, intelligent expression on the girl's face, at that moment extremely like her mother's. The husband, with his serious, unforgiving expression, nodded affirmatively: *Clearly, that's it.* He took a small knife out of his pocket and passed it, with the corn bread, to the visitor, explaining in a few words how "down there" the Guild men were demanding the clear-cutting of the pines, and paying a ridiculously low price for them. Now people mistrusted everyone who came from away, and it must have been out of suspicion that they hadn't shown him the way. If Zé Cavalinho had indicated the way it's because he knew that someone was going to come looking for Manuel Rato. *Here's the business card of The Guild,* the visitor thought as he recalled the devastation he had encountered in the pine forest and Cavalinho's comment, *Now that's one very interesting story.*

The visitor cut a piece of corn bread and started eating it without saying anything, focusing on the knife and the wedge of corn bread. Standing in front of him, the man of the house, now silent, stared at him attentively. He noticed his messy hair stuck to his forehead, his involuntary energy chewing the food and the haste with which he swallowed. He saw the clothes and shoes soaked with water and mud, the awkward position of his legs, one extended out on the floor and the other splayed out to the other side, a sign of intense fatigue.

"Eat! Eat!" he insisted.

8

The wife and girl having left the room, the man of the house finally removed the sack from his head, uncovering a hat that many years before must have been black. Sitting down, he also took off his hat and placed it on the floor on top of the sack. His wide, arched forehead, whose color was lighter than that of his face, somewhat softened his especially gruff look, accentuated by the depth of his facial coloration, his black, close-cut mustache, the strong creases in his face and the wrinkled eyebrows.

"This is our first contact," the visitor said calmly, concisely and dispassionately. "It would be good if you gave me an idea of what there is here, how many you are, what possibilities for work that you see, and how many copies of our press you want."

Manuel Rato placed his bony, nervous hands on his knees. "I don't know if you know I'm not a peasant," he began. "I'm working in the countryside now on a little property of my wife's, because there's no way I could be always separated from her and my daughter. But I was always a factory worker and I never spent much time here. Most recently I worked in civil construction in Lisbon. It was there that I left the paper token that you brought."

He fell silent for a moment and his face tightened even more in a visible effort to gather his thoughts.

"As you see, it's very small and isolated here. Everyone has their little foothold, but what they have isn't enough to live on. Not to live well or badly—just not to live at all. The situation in the other houses is no better than in this one. So everyone has to find outside work. Some work in street repair. Others do day jobs on the rich people's estates. But all these jobs around here don't last long and are badly paid. As a result, there's not a house here where someone or other isn't going out to seasonal work in the fields. In a few weeks there'll be the olive harvest. Then there'll be the weeding of the rice fields, and then the wheat harvest in the South. Some spend more time away than at home. My wife and daughter have also gone, though I'd like it if they never had to."

The voice was calm, the tone as energetic as his face. Manuel Rato grabbed hold of a burnt splinter of wood and started making overlapping lines in the ashes on the hearth.

"What can I do, my friend? Many times I think it would be better to let this land go to seed and make a new life far away. But try saying it out loud! Could you convince her to abandon this? Me neither. She works the fields like a man, and the little one does the same. Sometimes she's gone off to field work and all she worries about is saving up to pay the taxes, or the interest on some little debt—in short, to maintain the little that her father left her. We've arrived at a place, my friend, where instead of the land giving people independence, it turns them into the most dependent of creatures. All around here, that's the way it is. And there you have it."

Manuel Rato stopped talking for a while. His face looked extremely disturbed now, and he drew an enormous circle in the ashes. His new friend placed a notepad on his knees and wrote something down with a trembling hand.

"As far as other comrades here, I'm the only one," Manuel Rato continued. "Down there are lots of people, but I don't know anyone who's ready. Cavalinho reads our paper and could do something if he wasn't such a drunk. So there's no use thinking about him. Right around here everyone's against the government, but up to now they're very immature. Maybe it's me that doesn't know how to do it, but I've been here more than sixty days and haven't made a single recruitment."

Manuel Rato put aside the burnt stick of wood and for the first time since he had started talking looked at his comrade. The visitor looked straight back, his eyes fixed and waiting, one hand supporting his chin, which also trembled.

"As for the press," continued the homeowner, taking hold of the splinter again and recommencing his instinctive line drawings, "there's two copies of *Avante!*, one for me and the other for Cavalinho. It would be good, when you come back here, if you could leave me ten or twenty, even if they're out of date. When I came from Lisbon, I brought quite a few and every week I went out at night here and there, even two leagues away from home, and I'd leave a few hanging in the branches of trees or slipped under doors. It had some impact, because a guy who works down there in road repair had heard people talking about it. That's the only thing that can be done here."

With that, he dropped the piece of wood, dusted off his hands and called his wife. When Joana appeared, he merely said, ""Bring it."

Joana certainly guessed what, for she shortly brought "it." With her eyes shining from that pretty but worrisome face, she pulled a little package from her apron pocket.

"You can go," said the man.

How could she obey him? Together with her daughter, who also came to see, she remained standing in the doorway rather solemnly, watching her husband carefully unwrap the paper and listening to him talking in his calm manner.

"I'm paying for my *Avante!* and for the friend we spoke of. As for my dues, the last time I paid was in Lisbon, so I'm nine weeks behind. Here's one *escudo* for the paper and four and a half *escudos* for the dues. There's one *escudo* left, which is for the back issues, but that'll be for the next time."

And slowly wrapping the money back into the paper, he handed the package to his wife, who approached again. "Put it away," he said.

The comrade placed the money in his change purse and, with a cold tremor still in his hands, wrote something on his notepad with difficulty. Glowing with pride, the woman now seemed younger. She gazed at her husband with loving eyes, and her entire face, thin and pretty, looked happy.

9

The two men were getting set to continue their conversation when the woman returned, followed by the girl, each one with an apronful of wood. They started lighting a fire.

"Now?" asked Manuel Rato.

Without letting up on her blowing on the kindling, Joana moved her head in the direction of the visitor, who was making unsuccessful efforts to bring his shivers under control.

"Yes, I got a chill," he mumbled in discomfort.

Suddenly the wood started crackling as if salt had been tossed into the fire. The flames rose frighteningly. Moving lithely on her bare feet, the girl placed a pot on the two bricks and closed the street door. The men remained by themselves, illuminated by the red of the fire.

"So, friend," the visitor began. But he couldn't go on, his tongue and jaws frozen by the cold. As much as he tried, he couldn't get another word out.

Manuel Rato went to find more sticks of wood, and the visitor, who had in the meantime taken his shoes off, removed his jacket and placed it to dry out by the heat of the hearth.

For a long time they stayed quiet. Watching the fire with unaccustomed fixity, Manuel Rato recalled the two times, still in Lisbon, when he had met with Party functionaries. He remembered the long explications they had delivered and now he expected the same kind of exposition from the visitor, deliberate and sound, from which he certainly could learn a great deal. They listened to the snapping fire and the rain drumming on the tile roof. Finally, though speaking with difficulty and still shaking with tremors, the visitor spoke.

"Yes," he began, "this is a small, isolated place. But down there in V—, well, that's an important center. It's there we should be directing our attention. The initiative of going out in the night leaving papers in distant settlements is very positive. The basic thing, though, is to establish a Party organization in V—. That's it, my friend."

Manuel Rato was expecting the other to go on. After all that he himself had said, and reflecting on the long dissertations from the two Party functionaries he had met, and considering that the comrade would not have traveled such a long way just to tell him "that's it," he was counting on a lengthy speech. But no. The comrade was rubbing his hands before the flames, and from the way he did it, it looked like he had said everything.

"Did you finish?" Manuel Rato asked.

"Yes, I finished," the comrade responded, still rubbing his hands together.

The head of the house then started talking some more. He had forgotten to say that within a month and a half or two months he would be leaving Vale da Égua again to go work in some mine in the North. They should figure out a new token so he could be located there, either by the Party organization in the mine if there was one or by a Party delegate if there wasn't. In two months' time he didn't see the potential to get anything done in V—.

"There is one angle," the visitor said. "The question is if you know how to grab it. There's Zé Cavalinho."

Manuel Rato's eyes, focused on the fire, toward which he pushed the stray embers with a stick, almost disappeared under the shadow of his thick eyebrows. But no, Zé Cavalinho was not a worthy candidate. He was a good man, but he drank way too much and he didn't have the right judgment to influence, approach or cultivate sympathizers and new comrades.

"The hardest thing of all is to find that angle," the visitor replied. "We have it. Now we have to make use of it."

Interrupting their talk, the girl appeared with a pottery platter and threw chopped kale and potatoes into the pot. A cloud of steam got lost in the darkness of the roof, spreading a gentle smell of hot animal fat. The lulling sound of boiling stopped.

The two men went on talking for a long time. It was well after nightfall before the woman and the girl returned.

"It's time," the woman said, smiling toward the guest. And with her eyes on the pot, she used a fork to push a bunch of vegetables into a ladle. Then, raising the ladle and blowing on it, she used her clear white teeth to bite off the hanging, steaming strands of kale.

The girl removed the pot from the fire. The woman left and came back with two bowls. Her black eyes shone strangely in that thin, restless face as she cut two big pieces of corn bread that she also served. The mother and daughter remained standing next to the men. The girl smiled continuously, holding onto her mother's shoulder.

The men ate their soup, and only after them the woman and girl ate from the same bowls. When the soup had been eaten, Joana pulled a piece of pork belly from the pot, placed it on a slice of corn bread and handed it to the visitor. The visitor glanced at Manuel Rato as if to ask, *And all of you?* Manuel Rato responded to the look saying, "You're the one who needs it most today, friend."

In silence, his serious expression unchanged, the comrade started eating the corn bread with pork fat.

Visibly satisfied, Manuel Rato stood up, left for a few moments and came back with a wooden board that he placed on the earthen floor next to the hearth. "Sit there!" he said to his wife and daughter.

They settled themselves on the plank, and the three of them silently observed the comrade eating.

10

The rain drummed endlessly on the tile roof. The woman deposited a mountain of logs and kindling next to the hearth. When the fire was dying down, she threw more wood on it. The light came back to life for a time, and shadows of big deformed heads danced on the walls. After they ate, Manuel Rato asked the visitor to relate something about the Soviet Union. "She doesn't believe me," he explained.

As the comrade eyed the little girl questioning if he should speak in front of a child, Manuel reassured him. "The girl is safe and she's already of an age to learn."

As though moved by her father's words, Isabel's cheeks, ears and eyes filled with pride, and she adjusted herself more comfortably on the plank she was sitting on, turned toward the visitor and gently leaned her head forward on her long, white and tender neck. *What were you thinking?* her slender, proud little figure asked.

The visitor had been roaming through this area for a week, walking or cycling hours on end, day and night, almost without sleeping or eating. He felt exhausted, wanting only to lie down, bundle up and sleep. A blanket and some sheltered, quiet corner was his greatest desire at that moment—so powerful and insistent that he looked upon the earthen floor next to the hearth as if it were waiting for him and calling him. The water that drenched his clothes almost seemed to drench his brain as well, grinding his thoughts into a confused, indecipherable pulp. But one question after another came at him, and Manuel Rato, in his quiet voice, made some observations and carried the conversation forward. Joana, with her insatiable thirst, asked more and more questions, her lovely thin face animated by the responses. The comrade was reviving, and the talk extended into the night.

Struck by the flames' glow, the girl's face shone with delight and intelligence. It seemed she drank in and approved every word. But who could guess her thoughts? How could anyone know that only from time to time was she paying close attention to what was being said? And that what she understood wasn't so much the problems discussed and the responses given, but more a stimulus to her own thoughts? *Yeah, it's all very nice,* she thought. *Mother sitting down with Father and with this friend and all of them talking about these things. But why does Mother say I could wind up marrying Tónio da Carriça if he's also rich? No, I don't want to marry Tónio and not a rich man anyhow. I want to marry a man like my father or like this friend (who is very nice, yes, very, very nice), who would be good and think about the welfare of the poor, and doesn't beat his wife and would talk with her like we're doing here now. I might be a poor little girl, but Mother is also poor. And how can you put a price on the husband she has? How can you?* And the girl's eyes sparkled more and more with enthusiasm and approval.

The night got later, and Joana asked to pause the conversation a little. She left, with the girl beside her. When the women returned a few moments later, the comrade was in a deep sleep.

"Come on, friend," said Manuel Rato.

The comrade didn't respond. Only when Manuel Rato shook him did he open his eyes wide—but only out of shock, as he couldn't see. Manuel Rato almost dragged him asleep to the other room, where he helped him stretch out on the only bed in the house. The visitor had some fleeting awareness of that, but didn't notice the blanket with which they covered him.

Three hours later, Manuel Rato called him. "It's time." He said it four times with no result. Only by shaking him violently was he able to awaken him.

The comrade sat up in bed, in the dark, still without understanding what had happened, where he was and how unfair it was to yank him out of his peaceful sleep that didn't seem to have lasted for more than a minute.

In the next room, Joana continued to sit on the plank, next to the remains of the fire, just as she was the night before, but now her eyes were even more bright from excitement and insomnia. Encircled, with her head in her mother's lap, Isabel slept. Manuel Rato checked the tires on the bicycle.

A cold breeze came with the early morning. A drizzle mixed with a thick, low cloud clung to everything. The two men walked in silence for almost an hour through pine forests and peaceful fields. As it started clearing up, they reached a paved road.

"I'll return in two weeks," the comrade said. "Prepare for my contact with Cavalinho. And remember: The fundamental task is to create an organization in V—."

And drawing the little collar up on his neck, he straightened his hat, jumped on the bicycle and left.

11

At eight a.m., in a church courtyard, he was speaking with a short, chubby little man in a worker's overalls. He handed him papers, conversed a few minutes, received papers and left. At 10 a.m. he entered the grocery store of a small village. The grocer simply told him, "Nothing," and he left. At mid-day he was a hundred or so meters from a lumber factory adjacent to the street. Three workers leaving their shifts there sought him out and, in the course of their conversation he said several times, "The Committee should not be imposed. It's the workers who should choose it or at least consider it well-chosen." An hour later he was in an olive grove talking with two peasants and he insisted: "You *can* put honest people in the leadership of the People's House, even if it's state-sponsored. What's important is to believe in your power to do so." Mid-afternoon he sat down on a bench in the little workshop of a shoemaker in another town and spoke with cold severity: "We had agreed that the Local Committee would meet today. We've been working on this for two months." Some time later, on the bank of a brook, a woman surprised him under a tree as he was shaving. She crossed herself and walked away, bewildered, always looking behind her.

As night fell, he got off his bicycle under a falling rain, by a little tavern at the side of the road. He went in, propped his bicycle in one corner, sat at a table and asked for a quarter loaf of bread, white cheese and a glass of wine. It was the first time he had eaten all day and he made an effort to chew and swallow slowly. One hope excited him: a good meal that was perhaps waiting for him at the lawyer's house.

The tavern keeper eyed him curiously, finding something strange about that customer. On the one hand, his clothes and hat were all rumpled and soaked; and on the other hand, his face was shaved and good-looking, his gaze was normal, he was well-mannered and sure of himself, and his voice was confident. On one hand, something in his expression, his pallor, the dark circles around his eyes, his gestures, the way he fell into his chair and extended his legs, spoke of a deep sense of fatigue. On the other hand, despite all of that, he exhibited formidable energy and physical vigor. The taverner didn't have a lot of time to think, however. Having eaten his bread and cheese and imbibed his wine, the customer paid and left.

That night he arrived at a city of new buildings all bright with electric lighting. On a narrow street, he hesitated a bit and finally knocked on the door of a humble house, in front of which an empty automobile was parked. He recalled Ramos's phrase when he brought him there the first time: "There's even an automobile at the door," he said giddily, with a joking laugh, alluding to the fact that the owner of the house was a professional driver. A woman came to open the door, and she called into the house, "Afonso!"

A tall, willowy figure appeared. Without a word, he took the bicycle and carried it inside. He came right back and kissed the woman.

"Don't be late!" she said in a supplicating tone.

The two men walked out onto the street in silence. At the end of the street they set out on a route that followed irregular paths between yards. Afonso was markedly taller, although slightly curved, and walked in a long, rhythmic, almost lazy stride. They crossed a well-lit street and passed onto a new route, almost invisible, onto an empty terrain with a somber atmosphere, punctuated sadly by the distant line of lights from the city. After a few minutes, they hopped over a low wall in a field and headed toward a house distinguished by lighted cracks around one window. Afonso tapped his fingers on the window pane. Low voices could be heard in the house. The lighted cracks disappeared, the door opened cautiously, and a voice in the dark whispered, "Come in."

When the door closed, the electric light went on again. A dark-haired man in a blue work shirt stood smiling and held out his long, heavy hand to the newcomers. Seated at the table were another two men. Behind the thick eyeglass lenses of one of them, the intelligent, questioning eyes seemed to eat his whole face. The other, with carefully combed hair and his elbow on the table, supported his chin in his hand, which held a lit cigarette. Now in the light, Afonso appeared extremely young. A rebel lock of hair fell over his forehead, and across his face loomed an uncertain expression of melancholy goodness.

"As always," said the man in the work shirt, "Comrade Vaz arrives on schedule."

They all sat down and began their meeting.

12

In a nearby town, every Monday, the rural workers gathered at the marketplace to be hired. Bosses and managers came and offered wages like someone at a fair announcing the price for cattle.

"It's our duty to put an end to these vestiges of servitude!" the carpenter Marques had said some time back, in a sharp, incisive tone with his eyes shining behind his thick lenses.

Everyone agreed. Afonso, who supervised the comrades of the town, gave instructions to that effect. From then on the day workers would not place even a foot in the marketplace for day worker hands, forcing the bosses to go find them in their own houses.

But José Sagarra in the village categorically opposed that decision. "In the marketplace we're all together and we can set our own price," he said in his nasal voice. "If each of us waits in our own house, or if we go knocking on the bosses' door, they grab us separately and impose on us the prices they want. Doing away with the marketplace would lower our daily wage, end our lunch breaks, our smoking breaks and our gratuity, and it would take work away from the older and weaker ones."

Afonso insisted on fulfilling the planned approach. But José Sagarra, awkwardly waving his hands without knowing where to put them, maintained his own opinion. "No, no, no! This is a serious mistake!" Since Afonso was not able to carry the resolution, the Regional Committee decided to call the comrade to a meeting and persuade him. On the appointed day, José Sagarra showed up with a surly chip on his shoulder, looking sideways at the unknown comrades. Each one in turn—first Marques the carpenter with his eyes shining behind his glasses, then the retail employee Vítor speaking haughtily, then the electrician Cesário, with a big smile on his long, dark face, then Afonso again—insisted on the necessity of ending the marketplace of human beings as a medieval institution that degraded the workers. José Sagarra repeated what he had already said to Afonso and added nothing more. He lowered his eyes and, to each of the others' arguments, limited himself to shrugging his shoulders and altering the position of his arms and hands.

"Listen, comrade," Marques told him at last, peering out observantly from behind his lenses, "Do you know how to read?"

José Sagarra nodded affirmatively. "A little," he said.

"How many years are you in the Party?"

"Just one."

"So it would seem," the carpenter said. "Why don't you listen to the opinion of comrades with more experience than you who have more knowledge, more time in the Party and more responsibility?"

Everyone was waiting for his response, but José Sagarra only shrugged his shoulders again. They thought he wouldn't respond at all, when suddenly he raised his thin, freckled head and unexpectedly revealed his eyes of a pure, luminous blue that a small blemish couldn't obscure. "Very well, then, the Central Committee can settle it," he pronounced in a quiet voice that was nevertheless afire with passion.

As the comrades did not clearly understand what he wanted, he repeated: "Let the Central Committee settle it!" In the way he said it, it was implied that without the Central Committee resolving it, there was nothing to be done; and if the Central Committee resolved it unfavorably to his opinion, he would comply but nevertheless that would be a huge blunder that could do serious damage, for which the comrades would take responsibility.

The Regional Committee met again and now Marques had a hard time believing what Vaz reported. The Secretariat sided with José Sagarra, opposing the decision by the Regional Committee. But not only that. Basing itself on the experiences of various places in that region and in others, the Secretariat not only considered that everything should be done to maintain the marketplaces, but that an effort should be made to transform them into tools of struggle for rural wage-earners. It advised establishing in every marketplace a Marketplace Committee, elected by the workers, to deal with the bosses, foremen and managers over working conditions. In one paragraph, it criticized the Regional Committee and other organisms for their deficient work in the rural sector, for their lack of familiarity with the problems of farm workers, and for the imprudence of their decisions and bureaucratic methods of work.

Extremely pale and constantly fiddling with the pencil behind his ear, the carpenter Marques followed Vaz's report with obvious impatience. "These committees will only wind up burning people out," he said at the end.

Vítor also did not look convinced. "Workers in the field are not prepared for that," he commented as he blew smoke from his cigarette. "No one's going to convince me that the marketplaces are a progressive institution."

Cesário smiled and said, "Let's do as the comrades have told us. We still have a lot to learn."

Afonso felt perturbed. The decision from on high seemed well-founded, although he doubted it would be successful in practice. But it was hard for him to suddenly switch an opinion that he had defended so forcefully. The criticism against the Regional Committee shocked him, as everyone had just tried to do the right thing. He read profound discontent in Marques's face, and to an extent he shared it, for he could never forget that Marques was a longtime militant who by then had suffered great ordeals in prison. But he expressed agreement with Vaz all the same, promising to carry out the resolution.

Vaz had one more thing to say on the subject: He had also been instructed to speak directly with José Sagarra. On hearing this, Marques laughed in an openly mocking attitude. Turning toward him, Vaz stared at him with fixed disapproval. Marques's laughter died out, but behind those thick lenses his intelligent eyes resisted Vaz's gaze. Before moving on to other issues, Marques added, "The comrades on the Central Committee are way, way up there, and they're not always well informed."

Vítor never moved his chin from the hand it rested on. Through a fog of smoke he turned his eyes ironically toward Vaz to watch his reaction. As if he had heard nothing, Vaz went on to the next point, but Marques interrupted him: "I still want to say a couple more words. If Comrade Ramos were here, it wouldn't have turned out this way."

Close to 10 o'clock they declared the meeting adjourned, and Vaz pulled Afonso over to one corner. "Did you talk with your girl-friend?" he asked.

Afonso blushed. "I haven't been able to ask her yet."

Vaz stayed silent for a few moments, his expression unchanging, his eyes riveted on his comrade. He was clearly hesitant to show his dubiousness at what Afonso was saying. "Didn't you tell me that your friend said she was inclined to go underground on her own initiative?"

"Yes," Afonso said, blushing again. "But I haven't had the chance to talk about it with her."

Vaz kept his peace once more. Only the muscles contracting in his face were aroused. "Very well," he said finally. "The next time I come here, I'd like you to set up a meeting between me and your friend. If I don't come, Ramos will come and handle everything."

Afonso nodded his youthful, kind face. But there was something profoundly pleading in him when Vaz gave him the cordial pat on the arm that ended the conversation. "So, agreed, eh?"

They returned to Afonso's house by the same path. His mother was waiting for him at the window. Vaz grabbed his bicycle, made sure his briefcase was well secured to the frame, tucked his pant legs into his socks, hitched his jacket collar up his neck, adjusted his hat and left.

13

One hour later, several leagues away, he found himself seated in the lawyer's office. It was already 11:30 at night, but the comrade deemed it the best time for a meeting if they were not to be observed. It wasn't rare for him to stay late, and no one would be coming to bother them.

The lawyer was a short man with a lean face, dark, creased skin, and a mane of wavy hair that highlighted some bright white strands. Seated in an armchair in a pose of utmost self-confidence, he spoke with heightened articulation. "No one more than I appreciates the efforts of the comrades. It does seem to me, however, that their work in practice doesn't correspond to an acceptable theoretical level. The publications might be very useful in certain places, I don't disagree.

But for people of some education, they have a negative effect. The paper always seems to say the same thing, and the writing is a poor Portuguese where it's common to find spelling errors. There aren't any articles on the level of theory or doctrine, especially about economics and political economy."

Vaz felt exhausted. The armchair he was sitting in made him even sleepier. A heavy weight fell onto his eyelids, a deep anxiety clutched at his chest and filled him with the absurd desire to lay himself out right there on the office floor, on that carpet he imagined would be soft and warm.

The lawyer spoke leisurely, from time to time running his hand through his wavy hair and doubling down on his criticism of Party work. It was obvious he had carefully prepared his speech and had been eager for quite some time to deliver it. Vaz decided to wait until he had finished before addressing some practical questions and then being able to rest a little. Without willing it, his imagination traveled to the clean, comfortable bed that surely awaited him that night in the lawyer's house, and the dinner he would offer him. As much as he forced himself to follow the lawyer's oration, he now envisioned before him fresh sheets and a pillow, a nice bread and a hot, sweet drink.

After almost an hour, the lawyer stood up, stretched his limbs and smiled. He looked pleased with himself, and certain of the over-whelming effect of his words. "We're finished, no?" he said, meaning that the meeting was over.

"Just a couple of little things to check up on," Vaz said, noticing with some surprise the sudden expression of annoyance these words evoked. "How many papers do you want?" he asked, speaking more formally than he ordinarily would with his comrades. "Is it just for yourself, or for anyone else as well?"

No, there was no one else, the lawyer replied, recognizing the wrongness in getting just one copy for himself. The comrades had to know how touchy this was for him. Everyone in the area knew he was a Communist, and for that reason it would be imprudent—criminal actually, and disrespectful of the rules of secrecy—for him to receive clandestine newspapers.

As though fatigue and drowsiness had been brushed by the hand he passed over his forehead, Vaz's eyes now regarded the lawyer with serenity and a steady gaze. His serious, impassive features barely concealed the effort to restrain himself. "Good, my friend. Another thing. We had discussed gathering data in the case of the civil governor's shady dealings with the City Council. What's happening with that?"

The lawyer sat on the edge of his desk and lit a cigarette. In slow movements, so slow they seemed to Vaz designed to gain time to think of a response, he blew out the match, crushed it in the ashtray, and took a few drags. "It wasn't possible," he said finally. "Besides, the shady business was not what people initially said it was. Matters like this are very delicate, isn't that so?" And the lawyer attempted a smile, confident in his wisdom. But in his lowered eyes, a glare danced of something new, fleeting and uncertain.

Vaz did not reply. His face and eyes retained their reserve. "Good, my friend," he said again. "Sorry for taking more of your time, but there's one other small thing. Do you have the *Government Journal* you'd agreed to purchase? Could you give it to me?"

At every step of the way, the lawyer's face manifested his uneasiness. In a brusque gesture that seemed a little theatrical, he slapped a palm to his forehead. "I completely forgot!" he admitted, shaking his head. "I've had so much to do, so much going on in my life, I forgot completely. Besides—"

Before he could go on justifying himself, Vaz cut him off cold and changed the subject. Now he seemed to be in a hurry to wind up the conversation. His face remained impassive but in his voice, once he began to speak again, he addressed his comrade more familiarly and with an undercurrent of displeasure and scorn. "Listen. comrade. Am I sleeping at your house or right here?"

Now a truly agitated mood crossed the lawyer's face. He had lost the composure and assurance with which he had received Vaz and laid out his ideas. He pulled a chair next to Vaz, seated himself leaning forward, made a gesture toward giving him a pat on the leg, and then spoke in a whiny, complaining voice. Vaz had to understand the situation. To stay there would be extremely foolish. The cleaning woman would arrive at seven in the morning, and if he left beforehand, he could be spotted and apprehended as a thief. As for his house, unfortunately he had a bourgeois family, his wife didn't comprehend these things, he had a maid, so the comrade had to appreciate—isn't that true? The lawyer's diction, normally so fluent and well articulated, became confused, hesitant and pathetic.

Vaz stood up. His thoughts carried him far away. He saw before him Manuel Rato's wife sitting on the floor next to the remains at the hearth, her eyes shining from insomnia and happiness, and the daughter nestled asleep next to her mother. The image was so clear and reassuring that a brief smile flowered on his serious countenance. The lawyer interpreted this smile as acceptance of his explanation and calmed down a little.

"Good," said Vaz, extending his hand. "Be well!"

The lawyer accompanied him down the corridor, where Vaz had left the bicycle, and peeped out to see if the road was clear. As Vaz prepared to depart into the shadows, the lawyer suddenly felt the onslaught of a multitude of insistent and dreadful thoughts.

"Friend!" he called after him, and as Vaz turned around, he lifted his hand to the inside pocket of his jacket, saying, "Maybe you need some money?"

Vaz didn't answer and headed out onto the street. The lawyer returned to his desk, lit another cigarette and smoked it savagely, and after pacing back and forth a few times, opened the window curtain and stood there looking out at the dark, deserted street. The rain had started again.

14

Only the following morning could Vaz go to the Pereiras' house. To get there would take just over an hour. And he had more than five hours. He couldn't even think about finding a pension for the night. It was too late and it would provoke dangerous suspicions. Besides that, he was self-conscious about the terrible shape of his clothes and shoes, soaked by water and mud, all crinkled and shabby. He felt so weak from hunger and from lack of sleep that he couldn't go walking around until the end of the night. He had to rest, even if it meant lying down in a ditch in the mud. It had been more than a week since he began his tour of this area, and during that week he had spent two sleepless nights, and on none of the others did he sleep more than three or four hours. He had pedaled hundreds of kilometers on his bicycle, gone league after league on foot, and all this eating an average of one small meal a day.

Then he remembered an encounter months before near that road, alongside a tranquil brook, in the shadow of the ruins of an old aqueduct. It was a bright sunny afternoon and with his comrades he had eaten a big crumbly bread with a bright yellow omelet sprinkled with green parsley. The memory brought him there. Slipping in the mud on a by-way, he made it to the brook and saw the dark blur of the aqueduct. He propped his bike up, found a stone and sat down. The stone was wet and cold, the ground a marsh. The arch of the aqueduct hardly served to shelter him from the rain, driven by a wind that gusted in soft, cold and silent flurries. In the dark of the night he made out the sad outline of two willow trees and heard the water bubbling in the stream.

He gathered up his jacket collar, pulled his hat down to his ears and, supporting his elbows on his knees, buried his face in his hands. He still saw Manuel Rato's wife and daughter nesting on the earthen floor near the embers of the hearth and then fell into the void of a doleful slumber, constantly interrupted and constantly triumphant. Dozens of times he woke, and after brief instants of lucidity when his hearing sharpened to the sound of the water in the stream and his skin shuddered in the wind and the rain, he fell back again, also for just brief instants, into a heavy stupor. Each time he woke, the image came to him of some comrade, or of his girlfriend with her thin, sad face, and voice and gestures so delicate and tender. And every time he went back to sleep, the very same images appeared in his dreams.

When morning began to break, he was trembling from the cold and his weakness, and he got back on his way. But he couldn't say if he had been sleeping the whole time next to the aqueduct ruins or if he had ever got to sleep at all.

15

Pereira wasn't home, but he wouldn't be long, said Conceição, in a singing drawl with her arms folded over her chest. She was a full-figured and ruddy-faced woman with bright white teeth that were always flashing, black curly hair pulled up behind her fleshy pink ears, and rolled back in a sizable bun secured with barrettes.

"Would you like some coffee?" she asked, changing the subject. As Vaz nodded yes, she got up and added, "But first come see my baby boy."

Yanking at his arm, she practically forced him to get up too and led him to another room. "Shhhh!" Step by step, ever watchful of her guest and lifting her finger to her nose to ask silence, she approached a small wicker basket and raised the cloth covering it. Amidst a pile of clothing, a minuscule face was hidden, wrinkled and purplish, wrapped in an enormous white bonnet. Next to its face the baby held its closed fist, also purple and shriveled, with fingers so tiny and fragile one might have felt afraid to touch them.

"Beautiful, huh?" Conceição whispered. Slowly and cautiously she lowered herself and kissed that adorable little hand.

When they returned to the kitchen, as she lit the portable oil stove, she asked, "Have you heard anything about The Friend?"

Two years earlier, shortly after they married, Pereira showed up at home late one night accompanied by an unfamiliar man. He had come to spend a few days with them, but no one in the neighborhood should know about his presence there. Conceição regarded the intruder with mistrust. The next day after lunch, when he offered to dry the dishes, she couldn't hold back from exclaiming, "What nonsense!"

The unknown man only smiled and dried the dishes. He was tall and thin, with a long face marked by deep furrows and a forehead that vanished into his incipient baldness. His whole face was touched by such a profoundly peaceful and friendly expression that any feeling of antipathy toward him was unthinkable. He talked little, but when he did, he spoke about things in his low, serious voice so clearly and well that when he stopped, Conceição felt sad that he didn't continue talking, for she had never heard anyone speak like that. Seeing him with his calm demeanor, so friendly and happy, she could hardly imagine him to be a man burdened by responsibilities and passing through an extraordinarily difficult situation. Her husband told her that The Friend had just escaped from a stockade. The police had attacked his house and pursued him with gunshots, conducting a manhunt for him throughout the region. He spent five days in their custody, writing most of the time, always making his bed, quietly helping to peel potatoes or dry the dishes, and showing interest in everything with his discreet questions and frank opinions. At the end of five days, in the dark before dawn, he escaped, accompanied by a comrade who came to retrieve him, leaving behind ties of admiration and mutual understanding that he had nurtured. For several days, Pereira could only sigh, while Conceição wiped her eyes from time to time with her closed hand.

"If they catch him, they'll kill him," Pereira had said.

Conceição found it impossible to understand how anyone could pursue and seek to kill such a man.

That visit tied the Pereiras definitively to the Party. The Pereira house at first served as a secure site in the underground system and later, when Pereira became responsible for the local organization, it became the contact point for the controller comrade with the organization. In those two years, several Party functionaries had visited regularly. But the fond memory for "The Friend" never died. All the others had a name. That one, to them, remained always "The Friend." The first time Vaz went there, he didn't respond when they asked about him, because he didn't know whom they were speaking about, and the Pereiras also couldn't say any more because they didn't know anything more. Later on, Vaz asked the leadership and the Pereiras got to know who the comrade was, his name and his best-known pseudonym, but never used either one. To them the friend was always "The Friend."

Vaz was just finishing his coffee when Pereira returned. He was a short, sturdy man dark with a deeply tanned face and cool green eyes like a cat's.

"They're coming!" he said as he entered.

16

Aside from Pereira, Jerónimo and Gaspar also took part in the Local Committee. Jerónimo was a strong man in his fifties who moved deliberately; he had very short hair, white and thinning, the clear, loose skin of his face covered by an irregular outgrowth of beard, with cheerless gray eyes, and a drooping, disdainful lower lip. He was the oldest of the comrades; he had served time in prison and with his moderated, patronizing voice never looked directly at the other person when he spoke.

Gaspar was quite tall, with a serious, long countenance, always sucking his narrow lips, giving him the impression of self-assurance and decisiveness. He was one of those figures that call attention to themselves by their physique and their attire: On any Sunday he would less likely pass for a worker that he actually was than for some public employee or schoolteacher. He spoke fluently and expressively, with visible pleasure that he took in hearing his own voice. Gaspar was a worker at Cicol, the biggest factory in the area. Among the various worker committees that had been created in different enterprises, the most active by far was the one at Cicol. Gaspar personally chose the other members of the committee, and it was he who several times led them into the main office to present the demands that he himself had formulated. The management was taken aback by the breadth and organization of the movement and promised the asked-for raise in wages, as well as agreeing right away to some smaller needs.

"They think they're only dealing with ignoramuses," Gaspar was saying now at the Local Committee meeting. "But if the workers show up knowing what they want and explaining in detail what they're asking for, the company is forced to agree."

Gaspar described their victory with evident pride, highlighting his personal role with no pretense of modesty, because he was convinced that their rapid success belonged to him and his arguments.

"And what were the other employees doing while the committee was in the main office?" Vaz asked.

Gaspar tightened his lips, as he habitually did when he'd begin to speak. "They continued working naturally," he answered.

Vaz brought out the advantages of having the employees suspend their work and gather outside the main office while the committee was inside, but Gaspar disagreed firmly. "That would only complicate matters. If we get a good result this way, why should we do it any other way?"

"Success is not always the best proof of the correctness of an approach," said Vaz, insisting on his point of view.

Pereira thought like Gaspar and, when he spoke, regretted that he did not have his friend's gifts. He spoke as though Vaz's opinion had attacked and personally humiliated Gaspar and he felt the duty to defend him.

As for Jerónimo, it wasn't very clear what his position was. "Comrade Gaspar," he said, looking distractedly toward the window with his drooping, scornful lip, "is a most outstanding comrade owing to his gifts. And that's the danger. If the comrade's not there, the organization loses fifty percent."

And after a pause he corrected himself: "Maybe even sixty percent."

Such words were high praise for Gaspar, that in a way also implied an ironic criticism of his methods of work.

Gaspar appeared not to notice either the criticism or the irony. Hearing Jerónimo's words with obvious pleasure, he continued defending his opinion, insisting on the successful achievement. "If people believe some other way will produce better results, let them do things their way. But at Cicol, let me continue doing it my way."

Providing further backup, he cited the progress in the Party cell at the factory where, besides circulating thirty copies of the paper, they already had a dozen members. "And these aren't just casual members. I know them all and I recruited them to the Party myself."

"You've done quite a bit, friend," said Vaz. "As Comrade Jerónimo says, that's the danger."

17

By midday Gaspar and Jerónimo had left, and Vaz stayed for lunch with the Pereiras. Conceição brought out a cod steak for each of them and an enormous pot of potatoes that normally would serve half a dozen people. The Pereiras well knew the life of Party functionaries and conscientiously aimed to fill their bellies when they came to visit. There was no longer any question about that. But if a stranger would attend that lunch, they would find it truly extraordinary. They would be surprised to see Vaz pile up an incredible mountain of potatoes on his plate and devour them like a glutton in short shrift, along with pieces of fish, bites of bread and gulps of wine poured out for him in a little pink glass she reserved exclusively for the comrades. The surprise would turn to shock seeing Vaz return to the pot, serve himself another whole pile of potatoes and eat them with the same pleasure as the first, as the couple looked on calmly and coolly. The shock would rise to the level of indignation when Vaz, after destroying his second serving of potatoes, went back to the pot again, served himself some more, hesitating briefly seeing there were still a half dozen at the bottom, and ended up taking those too. He unexpectedly laughed to his friends, saying, "No one's good for anything if they don't have their health!"

The first time Pereira told Conceição that the comrades were hungry and she needed to feed them abundantly when they came to the house, Conceição cooked a ton of potatoes with fish. Pereira invited the comrade to help himself. Conceição watched as the comrade ate everything and could have eaten more. The next time she made more and was amazed that even that didn't conquer his hunger. *How could this man eat so many potatoes?* she thought. Only later did she come to understand the meaning of deferred hunger in healthy, energetic bodies, the hunger from months and years of intense work. So now, when she heard tell of a comrade who climbed a fig tree and ate a hundred and fifty figs at one sitting, and another who consumed two generous dinners in succession, "so as not to disappoint either of the two families that invited him," or when she saw Vaz polish off a whole pot of potatoes that in truth would have been enough for half a dozen people, she found it natural, and only felt sorry she was not in a position to offer more substantial, tastier meals.

After lunch Conceição brought out Vaz's clothes, all dried out and ironed, and Vaz made ready to leave. When he said goodbye, Conceição grabbed him by the arm and almost shouted, "What? You're taking off without seeing my boy?" And she pulled him, raising a finger to her nose to impose silence.

18

That was the last meeting of the day. Now he had to get home. At 10 o'clock that night, on the dark, open road, he perched on his saddle, pushed off with his pedals and gladly appreciated the squeal of the tires on the wet asphalt. From time to time a car approaching from the opposite direction blinded him with its headlights. At those moments he hugged to the right and made a point of looking only at the curb until the tornado of the speeding automobile passed. From a tavern in a well-lit stretch a radio blasted. Three boys saluted him. A pair of lovers pinned to a wall unclasped themselves seeing his bicycle's night light. In the roadside gutter a stray dog's pair of eyes glistened. All these little incidents seemed worthy of Vaz's attention and notice. Only when he got to the rise with the olive trees did he take note of his own fatigue. He didn't go farther than the first milestone. His legs were giving out, his body was drenched with sweat, and he breathed deeply as though the air could wrench the growing anxiousness out of his chest. Having traveled more than a hundred kilometers on a bicycle, against the wind and through a number of rainstorms, the potatoes he had eaten at mid-day had been ingested and digested, and now his weary organism was begging for some reinforcement. *I have to eat something,* he thought. And he remembered that a league and a half farther on he'd surely find that curious man's little store open. At the crest of the hill he let go and coasted down.

The fresh, moist breeze thrashed his face and neck and penetrated his fists and upper arms, reinvigorating his exhausted body. It wouldn't be long before he'd be eating a quarter loaf of bread with whatever else they had, and the rest would go better.

The store was closed. On the black, silent village street he saw nary a soul. At that point Vaz envisioned before him the whole long trek home. He saw the steep hills he'd have to climb and the kilometers he'd be forced to walk his bike, and the rocky roads punctuated by ruts that would make him brake constantly and throw him off course. He saw the settlements, the tiny dwellings, the forests, the bridges. And feeling the listlessness of his body and his growing desire to lie down and cover himself, he recalled the indignant face of a comrade doctor objecting to their work regimen in the last couple of years: *You're going to kill yourselves!*

He felt a genuine aversion on that stretch. It was two kilometers of flat plain with only the rare tree alongside the way, without a house or a milestone or distinguishing feature. Now the only sounds he could hear were the frogs in the marshes and his generator, sweet and monotonous. The entire weight of his exhaustion fell onto his eyes. The doctor wasn't right. There are many ways to die. He saw him as if it had been today. He seemed angry, then he smiled.

Whoa! The wheel twisted. He tried to steady it but a powerful force threw him into the air until he fell to the ground, while the bicycle rolled into the gutter in a wild somersault. The headlight went out. In the depth of night, through which only very far away could he see a twinkling of lights, once again he heard the lazy croaking of frogs at their leisure.

The generator worked. He tested his hurt shoulder, straightened out the handlebars, and proceeded for a while on foot, noisily slapping the pavement with his boots to drive away his sleepiness.

In the first village there was a fountain. He set his bike down, pulled off his cap and washed his face over and over again with palmfuls of water. A figure appeared, stopped to watch him, mumbled a few words and faded back into the darkness to the dragging sound of wooden shoes.

That made him feel better. But after the midnight hour he came to a long bridge that separated the two halves of a village and he thought about the sudden steep road ahead. He doubled over with fatigue and his chest tightened like a vise. If all went well, he wouldn't arrive home before three o'clock. And now he had a good number of kilometers before him to walk his bicycle. One time when he got to this place, another cyclist with a basket on his luggage rack briefly met up with him, and when Vaz dismounted, he did too.

"The rest stop is at the cork tree!" said the unknown man, his eyes burning with lively irony.

Then he saw there was indeed a solitary dwarf cork tree and subsequently took it as a reference point to get off.

As he traveled, the few lights in the village next to the bridge appeared ever farther below. He already knew by heart all the irregularities on the road, the slope's incline meter by meter, the patches with holes or sandy pavement or loose gravel, and the grassy terrain alongside that made for smooth going. As much as he tried to take advantage of the time thinking about useful things, he couldn't divert his attention from the road he was negotiating, imagining the desolate landscape the night held hidden from sight and the white wall awaiting him at the top of the first angle of the rise. Then he'd see that straight row of three trees, and the sandy curve, and that flat section with the little house where a little girl once said goodbye to him, and that deceptively curved slope whose angle of incline was much greater than it appeared, and then that long stretch of road that snaked across the plain, then the little village, the first sign of life after three kilometers of desert, and then rising again, up, up, up to the summit with the mills. When he got to that spot and felt the cold night wind from the north caressing his sweaty skin, he would think, *I'll soon be home.* And with renewed energy and elation he'd throw himself into the last hour and a half of his journey, another thirty kilometers of hard, difficult road.

There was still quite a way to go before he was "home." Some timid lights from the village next to the bridge could still be seen below, way below, as though buried in the formless mass of night. He guessed down below at the meandering course of the stream and of the hills eyeing each other from their heights along the valley curves. He paused for a moment. Neither wind nor rain, nor any human voice nor bird cry, nothing disturbed the beautiful, tragic night silence. But when he got to the white wall, the full effect of the mills came beating into his ears: *Wheww, wheww, wheww....*

How happy he was to receive that announcement from on high. It wasn't just the anticipation of the moment when he would have conquered the long climb. It was also the friendly company in the barren wilderness. Well he knew that song, sometimes tenuous and smothered by the hills between, other times daring and full-throated as if the whole firmament belonged to it, sometimes sad and fleeting, other times threatening and proud, and always ever nearer, more present, more enchanting. It would not leave him until he reached the top. Despite both his recurring weariness, hunger and need for sleep and the tiresomely dense dark of night, he felt rocked in the cradle of that strange song and thought even if only for that it was worth passing through there in the dead of the night. *Oh, Portugal! How beautiful you are, in the embracing diversity of your landscape, the purity and whimsy of your skies, the melancholy goodness of your people! Oh, Portugal, beloved country! You will emerge from your long nightmare, you will surely leave it behind. Your people are waking up and struggling. The Party has finally reached the greatness of your people.*

The mills sang in the night. The sweet smell of damp earth and vegetation spread through the black air. Vaz huffed and puffed as he walked on in his steady, dragging pace, and his eyelids drooped ever more. Was he still awake, or sleepwalking?

Chapter *II*

1

The little houses spread out, quiet and reticent, on both sides of the road. Some grouped together, separated by a few meters of land or stone walls. The others seemed like they sought to avoid company, surrounded by pine and olive trees, perched on a slight elevation or submerged in the dusty green of fig trees and briers.

Next to the street stood the house of Miss Ermelinda. The nearest house, a good thirty meters away across an olive grove, had recently been rented to a family from Lisbon. Ermelinda was involved in this. One day two guys appeared at her door with bicycles in hand, asking if the house was for rent. Not that attractive and profoundly meticulous, Ermelinda had left her younger years far behind. But she loved to gossip and joke around, especially with nice young men, which these two were. So she was interested in them and went to retrieve the key from the sister of the owner, and she herself showed them the house. One of the men had a wide face and clear skin, with a serious expression and eyes of unusual intensity. He spoke quietly and responded to every question quickly and assuredly. She asked where he was from, what he did, if his parents were still living, if he was planning to stay for a long time or just a while, if he was sick, if he would be using the local bus, if they also had rationing in Lisbon. And this man, with his clear, fixed gaze, answered all her questions to her satisfaction.

But it's strange, Ermelinda would later recount, *everything I asked he answered, but I wound up not knowing anything.* Only when she asked how they were going to bring their baggage did she receive a concrete answer that she could remember. The one who provided it was the other man, tall, dark, with delicate features and a happy attitude, who spoke in a jocular manner that, along with the mischievous way he looked at her, pleased Ermelinda very much.

"Baggage?" he said. "It's on our bicycles."

Ermelinda laughed out loud, and the dark man, giving her a friendly pat on the back, laughed too.

One morning Ermelinda opened her window and saw people in the neighboring house. "They came last night and I didn't see anything!" she said to her husband in a whisper reserved for great confidentiality.

The husband was quite different from Ermelinda. He always left it to her to look after their little patch of property. He worked at home as a shoemaker, at his own pace, with his lips always in position to whistle quietly to himself. She talked rapidly and excitedly; he was a quiet man of few words. She had dusky skin, a muscular body, flat chest and energetic manners; he was built softly, full-figured without being fat, white-skinned and of calm temperament, with a number of black moles on his face that looked painted on. He was still yawning, not quite satisfied with his sleep.

"They came last night!" Ermelinda said again, intimating with her repetition some questions, doubts, curiosity and designs.

Her husband only replied, in his slow drawl that seemed to echo in his mouth, "And so-o-o?"

That afternoon Ermelinda met up with Amélia and asked if she had heard the neighbors arriving. Amélia furrowed her eyebrows, as always, and answered, "Ermelinda, I couldn't care less about the lives of other people."

Miss Ermelinda walked off muttering and looking at the pathway ground with uncommon attentiveness. "What bothers me," she said when she arrived home, "is that I neither heard the car nor do I see any sign of the wheels. They couldn't have come by foot."

The husband enjoyed seeing her irritated and kidded her deeply and slowly, "Boo hoo hoo."

Meanwhile, Ermelinda liked her new neighbors. They were educated but not smug, level-headed people. Sometimes, in the summer, families came from Lisbon. If anything, they got along well with the Pim-Pa-Pum, the wealthiest people in the area, the name Ermelinda gave them because they couldn't hear any noise on the street without immediately jumping to the window, sticking their heads out, turning their necks and peeping out in every direction. The new neighbors were just a couple, although the Senhora's brother often visited them, the nice tall, dark man who gave her the answer about the bicycles. They were friendly toward everyone and the Senhora never passed the children by without saying a few caring words. Still, they led a very isolated life. Days passed when only the Senhora showed up at the door or window, to shake out a cloth with gentle motions, or to look up at the trees and sky for a few moments with a sad face.

2

Miss Ermelinda wrapped herself in an old shawl, sat on her doorstep and looked at the open lighted window of the next house. She didn't see any shadow passing in front of the lamp, nor hear any sound of voices. Only the steady light indicated the presence of anyone. Her husband, his jacket over his shoulders, came and sat by her side, remaining there similarly attracted by the illuminated frame of the neighbors' window. On the other side, they could barely discern the white strip of the road coming down through the shadowy blur of trees until evaporating down below on the big curve. Now and then they could hear a distant voice or the howl of a dog. Then the silence in the dark, humid, tepid air returned.

Suddenly from the hill facing the other side of the road, where you could barely see Ernesto's cottage, raised voices could be heard. Then everything receded into silence, and the night went empty and peaceful again. Only from the direction of Uncle Luís's cottage, Rogue was barking roughly and excitedly. Ermelinda's husband was yawning already and, stretching his arms in the darkness, he stood up to go to bed. A woman's full, distinct cry reached them. "He-e-lp! He-e-e-lp!"

A tangle of women's and children's voices followed the shout. It seemed as though from the top of the road the houses had grown closer, and the whole atmosphere was bubbling as the shouting spread. Ermelinda leaped up, looked at her husband, looked at the neighbors' lighted window, and shouted, "Senhor Francisco! Senhor Francisco!"

The Senhora's outline appeared at the lighted window and then a man's figure. And as the shouts of distress continued coming from the facing hill, Senhor Francisco's calm voice came to her: "What is it?"

"Help, Senhor Francisco, someone's getting murdered!"

The shadows disappeared from the window. The Senhora's returned as she leaned on the window sill. Then two figures came through the olive trees in a long stride. *Two?* Ermelinda thought. *I didn't see that they had any visitors.* Shortly after, the shouting ceased and everything retreated to quiet, darkness and mystery. Only here and there, dispersed through the night, could you hear voices frightened by the shouting emerging from the other houses.

"If it was me, I wouldn't go there," Ermelinda's husband said in his husky voice.

"You wouldn't go?" his wife hissed, her face right into his as though she wanted to flay him with the whip of her words. "You didn't go, you chicken!"

The husband forced a smile. "Boo hoo hoo." And then they heard the sound of gravel on the path in front. The sound was clearer as steps crossed the street and two figures close together, one apparently supporting the other, passed through the olive grove toward the neighbors' house. The figures slipped behind the house, the Senhora's shadow retreated from the window, and then the lamp was moved and the light danced inside the room until it disappeared.

More steps were heard, a new figure came from the road and passed through the olive trees on the same path.

The two of them held their tongues as night settled in, now sinister and unrevealing for the lack of the lighted window. From afar, Rogue started barking again, raw and excited. Time passed and no one reappeared.

"I'm going there!" said Miss Ermelinda, just to say something.

When her husband muttered, "What do you want to stick your nose in for?" she made her decision and crossed the olive grove, crunching the stubble in her hurried, nervous steps. At the back of the house, under the kitchen door, a strip of light shone. She knocked. They opened the door. And what she saw left her speechless.

At the table, Ernesto was seated with a steaming cup of coffee before him. He glared at the cup with deep concentration and occasionally lifted his angry eyes, looked at one, then the other, and returned his gaze to the cup. After opening the door and telling her to come in, Senhor Francisco went and stood by the chimney with his face paler than usual, and watched the Senhora with attention. The Senhora's brother, leaning by the window sill, standing a little apart, seemed amused. Ernesto's wife was also seated at the table, her black eyes and hair contrasting with her pretty white skin. She had her littlest daughter on her lap and, standing at her shoulder, a sleepy, bored-looking boy who looked like her. Anica tried to grab hold of her coffee cup with both hands, but scalded herself, saying, "Oh! Oh!" angrily, and blew on them to cool them off, clapped her hands and laughed.

And the Senhora, in front of Ernesto, turned her thin, sad face toward Anica and said to her, seriously and tenderly, "Wait a minute, honey, until it cools down."

Miss Ermelinda, gathering by the derisive looks from Senhora's brother, that she was a fifth wheel, had to return home without knowing or understanding anything.

3

This is what happened. They were at the Frog's gate.

"Children wear you out," said Ernesto's wife. "I have three kids and I look like an old lady."

Leaning against the wall, the Frog laughed. "You may look like an old lady, but you're a lot better looking than a lot of young ones."

They talked a little while longer. Everyone had said their good-nights when Ernesto turned toward the Frog. "Repeat what you said before."

The Frog stammered something and laughed, not knowing if Ernesto was serious or joking. But Ernesto had taken great offense at it. He clearly saw how the Frog ogled his wife. Frog, yes, and all the others too. Seeing it, he became incensed over his wife's cool, white skin and her provocative black eyes and hair. That's what he loved about her, yet the very thing he could not forgive her for. Now, with a bit of wine exposing old jealousies, he insulted his wife, insulted the Frog and started advancing on him threateningly. The women shouted and dragged him back home. When all seemed to have quieted down, Ernesto in a violent move ran to his tool shed and grabbed a small hoe.

Prudently, the Frog went into the enclosed patio, took hold of a thick pole and closed the gate. With a great hullabaloo the women and children piled up to block Ernesto's way. In one moment, when the Frog's wife fell to the floor shrieking and Ernesto took a few steps back to launch a new assault, a figure emerged from the shadows, seized his armed hand and lifted his arm behind him, and the unknown voice breathed into his ear. "Calm down, okay?"

Ernesto bucked and tried to free himself, and tried again even more desperately. But the unknown man, taller than him, kept pace with his movements almost effortlessly, keeping his arm in a tight hold. Ernesto glanced at another man's figure a few feet away who, from his stance, undoubtedly was preparing to intervene. A sudden memory came to him of what was happening. *I'm apprehended*, he thought. Years before, he had been apprehended on the street in Lisbon and then too the police grabbed his arm in that same hold.

"Take that thing from his hand," said the second man to the one holding him.

Ernesto felt strong hands vigorously prying his fingers and twisting them until he dropped the hoe to the ground. The unknown man pushed down the footpath while the other man spoke to Ernesto's wife, as Ernesto pleaded to know where they were taking him. Tripping across the pebbled ground, Ernesto experienced a mixture of rage, shame, relief and curiosity. *Let's see what will happen,* he figured.

The door opened and the thin face of a serious, smart woman could be seen in the lamplight. They ordered him to enter and he did. They ordered him to sit, and he sat. Were these really police? Was he arrested? And if so, would a police transport be coming to pick him up? The taller man, who had grabbed him in the arm-lock, handed him some loose tobacco and rolling papers. Wanting to decline them, Ernesto nevertheless found himself with the tobacco and papers in his hands. As he listened to the wheeze of the oil heater in the hearth, he started awkwardly rolling a cigarette. It was so thick he could barely close the paper around it. Ernesto flushed up to his ears not understanding how he could even have taken so much tobacco.

Shortly afterward, his wife arrived holding Anica in her arms and João grabbing one arm. They offered him a seat. Ernesto continued to feel the humiliation of surprise and shame, but the owners of the house appeared not to notice it. They didn't speak to him and just talked with Anica. The woman of the house put out the heater and Ernesto heard the lid of a coffeemaker, and soon the appealing smell of coffee reached his senses. His wife smiled that the danger had passed, and her skin looked even whiter and her eyes and hair looked even blacker and shinier, and that pleased Ernesto now though he didn't know why. The lady of the house, with a smile that contrasted with her sad expression, asked how old Anica was, gave her a tentative caress with her fingertips, and pouring her a cup of coffee, placed the spoon with the sugar dregs in her mouth. Anica hesitated, sucked on the spoon and giggled. And Ernesto, raising the mug of coffee that had been placed in front of him, looked at Anica, looked at that unknown woman and felt his despair diminishing and his love of life coming back. He was tempted to smile, but he suppressed it as being inappropriate, and furrowed his eyebrows even more fiercely.

Ernesto's wife delicately declined the coffee, and her son refused it angrily. Miss Ermelinda came, her eyes burning with curiosity, and then left. Ernesto drank his coffee. No one addressed a word to him. Only the woman of the house, when she put the bag of sugar before him and stared at him with sad eyes, said, "Help yourself."

And he, out of politeness, helped himself. At any moment he was expecting to hear some reference to his behavior, and was even prepared for interrogation, blame and insults. Nothing. Not even the woman of the house asked what had happened.

"Listen, dear child," she said to Anica as they stood up half an hour later, "whenever you want, come visit me. Agreed?" And once again she gave her a fleeting caress with her fingertips, a gesture that showed both the desire and the dread of affection, that also reflected the same contrast between her smile and her overall melancholy.

Anica responded firmly and warmly, "Agreed."

4

After Ernesto left with his wife and children, the senhora went to the window to watch them go down through the olive trees, and the two men headed into a room inside whose air smelled strongly of tobacco.

The lamplight spread lazily into the corners of the room. A man with his chest draped across the table had a round, ruddy face, graying hair and tortoise-shell eyeglasses. From the lassitude of his position on the chair, you could tell he had been there a long time, trying not to make any noise that would betray his presence, and had gone numb from his absolute immobility. His sleepy eyes, daunted by the light, peered coyly at the newcomers over the top of his lenses. In one corner, a thin young man with a tiny black mustache stretched out belly-up on a bed, his hands behind his neck. He remained still for a few more moments. Then he got up in an agile leap and approached the table with a big smile across his face, his mischievous eyes surrounded by tiny creases. He seemed to be eagerly anticipating the news they would be giving him.

It was the first meeting of the Party organism created to direct the activity across a vast area, up until then the sole responsibility of Vaz—Senhor Francisco, as they called him where he was living—helped and supervised by Ramos, who had accompanied Vaz when he went to rent this house, passing himself off as his brother-in-law when he visited. The evolution of the organism had made it impossible for only one comrade to handle. The establishment of leadership organisms for locales only recently connected to the Party was especially hard, since they were dealing with new, inexperienced cadres. In larger centers, where the Party had stronger roots, actual Regional Committees assumed charge of the work in several places. But in most cases, to continue advancing, and to pay close attention to the contacts that were arising all the time and integrate them organically, it was necessary that the major part of the work be handed over to people entirely dedicated to that activity. Thus it was decided, and they were designated, that comrades António and Paulo would work with Vaz. Ramos would absent himself from contact with the cells at the base level but would continue to supervise the sector.

While Ramos recounted what had happened with Ernesto in upbeat, accelerated tones, António listened to the story, slowly smoothing his mustache, his little eyes shining with malicious satisfaction. Paulo looked tired, his eyelids lowered as he calmly leafed through an appointment book, as though he had no interest in hearing the story and wished to show as much to the others.

"That's it," Ramos concluded. "The man had his coffee and went home. Here in this area Vaz found a friend who could be helpful to him in any situation, and we must now get down to our work, because we've already lost more than half an hour."

With his round face more flushed than usual, Paulo raised his timid eyes above his tortoise-shell frame for an instant, as though he wanted to say something, but returned to his calendar, turning its pages with his short, stubby fingers with nails that were cut very close.

"We had just finished giving a quick overview of the organization," said Ramos, continuing with the interrupted meeting. "Does someone else want to speak?"

Paulo turned to look around at the other comrades with a questioning glance, which Ramos did not notice, but which Vaz did.

"One moment," Vaz said in his even-keeled voice. "I would like to say a few words about what just happened. It seems to me that Ramos and I ere too rash."

Paulo looked at his comrades over his glasses, as if to query if anyone could doubt the correctness of Vaz's words.

Ramos doubted. "Let's not make something tragic out of it," he said. "As for myself, that's all it was. They called for help and I came. I saw the man with the hoe and I took it from him. I saw that if he stayed there, he'd end up going after the other guy, and I brought him in here to calm down. It all went well, and it considerably strengthened the underground nature of this house. It's very important that we have people who owe us favors, and the one today is of no small account. Besides which, dear comrades," he added smiling, "it's always pleasant to exercise your muscles. Shall we continue our work?"

António smiled with satisfaction. Paulo looked at Vaz.

"A couple more words," said Vaz slowly. "Things could have gone very differently and whether it's because they wanted to present us as witnesses or because we saw ourselves directly involved in the issue, we could have placed the security of this house in danger. We were too impetuous."

"Shall we continue with our work?" Ramos insisted. His tone now was hard and cutting.

"We can continue," Vaz pronounced calmly, fixing his steady gaze directly on Ramos. "But you're making a big mistake not recognizing such an obvious thing."

"In addition, we were here," Paulo underlined, blushing and looking at the others as if to beg pardon for speaking up.

"Shall we continue?" Ramos asked for the third time. They continued.

An hour later, Vaz's companion entered the room. She placed a coffee pot on the table, two mugs, two cups, and a bag of sugar with the soup spoon stuck inside.

"Hey, my friend," Ramos said, placing his hand on her shoulder. "Are the spoons also rationed?"

She slipped her shoulder away and didn't answer. Before she left, looking at Vaz with her sad smile, she slowly passed her hand through her hair. Vaz followed her with an observant eye and for an instant remained staring at the closed door, thinking something confusing and far away.

5

There were a number of items on the agenda: To present an overview of all the aspects of activity in the sector so that the new comrades, António and Paulo, would be up to date before throwing themselves into the work. They needed to distribute tasks among the three of them, choosing which organization each one would be responsible for. To make decisions about a series of struggles in progress. To decide on the political orientation in a few delicate cases of cadres, such as on the Regional Committee, where some friends, influenced by the carpenter Marques, continued to manifest serious misunderstandings about the day labor market, attributing the adopted orientation to poor work by Vaz and asking that Ramos be there. And to agree finally on the difficult and urgent problem of "installations," that is, the clandestine houses where comrades lived.

In fact, with the exception of Ramos, who was not technically in the sector and had his installation somewhere else entirely, of the three comrades in the new organism only Vaz had a companion and a house "installed." António's situation required an urgent solution. For two years he had been a Party functionary. In the region he came from he always lived in rented rooms. Removed from that region, where his location had been compromised and his security was in danger, he arrived precipitously in the new sector and was now living in Vaz's house, keeping his presence completely secret in the area and experiencing extreme difficulty in leaving and returning without being seen. Aside from that, the leadership opposed two Party functionaries with organizational tasks permanently living in the same house. So it was necessary to find a new installation for him immediately. Vaz had already spoken with the woman comrade whom Afonso had introduced to him. António went to find a house. As Ramos had to go to the Regional Committee—of which Afonso and Marques were members—and as Vaz had to connect António to other organizations and lend assistance without delay to struggles that had been his task, they decided that Ramos should take advantage of the visit to the Regional Committee to bring the woman and connect her to António who, for his part, would bring her to the already rented house.

As for Paulo's installation, that was temporarily resolved, and Ramos was in no special rush to alter it. Paulo was living in the home of a baker in a little village, introduced and known to the neighbors as a family member who had business in the region and would be living there for a few weeks. But according to Paulo, he could only work at night. The house was tiny, without a room where he could do as he pleased. People, either family members or customers, were popping in at all times with personal questions and, above all, there were four children in the house who never gave him a minute's peace. They got into his books and wanted to get into his papers, they pestered him, rattled him, grabbed him, challenged him to play with them, annoyed and roughhoused with him, constantly playing pranks on him, and trying, though so far without success, to steal his eyeglasses right from his nose.

"Grin and bear it, old man," said Ramos, laughing and speaking at the same time in his unique way of making his every word a kind of rumbling laugh. "You need it as part of your training."

Paulo timidly peered at him over the top of his glasses and said nothing in response. He clearly was not satisfied from this not taking his installation more seriously.

Ramos's failure to give his attention to this problem did not flow only from the idea that Paulo's installation was fine or from the difficulties of finding something better. It flowed mainly from the idea that Paulo did not have the skills to be a Party functionary and that, within a short time, to the extent that he wasn't up to the requirements of his new assignments, it would be seen that he, Ramos, was right in the discussions he had with the Secretariat. Ramos did not deny that Paulo was an honest comrade, for, after all, he had known him for many years. But to him, to Ramos, whose least gestures and poses immediately revealed a far from common fieriness, a quickness and audacity in his decisions, optimism in confronting hardships and dangers, to him, the timid Comrade Paulo, unsure of his own opinions, blushing at any criticism, and soft, soft, soft as mashed potatoes, could not rise to the necessities of a Party functionary's life and activity. For that same reason, too, when it came to distributing control over the organizations in the sector among the three comrades, Ramos tried to assign to Paulo only the simplest things with no long-range implications, such as dealing with the lawyer who didn't even want to read the press, or Manuel Rato isolated out in his little village, or the shoemaker who had promised months before to call a meeting of the Local Committee.

"The easiest things, the most manageable," he said ironically, without observing the imploring look Paulo gave him over his glasses.

Although this was only the third time he had met Paulo, Vaz also shared Ramos's doubts: The comrade would hardly do the job. Noticing Paulo's diffident eyes and the way his face reddened as the tasks were handed out, he concluded that the comrade himself believed he didn't have the right assets. It was so obvious that Vaz himself felt ashamed for Paulo's embarrassment.

"I'll help you any way I can," he said by way of consolation.

6

Early in the morning, before the meeting began, Vaz stood at the kitchen door watching his companion. Rose had some outside and lit the charcoal stove, and as the wind stirred up the embers, she seated herself on the doorway stair. In a typical pose for her, she placed her elbow on her knee, held her chin in her hand and remained still, distractedly eyeing the farthest curve in the road. They'd been living together for three years, considering themselves content with one another, appreciating and respecting each other. Nevertheless, Vaz sensed that something in Rosa's life and manner still escaped him. When they decided to join their lives together, Rosa, in her calm tone and a sad expression on her face, said, "Listen, José—" (at that time, Vaz was not Vaz yet, and not even Francisco) "Listen, José, I love you as I've never loved anyone and I feel certain you'll be happy with me. But let's agree on one thing: Let us not speak of the past. Not mine and not yours. There's nothing I can possibly be ashamed of, but you know I had been with someone and I prefer to never talk about it."

Over the three years they'd lived together they always honored that agreement. Rosa was devoted both as a woman and as a comrade. Vaz grew more and more fond of her, and thought to himself how lucky he was to have met such a companion. But despite their mutual trust and understanding, their tenderness and respect, a strange presence always showed up whenever Rosa got distracted, in her melancholy, in her way of looking and touching. This presence constantly captured Vaz's attention: Against his own will, he found himself observing his companion and trying to figure it out.

For a long time, Vaz thought he had found the secret of Elisa's ways (at that time Rosa also was not yet Rosa) in the memory of the first man she had been with. Vaz had met Rosa in Party life, a solid comrade with much experience behind her, but he never heard anything about her past personal life. He was completely in the dark about the man, or the men, who had passed through Rosa's life. The memory of a great love in her past—for some time that seemed to Vaz to be that imponderable presence in Rosa's spirit. One day he decided to mention it.

For a few moments Rosa didn't speak. With her sad eyes vaguely reflecting very distant memories, she knit her brows in an effort to pay attention. Then she seemed to come back from very far away, looked at Vaz's face, peered into his eyes, looked at his face again, and her sad expression came alive with a sincere smile. Bringing her face up to his, she embraced him for a long time, quietly, as a friend, saying only, "Silly. Silly boy."

From that instant Vaz became convinced that Rosa loved him as she had never loved anyone.

Then he began noticing Rosa's interest in children, in the shy, almost fearful way she coddled them. He saw how frequently, when she was speaking with one of them, she would suddenly shake her head as if to wave away some unwelcome thought. He concluded that invisible presence was her sorrow over not having a child. When he arrived at that conclusion he kept it to himself. Under current circumstances in Party life, for security reasons, for financial hardships, and more than anything the uncertainty of the future, he deemed it his responsibility to avoid having children. He never spoke of this to Rosa, instead encouraging her to make friends with the neighbors' children. But the problem was not resolved. At every turn, he was reminded of it by his companion's sad face, her distant gaze, her distractedness, and in the almost maternal way she treated him. Now, on the threshold of the door, seeing her with her chin resting in her hand and her eyes fixed on the curve of the road, while alongside her in the stove the charcoal was being fanned by the breeze, Vaz once again thought there was still something lacking before Rosa's life was completely bound to his.

And if truth be told, at that moment Rosa's thoughts were indeed very far away, going back, way back in years. At that time her mother was still alive. Rosa didn't have work in the factory and was staying home. The two women had been silent for a long time, sitting next to each other sewing up the holes and rents in their ragged clothing. All of a sudden, Rosa lifted her eyes off her sewing, looked at her mother and let out a wild guffaw. There was something so unreal and unusual about that laugh that the mother, not knowing quite why, felt deeply disturbed. And also lifting her gaze off her sewing, she looked into her daughter's burning eyes, brimming with desperation, and shining feverishly in her wrinkled face.

"What's the matter, daughter?" Her work started to tremble in her hands.

The response came immediately and decisively. "I'll kill myself!"

Rustled by the wind, the charcoal crackled in the stove, throwing off a flurry of bright sparks. Rosa shook her head and removed her hand from her chin.

"Have you been there all this time?" she asked, seeing Vaz leaning in the door's shadow. She rose, approached him and placed a soft, chaste kiss on his cheek.

Vaz looked at her intently, then went in to see his comrades.

7

Late that night, after discussing the struggles in progress, they saw the need to issue a manifesto. It would describe the successes achieved in some factories, the wage raises won by committees chosen and supported by the workers, and would try bringing those experiences to factories where they had no contacts. The meeting was suspended while Ramos, lowering his excited face in deep concentration to the table, drafted the manifesto.

Although she did not belong to the cell, Rosa attended this part of the meeting because, by higher-level decision, the companions in these clandestine houses should attend meetings held there at least when matters of a general nature were under discussion. As soon as the meeting was suspended, António handed her a piece of paper. Rosa gave him that same sad, attentive smile she gave to the children and looked. It was a rough, awkward image of a heroic woman holding a big stick, with police and fat-bellied bourgeois either dead or wounded at her feet. Below, in carefully designed letters, it read: "The new baker woman of Aljubarrota." The humor in the drawing was in the fact that the brave, athletic woman was supposed to be Rosa. Although this one was skinny and wrinkled, it could clearly be seen because "the new baker woman of Aljubarrota" had one finger sticking out wrapped in a bandage, just like Rosa, who had cut herself a few days before chopping onions.

"You can't deny it looks like you," António said, his black eyes glinting maliciously.

A childlike smile that clashed with his graying hair lit up Paulo's face. "It's not bad," he said, and then shut up, not wishing to irritate the artist, and seeing he was being unkind toward his woman comrade.

"Let me see, let me see," said Ramos, pausing his writing on the manifesto. He looked at the drawing, then at Rosa, like someone comparing a portrait with the sitter. "Yes, the finger is similar."

Vaz walked to his bed, lay down and slept deeply. Seeing his wan face and his panting chest, Rosa recalled how a few days earlier he had arrived home late at night practically dead of fatigue, his lips white and his eyes sunken, and after washing up—his trunk, face and feet—and devouring two plates of reheated soup, still he went into his work room to do what he always did when he arrived home no matter what the hour: put all his papers in order on the table, write down his expenses outside the house, read the wartime communiqués and shift the little flags on the map of the Russian front. It was that superhuman energy that Rosa most admired in her companion. Seeing him now, laid out asleep, while his comrades laughed and joked, she heard their amusement and chuckles as an unfair judgment of Vaz, accusing him of weakness and laziness. For that reason, slightly annoyed as she always was with Ramos's humor, she got up and covered her companion's legs with a jacket.

When Ramos finished his work, they woke Vaz up, read the manifesto and, following the group members' suggestions, made a number of alterations. Ramos handed the manuscript to Rosa. "There, you have something to amuse yourself with tomorrow," he said. "It's ready for you to cut the stencil. António will take it from there."

As they were now about to confer on matters of a more secret nature, they told Rosa to leave and go to bed. Minutes later they heard typing on the machine. "Our friend doesn't lose any time," said Paulo.

For half an hour they heard tapping on the machine. Then the rest of the house fell silent. The four men worked into the night. They spoke in low voices and only once in a while, if the discussion heated up, did their voices rise and leave the room.

"No, comrade,"said Ramos, elevating his voice toward Paulo, who looked at him humbly over the top of his glasses. "That's not the way we should talk about problems. When an obstacle arises, our first obligation is to try and find a way to overcome it. The rest is just chatter."

"Don't talk so loud," António said, "you'll wake our friend."

Ramos lowered his voice, but even though stifled and contained, he sounded even more excited. *In everything Paulo says and does*, Ramos thought, *it always shows his timidity. He's soft and weak, like mashed potatoes. He's not going to get very far.*

Early in the morning, when it was still dark, they considered their work finished. Paulo and Ramos gathered their things, got dressed and ready to leave. When they passed through the corridor they found the light on in the kitchen.

Rosa had worked all through the night. Her tired, imperturbable face looked even more delicate. Holding her bandaged finger out exaggeratedly so as not to soil it, she passed the black ink cylinder over the template on the copier and, lifting the template, retrieved the copies that she had piled at her side.

"Are a thousand enough?" she asked Ramos, her voice raw and disagreeable, almost aggressive.

8

For some time Vaz had witnessed Rosa's impatience and ill-will toward Ramos. Attentive and friendly toward all the comrades as she was, though not especially an intimate, she demonstrated extreme reserve talking with Ramos. In his pleasant or expressive mood, or just simply being in his presence, something put her into a bad mood. One day Vaz brought it up, asking if she had anything against the comrade. Rosa thought for a few moments. "No, I don't," she answered at last. "I've known him for many years and I know he's a good comrade worthy of respect."

With that the conversation ended.

In truth, who could deny Ramos his good qualities? Episodes from his life were often recounted among members of the Party. It was known that he had fought in the Spanish Civil War and had been among the first to enter the Montaña barracks at the time of the fascist uprising in Madrid. It was also known that he had been imprisoned several times—and escaped once—and each time he had been flogged and tortured. People retold the answers he gave to the police, some of them earning him violent beatings. One time, for example, when he was in solitary confinement in a hole underground, humid, suffocating, with no light or ventilation, they found him steak naked. *What are you doing all naked in there?* the guard inquired. *What a question!* Ramos answered. *Can't you see I'm taking a sunbath?* A lot of such stories circulated, all of them portraying a vigorous, courageous, dynamic man of inalterable good disposition and cheer even in the most difficult situations. But many times the comrades closest to him, with whom he was on the most intimate terms, noticed the ease with which he could anger, and how his good disposition in reality then concealed an unconquerable bad temper. At times like that, his jokes were harsh and even cruel, unjustly hurting others.

Rosa claimed she had nothing against Ramos. But the difference in the way she treated him and the way she treated the other comrades was undeniable. António was in the house just two weeks, yet Rosa gave him attention and affection such as Vaz had never seen her give Ramos. Vaz never noticed when this habit began, but whenever António left the house, he took his leave giving Rosa a kiss on the cheek, and Rosa kissed him in return. In Ramos's case, it sufficed for him to place his hand on her shoulder, a gesture he made frequently with anyone, and she would turn away, her face contracted in abhorrence.

Vaz returned to the subject. "How come you always talk to Ramos with such ill will?"

Rosa half-closed her eyes in thought. For a time it looked as though she had escaped far away to that past that Vaz didn't know.

"I don't like the way he looks at women," she answered finally.

9

Seated on the kitchen doorstep, resting her elbow on her knee and her chin in her hand, Rosa watches the last curve in the road.

She remembers it as though it were today. She was just sixteen and he was already over thirty. He called her on the pretext of asking for something and placed his hand on her shoulder in a paternal gesture, a heavy hand with clean fingernails that grasped her flesh. From his face of finely drawn features, his bright ecstatic eyes did not look into hers, but rather searched her mouth and her ears now reddening with shame.

"You're making a mistake not wanting it," he said.

Seeing a sad shadow pass across his generally such joyful eyes, sensing with that hand every intention of intimacy, Rosa felt that in fact she was making a mistake in not wanting it. Oh, how stupid she was then!

A sudden close sound yanked Rosa's gaze away from the last curve of the road and her distant past. A few meters away, regarding her intently, was a bitch, dirty white, small and skeletal. Right away Rosa saw its eyes, red like a rabbit's, and her enormous teats hanging disproportionately from that tiny body.

Vaz, who had been reading the newspaper at the kitchen table, got up and went out to see what was going on. "Shoo! Get out of here!" And he moved as if he were about to throw something.

The little dog took a couple of steps but did not seem impressed by the threat. She continued to look at them with curiosity.

"Are you hungry, girl?" Rosa asked in her sweet, sad voice. "Haven't eaten anything today, huh?"

The dog's muzzle responded well to the friendly tone of that voice, her drooping ears stiffened in one jolt, and her eyes fluttered with glee and intelligence.

"It looks like she understands," Rosa smiled.

Vaz went back inside. The bitch lay down a few meters from the door, her muzzle tucked under her front paws, enjoying the sun and looking up without for one moment losing sight of the woman sitting on the doorstep. Rosa had seen her more than once already next to Miss Ermelinda's house, but didn't know whose she was. "Hey, you!" she asked. "Who do you belong to?"

The dog raised her head, her ears once again stiff, a flash of joy passed once again over her eyes, and she started rhythmically tapping the ground with her tail, a wretched, dirty, yellowish white tail.

"She's ugly, but she's a hoot," Vaz observed, returning to the door.

After a while, when they left for a nearby house to purchase potatoes, they told her, "If you want, come with us."

The hound rose in one movement and followed them, almost dragging her misshapen teats on the ground. When they got back to the house, they gave her a hunk of bread, and from then on they remained friends.

10

This was the second time since the meeting that Miss Ermelinda knocked on their door. The first time, on the pretext of bringing the latest news about the brouhaha with Ernesto, she came to confirm if the versions that were circulating in the area were true. Now she appeared minutes after Vaz had left, as if she had wanted to corner Rosa alone.

"I came to bring you this bunch of parsley," she said, explaining herself. "Can you use it?"

"Listen to this," she went on in her alarmist metallic voice. "Today I went to town and I wanted to buy a bit of salt pork. It was more salt than pork! 'Listen man,' I told him, 'not only is the pork so expensive, but even at that, it's so full of salt!' You want to know what he answered me? 'You think it's expensive?' he answered. 'Then don't get the salt pork, put your money in the pot, and watch how much fat it adds.'"

Ermelinda wanted to show how indignant she was, but the joke was stronger than the indignation, and she couldn't contain her howl of laughter.

What does she want? Rosa asked herself. *She didn't come here to give me some sprigs of parsley or to tell me that story.*

"Everything's so expensive," Rosa said, "and on top of that they doctor foodstuffs in all kinds of ways."

"Well," Ermelinda replied. "I really have to admire how you manage to run a household without rations," and she fixed her sideways gaze on her neighbor with the sharp, penetrating eyes on her dark face. "Oh, yes!" she added without a pause. "True, you get your rations in Lisbon."

It was clear from the way she said it that she didn't believe it. *Why is she talking about this?* Rosa thought. *There's something behind it.*

"That's it exactly," said Rosa. "Our grocer in Lisbon always puts some things together for us on a regular basis, and my husband and brother are able to pick up a little extra thing or two on the way."

She pronounced this with such conviction that she had to congratulate herself. Miss Ermelinda seemed to share this admiration because she remained silent for a few moments just looking at her. Then her eyes smiled, as she realized that Rosa's answer instead of throwing her off, opened up a new path for her.

"You're lucky. You have your husband always going to the city and you have your brother who shows up whenever he can, by day or by night—."

These words, "by day or by night," were said purposefully. Rosa thought, *This is the issue.* And she understood that seeking her out to learn things, Ermelinda was holding trump cards to play from her hand.

"Yes," Rosa answered in her sad, calm voice as always. "I owe a lot to my brother."

She quickly tried to find an explanation for Ramos's nighttime arrivals which, Rosa perceived now, had been noted. But a reasonable explanation did not occur to her, and Rosa preferred to show her confidence in not answering directly. Miss Ermelinda's piercing eyes glowered at her insolently, as if to ask, *So, you won't explain?*

"You just told me what happened to you when you went to buy salt pork. Do you want to know how my brother buys meat? He enters a butcher shop and says, for example, 'Give me half a kilo of the 14$40 meat.' And when the butcher sets it up to cut, my brother stops him and repeats, 'I said 14 *escudos* 40 *centavos*.' Most of the time the butcher sets that piece aside that he was going to cut and proceeds to cut a better one. Now, don't think my brother knows anything about meat. No, he doesn't. But since he lets it be known that he understands, they are afraid to cheat him and they always sell him the best."

This little story normally would have delighted Ermelinda. This time, it seemed she didn't like it. *This wasn't what she was looking for*, Rosa figured, *but this was what she'd get*. Miss Ermelinda didn't give up so easily and went back a little in the conversation to pick up the lost thread.

"Well, as I say, you are lucky. We peasants, we don't have friends in the city, we're denied food, they steal from us on the weight and the quality, and even cheat us on the price controls. But you have your husband, you have your brother, you have friends of your husband and your brother, and obviously that's a lot different."

Friends of your husband and your brother, said Ermelinda. So it wasn't just about Ramos. Miss Ermelinda knew or suspected something more. Had she noted, through some carelessness, the presence of António in the house? Or his exits and entrances, however infrequent? Or that Paulo had left with Ramos after the meeting? Or did those disturbing words "friends of your husband and your brother" reflect a specific mistrust of political activity on Vaz and Ramos's part? Now it was she, Rosa, who absolutely needed to draw things out of Miss Ermelinda, for it was a matter of security for the house.

"Am I lucky?" she said, changing the direction of the conversation. "I would be lucky if I had my husband and my brother always at my side. But as you know, my brother only rarely comes here, and my husband has to make a living so he spends much of the time away from home. So I'm almost always alone. It's a poor excuse for luck, what I have."

Ermelinda remained quiet, thinking. *No*, Rosa thought, *she doesn't suspect António's presence in the house*. And with that thought, the sudden, manic fright came over her that António at that moment might make some noise inside or would have to cough. Despite her outer calm, she felt her heart beating fast and feared that Ermelinda would see it.

Then she sharpened her ear and noticed without the shadow of a doubt that Miss Ermelinda was not trying to listen hard. *No, she doesn't suspect it,* she thought.

Ermelinda let out a sudden laugh and asked, "The bitch was here, wasn't she?"

To Rosa, in her nervous state, this question seemed to be saying, *When I wanted to draw you out, you didn't want to give me anything. Now that you want to draw me out, I'm not giving anything to you.*

"Yes, she was," Rosa said.

"Do you know what the Pim-Pa-Pum are saying?" Ermelinda's eyes lit up with irony and malice. "They say you don't raise children to go serve in other people's houses." And she laughed heartily again.

Rosa did not entirely understand the meaning of the expression, but she did get that the bitch belonged to the Pim-Pa-Pum and that they looked upon her hanging out by the door with displeasure.

"The animal is going around hungry," she couldn't help herself saying.

"They don't give a damn about the bitch!" Ermelinda exploded, getting more and more excited. "It would have died a long time ago if it only ate what they give her. While she was wandering around, now at this door and now at another, they didn't even think about the bitch because no one wanted her. Now that they think the bitch was able to find a new owner, they don't want to lose their property rights over this rich prize. That's how they are"—and Ermelinda closed her fist to indicate the stinginess of the wealthiest women in the area—"and if you'll forgive me for saying so, they wouldn't even give a piece of shit to the poor. They eat salt pork to their heart's delight, and that says it all."

Her dark features wrinkled and her eyes lit up even more.

"Let them talk," she added. "If the bitch is okay here, it's because she's well treated, and if they want her in their house, then give her something to eat! Don't you pay any mind to what they say."

These words soothed Rosa somewhat. They showed that apart from her suspicions and curiosity, Miss Ermelinda remained sympathetic toward her neighbors and took their part against the malicious gossipers around her. But Rosa still didn't know just what suspicious things had been observed in the life of this house.

"Well," Ermelinda said, rising to her feet, "I have to go look after my Tender Rabbit," as she referred to her husband when talking with strangers.

When she left, Rosa immediately went in to recount the conversation to António. He agreed that Ermelinda, or someone she talked with, had suspicions about the life going on in the house and had certainly noticed strange things, possibly arrivals and departures by night.

The grocer, who was a cousin of the Pim-Pa-Pum and had heard about the scuffle with Ernesto, sought Amélia out that night to ask her a question about the neighbors. If there was one thing Amélia did not like, it was talking about other people's lives. She told the grocer she knew nothing about Senhor Francisco or the Rosa girl, and left it at that. To some question that the grocer asked her, she just frowned and muttered, "Revenue inspectors? No."

Chapter **III**

1

"Women comrades are necessary in the ranks," said Marques the carpenter, his intelligent eyes shining from behind his lenses. "If they take away the few we have, how can they later criticize us for not developing women's work?"

Afonso received these words with enthusiasm. Until then he had believed the single reason for his discontent at Maria's going underground was of a personal nature: He loved Maria, Maria loved him, and the new life that Maria was about to enter admitted the danger of a definitive separation. In the final analysis, he more than anyone had contributed to this. It was he who had cultivated a dedication to the Party in Maria. It was he who, after a conversation with Ramos, spoke with her about the need for strong, courageous women to set up clandestine houses. It was he who communicated Maria's words to Vaz when she affirmed she was prepared for such an assignment. Yes, it was he who, step by step, prepared for the event he least desired—the removal of Maria, possibly forever. He now understood that what led him to this was in great part his vanity over being loved by such a woman. He also understood that for some time he thought it was a question of demonstrations of dedication in words alone, affirmations to declare and nothing more. Later, when he saw that the comrades were taking her at her word, he tried to retreat, walking back his conversations with Maria and privately hoping that Maria would retreat as well. But no. He saw, to his surprise, that Maria accepted the news with tranquility. Since Maria had joined the Party, there had been a kind of competition between them as to their dedication, a competition strictly tied to the mutual feelings they both had. Afonso's intense Party activity was largely driven by his desire to rise in Maria's sights. And in Maria's activity, he also thought he saw the desire to please him, Afonso. Maria had won the competition. Afonso now saw with a certain resentment

61

that it was truly the love for the Party that moved Maria, and his dis-enchantment forced him to admit that her feeling for him, Afonso, was an expression of love for the Party.

In the long, sad conversation they had on Sunday, she grabbed the end of his tie and told him, in that special, very personal way of hers, "So, my dear friend? What are our problems compared with those of the Party? Come on, don't be angry, be happy."

And he, the comrade on the Regional Committee, Comrade Maria's supervisor, bemoaned the fact that she had carried her ded-ication this far, and felt disillusioned when he perceived not the slightest hesitation from her about their imminent separation.

This is when Marques brought up a political argument against Maria's leaving, an argument that he had never recalled before, that could apply not only to Maria but to other more highly placed comrades. "The problem," Marques expounded, "is putting people in charge of the ranks who do not have enough preparation. The Central Committee is way, way up there" (this phrase was one of Marques's favorites). "Not being well informed, it cannot decide properly. In this case, on the one hand, Comrade Maria goes away and the movement in the jute factory is as good as lost. On the other hand, Maria is a very fine woman, full of spirit and good intentions, but from there to being prepared for a life underground is a great distance. Our regional organization suffers, and the comrades in the leadership, instead of solving difficulties, will probably just create new problems."

All this sounded so clear and well-founded to Afonso that he wondered why it had never occurred to him. Once again he recog-nized the superiority of Comrade Marques, proving with a mixture of admiration and restlessness how in many respects Marques saw things better than the comrades at higher levels. It had already struck him (and continued to) that on the question of the day laborers Marques was right, not José Sagarra, Vaz and the Party leadership. Now, in the case of Maria, Marques once more opened his eyes. *We want to handle things so seriously,* Afonso reasoned. *We worry so much about not giving weight to our personal interests, that we end up not seeing what's in front of our eyes out of fear we'll be judged for being persuaded by our personal interests.* The error, the big error, was not having sought out and consulted with Marques, not having heard his opinion, in spite of Vaz having said it was not a matter to bring to the Regional Committee.

Now it was too late. Vaz had gone to speak with Maria and all was set for either Vaz or Ramos to pick her up. Afonso mournfully awaited that day. Confused, he lost his motivation for everything. At the shop, the boss was always calling attention to his carelessness. He forgot to show up for meetings. He almost didn't eat. At home, his father looked at him askance and in a sour mood. His mother watched his movements closely, thinking her son had some dissatisfaction related to his political activity, caressing him more often and straightening the lock of hair that daringly fell over his forehead. She told him gently, "Let them go, my son, they don't deserve your sacrifices."

Afonso wondered how she could have guessed what was going on in his soul.

2

If you asked the guys if Maria was pretty, everyone would be baffled. If you asked if they liked Maria, everyone without hesitation would say yes. In one form or another, to one degree or another, at some level or another, guys who knew her had been in love with her. Was it her way of walking that seduced them? That unhurried stride, with her legs close together, seesawing modestly with each step? Was it her black, moist eyes, over which those eyelids with the long eyelashes slowly swept? Was it her suave singing voice that seemed to ask but always commanded? Or was it her childlike gestures like that one grabbing Afonso's tie or his open shirt collar to say, for example, "No, dear friend, you're not right. If we all just looked after only ourselves, who would get things done? You'll do it tomorrow, right?"

Afonso first became conscious of his interest in Maria in an incident with Higino, a stuffy little man with pale skin and shiny hair, who had been a boss of the local opposition and because of it imprisoned various times. It's not at all clear what precisely was his thinking, but he spoke well of the Soviet Union and badly of the dictatorship of the proletariat, well of the Communists abroad and poorly of the Portuguese Communists. When the Party started gaining influence among the local working class, Higino would say he was getting old, that there were no longer any capable people, that it was all just a joke now. He focused his activity in the doorway to a bookstore where, with an appointment book under his arm, he spent his afternoons surrounded by two or three admirers. One day, when he saw Maria, Afonso and Marques walk by, he said to his followers, "With members like these, the Party is doing some formidable recruiting."

He didn't say it so softly that Afonso didn't hear him, and in the fisticuffs that followed, Higino lost two teeth. For some strange reason, he stopped speaking positively of the Soviet Union and the foreign Communists. As for Afonso, he realized he reacted that way not just over the offense toward the Party but for the offense directed to the beloved girl. That evening, when he took his leave of Maria, she lifted her arm to straighten out his wayward lock of hair. *She loves me*, Afonso thought.

Maria lived with a brother and his wife, an older sister and their father. The mother had died long before. The father was an old anarchist. But in the last years that he worked, he would often say to his friends, "I was always an anarchist, and I'll die an anarchist. I don't agree with the system of government that the Communists support, nor with many things in their theory and organization. But they're the people winning the hearts of the youth and in the end they're the only ones doing anything. To be against them is to stand with the bosses and fascism against the workers. And that I will never do."

Then came the stroke that immobilized him. Now only with great effort did he move, leaning on a cane, and only with great difficulty could he articulate a few words. In half a dozen years he aged considerably and lately just stayed at home, watching his older daughter and daughter-in-law take up the slack. When Maria came home from the factory, she went right to her dad to give him a kiss and say a few words. For the old man, this was the best moment of the day, the moment he waited for impatiently and tearfully, gnawing the white hairs of his mustache in a prolonged tremor that might have been his attempt to speak, or the horrible feeling that came when his mouth would not articulate the words he wanted to express. The day of the incident between Afonso and Higino, when she got home, Maria sat next to her father, kissed him on the forehead, adjusted the pillow he was reclining on, and told him, "So, Gramps?"—that's how she addressed him—"You know what? Your little dove's going to have a boyfriend. A very brave man!"

Maria didn't withhold secrets from her father. Now she related her feelings toward Afonso, and the incident with Higino, as she had told him about the first struggle she'd participated in at the jute factory, her first enrollment with the Young Communist League, the first committee she belonged to, and even her entrance into the Party.

"Listen, Grampsy," she said to him that time. "You were always an anarchist, but I know you'll be able to understand me. I just joined the Communist Party. What do you think? Good or bad?"

The old man sat nibbling on his mustache, his eyes fixed on her, brimming with tears. Maria, who knew him well, saw them clearly as tears of approval.

More difficult, far more so, was communicating to him her decision to dedicate herself to the revolutionary life. Now it was a question not just of the struggle, but of abandoning her aged father, the father she adored and to whom she was his greatest joy. She told it to him in her half-mischievous, half-ingenuous manner, and repeated it several times on different occasions so he would believe her. Her brother, sister and sister-in-law kidded her so long as they suspected she was joking, then declared open war when they understood she was serious. But the old man, silent in his armchair, shot them disapproving glances and supported Maria. Maria straightened his pillow, combed his hair, caressed his face and told him, "I love you more and more, Grampsy. You're worth more than all of them put together. You get younger and younger all the time, you know?"

Then came the lengthy conversation with Vaz who, in the unemotional terms that he habitually used, explained to her how a Party house functioned and what her tasks would be. Vaz set the date on which either he or Ramos would come to get her and she should have her things ready—one small suitcase or basket. "Take only what you think most necessary. We'll arrange for anything else you need."

After that talk, which gave a new and entirely different direction to her life, Maria was with Afonso in the garden and kissed him for the first time, a sad, restrained kiss that bespoke nothing of passion and youth. They walked in silence to Maria's door and then she said, "This is it, dear friend. If no one made any sacrifices, how could we move forward?"

She looked at him with tears welling in her eyes, her black eyelashes aloof and, leaving Afonso crushed and desolate, ran into the house.

With his permanent tremor, the old man moved his lips as if he were trying to chew. He looked at his daughter, waiting for the usual caress and words and right away noticed something strange in her. But before he could guess what was the matter, Maria ran to him. "Oh, father! Dear, dear father!" And she embraced him, reduced to convulsive sobbing.

3

Ramos appeared on the appointed day.

"It's a good thing you came," said Marques with visible satisfaction. "Let's see if we can still fix a few stupidities."

Ramos had come essentially to talk with Marques, the oldest comrade in the local organization and member of the Regional Committee. Marques had expressly asked to speak with him because he did not agree with the directives given or transmitted by Vaz. The question was about the marketplace for the day laborers. Marques continued to believe that the markets were a reactionary institution and that the formation of marketplace committees and the struggle in the markets, rather than leading to successes would only carry hardships, alienation from the farmworkers, and repression against the best comrades.

Marques lived with his mother, a skinny old lady with big distrustful eyes who for no apparent reason circulated throughout the house pacing in silence. Marques brought his friend to his room where the map on the wall and a small table with neatly arranged books and papers contrasted with the disorder of everything else: the bed unmade, a saw and a plane across the pillow, trousers and socks crumpled on a bench, and boots full of dried mud in the middle of the floor. Marques pulled the old blanket over the pillow and, offering the chair to his friend, sat on the edge of the bed.

"If the Central Committee had decent information it would never have handed out such directives. The results are there to see."

His eyes shining behind his lenses and dominating his thin face, he drew from his pocket a greenish paper in a slow-moving gesture, unfolded it carefully and placed it in front of Ramos. It was a posted decree from the Civil Government still bearing evidence of paste and whitewash. The decree established heavy fines for rural landowners who paid more than fifteen *escudos* a day.

Impatiently, barely containing his tongue, Marques eyed Ramos as he read the decree. When Ramos got to the end, Marques continued in a burning, authoritative tone. "There you have it—the first result. Instead of the hoped-for raise in wages, immediate repression and setting a maximum wage."

Ramos did not seem impressed by Marques's rant. He asked first what the farmworkers were saying. Marques reported that the Party organization—which had sent them the decree—had the same opinion. Ramos placed his hand on his comrade's shoulder and said, "The comrades see it wrong and you see it wrong, old man. What you are presenting in defense of your opinion is, on the contrary, the best proof of the Party's correct orientation. And what a proof it is, my friend!"

Ramos remained quiet for a few moments, as if enjoying Marques's contrary expression and the sight of his eyes like hot coals behind his lenses.

"You see it wrong," he repeated. "The intervention by the Civil Government, establishing fines for landowners who pay more, shows without a doubt that the farmworkers are demanding and winning higher wages. You don't need glasses to see that."

Saying those last words half speaking, half laughing, Ramos patted Marques's shoulder, a friendly, protective, condescending pat that he immediately saw was not well received. Marques's annoyed gesture seemed to say, *You are mistaken if you think you have said the last word.*

"Answer me this," said Marques in a slightly trembling voice. "Is it or is it not true that, threatened by the State itself if they pay more, the landowners, not just out of fear, won't pay more, but they'll have a beautiful excuse to justify their refusal in the face of the workers? Is it or is it not true that we are seeing a ruling-class offensive against the workers?"

Regarding him sideways, Ramos appeared amused by Marques's state of excitement. "No, it is not true. You're not even noticing that the threats are directed not against the workers but against the owners themselves. You know what that decree signifies? It signifies that the big landowners, the biggest landowners, are terrified by the victories the farmworkers have gained. Everywhere, they're seeing owners forced to give in to the workers' demands, and want to organize the reaction and put the brakes on this backsliding of their own class. This decree should be shown to all the workers as a sign of the gains they've won following the correct line of the Party. My friend, the path is as we've said: Establish market committees, and in the market, through the committees, demand higher wages. What you and the Regional Committee have to do is give the greatest possible assistance to the peasant organizations to carry this policy forward."

After a brief silence, as though he had not seen Marques's annoyed gesture a few minutes earlier, Ramos placed his hand again on his shoulder and in the same condescending tone said, "You've blundered, old man, and now you have to acknowledge your mistake."

A somber Marques held his tongue. When he spoke again, he did not allude to the issue of the day laborers' marketplace. "A lot of times," he began, "if we make mistakes, it's because we don't have the help we need. The Regional Committees need politically prepared supervisors who know how to explain things, who know how to defend decisions, not supervisors who are just mailmen taking and delivering reports from the base and instructions from the leadership—and all too often distorting them!"

Marques's intelligent eyes scoped out Ramos as if asking, *Should I go further?* And the slightly amused smile that broke out on Ramos's mouth seemed to answer, *Say it, say it, I already see where you're going.*

Marques took a few deep breaths and then spoke for a long time. According to him, Vaz was not qualified for his job. He framed problems in a dry, bureaucratic manner, imposing the decisions of the

Central Committee without adequately explaining them. He didn't know how to deal with doubts or arguments from the comrades. Marques cited case after case, which he had obviously kept and catalogued assiduously. "Speaking frankly," Marques concluded, "any one of the comrades on the Regional Committee has a more solid political education than Comrade Vaz who's leading them."

"So it appears to you," Ramos said flatly.

"It's not just my opinion," Marques answered. "Comrade Vítor thinks as I do."

"Comrade Vítor?" Ramos asked, as though he meant, *What, that great authority?* as he recalled Vítor supporting his chin on his hand and exhaling lazy spools of smoke.

The two remained quiet again. Marques's eyes shone bright as coals in his pale face, and Ramos adopted a sudden, severe concentrated expression.

"Anything else?" Ramos inquired.

"Yes, there is," Marques replied petulantly. And he referred to the women's work in the sector, the movement at the jute factory, the gap that would be felt from the mistake in taking Maria away. "The movement at the Jute can be considered wiped out," he concluded.

"And what measures did you take anticipating Maria's departure?" Ramos asked.

"Measures? What measures?"

Their voices rose and resounded throughout the house. The old lady came to the door, silent, with her big distrustful eyes.

"Sorry," Marques said to her, and lowered his voice.

When Ramos made a discernible effort to also lower his voice, it gave him a more excited timbre. He spoke first of women's work in the sector, of the need and potential for assuring the continuity of the movement at the Jute after Maria's departure, and of the need for all the cells and units of the Party to consider it their sacred duty to help the central apparatus.

"The egoism in the sector, the localism, is still one of the great evils we struggle with. There are comrades who forget they're members of the Party," he added sarcastically, "so they can pass themselves off as members of the local branch of the Green Village of Shallow Bowls or the New House of Friars."

The two men conversed well into the night. Later they stretched out on the bed and covered themselves with the same blanket. Ramos fell asleep immediately. Marques lay there for a long time with his eyes open, peering into the dark.

Early in the morning, in the pre-dawn half-light, Marques got ready to leave. Ramos shaved and looked well-rested.

"All right, old man," he said, smiling and putting his hand on Marques's shoulder. "We'll have another crack at hashing all of this over again sometime."

"Yes, we will, we will—" Marques responded, his eyes shooting through his thick lenses, his face wan from sleeplessness.

Ramos spent the morning at Marques's house, writing. Before midday, Afonso appeared to pick him up and introduce him to Maria.

4

The train jerked along slowly. At each station it made an unexplained lengthy stop. You could hear the huffing and puffing of the old locomotive, a whistle, a bugle blast, the jolt of rail cars, followed by sad silences sticking to the nighttime shadows. Aside from the freight cars there was only one car dimly lit by cheerless oil lamps. In the compartment, three passengers traveled—on one side, an old man with his arms resting on a sack on his knees, his head hanging almost as if unhinged to his emaciated neck, dancing to the rhythm of the train's progress. On the other side, seated face to face, Ramos and Maria.

Her neck supported against the wooden partition, her eyes riveted onto the handsome face of her comrade, Maria is recalling the events of that extraordinary day. She sees Afonso's consternation, and his despairing mood at being left behind, disappearing ever more into the distance in the middle of that deserted road. She sees Ramos's spry, decisive movements as he boards the jitney, carrying her suitcase in one hand and his briefcase in the other. She sees herself getting off in the middle of the muddy road lined with pine trees. She then sees herself sitting in a pine forest with the comrade, eating provisions he had purchased somewhere. She sees the curves in the road where they'd been walking for a long time, sitting down to rest from time to time, until they reached the little station.

She sees herself then, by night already, seated next to Ramos in the sorry, dark waiting room, him getting up and returning with bread, cheese and a bottle of water. Finally, in a clatter of metal and steam, she sees the locomotive and the train. Of all that she remembers, only one thing did she try to remove from her memory: the face of her old father, quietly nibbling the tip-ends of his white mustache and, strangely enough for someone who was always crying even for no reason, not crying at the moment of farewell. When that image comes to mind, Maria immediately tries to send it away and not dwell on it. If she doesn't succeed, tears come to her eyes and she has to pull out her handkerchief to keep herself from bawling. Then comes Ramos's strong hand placed on her shoulder and there's his upbeat, confident voice: "How's it going, girl?"

How abandoned and alone she felt those first hours of the trip. How that jitney seemed so hateful and suffocating. How ugly and hostile that place on the road seemed where they got off. How many times during those hours did she ask herself how she could have decided to take such a step, and if she hadn't made a serious, irreparable mistake offering to live in a Party house. How many times, as if she had forgotten everything, did she find herself asking what she was doing with this tall, dark man who now ruled her fate.

But the hours passed, and Ramos spoke and laughed, and encouraged her, and told jokes about the food, and told stories, and looked straight at her with amused observation, and Maria calmed down and started to smile.

When they left the pine forest to get back on the road, they found a trench at the curb. "Can you jump?" Ramos asked.

Maria balked. No, she would not be able to jump. Ramos then jumped first, holding both the suitcase and briefcase. Now on the other side, he set the suitcase on the ground and, opening his arms, urged her. "Go!"

She jumped awkwardly. He held her for a moment. She felt her comrade's athletic body next to hers and, lifting her eyes, they met his, eyes that said something friendly, confused and disquieting to her. Maria blushed, lowered her eyelids with their long eyelashes, and pulled apart. But it seemed that a memory or an idea coming from far back and rushing now through her veins reached out to her from that man.

5

In the weak light of the railway car, Maria regards her comrade and feels a palpable pain for having to separate from him in a few hours. She was already so accustomed to his presence and his manner! Why couldn't she go live with him? After the awful farewells that morning, this new looming separation seems equally sad. Ramos had told her she would be going to live with another comrade. Ramos would do no more than accompany her to him. "And I'll never see you again?" Maria asked. Ramos laughed at the question and said, yes, she'd see him a lot, and kept looking at her with knowing amusement. Then Maria, somewhat confounded, brought the picture of Afonso back to mind. But Afonso, with the lock of hair drooped over his forehead, his gloomy moods and courteous manners, seemed far away, almost erased, weak and childlike, and over that image another superimposed itself—this one in front of her, this dark man, strong and good-natured, and she saw him placing her suitcase on the ground, opening his arms and saying "Go!" and her jumping and him holding her for a moment tight against him and looking at her, looking deep into her eyes. How would the new comrade be? Would it be Vaz? The idea that she might be living with a man like that frightened her, so officious with his words and expressions, and those fixed eyes so terribly cold and indifferent.

In the other corner of the compartment, the old man coughed, a rough, wet rattle.

"Are you tired?" Ramos asked her.

"A little—"

"Sit here," Ramos said, touching the place next to him. "Lean on my shoulder and you'll sleep better."

Following his suggestion, Maria got up and sat next to Ramos. She adjusted herself into the seat with her back toward him and covered her legs with her jacket. The old man coughed again. The train stopped, and for a long time, as if it had stalled just to idle, all that could be heard was the locomotive releasing steam in a lengthy, monotonous, tiring lull. Then, begrudgingly, it started up again. Exhausted by the events and hardships of the day, and by the train's vibration, Maria fell into a bizarre drowsiness in which she neither thought nor recalled anything, but always present were that poorly lit compartment and the old man coughing and Ramos's shoulder and arm into which more and more she sought succor. Her head slid toward the comrade's chest, and Maria vaguely sensed his face lightly touching her hair as a strong arm propped up her shoulder. At a railway stop in the middle of nowhere, the old man left the train. With only Ramos there, the semi-obscurity of the compartment seemed even more restful. How many times did she drift off to sleep? How many times, half-sleeping, half-awake, did she try to snuggle closer to her comrade for support and comfort? Now she had an arm lying across his long muscular thigh. She felt her comrade's chin resting on her head and she wanted it to stay there.

"Sleeping?" Ramos whispered.

"Huh?"

And she felt the hand leaving her shoulder, moving to her neck and nape, and slowly turning her head. She made no move to resist. In another second she saw her comrade's beautiful face up close and, in the low light that face had something unexpected, inviting and violent about it. Then, as though another person inside of her were compelling her movements, she suddenly disengaged herself and moved away. With his hand Ramos still tried to hold her but in one abrupt jump, Maria shook him off.

"What are you doing, my friend?"

Seated side by side, they remained for a moment looking at one another questioningly. Maria again saw Ramos's hand rising and his face taking on a hard, unattractive expression in which all at once she read deception and threat. She stood up and crossed to sit opposite him, in her former spot, lodging herself into the seat. Ramos said not a word. He crossed his arms, leaned his head back, closed his eyes and looked asleep, rocking with the train's seesawing motion.

How is this possible? Maria asked herself. Maybe from her sudden discomfort or from the cold night air, she was trembling all over.

She didn't know what surprised her most. Was it the comrade's attitude, or her not feeling any indignation or shame over it? No, she felt neither indignation nor shame. At that moment, she thought, she only felt sorry for him and nothing more.

6

Early in the morning they got off at an isolated station. A cold breeze was blowing and a white mist clung to the wooden shelter and to some lanky eucalyptus trees that rose mournfully alongside the rail line. They crossed the tracks to the road, and after a few meters met António.

Maria went on ahead and the other two comrades followed her in conversation. António had already been linked up to the local organizations and isolated comrades, he had gained direct knowledge of several struggles in progress, he got to know the Party cadres' issues, and had gotten commitments of new contacts and locales for support as dropoff points. The organization, which it fell to him to direct from now on, was broader and incomparably stronger than the whole sector he had previously worked in. António felt slightly distressed by the weakness of his earlier work in comparison with what he saw awaiting him in intensity and difficulty. He was astonished to learn that Vaz had not only created or developed all this organizational structure within the span of six months, that he, António, now would be directing. And moreover, Vaz had also been in charge of getting those organizations up and running that Paulo would now direct, not to mention the units Vaz himself would continue to lead, and which were in fact the most numerous, ranging across almost all the farmworker cells in the sector.

"How could Vaz have done so much?" António asked Ramos, as he had already asked himself numberless times.

"Understand, my friend," Ramos responded, "Vaz is not a man, he's a bull!"

António was enthusiastic over one cell above all, the one in the most important industrial center, to whose Local Committee Pereira, Gaspar and Jerónimo belonged. António met with the comrades and saw for himself it was a solid organization with deep roots, with an intense presence connected to the working masses, and with active, bright and resolute cadre. In many aspects they had more experience than he himself had, which led to his difficulty in helping them. Now he understood the reluctance of Vaz when it was decided to hand the direction of that organization over to António.

"You can't take on everything!" Ramos told him. "You already have most of the work with the farmworkers, and besides, this organization, considering the quality of its cadre and their work, is on its own two feet and doesn't need your help."

Vaz acquiesced to that, but still António understood his sense of loss in letting go of such an organization. "I never worked with such a good organization," António told Ramos.

"Yes, it's one of the good units in the Party," Ramos agreed.

"Gaspar is a tremendous cadre."

"Yes, he is. A great comrade."

A little ahead of them, enveloped in the fog, Maria walked on, tired, deprived of sleep, and dazed by the events of the last twenty-four hours. *Will they never stop talking?* she thought. She forged forward, listening from a short distance to the voices and steps behind her. When they had already walked hundreds of meters along the straight road leading out from the station, the bright white of some houses appeared in the breaking daylight of dawn. Maria thought, *Is it here?* And she looked back, her eyes asking the comrades. The two figures drew closer. In the mist, Ramos looked taller and broader, the other more spindly.

"Go on, go on," Ramos said.

After a good half hour of walking, Ramos called out to her. When the two men approached, Maria noticed that the suitcase had been handed over to António. Ramos placed a hand on Maria's shoulder, the other, with the briefcase on António's back. "Treat her well for me, you hear?"

Maria kept her eyes wide open, staring at Ramos, who now suddenly looked as though he'd aged considerably. And to Ramos, Maria also looked different, neither attractive nor even pretty.

He extended his hand. "Be well, my friend. Forget about it, huh?" Ramos grasped her delicate, thin hand and, turning around, went back the other way in a quick, deliberate stride.

"Let's go, friend," said António. Maria started walking at his side.

7

More than a league from the rail stop, they sat down on a slope where they could view the railway line. The house was nearby, but it was necessary to wait there until the morning train should pass to explain the time of their arrival to the neighbors.

Maria was no longer asking herself the same questions she had wondered about before: *What would the house be like? What kind of place would it be? How would the neighbors be?* She didn't even seem in a rush to take a good look at the comrade she would be living with. She noticed only that he wore a little mustache. She was eager to arrive, close her eyes and rest.

António didn't talk much. Once in a while, in a friendly, delicate voice he'd ask the odd question, sometimes repeating it: Are you tired? Did you eat something yesterday? Did you manage to sleep on the train? Are your legs hurting? Are you cold? Maria responded in kind with a minimum of words: A little. I ate. I slept some. So-so. No.

The train arrived, full of its haughty aura, leaving behind it a confused disturbance in the air and a ragged blanket of steam that mixed with the fog, sticking stubbornly onto the trees or depressingly lowering to the ground. Then it stopped a couple of hundred meters ahead, with a mournful whistle.

"We can go," said António.

Next to some houses, he told her to wait. He stepped into a narrow alley and came out with a heavy suitcase. "You take my briefcase," he told her. "I'll take the suitcases."

Maria insisted on carrying her own.

"Later. Farther on," he said. "When I get tired, I'll tell you."

António had said the house was near, certainly to encourage her. They got onto a side road which opened onto a street with big pits full of sand, followed the street, cut through another by-lane, and were leaving behind the few isolated cottages. They passed two small settlements, and Maria never heard the words she had been anticipating at any moment: *We're here!* By her side she only heard António's panting breath. Occasionally she asked, "Shall I take my suitcase now?"

"Not yet," António responded. "When I get tired."

He had already paused several times to put the suitcases down for a few moments and switch the heavier one to his other hand.

From his voice and his pace it was clear that he was exerting himself with difficulty. Finally, he stopped, breathing heavily as he placed the suitcases on the ground once more. Maria looked at him head-on for the first time: A pair of smiling eyes peered out from under the brim of the shabby hat that was too big for him.

Farther on, at the side of the road they were now walking, they saw a large shed with a tile roof set on beams blackened by age and weather. Underneath the roof a group of men were sitting. One was reading the newspaper. At the sight of the newcomers, one short man in shirtsleeves approached them. "Is it today?" he asked.

"Yes, we just arrived," said António.

"Did it arrive on time?" the man asked.

"Five minutes late," António replied.

That man had given António directions when he came looking for a house. He had accompanied him to the next village and then brought him to his wine cellar, where he insisted on António's sampling his goods.

"Is this your wife?" he asked.

"Yes, it is!" António answered, and saw that Maria was blushing.

"Are you better?" the man inquired, because António had explained their coming here on account of health reasons.

"Better, thank you."

The men under the roof watched the three of them. The one reading the newspaper was a strange type with a long beard and rags for clothes, with rips so long you'd think he'd made them on purpose to show off his chubby arms and his fat, hairy chest. He examined Maria lewdly, sizing her up from top to bottom and, paying no attention to the others' impatience for him to continue reading, followed her with his eyes until she disappeared from view.

In the village, faces came to the doorways. One woman greeted António. Two boys started walking alongside him. At long last Maria heard the words she'd been hoping to hear for so long: "We're here!"

It was a humble, ordinary little house, with a door and a window in front. António put the key in the door and they entered. Inside, in the dark, not knowing what to do, Maria froze. In the silence of the house one could hear only the painful creaking of rusty latches. A light appeared at the far end of the house, and António returned to the entry room, grabbed the suitcases and, seeing Maria quiet and indecisive, said—as he had said when they separated from Ramos— "Let's go, friend."

In the kitchen, she sank onto a stool and looked around, perplexed and reserved.

The house was tiny, with only two beds, two tables, three chairs and three stools for furniture, but it had been freshly whitewashed and the wooden doors exuded a pleasant smell of resin. António had already brought kitchenware and a few staples, and now, in the heavy suitcase he was toting some bedsheets. To a degree, this alleviated Maria's worries.

What truly scared her was the sense of constriction she felt, seeing herself alone in the small cottage with an unfamiliar comrade, a young man who had introduced her as his wife. Her constriction was even greater because she guessed the comrade she was going to live with felt the same. They both seemed embarrassed about the false pretense, and all their words and attitudes expressed an inevitable unease. Besides the kitchen, the house had only two rooms: one at the front on the street, the other, like the kitchen, that opened onto a walled patio. António suggested he'd stay in the back room because that's where he would be working and receiving friends. On saying that, however, another idea arose within each of them—that to the visitors they would have to play the role of two people who slept in the same bed. Guesses, expectations, doubts, the problems of housemates, norms of conduct, all these commingled in that instant in the minds of the two young activists. In sullen confusion, they kept their silence.

8

The next morning, António departed. With the thought of being by herself for five days, Maria felt instant relief seeing herself doing as she pleased in the entire house without the presence of the comrade. That very first day several visitors appeared.

She had just returned from the bakery and was making her coffee with the kitchen door open, when she saw the head of a woman of uncertain age and description, enveloped in an enormous shawl, popping up over the patio wall. The head turned from one side to the other, and when she focused on the kitchen door, the woman went "*Pssst!*" to call Maria's attention. Maria went out to the patio and the woman gestured for her to come closer. Maria stepped nearer, struck by the unusual features of the woman in the recesses of her shawl, her dark little eyes darting from one side to the other of her hooked nose that could have been the beak of a bird of prey.

"Do you want to buy?" she asked in a tenuous, low voice. And opening her shawl, she revealed a basket of fine-looking carrots.

Maria inquired the price, and the woman, who by then had covered the basket in the folds of her shawl, asked a ridiculously low amount for the whole bunch.

"All right," said Maria, and she went to fetch the money.

The purchase made her radiantly happy. Her pay, which António had told her was that of Party employees, was so low that she had already asked herself more than once how the pennies were going to last until the end of the month. Besides being so cheap, the carrots were of prime quality, mellow and tender. *We have carrots for half a dozen meals*, Maria figured, content with such an auspicious beginning of her life in a Party house. Still, she couldn't forget the woman's nimble little eyes as she peered out of the shadows in her big shawl. And she asked herself if it wasn't a little strange that the woman didn't just come to her front door.

As if in answer to that very thought, someone knocked on the door and Maria went to open it. It was that man she had seen the day before reading the newspaper under the tile roof. The monstrous rips in his clothing left his fat, hairy chest uncovered, his black beard almost covering his entire face. He had come to ask if they wanted his ration tokens for kerosene and olive oil.

"As you can see," he said, looking at himself from top to bottom, "for myself, I don't need them."

The man spoke in a very pleasant manner, with clear, correct words. Despite his rags and his vagabond look as someone without a pot to piss in, he held high his dignity and pride that fit his corpulent body. His imposing beard put into greater relief his clean white teeth. Maria refused his offer.

The man looked at her with a mixture of submission and insolence, lowered his head with an unexpectedly genteel air, and left.

Another visitor came from next door. Skeletal and famished, she complained about life, the lack of work and the poor treatment she got from her husband, and asked the senhora for any article of clothing she was no longer using.

The next woman, short, fat and obsequious, said she usually went to the town every Saturday and could bring the senhora, as she did for others, a cut of meat or whatever else she wanted. After her came a ruddy young woman offering to go fetch water from the fountain. Then came a woman offering corn straw for mattresses—and her daughter to wash clothes.

A man appeared saying the village was small and could not support one store, but there were two—one of them belonged to him, and would she please buy from him? Two children came, saying nothing, but opening their enormous eyes and drawing closer together as if wanting to defend themselves against some unforeseen assault. A smiling old man came, saying he was a cobbler. And a young fellow showed up selling goat's milk.

Almost all these people were dressed in dirty, worn-out clothes. Behind the smiles and the offers one could only guess at their long unmet needs. This entire parade of misery undid the happiness she felt with the purchase of her carrots. As night fell, viewing herself alone in the quiet of that little cottage, a deep sense of helplessness and abandonment overcame her. When António returned, he'd bring books and newspapers. As for reading during those five days, he had left her only a pamphlet with but a dozen pages, that Maria devoured when she first got up. Now she had nothing more to read. She had already washed her skirt and blouse, already scoured the pot, bowl and coffeepot, already scrubbed the tables and the chimney, already wiped off the iron bed frames, already washed the window glass, already cut paper to line the kitchen shelves.

The poor little house is in order, and her few clothes as well. And Maria still has four more days to endure, four long days and, even worse, four long winter nights, alone, completely alone, with nothing to do to occupy or distract her. She already sang, already cried, already remembered, already dreamed, already went back to the little pamphlet three, six, ten times, which by now she had already practically memorized, already organized and reorganized her things. Now she has before her an immense, empty time to get depressed and sad. It's the first time she has been in a house without a single other friendly person, without voices, without the sound of activity, without life. Vaz had told her she'd have to work a lot and if she had any desire to study, she'd not lack for help. But that would be much later, after António came back, and life in the house would return to its normal pace. Now Maria has four days in front of her, four long days and four long nights of solitude.

Do you hear me, Grampsy? Maria thinks, remembering her old father to whom she always brought her doubts, disappointments and joys. *Do you hear? Your daughter is very lonely and very unhappy, Grampsy. And the night-time is so ugly. The blowing of the wind is so ugly too! She knows the house that she winds up in is needed, that it provides a base for a persecuted comrade so he can work for the good of the people, that it will allow comrades to meet safely, keep their materials and create documents. She knows all this, Grampsy, and for that reason she's happy to fulfill her duty. But she's so lonely and so sad, beloved Gramps!*

9

The very afternoon of their arrival, António told her they were taking a little walk. Just outside the village, a hundred meters or so from the first houses, António stopped. "Take a good look at this wall," he said. "It's the first one on this side. So pay attention."

When they got to the end of the wall, he stopped again. "See this stone that's sticking out? Late Friday, come here and draw a cross with the blue pencil that I'll give you at the house. You won't make a mistake?"

That was the agreed-upon signal, then, by which on returning home António could be certain there was no problem. It was a measure undertaken in all the Party houses to avoid repeat incidents of previous disasters. The police invaded Party houses in the comrades' absence, and when they returned they fell right into the wolf's den.

Late that Friday afternoon, Maria left to place the signal. At António's direction, should anyone speak with her about it, she would explain her going out of the village saying she was going to buy some herbs at the house with the tile roof where on the day of her arrival she had seen the bearded bum reading the newspaper to the peasants. She found no one on the way, inscribed the signal, returned to the house and prepared a stew of potatoes and carrots with a sense of satisfaction she had not known for the last four days. When the food was almost done, she spread out on the kitchen table a cloth she had washed and bleached during those days, placed two dishes one opposite the other, two leaden spoons, two glasses, the bread and knife to one side, and in the middle of the table a little clay jar with a spray of mimosa leaves she had gathered by the side of the road. She stood for a moment studying the table and humming to herself. Then she went to the kitchen door to look out. The daylight was dying now in the humid atmosphere. In the distance, objects were losing the clarity of their shape. It seemed like some invisible hand was spreading a mist of silence and melancholy through the air. In the preceding days, these moments were the most anguished for Maria, almost prompting fear and horror at the coming of the interminable night. Now she was hoping night would fall very quickly, wrapping the village in darkness.

"I'll arrive shortly after it gets dark," António had said.

When the night had closed in completely, Maria broke two eggs into the stew and stood watching them through the aromatic steam, seeing them grow solid, and listening, as though the poaching eggs were assuredly the announcement of António's arrival. In fact, she did hear steps in the street. Maria waited. But no, it wasn't him yet. She pulled two pieces of charcoal from the stove, put them out in the sink and placed them in the dustpan. The fading flame barely kept the stew bubbling. All was ready now, awaiting the comrade's arrival. He was so late! Maria went to look out the front window. As the neighbor was at her door, and it was not a good time to start up a conversation, Maria retreated back inside.

In the kitchen she adjusted the placement of the spoons, wiped the plates with a cloth, although they were already impeccably clean, and thinking she once again heard steps in the street, sharpened her ears. How disheartening to hear footsteps approaching when you're waiting for someone! How long it takes for them to confirm or to dash your hope! Whoever it was continued on their way. *Why is he taking so long?* Maria asked herself. And suddenly dark thoughts possessed her. What if he'd been arrested? Or if something had happened to him? How would she find out? What should she do in case he didn't appear? Wait until some other comrade came? But that would be impossible, for António had told her that no other comrade knew about the house yet. How many days should she wait? And then, who would she go to? How slowly the time passes! How endless is every minute of anxiety and concern! How the heart leaps at the least sound from the outside! Time passes, and the modest little table, that she had set with such joy, and the carrots and potatoes with eggs that had given her such happiness, were now sad things like beautiful reminders of departed people. Maria lowers the lamp light and goes to lie down on her back on the bed. She lies with her eyes open, her ears tuned, feeling unprotected in the emptiness of the house. Now, with the relaxation, the darkness and the expectancy assume ever larger proportions as everything else recedes into nothingness. She's lying there like that for a time that seems like hours and hours, counted by that strange clock where the clicks of the woodworm mark the beat in an unsettling quiet.

Then there's a knock, the door opens, she sees António with a bicycle in his hands. No, this is not some unknown young man whose presence under the same roof frightens and troubles her. It's an old friend, an old comrade.

"Finally, dear friend, it's you!"

And she ran to help him put the bicycle in the back room, and find a place for his hat, and help him untie a big bundle of baggage, and draw water in the sink for him to wash up, and give him a towel to dry off, and finally to put on the table a beautiful bowl of still steaming carrots, potatoes and eggs.

António is drawn and exhausted. But his eyes, circled by creases, smile at his comrade with such deep contentment that Maria smiles too and doesn't stop.

Chapter *IV*

1

Paulo seemed very reticent. Regarding his comrades timidly, he contributed to the discussions only by asking a few questions, many of them a simple request for information. Others, to Vaz, sounded almost senseless. He asked the lawyer, for example, if he generally got up early and if he usually went out evenings with his wife. He asked Manuel Rato if he had been at home when his daughter was born. *Well,* Vaz thought, *let's see if our friend can handle the work.* As he studied his bashful mannerisms and his grizzled hair, he recalled that the comrade had spent five years in prison and felt sorry for him. He'd probably fall short on his new assignments.

Some little incidents on that first trip were rather perplexing, however. One time, about two in the afternoon, they stopped to rest in the outskirts of a town. They had already conducted two outdoor conversations in the morning, had walked a long way, and were now killing some time before meeting a comrade in town after five. They had eaten something only early that morning, and Vaz proposed that they wait until five o'clock, because the comrade might offer them something at his house and thus they wouldn't have to spend Party money. But, looking at Paulo, he saw him so enervated and wiped out, that he said, "I see you're pretty tired, comrade. Let's go to a bar and get a bite to eat."

Paulo remained seated and didn't move. "Let's wait," he said.

Out of concern, Vaz repeated his suggestion to find a bar and stood up.

Paulo said again, "Let's wait," and stayed in the same position, peering over his glasses, as though asking pardon for his obstinacy.

And at the end of the trip, after the meeting in the field with the local committee, as they stepped onto the old road at the entrance to the town, Vaz once more noticed Paulo's severe fatigue. "I don't like to use the train station when I don't have to," he turned to his comrade and said. "It's nothing in particular, but I don't think it's prudent. When I'm not traveling by bicycle, I always go on foot to the next rail stop. But it's a good four kilometers away, and you're tired. Once won't hurt."

Paulo gave him a humble, almost imploring look. At that moment he appeared much, much older. "Is this the road?" he asked. And after Vaz's affirmative, he turned his back on the town and started walking again, in his pace of short, lumbering steps.

No, Vaz mused with some surprise, *he's not as soft as he seems.*

2

Paulo returned home just a while ago. It's night. From the bakery came a comforting smell of burning grape wood, and from the patio the sound of water flowing from an open spigot. The children are sleeping, and Paulo can work now in peace. At his side a glass of water, a nice roll and fresh cheese that Madalena had brought him when he arrived. As he writes, he eats in discreet little nibbles interspersed with small sips of water that he drinks noiselessly. Sometimes he just sits ruminating, in his stocky hand a pencil that he taps slowly on his upper lip. Then, readjusting himself in the chair, he examines the bread over his glasses, takes another little bite, and continues writing.

Paulo is happy with the assignments he has been given. How different was the work before he was taken prisoner years before! At that time he distributed the paper, and his energies were consumed with contacts and more contacts, whose sole purpose was just keeping the contacts live. Now, the smallest cells and contacts were all oriented toward the practical work of getting the masses in motion and organizational growth. To be sure, he had been entrusted with certain unrewarding tasks: contact with a place whose Local Committee hadn't met for more than two months, although its chair was always promising it by the next time Paulo, as the Party worker, would return; contact with the lawyer, all by himself in his area, whom Vaz had dismissed as "a chatterbox who does nothing"; and then the contact with Manuel Rato, which forced him to go way out of his way for few prospects other than just not losing sight of this comrade and trying with his help him to "penetrate" the large nearby village. Paulo thought about this last contact a lot, though, and when he did, turned slightly meditative.

Manuel Rato came to see them at the side of the road. He did not come alone. His daughter accompanied him, her braids tied in an arc behind her neck, and in a chintz outfit with a tiny floral print and white collar. Everything about her—her face, hair, her hands and dress—looked exceptionally clean, with a natural, visible freshness that only rarely leaps out to other people's eyes. Manuel Rato explained his daughter's presence: "It's good for the girl to get used to us," he said.

These tender words contrasted with his hardened visage, whose imposing black mustache lent him a military air, and in them one could grasp a deep, intimate satisfaction and the loving aspiration to make of his daughter a comrade. Isabel smiled, straightening her firm, slim torso and viewing the other comrades with affection. *It's so they understand*, she seemed to say. *You think I'm just a child. No, I'm not a child, I am a young woman ready to assist you, one of your own comrades, as you see.* And indeed anyone who saw her couldn't help but share those sentiments.

Vaz introduced Paulo to Manuel Rato, and the three men walked through the pine forest toward Vale da Égua. Isabel walked a little ahead, stopping whenever the men stopped and turning her smiling face back toward them.

Ah! Paulo thought. *What I wouldn't give to have a daughter like that!*

That was honestly Paulo's thinking. But if it weren't for his age, his white hair, his body weathered by long years of privation and prison, perhaps he might have thought, *Ah! What I wouldn't give to have a wife like that!*

Now Paulo is documenting the cells and contacts he had been entrusted with, thinking what he should do to help the comrades, and writing up a project for a list of demands. Out of all his travels, his trekking, the meals—and the lack of them—his sleepovers and his all-night sessions, nothing raises his spirits, except in the most general sense of banal, everyday things of no interest.

Yet many active, healthy people, if they had even once in their lifetime made the effort that he exerted in those days, would have considered it the greatest accomplishment of their whole life.

3

Paulo worked far into the night. His excitement over the first contacts with the organizations for which he had been given responsibility did not allow him to sleep. One minute lost seemed to him at that moment one minute stolen from the Party. He didn't even remember how many nights he hadn't gotten enough sleep. He saw the relentless work rhythm of the others. He recalled Rosa, thin and weak from exhaustion, giving up her night printing manifestos. He envisioned Vaz before him, pale and full of energy, never defeated by steps, fatigue and deprivation. He heard Ramos mocking the hardships of life. And he felt himself swept up in this great collective effort. So, after he wrote the list of demands and made various notes concerning his new assignments, despite it being two in the morning and being worn out, he continued reading, after several days' interruption, a book by Lenin. No, he couldn't lose time.

Going out to the patio and seeing, so late, the light on in Paulo's room, Evaristo, the owner of the house, all covered by flour dust, came to ask if he needed anything. He was a strong man, with hairy arms and chest like an ape that contrasted with a round, rosy face and his skin, smooth, bright and closely shaved. He still had bits of dough stuck to the hair on his arms and was carrying an earthenware jug. "You're sure you don't need anything?" he asked again.

"No, no, nothing," Paulo answered. "Does it bother you having my light on so late?"

"Bother me? Why?" said Evaristo. "The young guy is the one who might notice it"—he referred to a laborer who worked with him in the bakery at night—"but some explanation can always be found and there's nothing to worry about that. It's true it uses a little more kerosene. But it's necessary, and so be it."

Evaristo left. Paulo went on reading. He senses a growing weight in his head, and thoughts stray from his reading in all directions. He thinks about the two children sleeping, above all about Rita with her two pinned braids, the list of demands, Vaz, Rosa, Manuel Rato's daughter, his long-gone youth, prison. Disordered pictures and images loom up between him and the book. Then, throughout the house, wafts the aroma at once acidic and sweet of warm bread. And that smell carries with it memories of the distant island where he had been born and where he had never returned since the age of twelve, when he left by himself for Lisbon to work in a shop, the island where his father and mother had died and from which nothing more remained than his childhood memories. That odor of baking bread, although more acidic, was the characteristic smell of his parents' home.

His mother prepared the dough, kneaded it and, making a cross on top of it, placed a clove of garlic in the center and chanted:

> *Mother Martha queen of cooks,*
> *Patroness of viands and cheeses,*
> *On each and every path you look*
> *There you'll find Our Lord Christ Jesus.*
> *And with Him find the saving grace*

Of God come down to us on Earth.
And quickly may this poor bread chase
All evil from this humble hearth.

Then she covered the dough with a towel, placed all the shawls, mantles and blankets in the house on top of it, added some men's pants turned inside out when she had doubts about the dough, and she heated the oven with dry branches, and called the spirits in hopes of a good bake: *All evil from this humble hearth!* He would go out to the yard and fetch the dustpan and broom that always lay against the chimney. When he returned, he swept the oven while his mother took a bowl of flour and sprinkled it over the loaves and placed them on a layer of herbal leaves in the oven.

With the bread now baking, his mother told him, "Chico"—at that time Paulo was not yet Paulo—"Wake up the loaves, my son!"

He opened the oven door and touched the loaves with a wand to poke little holes in each one. "May God awaken you and open your eyes! May God awaken you and open your eyes! May God awaken you and open your eyes!"

How long ago was all that! And it was all so vivid in his memory, awakened by the smell of fresh baked bread that radiated ever more intensely all through the house.

By now Paulo is not reading any longer. His head falls forward, resting on his stocky hands, his eyeglasses slip farther down his nose, and his eyes, almost closed, are not seeing any more.

One day—the baking finished and the bread, covered by a mantle, placed on the table—father came home. He had gone to purchase a black goat to exorcise bovine fever and seemed spent from his long trek. Unlike himself, he sat down and propped himself on the table as if wanting to breathe in the warm aura of the baked cornmeal. Suddenly, mother shouted, "What's the matter, husband?"

Paulo watched his father grow more and more pale, remove his hand from the edge of the table, make a gesture as if trying to raise it, and then fall onto the floor, his body at the same time soft and firm like a sack of flour. In another moment he was dead. At the vigil over the body, Paulo only saw the neighbors expanding their nostrils, inhaling whiffs of the warm bread.

"You fell asleep!" said Evaristo, who returned with a loaf fresh out of the oven to offer his friend.

"Huhh?" a startled Paulo murmured. Standing up awkwardly, he dragged himself with stumbling steps to his bed, sat on it and told Evaristo, "Put out the light, please."

Evaristo placed the bread on the table, blew out the lamp and left.

Paulo didn't even hear the door close. He dropped to his side on the bed and slept deeply, his breath rhythmic and raw, which soon turned into loud snoring.

4

Leaving Delita and Zeca in the patio, Rita and Elsa are at the door to Paulo's room. Rita is four years old, Elsa two. Rita wears two braids with red ribbons and has enormous round eyes like a doll's. Elsa has her hair pulled up and tied on the top of her head with a string. Rita leans against the closed door and holds her hand out to her little sister. Elsa waits patiently because she knows that when Rita initiates something, good things will happen.

"Cousin," Rita says in a supplicating tone. "Nice cousin, open the door."

From the other side of the door not a sound is heard. The little girls remain quiet for a few moments.

"Cousin," Rita says again. "Open the door! Nice cousin, handsome cousin, good cousin, open."

Elsa raises her glance to her sister and her eyes ask, *Well? No more?*

"Beloved cousin, adored cousin, open!" Rita urges.

Zeca is heard whining in the patio, and right afterward, Delita's teasing voice: "You can't do it! You can't do it!"

"Cousin," Rita insists, her tone now somewhat petulant, "open the door." Nothing happens. An unexpected crease carves the girl's forehead. "Cousin, you rascal cousin, open."

As a response does not come, Rita lets go of Elsa's hand and starts to knock on the wooden door with her two fists, pounding over and over again, and with each bang saying the same words in a cadence: "Ugly cousin! Bad cousin! Rascal cousin! Ugly cousin! Bad cousin! Rascal cousin!"

Elsa tries to imitate her sister and seeing the grand moment coming, bursts out in laughter and shouting.

"What is it?" Paulo half-opens the door brusquely awakened, uncombed, his gray hair askew, without eyeglasses, peering at the children with his extremely weak, myopic orbs.

And as always, the children entered. And as always, they were soon joined by Delita, a little girl of seven, thin and tousled, and Zeca, five, a fat pink little boy. And as always, without knowing how to entertain the children, Paulo satisfies their every whim (except pulling the glasses from his nose). He shows them illustrations, draws little figures, puts two of them on his knees and plays horsey, forms his own hands into frightening machines that always open and shut, letting the children slap his hands with their little palms and run away for fear of getting captured. Only raucous laughter can be heard from Paulo's room, shouts of glee, of surprise, of wonderment, from the four little devils. And as always, only after half an hour or an hour, Madalena appears.

"Hey, kids, didn't I tell you to leave your cousin in peace?"

The children escape like a flock of surprised birds, trying to flee Madalena flailing about attempting to render smacks on their tushies.

Paulo is by himself now, cleans his glasses and laments the lost time. *It always happens! Either they don't let me rest or they don't let me work. What I really needed was a house without kids!* Paulo truly believes that and repeats it to himself so often that he ends up convinced by the idea that only in a house without children would he feel truly good.

But at times when he dreams of a Portugal freed of fascism, he always sees himself in a little house surrounded by a little orchard; and the great pleasure he feels imagining that orchard is seeing children coming in and gathering fruit. It's then that he pictures himself happy and content, listening in turn to the laughter and the shouting of the young ones around him, laughter and shouting like—exactly like—that of Rita, Elsa, Delita and Zeca, the very ones that right now he thinks he'd like to be free of.

One day Madalena's sister came to pick up the children to go spend the morning with one of her daughters who was having a birthday. After a while, in the silence of the house, Madalena heard the soft brush of Paulo's slippers. He paused in his door frame, looking at her uneasily over his glasses. "The children?" he asked.

And when he learned where they had gone, he returned to his room shuffling his slippers.

5

Three weeks after having gone to Vale da Égua for the first time, Paulo went there again. He got off the jitney on the tar road and cut through the path Manuel Rato had shown him. It was a rough course whose only markers were the deep ruts in the earth from wagon wheels, reaching into long, dangerous curves among the pines and gently edging up against the soft slopes of the hills. It was a bright, chilly day: The sun shone in the pure blue of the sky, and a cutting nor'easter blew aggressively.

Walking with his usual irregular pacing, Paulo saw two ox-drawn wagons pass him by, loaded with wood, and then he remembered some of the conversation he overheard on the jitney. He made the trip on the last benches, in a kind of "third class" jitney seating, where people of means would sit only as a last resort and which many peasants sought out even if there were available seats up front. The jitney was full, and two field workers were talking in a subdued voice.

"You want to know what the Council on Cattle Products is?" one of them asked, a small, thin and nervous man with a mustache and eyes as black as his hat and vest. "Want to know? Well, I'll tell you. Before, sausage was 24 *escudos*, and they paid 250 for 15 kilos of live pork. Now sausage is more than 30 and they don't want to pay 200 for the 15 kilos of live pork. The consumer pays more and the producer receives less. And there, my friend, you have it: That's the Council."

The other man was 50 or so, with a serious, lined face. While the first one was talking, the older one nodded affirmatively at each point, producing some guttural sounds. When the first man finished, he looked around to see what kind of fellow passengers were seated near them, and paused for a moment scrutinizing Paulo. His impression was not unfavorable, so the second man decided to speak:

"All this with the Councils and the Guilds only goes to harm the little guy. If they allowed the farmer to sell to whoever they want, the farmer would earn more and the consumer would pay less. No, siree! They obligate him by force to sell to them, they're the ones who set the price and then they sell for three or four times more. That way, when the farmer sells, the prices are always low, and when he buys they're always high. Councils and Guilds just serve to screw the little man."

The man stopped for a moment, looked around and fixed his gaze on Paulo briefly before going on: "Look at what's going on with the pine forest. The Guild comes, marks the trees it wants without any explanation to the owner, and pays 24$40 a meter. And you know how much they sell it to the factories for? 65, 70 and even 80 *escudos* a meter."

Thus Paulo became aware of the peasants' unhappiness about the corporate state's economic entities and understood the need to guide and organize this discontent. But how? Knowledge of these problems came to him by chance on a jitney ride, and not by way of a Party organization. Only days before, when he had taken charge of his cells, did he assess the progress of the Party. He believed that the Party had in fact assumed a determining role in the struggle of all the people. Bot now it seemed to him that there was much, so much to do to get there. The Party suddenly seemed so disconnected from the peasants, not knowing their problems, not knowing how to help them. The peasants were forced to sell a cubic meter of pinewood for 24 *escudos*, that the Guild would turn around and sell for 65 or more.

But what to do? Hauling the wood directly to the consumer was certainly not viable. Paulo felt the need to better understand this whole issue, but where to gather information? In the jitney, when he decided to ask a question, the men responded evasively and changed the subject. Now he'd speak with Manuel Rato, but the last time he went to Vale da Égua with Vaz, Manuel Rato knew little about it. Paulo walks on in his ungainly manner, absorbed in his thoughts, not coming up with a plan to better inform himself and act.

He had no idea that from one moment to the next he would be given new information in real life, and important enlightenment.

6

Raised voices rang through the pine forest. The nor'easter imposed its own strange highs and lows, distorting the direction of the voices and confounding them with its own whistling and the sighing of branches. Suddenly, in a fold of the terrain, next to what was once a grove, Paulo came upon the men who were arguing. These several men were standing next to an ox-drawn wagon loaded with wood. The oxen were drooling from exertion, showing complete indifference to the conversation in their great patient eyes. The men found it perfectly natural that an unknown person should show up and approach, for no one made an issue of it.

"It was the fault of the lumbermen!" said one wearing a green hat and a coat with a fur collar, eyeing another wearing a wool field jacket. "We only designated twenty-five percent."

"But you cut twice that and only the best trees!" responded a third man in a vest and shirtsleeves, his voice trembling with aroused emotions of rage. "A fourth is already an abuse, but even that's not enough for you. You destroyed my forest."

"We only designated the twenty-five percent," insisted the man with the fur-collar coat. "But if the woodcutters cut more, then you'll be paid more."

"A fortune!" replied the other with disgust. "You people have no respect for anyone's property. You could have designated something reasonable, but no. You cut down all the best trees. Trees goof for boards, and sold for this price."

"We only designated twenty-five percent," the man with the fur-collar coat said for the third time, turning aside, gazing far away and showing he considered the conversation ended.

"You make your laws against the poor," said a tall, thin peasant with a sparse blond beard and steady, dull eyes, "but when the laws don't suit you, you're the first to disobey them."

"I've already told you a thousand times it was the lumberjacks," his opponent shouted, his patience worn out. "And you know what else? You're not happy? Go complain to Salazar."

The fur-collar guy, seeking an approving look from the man in the wool field jacket for this last sally, turned his back to the peasants and, followed by the one with the field jacket, to whom he said something quietly that drew a laugh, walked away quickly through the pines.

Next to the wagon with the oxen remained only the driver, the owner of the destroyed forest and the peasant with the blond beard, who was now trying to close his shirt at the neck to protect himself from the bitter wind.

The forest owner sat down on a tree stump and, crushing his chin into his two closed fists, looked out on the sad field of stumps and the lengths of wood strewn over the vast clearing. The wagon started off in a sudden jerk, only to slow down again creaking. The peasant with the thin blond beard walked some meters away and stood inexplicably quiet in the middle of what had been the forest.

"Is this the best way to Vale da Égua?" Paulo asked.

"I'm going that way too," said the owner with a sigh, and stood up with difficulty.

7

They saw strange developments as they walked through the pine forest. In some places, axed trees were cracking and falling, ending their descent with a deafening, earthshaking crash. In other places, the lumbermen were sawing the trunks into logs and cubic meter pieces. Here a man with a can of paint the color of the purchasing company went around with a brush swabbing the ends of the already cut and measured cubes. Over there someone else daubed the color of their factory. Farther on, the men with the fur-collar coat and the field jacket, circling through a dense thicket of pines, placed a notch on the trees the lumberjacks would cut or, with the other end of their little hatchet, impressed the Guild seal onto the top of the cubes. On some heaps you could see a cube placed crosswise, indicating an area not open for cutting, that is, the drivers could not yet

carry away the wood. Spaced out here and there were oxcarts carrying loads of wood. Other wagons passed by slowly, their wheels
grating and screeching as the animals trod their path in surprising
silence.

From his companion on the walk, Paulo came to comprehend
the principal motives for the peasants' complaints. The obligatory
cutting of twenty-five out of every hundred pine trees, marked by
the men from the Guild without the participation of the owners,
represented a great decline in property values. But often they went
beyond twenty-five percent, sometimes with no explanation whatsoever, other times saying they had made a mistake, and still other
times shielding themselves with legal technicalities. Then there was
the price: a scandalous theft from the small owners, forced to sell to
the Guild at 24 *escudos* per cubic meter so that the Guild—acting only
as an intermediary imposed by the government and incurring as its
sole expense 2.5 *escudos* per meter paid to the lumberjacks from the
cutting to the loading—could sell the wood on the ground to the factories at 65 and more. When it was for the factories, it was not so bad.
When the wood was for the train company, for railroad sleepers, the
Guild people singled out the oldest, most mature pines of much
higher value, yet paid at the same price. On top of all this, other
abuses included mixing wood from neighboring property owners
before measuring and paying so that neither one received what they
were owed.

"And what do the owners do?" Paulo asked.

"What do you mean, what do we do?" the man replied.

"What do you do to stop the robbery?"

The man sighed. "What can we do? In other places they went to
talk with the civil governor, but nothing changed. In fact, he listened,
then turned around and paid no attention, saying that to avoid mixing the owners' woods, they should mark the boundaries before
the cutting began. But that was for those who protested, and they
wouldn't have a reason to protest again because by then almost all
the trees had been cut down and carted away. Here we mark the
boundaries and they go ahead and mix the woods anyway. What can
we do?" the man repeated.

"Why not get together and all of you go and protest?" Paulo asked.

"Protest? To whom? Make ourselves look like idiots like the
others? And if we can't protest, what more can we do? Look, you
saw that blond guy? The fight began with him. They destroyed his
pine forest right next to mine. And he said to Valadinhas, 'You took
mine away. But I guarantee you won't touch the other one.' But what
can he do? Something foolish—or violent?"

After a few moments of silence, the man continued. "What else can we do? Whoever holds the power rules the roost."

The man's words couldn't be more humble and resigned. But behind the meekness of the words, one could detect a discontent bordering on despair. They continued on their way without further words. Paulo recognized that complaining to the authorities was not the right approach for this struggle. Only a few of the small owners could pick up and travel to the city many kilometers away. And once there, either they wouldn't be received bye the authorities or no one would lend them any importance. So, what to do? Paulo looked at his defeated walking companion and he himself felt the formidable, brutal, hateful weight of the whole fascist state machine crushing the small, isolated farmers and plundering them mercilessly.

8

Manuel Rato confirmed what the pine forest owner had said. The government was extending its claws ever farther out from the towns and roads, bringing the interior to destruction, ruin and despair. Within days, the poor pines of Vale da Égua, like those in other nearby places, would suffer this criminal rape. Nervously, rapidly, as the apples of her pretty face turned brighter and her face became more drawn with excitement, Manuel Rato's wife related what she had heard. Standing straight, with her hair combed into braids and her head held high and steady, Isabel attentively listened to the others with concern. In her reactions, as in a mirror, you could see the reflection of both her father's and her mother's expressions and words. As Paulo spoke, peering reticently over his eyeglasses, Isabel smiled.

"What you heard my wife say," Manuel Rato said, "you can hear from anyone around here. Everybody has their little pine trees, and by now this is affecting everyone. At this rate, in two weeks, maybe a month, they'll have reached Vale da Égua."

"What do you think can be done?" Paulo inquired.

"What can be done?" the wife responded, gaining color and smoothing her hair in quick, fidgety gestures. "Bring the people together and don't let the Guild tag or cut any more!"

Isabel glanced at Paulo as if to say, *Exactly. What do you think?* Manuel Rato also looked at Paulo, and though his eyebrows were vigorously drawn together in a single black line highlighting his broad forehead, whiter than his suntanned cheeks, his eyes manifested an evident pride in his wife's words.

They then discussed how to unite and appeal to the people spread out in the sparse local areas and the little cottages dispersed among the hills.

The wife and daughter lit the fire, put a pot of water on to boil, brought out a bowl, kale and potatoes, crouched on the floor alongside the men and started preparing the meal.

"The difficulty," said Manuel Rato, "is that each person by himself hasn't got the strength to defend his own pine trees, and it's hard to pull every one out of their houses to defend the pine forests of everyone else."

According to Paulo, the most important thing was to bring the people together on a certain day at a specific place and from there to proceed with everyone to wherever the Guild and the woodcutters were at that time. Manuel Rato, his wife, daughter and brother-in-law could start spreading the idea, but they would not be able to reach a critical number of people, nor did they have the personal influence that would ensure success.

"A little manifesto would help," said Manuel Rato.

They agreed then that Paulo would see if he could quickly get a manifesto printed, undated, calling for a gathering in the town of Mato, the largest in the area, so that when it was agreed the time had come to act, the manifesto could be distributed the night before.

"Me and my daughter can take charge of distributing it," said Manuel Rato, as Isabel gaped at her father, enthusiastic, grateful and happy.

The two comrades then went on to talk about other matters. One point they dwelled on had to do with the railway station village. At Vaz's recommendation, Paulo stressed the contact with Zé Cavalinho, and Manuel Rato insisted that when he left the area to go to the mines, he would leave with that contact established.

"Better slower and safer," he explained. "A lot of times to get someplace fast you have to go slow."

9

While the men were talking, the wife and daughter fixed dinner. As they only had two bowls and three spoons, they first served the two men their soup, just as they had done with Vaz the first time he came.

"Your wife and daughter?" Paulo asked, seeing just the two men had been served.

"They'll eat after," Manuel Rato said calmly.

When they'd finished the soup, Joana removed a chunk of salt pork from the pot and, as she had done with Vaz, placed it in Paulo's bowl. Manuel Rato cut a slice of corn bread and handed it to him.

Paulo blushed, looked humbly over his glasses, and spoke awkwardly. "No, comrades. I'll only eat what you eat." And he looked at them at once apologetic and obstinate: *I know you have your reasons*, he seemed to say, *and I humbly beg pardon if I offend you, but I won't eat.*

Joana made the restrained gesture of shrugging her shoulders and, blushing too, glanced at one and the other. Isabel grabbed her mother's arm and her smile faded. It seemed that in a split second the intimate comradeship of the previous conversation had evaporated.

"You're more in need of it today than we are," Manuel Rato said, as he had said to Vaz, and his broad white forehead leaned forward as his dark face contracted even more, almost wildly.

"No," Paulo repeated, his face reddening again. "Let's eat together." With that he held the bowl with the pork out to the wife. As soon as he had done so, he sensed that his action was received with displeasure. The woman looked at her husband, who nodded to her, and she, rather upset, emptied the salt pork once more into the pot and filled the two bowls with soup for herself and her daughter. The girl kneeled next to her father and started to eat, blowing noisy mouthfuls of air to break the now uncomfortable silence. Remaining standing and visibly ruffled, lightly shaking her head from time to time, Joana more than once straightened her hair in quick, nervous movements and began eating without raising her eyes from the bowl. When she did, she saw the visitor looking affectionately at the girl over his glasses. Her husband observed him and, from that hard countenance, behind the eyebrows more pursed than ever, Joana was quite certain of seeing his eyes wet with tears. And she guessed, to her surprise, that these were not the same tears such as she herself felt rising to her eyes, tears of shame, indignation and sadness, but tears that said, *Yes, comrade, this is our miserable life. There's nothing more I can offer you, nothing more. Thank you for understanding that and for knowing how to accept it.*

When the wife and daughter finished eating their soup, Paulo, looking at this family with humility, as if asking forgiveness for his behavior, cut the cornbread into four pieces, handed each one their mouthful of cornbread with a little piece of salt pork on top, and began munching on his portion, calmly and purposefully.

As you see, he seemed to be saying, *it's quite enough for the four of us and we'll all feel very satisfied.*

Only Isabel didn't get to finish her cornbread with salt pork. She had to concentrate her every effort on suppressing her laughter. But she didn't manage to. Though she tried burying her head in her mother's shoulder, her hysterical laughter that almost choked her in the end broke out high and joyful.

"She's crazy, this girl," the mother said. It was clear, though, that she supported those feelings of joyousness.

10

At dinner Paulo is observing the children closely. Delita is already eating like a grown person, well-behaved and confident. It's the mother who fixes and gives food to Elsa, inserting big spoonfuls into her mouth with a certain rude impatience. Zeca and Rita eat without much discernment, and have no one to put food into their mouths. They eat on their own, but what work it is! Rita grasps the spoon decisively, raises it directly to the level of her mouth, but that's when tragedy strikes: The spoon knocks against the side of her face or her chin and some of the soup spills back onto the dish, leaving the little girl's face smeared with kale and fat. Rita's eyes are so imploring seeing her mother's indifference—and that of the others in her affliction—that Paulo comes to her rescue with help.

"Let her be, let her be," Madalena says. "She's old enough to eat by herself."

But Paulo gives her another few spoonfuls, happy and moved to hear the child's deep sighs of satisfaction and to see her enormous eyes fixed tenderly and appreciably on him.

Looking at Rita, he recalls Isabel, laughing on her mother's shoulder without getting to eat the bread and pork. He's surprised to find similarities between Rita and Isabel. Similarities in what way he can't quite define, but there's something that strikes him in the same way and with the same intensity. It seems to him, too, that Rita and Isabel could not exist if the Party didn't exist, and that there's some mysterious connection between his revolutionary activity, the manifesto he drafted, the struggle of the pine forest smallholders, and the enchantment of both the child and the young woman.

Paulo doesn't grasp that it's in the love he feels for them that they are similar. And that love is grafted into every fiber of his activity as a revolutionary militant.

Chapter *V*

1

Vaz arrived home, washed up, ate something, tallied his money against his expenses, read the war communiqués, moved the little flags on the map and sat down at the table to organize his papers and write.

The last few weeks had shown some decisive steps forward in the struggle of rural wage earners. The creation of marketplace committees was spreading throughout the sector. Because of their actions at the markets, the rural workers are getting higher wages and forcing the bosses to give work to the older and weaker men formerly disparaged. The successes are becoming known and serve as a fuse for new initiatives. In many places the peasants form market committees, and in locales where there's no market they demand its creation. The reaction by the big landowners—to set maximum salaries and fines for whoever paid more—utterly flopped. Opposite from what Marques believed, the edict was simply ignored. Now Vaz is making efforts for the organization to stand with the mass movements so that out of the contacts established with farm workers without party affiliation to defend their immediate interests, new Party members may be recruited and new local cells created. Assessing the work realized so far with the new orientation toward the dayworkers' market, Vaz confirms that apart from several victories, dozens of rural proletarians were recruited, and contacts established with almost a dozen new places.

All would have been for the best if it weren't for what José Sagarra told him during their last conversation. In the most important zone of the sector, precisely the one with the largest concentration of rural workers, the Party organization and the movement are practically inert by virtue of the Regional Committee's intervention. It had been decided that José Sagarra take charge of the contacts with isolated peasants until then supervised by the Regional Committee. Afonso was to provide contacts. Nothing had yet been done.

"The first time, the comrade promised to bring me the contact two days later," said José Sagarra, "but he didn't show up for our meeting. Now I have to wait for him to appear because I don't know where to find him."

Vaz shortly visited Afonso's house. He was not home. He went to Marques's house to give him a written message. The house was closed, no one responded. As he had things to do elsewhere, he was obliged to leave matters as they were for another two weeks.

Vaz recalls, as if it were today, the Regional Committee meeting when he had introduced the directives about the dayworkers for the first time. Still ringing in his ears is Marques's laughter when he said he had instructions to speak personally with José Sagarra. He still sees the ironic look from Vítor, gazing out through his cloud of cigarette smoke. In Afonso's failure to appear for the meeting with José Sagarra, in the delay of the movement and of the peasant organization, Vaz suspected a passive resistance amongst the Regional comrades. *They're mistaken*, Vaz thinks, *roundly mistaken. If Afonso doesn't give the contacts to José Sagarra, I'm going to grab him and right away he'll go with me to all the locales. And he'll give them to me, I haven't the slightest doubt, he'll give them to me.*

Seated on the other side of the table from Vaz, Rosa suspends her reading briefly and looks closely at her companion. Vaz's calm, earnest face looks impassible, but in the clenching of his jaws and in the lack of enthusiasm in the least of his gestures, Rosa recognizes his deep anger.

"Did you place the signal?" Rosa asked, for Ramos was due to arrive that night.

"I did."

For his part, Vaz stares at Rosa's thin, sad face. He arrived home a good hour earlier after almost a week's absence and only now looks directly at his companion. Yes, he needs to talk with her, to know what happened in and around the house while he was away, and to give her a little attention and love. He reads these needs in her melancholy, intelligent eyes, and he himself is eager to make her happy. His first question to her already occurs to him, but then he remembers that he hadn't yet arranged all his things as is his old longtime habit when he arrives home.

"We'll talk shortly," he says. And he returned to his work.

2

"The bourgeoisie around here is now placing itself at our orders," said Rosa, when Vaz finally gave her his attention. Despite its ironic tone, she retained her usual melancholy.

And she recounted how when she went to the market to buy some sewing thread, the grocer welcomed her with exaggerated friendliness and in the end told her, "If you folks need anything, don't be shy. If it's something I can possibly get, of course. At least, I have my share in the rationing, and you're welcome to it."

Amélia was the only other person at the grocery store, the thin, nervous neighbor, always with her wrinkled brow and ornery attitude. Rosa left walking down the street with her, and Amélia said frankly and openly, "You know why he said that? It's because he's afraid your husband and your brother are revenue inspectors."

"Where do they come up with these stories?" Rosa asked.

Amélia shrugged her shoulders. "They're such thieves. Such thieves. Their conscience is so detestable—detestable, I tell you— they see ghosts everywhere."

Rosa later spoke with Miss Ermelinda and with Ernesto's wife. The thinking about the house was divided into two groups. On one side, the grocer, the Pim-Pa-Pum and in a way Ermelinda herself, were inclined to believe that Vaz was a revenue inspector or had some other similar kind of job. On the other side, Amélia, Ernesto's family and generally speaking, all the other neighbors believed in the explanation they had been given, or at least acted as though they believed, that Vaz was a publicity and sales agent for pharmaceutical products.

"Nothing else?" Vaz asked.

"Nothing else," said Rosa. And having said it, she remembered the bitch with the huge teats showing up now and again to visit (the Pim-Pa-Pum were surely by now used to it), and little Anica coming down from Ernesto's house and fearfully crossing the street to come talk with her. Rosa could relate all these little incidents—all of them significant in her life of solitude. But in truth, at the moment she has no spirit for conversation. She studies her companion's wan cheeks with concern and says, "You should take advantage of the time until Ramos comes to go lie down and rest a little."

Those words are on the mark, because Vaz is wiped out and because, when Ramos comes, they will be working far into the night. But in Rosa's expression, in a flash of barely perceptible astuteness, Vaz reads something more. He pulls the chair away from the table and extends his hands. "Come here!"

Rosa stands up, rounds the table, and draws close to him with an unexpected smile on her sad thin face, a confused and hesitant smile, as if she were begging pardon for being a woman.

3

Outside, near the house, a dog barked weakly. "You hear?" Rosa whispered. "Someone's coming."

Vaz didn't answer. He was breathing steadily and deeply. Carefully Rosa withdrew her arm from under her companion's trunk, and with equal solicitude removed his arm that was embracing her.

She heard steps next to the house at the kitchen door and three knocks sounded: one, two...three. Rosa got up, straightened out her clothes, took hold of the lamp and went to open the door.

"Don't make any noise," she told Ramos as he entered. "While you eat something, let's let him sleep."

Ramos went to the work room to deposit his briefcase, hung his old raincoat behind the door and his jacket on the back of a chair, placed the pistol he carried at his waist on the table after removing the bullet from its chamber, and returned to the kitchen, rolling his shirtsleeves up to wash.

"Hey," he said, returning from the lavatory with his hands and arms covered with froth and his teeth shining. "Where'd you get that guard dog?" His question came out half speaking, half laughing.

The poor bitch barked just once and, seeing the unfamiliar figure, approached affably with her enormous teats scraping the ground and her tail wagging.

As she dismantled the pan wrapped in newspapers to keep the food warm, Rosa recounted in a few calm, slow words—in marked contrast to Ramos's jibing—how the bitch had first shown up and how she was now in the habit of coming by every day. It was the first time Rosa had ever seen her around the house at night.

Ramos sat at the table, and Rosa filled a dish with kale soup.

"The thing that shocked me was how ferocious that animal is!" Ramos said. "Aside from being abnormally big, it has a horrifying yelp that would scare off the most brazen intruders. She came so close to me, and so aggressively, I couldn't decide if I should go back or not."

As he talked and laughed, Ramos loudly sipped spoonfuls of broth and tore off little bites of bread that he deposited into his mouth all at once.

"Beasts like that need to muzzled," he insisted.

Rosa sat down with him and took in the comrade's lively, happy, and beautiful face. When he laughed freely, something baffling, sad and oppressive possessed Rosa like, like—yes, very much like, not exactly in his features, but in his way of speaking and laughing, so spontaneous and communicative, in his manner of looking at things, so observant and provocative. It was those manners and ways that had captivated her in that other man—yes, that's what it was—and she could never forgive herself for it.

"Don't you think?" Ramos repeated for the third time, noting her cold, hostile stare.

"What did you ask?"

"Nothing, nothing," Ramos muttered.

"I'm sorry, friend," Rosa said in her sad, calm tone, "but I didn't hear you. What was it?"

"Nothing, nothing," Ramos said again.

Ramos finished eating his kale soup in silence and stood up. "Do you want to get Francisco?"

4

Vaz brought Ramos up to date on the most recent events. In the organization entrusted to António, at the most important industrial center, important struggles were in progress, especially at Cicol, where Gaspar worked. After a few small concessions, the factory bosses started down the path of intimidation. They fired the members of the Unity Committee, saying it was an illegal organization and that all issues needed to be dealt with by the union. Gaspar alone was not fired, no doubt because of his great prestige. They returned to the executive office with a new committee and, at his initiative, the workforce accompanied him, threatening to leave work if their colleagues weren't rehired. António held a meeting at Pereira's house with Gaspar and with Túlio, his right arm at Cicol, and came out very encouraged. Aside from the importance of the movement itself, new possibilities were opening up.

"The factory owners," Gaspar had said, "are always trying to throw me to the union, because the leadership of the union is a gang of fascists at the bosses' say-so. The union hall is more than fifty kilometers away. Any written demand we make, or any trip there by a committee, is the same as doing nothing. But if the Party can help me establish contact with other factories in other places, and if in those places the struggle can advance in each factory, then yes, at the same time we put pressure on the bosses in every factory we also force the fascist union leaders to present our demands to the government to be acceptable to the whole class, and we'll wind up kicking that pack of dogs to the side of the road. According to the statutes, elections are now at the beginning of the year. We should work for the statutes to be obeyed for the first time."

"In my opinion," Vaz now says to Ramos, "we should follow this approach. We have cells in three factories in our sector. In all of them there are movements in the works and there are already committees formed. It's time to start bringing together the movement for demands in industry, and this will also be the way we most rapidly reach new factories where we're seeking contacts. We've talked a lot about working within the fascist unions. It's time already to talk less and do more."

Ramos and Vaz then went on to exchange thoughts about Paulo's sector and the perspectives for struggle there among the smallholders of pine woods.

"Paulo's not as soft as he appears," said Vaz. "He gives the impression that it's hard for him to walk, but when you actually look, he's come a long way."

"I hope so!" said Ramos. But these words seemed to imply, *I'd very much like to believe what you're saying, but I can't.*

Vaz spoke of the need to print the manifesto that Paulo had written and asked Ramos if it were possible to do in a Party printshop.

Ramos read the proposed manifesto, and considered it fine. The technical part was the problem. "To do it in a clandestine Party printshop," Ramos said, "I have to wait two weeks for my meeting with the comrades from the Secretariat and, even if they approve and decide to do it, it will take a lot of time because of the contacts that need to be made and the problems of distribution it creates in the central apparatus. Seems to me it would be better to just do it on a copier machine and take care of it without wasting time."

"Okay," Vaz said, without even thinking he'd been spending yet another night without sleeping a wink, after five whole days without either rest or meals. "I'll be home tomorrow. I'll do it myself."

"It's not necessary that you do it," Ramos said. "It's not okay wanting to be the only ones doing everything. Rosa can do it." And he asked Vaz if he could summon his companion.

Awakened just after she had fallen asleep, Rosa came in with red eyes, her face pale and wrinkled, her hair uncombed.

"Friend," Ramos addressed her. "We need you tomorrow to cut a stencil for a manifesto and to put it through the copy machine, and you're the one to do it so we don't leave it for your companion to do. I'll need a copy to take with me. Can you type a copy now?"

Her hand resting on the table, Rosa looked at Ramos. Whether from the dreams she'd been having or from being interrupted out of her state of somnolence, she assumed an expression of attentive sympathy, which Ramos was not used to.

"The original?" she asked.

They gave it to her and told her she could install herself right there at the table to type it up. Rosa had already begun to type on the heavy machine as the two men continued their meeting, when from outside, near the door, they heard a weak barking. Rosa stopped typing. The two men went quiet and listened.

"It's best to go see," Rosa suggested.

Vaz got up, went to the kitchen and opened the door cautiously. Outside, a humid wind was blowing through the darkness, coming from the south. In the silence, the bitch started barking again. Avoiding making any noise, Vaz crept along the wall, reached the corner of the house and peered through the olive trees that descended toward the street. All was silent. The only thing that drew his attention was a light on in Ermelinda's house. So late! Totally still, his ears pricked, Vaz tried to find anything unusual amongst the blurry shapes of the olive trees. The whimpering dog came and leaned against his legs, remaining there, immobile also, as if to shelter herself from the night humidity. In the neighbor's house, the light went off. Now just darkness, humidity and silence.

"Nothing!" said Vaz when he came back inside. "Maybe someone in the cobbler's house went out. There was a light on."

"You got yourself a good one," Ramos said to Rosa, looking at her and still joking. "Your ferocious guard dog doesn't even miss the shadows in the night. It'll never leave you in peace."

For an instant, Rosa raised her eyes from the machine keyboard, without even a vestige of the engaged, sympathetic expression she showed him a few minutes earlier. She looked at him again with cold hostility.

How stupid I am, Ramos thought. *I know she doesn't like to joke around, and I keep doing it.*

5

In speaking of the distribution of the manifesto, Ramos raised the more general problem of distributing the press, suggesting new answers and new assignments.

"If we're talking about isolated contacts in dispersed areas, the responsible Party workers can continue doing this work. But in the larger, more consolidated oranizations it's necessary to secure another comrade just for that, as it's done in other regions where there's an apparatus for distribution. If he's resourceful, he could also have a copy machine in the house."

To Vaz's mind, these ideas complicated things uselessly. The Party had grown, true, since the arrival of Paulo and António to the sector.

But up until then, he alone, Vaz, had supervised far more contacts than any of the comrades had now, and it was he who brought the press all over the sector with never a slip-up or drawback.

It seemed Ramos had anticipated Vaz's thinking. "The Party leadership has resolved to do away with the one-man orchestra, old man," he said jovially. "I know that for my part, I too am still one. And you no less. With the development of the Party, that kind of activity, which at a certain moment was useful, necessary and indispensable, becomes an impediment to the progress of our work and a danger for its security and continuity."

While comprehending the rationale for such an approach, Vaz feared, however, that in many cases everything would proceed more slowly, with duplication of energy and expense, and without that ready, immediate solution of problems that he was used to. Even once the organism for leadership in the sector had been created, though it was not humanly possible for him to maintain the work by himself, it was only with regret that he gave Paulo and António the contact with organisms he himself had created and nurtured. As much as he valued the two comrades, he was always privately uneasy about what they would do, and suffered for not being able to execute those tasks himself that had fallen to them. One new comrade for distribution would perhaps be more secure. But it would certainly be less efficient. Experience had taught him to rely more on his own energy and his own initiative than on complicated organizational blueprints which easily spawned bureaucracy, resistance, and brakes of all kinds. He cited José Sagarra and the peasants.

"Look at that case. You've got a Regional Committee, local committees, and a numerous Party membership. Meanwhile, in the towns controlled by the Regional Committee not a single forward step has been made. Except for José Sagarra's town, which was under Regional Committee supervision but is connected directly to me, there has still not been a single marketplace committee established, there's no news of struggles for better wages, and there's been no progress organizing the farmworkers. On the other hand, aside from isolated contacts and the individual work of some comrades, elsewhere there's mass mobilization and organizational progress. In theory it should be just the opposite. The truth is that our strongest regional Party organization in that sector is the most inert and the most moribund of all."

Ramos agreed in part with Vaz. In fact, a Party worker brings to the organization a dynamism, a leadership and assistance that local cadres on the Regional Committee don't, owing to the demands of their professional lives. But you can't judge the efficiency of work procedures only by the most immediate results. Given the impossibility of constructing the Regional Committees with Party functionaries, the organizational work in vast sectors, based on the personal control of the three functionaries, charged on top of everything else with distribution of Party materials, doesn't offer enough security, nor guarantees timely, appropriate help.

"To the extent that the Party evolves, measures for decentralization will arise," Ramos insists. In the case you mention, the issue is not the existence of the Regional Committee but, if we admit that your appreciation of the cadres is correct, the level of understanding and the weaknesses of the comrades that constitute it."

"Exactly," Vaz broke in, as if he'd been waiting a long time for those words. "In my opinion, the Regional Committee is gumming up the works. Either we give it some new blood or we have to jump over it."

Ramos recalls the last conversation he had with Marques and his unfavorable opinion of Vaz. Ramos himself acknowledges serious deficiencies and gaps in understanding on the Regional Committee, but it seems to him that Vaz's rush to take radical measures stems in large part from personal ill-will, especially toward Marques, an old comrade with a proven record of sacrifice in prison—and a strong personality.

"Let's move more slowly," said Ramos. "Marques is an old comrade and the others too are getting up in years. In spite of everything, they're the best we've got."

"No, they're not the best we've got," Vaz interrupted gently. "José Sagarra would certainly do better work on the Regional Committee than anyone who's on it now. He has a spirit of sacrifice and a fire burning for the Party that Marques doesn't have, nor Vítor, even Afonso, and I won't say Cesário because even though he doesn't say much, he's the best of the four. As for myself, if we want the work to develop, we have to restructure the Regional Committee."

And after a pause he repeated: "Either we give it some new blood or we have to jump over it."

Ramos smiled. Vaz says Sagarra would do better work than any of the comrades of the Regional Committee, and Marques had said that any of the comrades on the Regional Committee would do better work than Vaz.

"Slower, slower," Ramos insists. "Look, after all, the Regional Committee is in charge of almost fifty members. Try to convince the comrades, have more discussions with them, make them see the need for more help to the cells, and you yourself come to an agreement with Afonso about turning the contacts over to Sagarra."

Vaz stayed mum for a few moments, his pale, serious face intensely concentrated, his gaze pinned to the flame on the lamp.

"Very well, then," he said finally. "That's what I will do. One thing I will say to you, however. The Regional Committee will stay as it is. But if Afonso doesn't give his farmworker contacts to José Sagarra and if we have to wait for them, the peasant movement is going to get stuck here, while it's advancing everywhere else. So I'm telling you, it will not get stuck. If Afonso doesn't hand over the contacts, one of these days he's going to find either me or José Sagarra taking care of them to start getting the farmworkers' struggle moving.

Looking at Vaz's sallow, resolute face, at his clear eyes and fixed gaze, and remembering the whole history of the Party's organizational development, Ramos was sure that indeed it would happen.

6

Night had fallen already when Vaz knocked on the door at Afonso's house.

"Ah!" Afonso's mother blurted on opening the door.

He was arrested! Vaz thought when he heard that unexpected exclamation. But immediately, as instantaneously as it had appeared, that foreboding vanished from his mind, and he thought he perceived in her exclamation not so much surprise or shock, but displeasure.

The woman ordinarily would call out to her son from the door and would stand there until Afonso came to put Vaz's bicycle indoors before leaving with his comrade. This time she acted differently. "I don't know if he's home," she said. "Wait a bit and I'll go see."

Closing the door most of the way, she retreated inside. Vaz thought he heard low, muffled speech, and then the sound of a door closing between him and the voices. In the house a deep silence ensued. He waited a while and was preparing to knock on the door again when it opened and the tall, willowy figure of Afonso appeared. Contrary to habit, he did not take the bicycle inside. He came out to the sidewalk and stood for a few moments.

"Shall we go?" Vaz asked. He didn't even inquire if he should put the bicycle inside because in the mother's exclamation, in the whispering inside the house, in the long wait, he realized there was some unknown, but significant, rationale. This was no mere forgetfulness.

They walked down the street up to the narrow path they'd usually take to Cesário's house.

"You missed your meeting with José Sagarra," Vaz began.

Afonso hesitated. "Yes, I did," he said finally. "I was being followed when I was going to the meeting site."

"Followed? How?"

Afonso related how lately, both in front of his workplace as in other spots around town, he had seen a guy named Chico Maneta, a scoundrel from the government's Portuguese Legion, who didn't start walking anywhere unless he, Afonso, also started. When he headed for his appointment with José Sagarra, he saw Maneta at the door of a tavern on the edge of town, very close to where the meeting was scheduled. So he decided not to go.

"Do you recall that I spoke to you about a suspicious guy who was following me at night sometimes? I'm convinced that was Chico Maneta."

"Why do you say that?" Vaz asked.

Afonso hesitated again. "It seems—" he said at last, "well, I have a hunch."

"This isn't a matter of hunches, my friend," Vaz retorted in a cool, cutting tone. What Afonso had told him didn't seem to have anything to do by way of explaining his missed appointment with José Sagarra. He saw in it Afonso's attempt to explain his not handing over the contacts with the farmworkers. "How come you didn't seek him out later?" he asked.

"I couldn't," Afonso explained. "We've had a lot of overtime and night work at the shop. Tomorrow, which is Sunday, I'm thinking of looking for him." Afonso said this with a straight face.

"When will you give him the contacts?" Vaz demanded again.

"I'll get together with him and take him to the different places. If he can get out of town tomorrow, we can probably do one right away."

Good, Vaz thought, *he is prepared to make the contacts. It's not as bad as I imagined.*

"I want to tell you one thing, quite frankly," Vaz said. "I was thinking that you had missed your date with José Sagarra out of bad faith in giving him the contacts with the peasants, because you guys have a poor opinion of the comrade and you weren't convinced of the correctness of the Party's approach. As for your explanation of why you failed to show up, I also want to say, frankly, that from what you told me I don't see sufficient reason for it."

Afonso kept his silence as they walked. In the shade, his slender body looked more bent than usual. When he spoke again, his voice was shaking audibly. "I'm not a liar, comrade. I see that I'm being observed, and if measures aren't taken, I can't be held responsible for what might happen."

"What measures?" Vaz asked.

"Here in this area I can't do anything more." Afonso spoke with an unusually excited inflection.

In that voice, and recalling what took place when Vaz had come to the house, Vaz perceived that Afonso was expressing some mature, well thought-out conclusions. There it was: Afonso did not want to do anything more! Pressure from his family? Discouragement?

"What do you want, then?" Vaz asked in an attitude heavy with judgment and scorn. "Do you want to leave the Party?"

"Leave the Party?!" Afonso broke in. His voice was heated and full of indignation.

7

No. Afonso was not thinking of leaving the Party now. He did think of it briefly in the days following Maria's departure. When he saw the jitney transporting her far away, maybe forever, his beloved young woman, he turned around sadly on the street, eyes misty, a weight in his chest, avoiding breaking out into sobs only thanks to the shock the developments had caused him. It was all so quick and unexpected. He felt as though he were seized and crushed by a powerful machine that had grabbed hold of him, inexorably dragged him toward giving up his own interests and desires, and led him to what he least wanted, which was to lose Maria. Why did he not react when he still had time? Why hadn't he fought for his happiness? To him, Vaz and Ramos looked like parts of that powerful machine, abusing his good faith and sincerity, to rob him of his most precious treasure. In that revelatory instant he wanted to free himself forever from the awesome obligations he had taken on, to no longer have to submit to men who, being his equals, yet felt they had the right to destroy his wellbeing and dreams, and to escape, escape, escape, to some desert place, quiet and isolated, where he could be alone with his pain.

That day he didn't return to his workplace, and went home to shut himself in his room, lying on the bed, his head pressed into his folded arms. His mother, who had been observing his state of mind for several days, sat on the edge of his bed without showing any misgivings about seeing him home during his working hours, without asking any questions, without any judgment. Though she knew nothing of what had happened, she spoke as though in truth she knew everything.

"Try not to dwell on it any more, son," she soothed him, as she lightly rested her hand in his hair. "As big a disappointment as it is, it can't destroy your life. You're young, and you'll find consolation for what's making you suffer now, and in a while from now you'll have forgotten what's burdening you now."

Afonso pulled her hand and placed it on his lips, and stayed like that with his eyes closed.

"Up to now you've only thought about others," his mother continued, sensing approval of her words in her son's gesture. "It's okay to think a little about yourself."

That day, and over the following days, Afonso was tempted by the idea of building a new life, where he'd take care of his own interests and his own pleasure, where he saw himself liberated from the oppressive worries that his Party activity created in him. For one basic reason, his mother did not succeed in convincing him: Because she could not give that which he most wanted, and that he wanted even more now that it was out of reach and for which he felt the loss.

Because of Maria, Afonso was about to lose the Party. It was also Maria who led him back to it.

8

In a tiny provincial city one might be oblivious to many things in people's personal life, their tastes and habits. One thing could not be disguised: Who is for the government and who is against the government. The fascists are pointed out publicly and, in the rare cases of fascist workers, they are the object of derision and isolation. Much of the time, the most iron-willed democrats and especially the Communist sympathizers are also known, above all to the fascists. At workplaces, or in off-hours, and even simply passing on the street, everyone observes those of the opposite party, or suspected of being, and follows them with their eyes. Some, however, do not restrict themselves to such hateful and distrusting looks. They observe, take note and report. If, for example, someone is seen frequently talking with Marques the carpenter, or if a group of factory workers is seen speaking late at night in low voices, or if a suspicious utterance is captured from the air, all this is communicated to the lieutenant at the National Republican Guard—the GNR—who would start investigating on his own and from time to time, if the substance justified it, report it to the political police.

Because of all this, it happened that Afonso would bump into fascists and sense their eye on him. In particular, he often ran into Chico Maneta, a loafer and legionnaire without profession or work, standing at the door of a bar or café, or at a street corner, or in front of the post office, the court or the market.

If Maria had not left, Afonso wouldn't lend any greater importance to these unfortunate encounters than he ever gave them.

Suddenly, without even realizing why, he started seeing the encounters as having a threatening character, and finding in them reason enough to skip meetings and reduce his activity. Mixed in with this, another idea was slowly taking root—the impossibility of pursuing his Party activity there, in that town, without imminent risk to his safety and freedom. In the end, this evolution in his thinking came to him in a flash, in complete and finished form: the necessity of going underground.

Certain self-recriminations occurred to him. Why hadn't he proposed to his comrades going into clandestine life with Maria? A month before, he wouldn't even have been able to pose such a question, because he felt too bound to his mother, his soil, his day-to-day habits. Now it seemed absurd not even to have considered that idea. Even when he was alone, he blushed over his indecision and lack of initiative, and over that single kiss he gave Maria and never would have given to anyone else. Yes, he could have cultivated a situation of intimacy with Maria to strengthen the proposal that both go underground together. Why didn't he do that? Yes, why not? Now Maria is living with another comrade, when she could be living with him, Afonso. Who knows? Maybe she had already created a personal arrangement with that unknown comrade when it was Afonso that she loved. That thought is so painful and so difficult to accept that Afonso feels the need to set it aside and to still believe that Maria's separation is not irremediable.

For several days, Afonso's mother believed she had successfully torn her son away from the dangers of his political activism. Now, with surprise and disquiet, she's seeing how, from one day to the next, he's starting to offer rude responses to her words, which only the day before he had received with interest, as if they were and had always been deeply abhorrent. When Afonso decided to see Vaz, she saw herself having lost the match.

That is why Afonso gets so indignant when Vaz asks him if he wants to leave the Party, and conveys his willingness to pass into underground work.

Relieved of the distrust that consumed him, Vaz recalled his conversation with Ramos about the need for a Party worker to handle distribution in the sector. He says, "I'll talk with the comrades. In any case, if you feel they're putting the squeeze on you, don't let yourself get caught."

They had arrived at the wall around Cesário's yard. As always, aside from the owner of the house, they also found Marques and Vítor.

9

To Vaz's huge surprise, Marques the carpenter not only agreed with the approach toward the dayworkers market, but offered a self-criticism for his previous attitude. "I recognize I was wrong," Marques said, in a voice affecting perfect calm, but betrayed by the fire in his eyes behind his thick lenses. "There's no doubt that the farmworkers' struggle is developing on the basis of the Party's approach. The duty of the Regional Committee is to rectify its mistakes and throw itself decisively into the peasants' mobilization and organization, according to the Central Committee's strategy."

Hearing these words, Cesário's dark face erupted into a broad smile. "That's wonderful that you think so," he said. "The comrades up there see more asleep than we see wide awake."

Marques's obstinate former position well deserved this comment, but Marques and Vítor received it with visible disapproval, even with irritation.

"I'm in complete agreement with Comrade Marques," said Vítor without removing his chin from the hand supporting it, and slowly exhaling a cloud of smoke. "We saw the problem wrong, and now we have to make up for lost time."

Vaz asked Afonso what he thought. Afonso seemed distracted. The loop of hair falling over his forehead gave a more youthful look to his melancholy face. "I agree with the comrades," he said simply.

Vaz then spoke briefly, underlining the positive attitude of comrades making self-criticism—although he, Vaz, did not find it quite adequate—and happily stressing the willingness to launch into the work and recover lost time. Vaz also had spoken with Afonso and, about the contacts that he was supposed to give to José Sagarra and hadn't yet, he was convinced that issue would now be resolved soon.

Hearing these words, Vítor shot Marques a questioning look through his cigarette smoke, as a vague smile crossed his lips. Marques in turn directed a quick look to Vítor. "Let's leave that to the end," Marques said. "Before anything else we should discuss practical measures the Regional Committee can take to correct its errors in the peasant sector."

Then Marques laid out a plan of work according to the larger Party approach. Marques's plan, in the end, recapitulated the general ideas expressed in the clandestine press with no reference to the concrete situation in the sector. It seemed to Vaz that Marques was merely wanting to show his agreement with the Party line and his complete understanding of it. It was almost as though he were teaching a class, giving the vaguest of recommendations and instructions, all very well framed, naturally, but with no consideration of the particulars in any locale.

"Sounds good," Vaz remarked when Marques had finished. "Let us hope that the comrades take this approach going forward."

Marques glanced at Vítor once again as if to ask *Now?* and said, "It seems to me that the immediate and fundamental practical measure for us to face is the issue of control. Up until now, Afonso has been in charge of almost all the contacts with the towns and villages. Despite his good intentions, he cannot get everyplace, and this has been one of the main reasons why our work has fallen back in that sector. In my opinion, management of the peasant cells and individual peasants should be handed over to other comrades. I'm not counting Cesário because he's already in charge of supervising the main factories in the city. But Comrade Vítor and I, perhaps with some help from Comrade Afonso, whose situation with people watching him may possibly force him to remove himself from work for some period, could reliably perform this assignment."

Vaz listened to this speech with a serious, impassive expression. But his bright eyes were fixed on Marques and his jaws were visibly tensing. Through his cigarette smoke, Vítor watched with interest.

"Very well," said Vaz drily. "Comrades Marques and Vítor will take over some peasant contacts. But those that Afonso was supposed to give to Sagarra will be given to Sagarra."

"Oh, no!" Marques almost shouted, his eyes fuming.

Vítor laughed, as if Vaz had just said the most ridiculous thing.

That's it! Vaz thought. *In the end we're in exactly the same place without having taken a single step.* And he recalled his conversation with Ramos and the words he had said: *Either we give the Regional Committee some new blood or we have to jump over it.*

Vaz insisted that those contacts be given to José Sagarra, that he himself, Vaz, was supervising, with an eye toward rapid mobilization and organization of the peasant sector. All this peasant work would later be linked to the Regional Committee, but in the present circumstances, that body was not prepared to lead it.

Marques, however, had carefully prepared for this session. With his intelligent eyes shining behind his glasses, he referred to systematic principles and methods of work recommended in Party publications, cited the great teachers of communism, and concluded by stating that Vaz's work behavior, jumping over the Regional Committee, pulling contacts with the Regional Committee and giving them to an ordinary comrade, was at the end of the day not a work plan for organization but for disorganization, of disempowering the leadership organs in the sector, and disintegrating the regional organization.

"The issue is very simple," Vaz responded, feeling Marques's hostility, as well as Vítor's, and apparently Afonso's. "When the Regional Committee controlled the few contacts we had in the sector, months and months went by without action, and there was no progress in the organization. Then came these wrong-headed recommendations concerning the dayworkers market, contrary to the Party's approach. Only for those reasons was it decided that one comrade from the leadership would take direct responsibility for the peasant sector. Since that work has come to be directly supervised by a Party worker (Vaz did not mention his own name) and led and driven by peasant cadres (Vaz did not mention José Sagarra's name), scores of movements and struggles have taken place, in many cases elevating conditions for the rural proletariat, and we recruited a substantial number of new Party members. So, comrades, not only will this work not be given to you at this time, but I also demand that Afonso hand over the contacts, especially two of them," and Vaz cited two locales.

Trying with visible effort to conserve his calm, Marques spoke further. "When we were defending an approach that we now acknowledge was wrong, it was still understood that the Party leadership would give other comrades supervision over the organizations in the peasant sector. Now that we recognize our mistake and not only say that we're in agreement with the Party line but have shown that we know it well and can put it into practice, nothing absolves the Regional Committee from exercising its control."

Vaz did not reply at once. Unmoved, he studied the reactions to Marques's words from the comrades. He paused a bit longer to catch the amused expression on Vítor's face.

"It seems that you comrades," he answered finally, "performed your self-criticism only as a supreme form of confusion and resistance, as merely a tactic to continue undermining the Party's activity in the peasant sector."

The argument became extremely heated. A few times Cesário, smiling and with nice words that clashed with the stormy atmosphere, tried to persuade Marques to agree with Vaz. Afonso said almost nothing, repeating only that he would do whatever was decided. Vitor intervened in support of Marques with his ironic, malicious asides. Marques argued long and hard for his point of view, answering Vaz point by point.

If in the end, respecting the general course of work among the peasants, Vaz agreed with the future activity of Marques and Vítor, he would not retreat one step on the two principal contacts to be given either to Sagarra or to himself.

"All right. That's what we'll do," Marques conceded finally, exhausted from the anger, his eyes still burning like hot coals behind his lenses. "But only because of Party discipline."

"Perfect," Vaz accepted, his voice cold and dry as he eyed his comrades intently. "Do this out of Party discipline, and it will work out very well."

These words sounded, to the ears of a still angry Marques, as if they were saying, *What we need here is for things to be done as I say. Your opinion is a matter of complete indifference to me.*

10

When Marques, Afonso and Vítor left, Cesário asked Vaz—who for the first time was spending the night in his house—to wait a little, and he went to the house next door, where his in-laws lived, to fetch his wife. As usual when there was a meeting, she went there for the evening. After a while he returned with the blond woman, tall and slender, with a bashful, sweet expression.

Cesário introduced her, and while the woman, her head inclined slightly forward, looked curiously at the guest and the papers he had on the table, Cesário had a wide smile plastered all across his dark face that seemed to ask, *So, what do you think of my woman?* He clearly and truly looked happy with her. When the woman left the room to set up Vaz's bed, Cesário, still smiling, said, "If I had to go underground one day, I know I'd have my wife right there with me."

Vaz remembered Rosa in that moment and said how important it was to have a good companion who thinks like us and stays with us in this difficult clandestine life. "If a woman doesn't understand or accept our struggle, if she's not prepared to help her companion with it and confront the dangers, uncertainties and hardships that the struggle involves, such a woman can't nor should be the companion of a militant. In my opinion, our comrades should marry early, but only marry a woman capable of understanding, accepting and assisting our struggle. Otherwise, the only way is to remain single."

"Yes," Cesário said, "it should be that way. Sadly, we still have comrades who, instead of trying to find an honest, uncomplicated, dedicated woman, only feel satisfied with prostitutes or scatterbrains."

Although Cesário had not mentioned any names, it appeared to Vaz that the comrade was not speaking only in generalities, but rather intended to refer to some specific instance in the regional organization.

"Why do you think Comrades Marques and Vítor are single?" Vaz asked.

With the sleeves of his denim shirt rolled up, Cesário crossed his dark arms. "Marques spent several years in prison, and came out rather sour on women, you know? He's not a kid any more, and women are afraid of him. As for Vítor—look, friend, I'd rather not talk about that."

This attitude surprised Vaz. He said he wasn't aiming to pry into anyone's life, but the Party needed to know about the lives and personal conduct of its members. That's the only reason he posed the question and pursued the conversation.

Cesário sighed, clearly upset. "You're going to think my opinion comes out of my family experience, because Vítor was courting my sister-in-law. The truth is that my sister-in-law is a serious and unpretentious gal, and today she's our best comrade in the jute factory, but he was deceiving her for two years and in the end he dropped her like a hot potato and started hooking up with some doll."

Cesário paused for a while. "To speak quite frankly, I judge it improper for a comrade to associate with women like that."

And he went on to describe her. She was employed at the post office. She flipped her enormous head of hair all the time, throwing it from side to side with a wrench of her neck, as if she was flinging her cape like a bullfighter in the ring, around anyone she was talking to or that she ran into on the street. Her peals of laughter could be heard fifty meters away, and she let them out not because she wanted to laugh but only to draw attention to herself and show off her teeth. "That's more of a mare than a woman," Cesário concluded.

Vaz did not rush to agree. In his view, so it seemed, the fact of being a little wacky, using a lot a makeup and laughing loudly did not mean she couldn't be a useful person.

"Useful!?" Cesário was shocked. And he revealed that all over the city people said she was the lover of a Portuguese Legion commander.

"So where does that leave us?" Vaz inquired. "Didn't you say Vítor was still involved with her? Is she Vítor's lover or the Legion commander's?"

"Both of them, friend, both! And maybe others too." He added that Vítor appeared with her in public, at the café, the movies, on the street. But that's not all. Vítor had been seen with other women of ill repute, in low-class cafés eating cake and drinking whatever.

"Look, what confidence can the comrades have in the Regional Committee, comrades who know Vítor and see him behaving like that? Hey, there are even those who say Vítor was spending money on himself that was designated for the Party."

"Have you talked with him about this?" asked Vaz.

"No. I never talked with him or anyone. It's only now that I'm saying it to you for the first time."

"It would be better if you had raised this issue with the Regional Committee. That's where it should be raised."

Cesário looked embarrassed. "Honestly, I don't think I'd be able to do that."

"I'll raise it, then, don't worry," Vaz said coldly with a trace of both mockery and threat.

11

Cesário had alerted Vaz that very early the next morning a comrade would come to the house who was from the most important factory in the city, and asked him if he wanted to avoid being seen.

"You can get around saying who I am and that I spent the night here, but there could be some advantage to meeting him," Vaz answered.

In that spirit, the thought came back to mind about the Regional Committee, now beefed up with the information from Cesário about Vítor's personal life: *Either new blood or we have to jump over it.*

He was a short, thin little man with a delicate face and constantly blinking eyes. In a cutting voice that took on a falsetto tone when he tried to talk faster or got excited, he related what had happened the previous afternoon.

"As you know, the big boss wanted to form a committee of boot-lickers, saying he wanted it alone to represent the workers at the factory and calling the other committee a bunch of undisciplined troublemakers. But who does he go and choose? Zé Augusto, who's the foreman, Joaquim Coxo, who's a rat running to wherever they take him, and who else? Yes, Borralha! Jeez, Borralha who never learned how to do anything but guzzle wine. Yesterday the boss ordered the workers to assemble and said the committee had been formed, all serious men, and whenever anyone thought there was something management should do they should take it up with this committee. Miguel jumped right in, saying a committee had already been established, chosen by everyone, and the one the boss was pointing to did not merit the workers' confidence. The big guy—we call him 'Top Hat'—burst in again, threatening and making a scene, and the guys got intimidated. 'All right, guys!' I said then. 'As for myself, I'm okay with this committee.' You should have seen Top Hat! He interrupted me right away, saying I was one of the best workers in the plant, how he always respected my ideas etcetera etcetera. 'Now Henriques here,' he said, 'he's a sensible man and it's a shame I didn't think of him.' 'Well,' I said then, 'I'm okay with the committee but I think it has to prove itself.' 'Yes, of course, of course,' Top Hat right away agrees, figuring our committee is dead and his is now recognized by the workers. 'Good,' I said. 'The proof can start right now: Let Borralha tell us how he's planning to approach his future work as a member of the committee.' Wow, you shoulda been there! 'Talk, Borralha!' someone shouted. 'Hey, Borralha, give us a speech, man, here's your chance!' said someone else. 'Go for it, Borralha, now or never!' a third guy called out. And Borralha, with that drunkard's snout of his, lowered his head and looked the crowd up and down and looked so ridiculous that everyone broke out laughing. 'Ah, Borralha, my heartbeat, you should be a government minister!' The racket was so huge, with everyone laughing so much, that Top Hat wound up escaping back into his office. Then Borralha, kicked out, yelled 'Dammit' and threw his cap on the ground. And we, the members of our committee, went after Top Hat. And he received us immediately. We didn't gain anything from our show of disrespect, but that's okay because he will receive us on Monday as we requested."

Vaz wrote down notes of what the comrade had just related, and asked a few more questions—how many workers there were, what were their main demands, and others—and said he was fascinated by the way they were conducting the struggle.

Henriques blinked a lot and smiled in satisfaction. "On Monday I already know what he's going to say to us. We asked for a raise of 5 *escudos*, and for all the broken glass in the windows to be fixed. As far as the windows go, he'll promise to have them fixed. But as for the 5 *escudos*, he'll say he can't. And then I'll tell him, 'You can't? Well, we can't either: without coal the steam machine doesn't move. No money, no work! Give us 5 and everything will continue to run smoothly. Don't give us, and we'll have to work slower."

"Terrific," said Vaz, who then, sorry he couldn't continue with the conversation, excused himself and left.

On the almost deserted streets, here and there men were standing, waiting for the women to pass by on the way to market or to mass. A milk seller was carefully setting up some shiny pottery jugs against the wall of a building. A stray cat watched from the top of the wall with its surprised, expectant eyes, plotting its path to jump and run.

Vaz was walking his bicycle along a little sloped street with irregular paving stones, and as he glanced to the side he suddenly saw Vítor leaning against the door of a cheap café. He was with some man Vaz didn't recognize and although both of them quickly turned their eyes away, Vaz was convinced they had been talking about him.

What's the meaning of this? Vaz asked himself. *A secret with a comrade? Gossip? Or what?*

And if he could have, he'd leap right over the three weeks remaining before the next Regional Committee meeting.

Chapter *VI*

1

"Holy cow! What a face!" Ramos exclaimed. "Inflamed corn? Heart-sick over something?"

It was neither, just a bad toothache. She had spent the last week clasping her jaws unable to do much of anything. She even tried a cigarette, she who was always complaining about tobacco and the bad smell it left in the house.

"You know what caused it?" said Ramos, as he removed his coat. "It's from eating so much sweets. Sugar is bad for your teeth."

Elbows on the table, his face illuminated by the oil lamp, his smiling eyes circled by wrinkles, António appreciated his comrade's joviality.

"It's not because I've eaten so many sweets," Maria responded in all seriousness. "Apart from the sugar we put in the coffee, no other sweets in the house."

She hadn't even finished speaking before Ramos exploded in a loud guffaw and lit a cigarette.

There was a knock on the door. Maria opened it. Tired, laden with briefcases and packages, Paulo and Vaz entered. Vaz took off his cap, which had left an impression on his pale forehead, two bright red lines.

"Are your teeth hurting too, old man?" Ramos asked, still laughing.

Thin and shrunken, his eye sockets sunken and mauve colored, Vaz didn't answer. As if he hadn't heard, he left the work room and went to the kitchen. He filled a bowl with water and drank it all in big gulps. He washed it, put it back in the place he found it and came back to join his comrades.

"You don't have any news of my father, do you?" Maria asked.

Truthfully, he didn't. He had forgotten completely about it. But even if he hadn't forgotten, there was nothing he could have done. On this trip into the city he had many important matters to discuss.

"Stay calm and rest assured, friend," Vaz ended the conversation. "The next time I come back here I will bring you news of your father."

"Believe him," Ramos said. "The hard part is anteing up. Since you've already anteed up, the prize is guaranteed."

Maria looked at him crestfallen and turned to Vaz. "You say I should stay calm, dear friend. That's fine to say. When I went underground, they told me I'd get regular news about my father. Until now I still haven't received any. One time it's for this reason, the next time it's something else, but no one's told me anything. How can I stay calm?"

"You would be right," Vaz admitted, "but it wasn't possible. I had important, urgent things to take care of."

"Important, urgent things, friend. And isn't it important and urgent to bring a nervous daughter news about her sick father? It's easy to say, 'Be calm and rest assured, I'll bring you news when I come back the next time.' But when are you returning here? A month from now? Three weeks? How can you tell me to be calm and rest assured, dear friend?"

Ramos raised his eyes from the table, where he'd been sorting papers, and directed himself to Vaz. "What a thrashing you got, old man!"

Paulo was also organizing his papers. Over his eyeglasses he looked out timidly to one and the other and with a slight tremor in his voice said, "The problem is something else, comrade."

Ramos did not pick up what he meant by that, and didn't ask. "Shall we begin?" he said matter-of-factly. His jovial tone had suddenly evaporated.

2

They worked all through the night, laying themselves down only for an hour in the wee hours as dawn approached. Maria made coffee and served everyone a piece of bread that would barely have been enough for one, then they returned to work. If they were going to depart before lunch, as they had planned, they had to work conscientiously. The rapid development in the sector required meticulous attention. They placed on the table innumerable problems concerning the masses in movement, the organization, and the cadre. They felt that if they kept up the current rhythm, within a short period the Party would be the true leader of the workers in the sector—in fact, and not just in theory. With some amazement they took stock of the transformation that in this period was flowing from their hands.

They had started with a small nucleus of comrades separated from the class and the masses. Now the class and the masses were beginning to follow and support the Party.

Still, not everything was roses. Some delicate problems were cropping up to cast a shadow over this picture. Among them, Vaz continues to give special importance to the situation in the Regional Committee, of which Marques is a member. Once again he brings the case to the discussion. In his view, it requires urgent measures. The Committee is not equipped to lead the region. Only Cesário is any good. Because of his being spied on, Afonso is now with one foot in and one foot out, and is proposing to become a Party worker. As for Marques, Vaz considers him the principal impediment to developing regional work.

"And with Vítor, there are a number of things we need to find out. But in any case, he's of little worth."

"Hold on! Hold on!" Ramos interrupted. "Anytime soon you'll be seeing enemies all over."

"Maybe," Vaz answered without a change of tone in his voice. "I don't have a crystal ball, but I can see. And what I see is enough to conclude that the Regional Committee has been in place too long. It doesn't function, nor does it allow others to function. The future will tell if there isn't even more corruption going on."

And he told them about the woman from the post office and the incident at the cheap café entrance.

"You don't need to be so mistrusting," Ramos countered. "If you want to clarify the incident, fine. But if you start off with the idea that Vítor pointed you out to some scoundrel, you can't make an objective analysis of the facts. It's dangerous to follow your impressions. We have to be broadminded. Our members are men, not dolls made of straw. The weight of influences from the society we live in falls on all of us. We shouldn't expect to make the revolution with ideal men."

"We need more serious people with a higher morality in the Party," said Paulo. "I don't really believe in the seriousness regarding the Party of people who aren't serious in their private lives."

"It's not with people like Vítor that we're able to move forward," said Vaz supportively. "We need more Cesários, more Sagarras, more Henriques, people who are more down to earth, honest and dedicated, and fewer smokers of unfiltered cigarettes."

At that precise moment Ramos was tapping a cigarette. An aggressive flash crossed over his eyes, as if Vaz had intended to attack him personally with those words. But Vaz's imperturbable expression discouraged Ramos from questioning him.

"In the final analysis," an impatient, ill-humored Ramos said, "what we're talking about is not so much the case of Vítor but our whole policy toward cadre. What's important for us to determine is if we should behave like an association of English Puritans, if we should be closed and sectarian, or if we should understand men as they are, with their hardships and defects, but also with the essential qualities that—"

"But we'd have to define what are the essential qualities—"

The argument got heated, and by the time they had agreed to end the meeting there were still many points they hadn't touched on. They decided to stay through the afternoon and called Maria.

"Good news," António told her. "You're always complaining that our friends are here for such a short time. Well, now you have them for the whole day. They're staying for lunch."

Everyone expected that Maria would receive this news happily. It would have been quite natural for her to say something like, *Oh, how wonderful, my friends, how nice you are*. But no. She was visibly upset and made no comment.

"It seems you're not pleased," said Ramos. "Could it be that you have a date arranged with your boyfriend?" Ramos meant the slovenly bum who read the newspaper, who had already been mentioned.

"No, my dear friends, I'm very pleased to have you here," Maria retorted and, as if belying her words, turned her back on the comrades and quickly left the room.

3

When she got to the kitchen she acted very strangely. It looked like she was making a police search, thorough, fast and frenetic. She combed the two drawers, fumbled in every corner, unwrapped everything that was wrapped, upended every pan, a basket and packing case. With the kitchen already completely dismantled, and always with her rapid, nervous movements, she started all over again from the beginning, repeating the same inspection. Kneeling on the floor, she was peering once again under the stove when a soft sound made her turn her head. Next to the door, with his emotionless face and cold, untroubled eyes, Vaz was observing her.

"Have you been standing there, friend?" asked Maria, her panting voice showing surprise. "I didn't hear you enter. Do you want something?"

Of the four comrades in the house, it was by Vaz that she least cared to be seen in that state, in the same way that it was Vaz with whom she least would have wanted to live. She felt respect for the comrade, but the way he expressed himself with his dour manners brought up a combination of resentment and constraint in her.

Vaz kept his silence for a few moments, looking about the kitchen with a cool gaze. Then he drank more water, which is what had brought him there. "Anything going on?" he asked after emptying a container.

Maria hesitated, her browed eyes fixed on the comrade, and suddenly, still on her knees, she folded herself over a chair, put her head in her arms and let out her tears. She truly wanted to suppress her crying, but the harder she tried, the more she broke into sobs.

Maria imagined Vaz behind her standing in the same position, without any show of interest or affection, with his unchanging expression and his clear eyes taking in the scene. None of the other comrades would be like that. António would have a kind word; Paulo would maybe remain silent but would come sit beside her on the floor; and Ramos, ah well, long ago he would have caressed her shoulder to give her confidence. Still, Maria felt that any of those gestures from the other comrades would only intensify her commotion and send her into another round of even more convulsive wailing, while Vaz's silence and immobility were ever so gradually diminishing, then finally snuffing out her impulse to cry. She raised her face.

"What is it, friend?" Vaz inquired again, not having moved from his spot, and speaking as though he had not just witnessed the crying jag.

Maria wiped her eyes with the back of her hands. "I have nothing to give you to eat," she answered abruptly. "I wasn't counting on you for lunch. I have nothing in the house."

"Is that all?" Vaz's voice sounded as imperturbable as his facial expression.

"I have absolutely nothing, friend. Not even potatoes or rice. All I have is a dozen small salted sardines and a quarter loaf of bread. What can I give you to eat?"

Taking a couple of gentle steps, Vaz approached Maria, crouching on the floor, and sat on the chair. "Can't you go buy something?"

"Buy? With what money!? I have exactly 1.2 *escudos* until the end of the month." Maria's voice, with its unfamiliar tone of indignation and irony, seemed to be saying, *Did you think you could upset me for not having things if I could have bought them? Go ahead, say it: 'Is that all!' Go on, keep being your impassive self now!*

"You still don't know me," said Vaz in the same steady voice. "I've had far more days without eating lunch than you can imagine. One more, one less, it doesn't matter. The other comrades would say the same. Don't worry. It's not worth it." With that, he stood up and returned to the work room.

Maria remained quiet a few minutes, distractedly taking in the disarray in the kitchen. Then, slowly, she started putting everything back in its place. She had just begun doing so when they called for her.

"Maria!" It was Ramos with his joyous, happy voice.

Maria went to the work room.

4

"What the hell?" said Ramos when she entered. "You had a little snack and left us behind without letting us have a taste?—"

"Don't talk like that, dear friend," she interrupted. "Don't be nasty."

"As it happens, I like it too," said Paulo. Blushing, peering out over his eyeglasses, his wispy white hair tumbling over his forehead, he spoke solemnly, as if to foreclose any idea that he might be trying to be ironic. His intention of consoling Maria was so obvious, though, that his declaration of appreciation for salted sardines didn't convince anyone.

"Okay," Ramos insisted, "so tell us everything you have in the house."

"Eleven small salted sardines and a quarter loaf of bread. Nothing more."

"I didn't realize we were so low," said António, feeling somewhat co-responsible. "Didn't we still have a good piece of that cod?"

"A good piece?" Maria threw back at him angrily. "You ate it yesterday, and there wasn't much of it then."

"What else?" Ramos asked.

"Nothing else," Maia insisted. "Actually, I have a few leftovers not worth mentioning—"

"Like what? Tell us! Or are you holding back on the best?"

"I'll tell you,"Maria answered with a slight, fleeting smile. "I also have two onions, a small bag of corn meal and a drop of oil."

"But just days ago we bought half a liter," António commented somberly. He was visibly embarrassed by the lengthy revelation of the financial situation in the house.

"And salt, don't you have salt?" Ramos asked, paying no attention to what António had just said.

"Yes, I have salt."

"With this we'll make a banquet! A genuine banquet!" Ramos laughed heartily.

"Show me, dear friend, because I don't know—" and Maria's lips began to tremble.

"Agreed! Come with me." And he took her to the kitchen where the two of them started whispering.

How odd! Three comrades were present who didn't live there, they saw the comrades of the house embarrassingly low in supplies, and no one offered their help. Something else no less odd: The comrades of the house didn't seem surprised by that lack of help. The fact was that although those men had more than enough money in their pockets to respond to those needs, and although some even had relatively large sums on them, not one of them had a penny they could call their own.

The two cooks returned after a short time, very excitedly. Maria ferreted though folders of papers and quickly hid something under her apron. Now she was smiling and it looked like she was about to say something amusing.

Vaz took hold of his pencil and turned toward her before she could speak. "Problem solved," he pronounced in his ever calm manner. "Could you let us continue working for just a little while?"

5

Maria, in the kitchen, is making surprising preparations. She scissors fanciful lace out of tissue paper in various colors. Out of two red leaves of paper she makes lovely table mats roughly a half-meter long. She cuts five squares of white paper, and trims their borders carefully. She pulls two planks off a soap box, washes them and sets them out to dry. She places a handful of pine needles on a plate. And she does all this while humming quietly and from time to time looking into the pot that's on the stove. Every time she lifts the lid, an eddy of vapor quickly rises to the ceiling, and a warm breeze of salt and something fusty wafts through the house.

She was looking in on the sardines one more time when Ramos appeared. He poised an arm on her back and his chin on her shoulder, and also leaned over the pot. "So?"

The sardines, however, are clearly of little interest to Ramos. From her hair to her feet, Maria feels the body of her comrade very close to hers. His face is so near that his eyelashes brush her face every time the comrade closes his eyes. Her ears burning, Maria doesn't object or withdraw. She accepts the contact with Ramos with the same determination with which he seeks it. She hopes that, like on the train the day she met him, her comrade's hand will leave her shoulder, seek out the nape of her neck and slowly rotate her head. She hopes again to see that inviting and violent expression, and she knows that this time she won't flee or separate from him in an angry gesture.

"So?" Ramos asks again. "Are they ready?"

"Almost," she answers faintly.

Ramos's hand leaves her shoulder. Maria's heart beats fast. *Now? Now?* But no. Ramos separates from his comrade with such indifference and self-assurance as if he were declaiming to an imaginary audience: *You are fools to make quick judgments. What is so extraordinary about placing a hand on a comrade's shoulder in order to look into a pot?* He steps to the table to see the planks, the pine needles, the pretty tissue paper designs. "Shall we do it?"

Vaz studies his papers while Paulo and António are all ears to what's happening in the kitchen, to Ramos and Maria's murmuring voices that reach them. They hear laughter and words in low voices. After the tinkle of spoons, silence and more laughter. António can't resist and runs to see.

But Maria hears his steps. Pushing the door, she sticks her nose through the crack and doesn't let him in. "Go away, dear friend. We're about to serve your banquet."

"I'm coming to help!" António says, his perky, wrinkle-lined eyes smiling slyly.

"No," Maria says firmly. "There's nothing for you to do here. Go away, because lunch is coming soon."

"Let me in," António implores. And as Maria doesn't answer, he tries to push the door in. With unexpected strength, Maria slams the door, latches it closed and laughs. "Wait, my friend, wait! Waiting will whet your appetite."

António bangs on the door once more, but gives up. He returns to the work room and starts reading a typed sheet with exaggerated attention.

6

It was sensational. Maria entered first. Five plates can be seen artfully arranged on the planks resting on big trays and beautifully decorated with tissue paper. Ramos followed her. With a white cloth skillfully molded on top of his head, he looks like the master chef. On one hand he lifts another improvised tray with even more beautiful decorations. In the middle of the tray rose a single dish with so many pine needles that it could be mistaken for an ersatz porcupine.

Maria's glance met that of António, which he slowly raised from his papers. But heavens, what a look! Now it was no longer the usual happy and mischievous look from lively eyes surrounded by wrinkles, but a sad, resentful look she had never seen on him.

They made room on the table. Maria and Ramos placed the trays down. Paulo laughed with his childish giggle. Vaz was supportive but not exuberantly. António looked at the plates. "How rich!" he exclaimed. "Cornmeal porridge and cooked sardines speared with pine needles!

Despite everything the meal was a happy one.

Ramos asked once again about Maria's "boyfriend," and António offered the latest news about him and the woman who sold them the carrots. She had come back again, always wrapped in her shawl, her dark little darting eyes peering out of the shadow. Quickly pulling the shawl aside, this time she showed an enormous yellow rabbit and for that too she asked a ridiculously low price. Excited about it, Maria wanted to show the rabbit to António, but only with reluctance did the woman allow her to take it.

"It's too cheap," said António. "This woman is strange. Don't buy it."

The vagabond came back too, displaying his beefy body through the rips in his clothing. He silently offered Maria an enormous orange. António also went to the door, but the bum, pretending not to notice him, kept ogling Maria with appreciative persistence.

"Where did you get that?" Maria asked.

Indicating fields faraway, the vagabond gestured clownishly wide and imposingly: "On my estates, senhora." And he walked away, full of self-importance.

António then decided to ask for information about the woman and the vagabond, and to that end he went to see the man from the tile roof who had guided him when he was searching for a house. The man received him gladly and brought him to the wine cellar to talk. Adjusting his eyes, he indignantly said the woman was a habitual thief who didn't own even a single stalk of kale.

"So that's it," António said. "I had good reason right away to distrust the low price of her carrots."

The man had a rollicking laugh. "You distrusted, but you ate them!" reprimanding him as if the carrots had been stolen from him—even though he didn't have any.

About the vagabond he told a long story. He simply appeared in these parts and stayed. They called him Elvas, because he claimed to be a native of Elvas, but his name was Damião. He'd been in prison, but no one knew why. Some suspected him for robbery, others homicide. People had asked him, but after his response they knew even less than before. Elvas bought the newspaper, and read and commented on it to the illiterate peasants. He wrote letters for them and helped them manage their accounts. For these little services, and out of pity, one gave him a bowl of soup, another a piece of bread, and someone else let him sleep on their hay. Elvas didn't accept these donations as alms, but as payment owed. Though he was a bum without a penny, he commanded a certain respect.

"Wherever you see him," the tile man concluded, "you pay no attention to him. But he is no fool. That's a man who has had an education—and bad luck in life."

António and Maria had purchased his rationing vouchers, but António did not like him, above all because of the constant pretexts he found to knock on their door, because of the rude way he looked Maria up and down, and because of his complete indifference, if not to say scorn, he displayed toward him, António.

"I don't like seeing a guy like that prowling around your door," said Paulo, thinking about the long days Maria was left alone in the house.

If Paulo had known Elvas, he would have liked him even less.

7

During the lunch, Maria drank some water and her expression turned to acute pain. She brought her hand to her face. The toothache had returned. Ramos told a number of jokes on the theme. Vaz listened, António laughed, and Maria smiled. Only Paulo expressed annoyance at the direction of the conversation. When Ramos let out a big burst of laughter after telling his next story, Paulo could not restrain himself any longer. "Joking around isn't going to solve anything," he said. "We have to do something for our friend."

Agreeably enough, Ramos stopped laughing, then turned to Paulo in a condescending tone: "Wanting to do something for our friend won't solve anything either, old man. What we need is the means to do it."

Paulo did not respond right away. With a shock of white hair fallen over his back, he glared at Ramos over his glasses. Seemingly, he had no response. Finally his words came out slightly timorous but convinced. "When you truly want to do something, it gets done. When you don't want to, justifications appear."

"So, do it!" Ramos said harshly.

"I will."

At the end of the meeting they looked at the situation. Paulo proposed the house of the lawyer with whom he was in contact.

"Who?" Ramos interrupted. "The blowhard?"

"Unfortunately," Vaz had to agree, "he's useless even for that."

"Maybe he can help," Paulo said with surprising assurance. And he recounted that he'd had long talks with the lawyer who, through Paulo, saw the potential for his wife to get interested in Party activity. The last time he'd seen him, the lawyer slowly stroked his wavy hair, smiled, and said with some satisfaction, "My *companion*"— the lawyer intended to say that word with all naturalness but it came out rather exaggeratedly, using Party-speak for underground workers but no doubt signaling that she really was his wife—"my *companion* would also like to help us. If some comrade needed to use our house for one or two days, or to spend a night, she's at the Party's orders."

Upon saying this, the expression on the lawyer's face suddenly became grim, and he nervously put out his cigarette in the ashtray. Paulo did not understand the sudden appearance of such a sour mood. Nor could he have understood it. How could he imagine that, in the lawyer's mind, the image came up at that moment of Vaz in the corridor outside his office disgustedly turning his back on him to go out into the rain late that night on his bicycle after he, the lawyer, had refused him shelter?

"You done good work!" said Ramos. That was a fact. Paulo had indeed. But that didn't stop Ramos from proceeding to his next bit of wisecracking. "So you brought the lawyer along. But you won't get the shoemaker." Ramos was referring to the comrade who months before had promised to call a meeting of the Local Committee without having done so all this time.

Paulo regarded Ramos over his glasses with his usual modesty. But a slight smile lit up his face. Vaz saw it and read, *We'll see, comrade*. Paulo's amused expression said, *We'll see if I get him or not.*

8

António came out yawning, mopish from his few hours of rest. He had still not recovered from the past few nights of poor sleep. At the kitchen table Maria was reading and writing. Absorbed in her work, she barely responded to António's "Good morning" with some unintelligible sounds and without raising her eyes. António waited a few moments for Maria to respond, but she went on reading and writing as if not noticing his presence.

"No coffee today?" António asked.

"Huhh?" Maria grunted.

"Aren't we eating in this house today?"

"One quick minute, just a minute," Maria said without sensing António's lousy mood and without putting her papers aside.

António waited "one quick minute," but since his comrade continued to be engrossed in work without any rush to attend to him, he went out, disgruntled, to the back patio. He waited for Maria to call him, or for her to follow him and ask him if anything was the matter—was he in a bad mood or sick, or was he still mad over her not paying him any attention? Standing at the wall, he looked out sadly over the dewy fields, not focusing or remarking on anything in particular, only waiting to hear his comrade's voice from inside the house, or hear her rapidly approaching steps. But Maria didn't say anything, nor did she come out to check on him. Eventually António returned inside and sat at one corner of the table.

"What are we eating today?"

His voice was so intrusive that Maria finally raised her eyes and brow. "How rude he is! Did some animal bite him or did he wake up on the wrong side of the bed?"

"What're we eating today?" he repeated. It seemed he was wanting to blame Maria for the hardships in the house.

"Don't worry, dear friend," Maria answered. "I'm giving you hot chocolate and toast now, hake with sprouts for lunch, and roast veal for dinner. Will that do?"

António understood that he was being ridiculous and that he had spoken in an unfair tone, but he didn't know how to correct himself.

Finally Maria served him coffee, without bread. And she informed him that lunch would be only a piece of bread with a few vegetables, and for dinner, coffee and a hunk of bread. Their few coins remaining she had spent on coffee and bread, unable to buy anything more. In an unexpected reaction and unforeseen temper, he disagreed with that use of the money. It would have been smarter to buy potatoes. She could have bought two kilos of potatoes, because potatoes are always more filling.

"Maybe you're right," Maria said. "But it is what it is. Today's the last day of the month and tomorrow you'll eat better."

"That's stupid!" António exploded. "Having money in your pocket to hand over tomorrow and go hungry today just so you don't touch that money! We could perfectly well give ourselves an advance of ten or twenty *escudos* from our next month's salary. There's no need to go hungry today."

"How can you say that?" Maria was indignant. "Haven't you yourself said there must be no deficits allowed in Party houses?"

"Rules are one thing, but schematicism is something else. Schematicism always leads to foolishness. If we advanced ourselves ten or twenty *escudos* of our salary for next month, which starts tomorrow, where's the harm? We'd just eat less ten or twenty *escudos'* worth next month, and that's it. Anything else is just stupidity."

Maria gazed at her comrade stupefied. "How can you say this, dear friend? How can you want to do what you prohibit for others?"

António shrugged his shoulders aggressively and spoke with cutting, offensive irony: "Comrade Maria now wants to teach 'Our Father' to the vicar."

Maia was stunned into silence. She picked up the dishes and put them away, then returned to her seat with her papers. "You're the one responsible for this house," she said at last. "Do as you wish, buy what you want and eat whatever you like. I will eat bread and vegetables and drink coffee. It's enough for me."

António said no more. He got up noisily and went to his room.

After a while, Maria went there and opened the door. Lying on his back on the bed, his hands behind his head, he stared at her, angrily and seriously, with the same look, precisely the same sad, resentful look that Maria had seen in him when she appeared with Ramos and the salted sardines.

She shook her head two or three times and went away, closing the door softly.

9

Paulo had it all set up. António and Maria went to the lawyer's office. He arrived shortly, in a hurry and smiling. He told them to enter his chambers, offered them armchairs, sat at his desk, leaned back and, placing his palms wide apart on the desk, smiled amiably.

"You'll have to wait a little. My *companion* will be here with you—" stressing the word, which still came out awkwardly.

"Did she get a doctor?" António asked.

The lawyer settled himself more comfortably into his easy chair and suavely ran his fingers through his wavy hair.

"There were several options to consider," he began, pausing frequently. "This is an insignificant town. Whoever can afford it gets treated elsewhere, and those who can't don'e get treated here or anywhere. I'll tell you a pertinent story. Some five years ago a young boy from Casal do Pereiro was out picking figs, he fell from the tree and landed on the ground unable to move. They called Dr. Cirilo and the old man came. He's a curious old guy who wears boots, goes around bareheaded and drinks water from public fountains."

The lawyer stopped for a moment to observe the effect of his words and his sense of irony. He must have been satisfied because he went on animatedly.

"The doctor examined the boy and pronounced his judgment: *Here, my friends, or the hospital—or the witch doctor!*

He chuckled, examined his clean, polished fingernails, and was about to continue when his office door opened, and in the threshold appeared a fine, strong woman dressed to perfection, whose shapely figure could be read under her amply proportioned white topcoat. From the door she shot a quick glance at the visitors, curious and rather imperious. Then, in rapid little steps, hammering the carpet with her nine-centimeter heels, she approached the desk and stopped suddenly to make a pirouette such as might announce the next number at a circus.

"We can go," she said decisively.

The lawyer, somewhat deflated for not being able to finish his story, made the solemn introductions. "*Our* comrades—my *companion.*" There was something unnatural and forced in these expressions.

Maria rose and extended her hand. The hand of the lawyer's wife, dainty with painted nails, came out instantly, at the end of a rounded arm of delicate skin, shaking and tinkling her metallic costume bracelets. "Very pleased," she said, looking Maria up and down, pausing her gaze a little longer on Maria's worn, out of style shoes.

With her arms gracelessly hanging by her sides, her little black jacket badly designed and showing signs of wear, Maria reddened. Then the lawyer's wife made a half turn on her high heels and, snapping her white topcoat open, displayed her beautiful wool pullover atop which, around her neck, glowed a necklace of white spheres.

"Oh, I haven't told you yet," she said to her husband apropos of nothing. "I was with Baby just now. This time it was a real disaster. Imagine! Remembering to fill it with gasoline—in the water tank!" And she let out a hearty, tuneful laugh, revealing her neck and her pearly white teeth.

The lawyer and António laughed with her. Maria felt disoriented and confused. She sensed that their raucous laughter came not from

the story of the gasoline and the water, but from herself—Maria—
from her uncomfortable position, from her distorted expression on
account of her toothache, from her threadbare outfit, from her arms
just dragging alongside her body, from her wimpy, poorly maintained hand that fearfully grasped the lawyer's wife's. Soon she was
feeling irrepressible dislike.

Impossible to explain the whole problem in details, the lawyer
then briefly laid out the plan: His *companion* (again he emphasized
this word with a very special inflection) would take Maria to the
dentist at the government public health service. Then the two of
them would come back and have lunch at the house. This idea had
come from the *companion*, who had handled and settled everything.
Would that be good?

They got ready to leave. Before leaving, though, the "wife" opened
her handsome leather handbag, riffled through it and withdrew a
light green handkerchief that released an intense perfume into the
air, raised it to the end of her nose, sniffled and put the handkerchief
back, and shut the handbag with a metallic click, which to Maria's
ears sounded like the gate to a house thwacking a poor man's back.

10

He was a short, chubby man with waxed hair fixed to his skull and
a wide, strangely flat face as if he were mashed against a pane of
glass. There were those who said he looked like an English pig, but
in fact pigs don't wear eyeglasses, and the dentist from the health
service did. He wore glasses without frames, the kind that give the
impression of culture and intelligence—at least in the minds of the
wearers. This surely influenced his choice. With such glasses and a
university diploma, one brother a priest and the other a government
functionary, the dentist performed his job completely as he wished.
The worst were the gossipers.

These maligners said, for example, that our man was a filthy pig.
They said that, after treating a patient, he'd take his dental tools to
a nearby sink and wash them with a small nailbrush, and that the
nailbrush also served other purposes, especially to draw blood and
pus from the vats full of wound dressings at the emergency medical center. So said the gossipers. But who could believe that? Was it
conceivable that a dentist from the health service, a medical professional, brother of a priest and a government functionary, member of
the National Union, would wash his tools with such a nailbrush and
then place them without any disinfectant in the mouth of the next
patient to come along? Maligners for sure. And revenge. Because if

we're speaking of revenge, it's appropriate to acknowledge there were reasons for it. For if conversation should start among those who gathered at the door of his consultation room, our man never missed a word nor interrupted his drudgery. Turning his pancake face to the door, his dilated eyes peering through his thick lenses, he continued giving treatment by feel. He examined, jiggled and wiggled, picked and pecked, scraped, dug, probed, opened cavities, until a groan from the patient called his attention away.

Naturally, things went differently in the rare instances when a person of some stature came for a consultation. Then, gracefully maneuvering his roly-poly figure, smiling and cheerful, he was all attentiveness, polite talk, alcohol wipes, disinfectants and Novocain. With one little finger in the air, his hands looked like feathers.

It was Maria's good fortune to arrive with the lawyer's wife. Surely more on account of her, rather than Maria's, though in any case it worked to Maria's advantage, the dentist treated her with deference. He took care to clean his tools over an alcohol flame, and he pulled her tooth with only a couple of jiggles, a couple of wiggles and then a few yanks. Perfect!

While the doctor proceeded with the extraction the lawyer's wife remained at the door, observing, holding her chin in and looking up and down. With a protective and condescending air, she introduced Maria as the daughter of a foreman in their employ. What else could she be if Maria was so poorly dressed? Maria realized this was the best way not to raise any suspicions but, not knowing quite why, the situation made her uncomfortable and bitter. Every once in a while the lawyer's wife tinkled her metal bracelets or let out a loud laugh not having to do with anything. Which only made Maria even sadder.

When the dentist finished his work, the lawyer's wife opened her big purse of lustrous leather in a showy gesture and, holding out a banknote at the end of her fingers, shut the handbag with the solid crack of the metal clasp. *I am here to protect the poor daughter of my foreman,* her gesture seemed to say. *As you see, I am an important and generous person.*

As she rinsed her mouth with the lukewarm violet disinfectant, Maria felt constrained and shameful. Why? Why? Wasn't the lawyer's wife there to help? Wasn't she risking her own freedom to bring her there? Wasn't the explanation she gave on Maria's behalf helpful? Yes, all true. But the feelings of constraint and bitterness were larger than her rationality.

The dentist gave the lady her change from the banknote. Again the bracelets tinkled and the purse closure snapped. The doctor bowed and scraped. On his flattened face was pasted a smile as waxy as his hair. The two women headed for the door. Maria, wrapped in her little black coat, caressed her jaw. The wife brazenly attacked the wooden floor with her nine-centimeter-high heels.

On the street, the lawyer's wife had them stop in front of a store window. "Beautiful stockings, aren't they?"

They looked magical to Maria—sheer, light, a matte ashy chestnut brown.

"They look good," she answered, blushing all the way to her ears, wondering if she had responded in words that came off insincere and indifferent.

They entered the shop. With more jangling of bracelets and new clacks of the handbag clasp, the lawyer's wife purchased the stockings.

Does this woman only think about herself and her folly? Maria wondered. The more she thought about it, the less compassion she felt for her—and the sadder she felt.

11

As soon as she came in from the street, the lawyer's wife changed into another knit sweater that even more distinctly gave shape to her firm, copious breasts. Her bracelets continued to jingle with every slight movement. The lawyer motioned with politesse and a smile for his guests to go first. António also showed his smiling, courtly manners asking the lawyer's wife to take the lead and giving her a little bow, which surprised and displeased Maria.

Never had Maria seen such a lovely dining room. Understated, light yellow furniture. Transparent white curtains with a discreet floral pattern. An enormous carpet all in soft blues. Little chairs with wicker seats. Two paintings with colorful designs. And the table! The dishes, napkins, everything so cheerful and well appointed! And so many spoons and so many glasses! All right next to each other in groups and rows. Why so many? Everything polished and shining! Amongst the porcelain laid out on the table her attention was especially drawn to the little brown jugs with a white stripe. How pretty one of those would look, as a little jar for flowers, on top of the soapbox that served as the night table in her sorry room at the Party house!

The toothache had passed. Only a slight, bothersome impression remained and the hot taste of the disinfectant. Coming out of the dentist's office, on their walk, Maria believed that considering the hunger she'd been experiencing over the past few days, she'd easily be able to eat three or four bowls of soup. All the more so the lavish lunch she was about to be served! Now, though, dazzled by that dining room, she couldn't say if she was hungry or not.

They sat at the table. A servant dressed in black with a white apron brought a steaming tureen from which the lady of the house served the thick brown soup that gave off a vague aroma of fish. Stunned by the ambiance, Maria barely noticed the aroma. The big problem she had at the moment was to figure out which of the spoons she was to eat the soup with.

"Don't you want it?" asked the friendly but firm lady of the house. And she handed Maria one of those little brown jugs striped in white. Maria took it and blushed again. She didn't know what she was supposed to do with the little jug, nor what was in it. What were those little blond cubes, and what purpose they served, she couldn't begin to say. The lady of the house once again came to her aid. "Don't you want to put some in your soup?"

Chagrined, Maria thanked her and said yes, and prepared to serve herself. But with what? Confounded, she used her fingertips to take a few of those blond cubes and drop them in her soup (they turned out to be croutons). *Oh, dammit!* She was so clumsy that she let four or five of them fall onto the immaculate tablecloth, which, in her imagination, would leave a number of stains.

"Is that all?" said the lady of the house, as if she had not noticed the disaster.

Maria declined politely, feeling tears of embarrassment well in her eyes.

"Hey!" the lawyer's wife said suddenly in a high, strident voice directed at her husband. "Do you know that crazy sister of yours went to Lisbon?" And she let out a high-pitched gale of laughter as though her sister-in-law going to Lisbon was something extremely funny.

Maybe there was something funny in it. But Maria heard that peal of laughter, like the other one she let out in the lawyer's office telling her story about some Baby, as directed toward her, toward Maria, now even more agitated over her inexperience eating at a table like that, by her clumsiness serving herself those blond cubes, by the accident she had letting some of them fall onto the tablecloth. Tense and ashamed to the point of tears as she felt, that lunch was beginning to turn into a kind of torture. She longed to get out of there the soonest possible.

The couple, and António, seemed not to notice anything. They conversed and laughed with great relish, speaking of things that Maria didn't understand, with words she didn't know—maybe owing to her state of confusion—and seemed so pleased with all their gossipy back and forth. But with all that was happening, what truly shocked Maria the most was António. Since he had stepped into the lawyer's house he seemed like a different person. In his behavior, his expressions, the way he tapped his cigarette on his left thumbnail, in the way he laughed and in the mannered tone in which he addressed the lords of the house. Even in the words he used that Maria didn't understand António sounded completely alien from the António she had known up to then: the simple, fraternal António of a humble Party house, and now the equal, on a complete par with the lawyer and his wife. Maria remembered that António had been a student who came from a family like that, maybe wealthier, and this too now heightened her resentment.

The servant came to carry away the soup plates. She then brought a beautiful platter with green vegetables, tiny bits of carrot, carmine radishes cut into flower shapes, and some invisible choice delicacy topped by a scorched cream. Everything at that lunch looked like a confusing mush. She barely heard the chatter that progressed excitedly around her. At a certain point, the lady of the house disengaged from the conversation, and in a voice that sounded somewhere between protective and joking, urged her, "Eat, eat!" But how could she possibly serve herself, balancing the platter in one hand and transferring to her plate, as she had seen the others doing, spoonfuls of unrecognizable food, dry potato fries that escaped from the platter as though they were alive, fine grains that fell apart and threatened to fall on the tablecloth at any moment? What sweet memories she recalled at that moment of her supremely modest Party house! What fondness—what saudades—she felt for those simple meals, those miserable salted sardines eaten with Ramos, with Paulo and Vaz, so plain, so honest, so natural.

At her side, with a smile and a jug in his hand, the lawyer poured for her. "Have no fear. It's a wine for ladies."

The waitress returned, took away plates and silverware, brought new plates and silverware, brought another platter (Maria never found out what that was), removed plates and silverware, brought dessert, fruit, coffee and chocolates. The air was redolent with a confusion of smells that melted into one—sweet creams, butter sauces, pastry and fruit.

They got up to leave. The animated conversation continued between the couple and António. As if she were the odd wheel, Maria didn't know where to put her hands. They had already said goodbye when the lawyer's wife tapped two fingers on her forehead in a demonstrative gesture. "Wait a minute, wait a minute!" And hammering with her high heels, she left the foyer.

She returned shortly and handed Maria a package. "Sorry. It's a souvenir."

Maria instantly recognized the package of stockings and blushed in confusion. In a fraction of a second she realized that in front of the shop window, her judgment had been wrong. Still, she didn't refuse the present only because she lacked the language for it. The lawyer's wife approached her and, placing her hands on her shoulders, gave her two loud kisses near her cheeks, without touching them with her lips so as not to smear her lipstick.

Maria and António left. For a long time they didn't speak. António seemed distracted and Maria glum. They took the train from the same little station where Maria and Ramos had taken it the day they went underground. They sat in the squalid waiting room.

"António," Maria said suddenly. "Can you buy bread and a bit of cheese? I'm starved."

"Starved?"

"Yes, can you buy a little cheese? Now we can do it. It's the first day of the month."

"But you're hungry?"

Yes, hungry. In spite of her privations over the last weeks, Maria, in her confusion and bashfulness, hardly touched that rich lunch at the lawyer's house. So involved in talking and enjoying each other's company, neither the lawyer, nor his wife nor António himself, had noticed that she hardly served herself anything and had left almost everything on her plate. Only one person noticed it. Only one person understood: the servant. But she had categorical orders from her masters not to engage in conversation with any visitors to the house.

12

They got off at the same stop where Maria and Ramos had left the train the day she went underground. But how different from that first image that she had remembered! Now it wasn't that sad early morning with a pale fog that clung to everything. It was a bright afternoon, a fresh breeze was blowing, and the eucalyptus trees alongside the railway line pointed gaily skyward. They left the main road and switched onto deserted paths. Only here and there did they spot an isolated peasant or two working the fields at great distances from one another. Occasionally one of them would look up from their work and gaze at them questioningly from far away.

Maria was now in a better mood, talking and laughing at what they saw—a dejected-looking mule, a tailless salamander running away as fast as it could, a line of red ants, a single lonely pine tree, an intrepid flock of sparrows. Now and then she strode arm in arm with her comrade and they walked along conversing contentedly.

Nearing their village, back on the road again, they saw walking toward them the heavy, imposing figure of Elvas. Through his rags, he offered his hairy chest to the open air, obviously enjoying the cool breeze stroking his body. As they passed him, António greeted him. "Good afternoon, Senhor Damião."

It was almost laughable. Everyone called him Elvas—even he was now referring to himself as such and could hardly imagine, when a few days earlier António had asked him his real name (which he actually knew already), that António would start calling him by it.

"Good afternoon, Senhor Lemos," he responded magnanimously, Lemos being the name António had given out in the area. Though he answered António, it was toward Maria that he directed his shameless gaze.

When they had gone a few more steps, Maria started to laugh with childish glee. "Ay, dear friend, now you startled him!" And she hung onto her comrade's arm shaking with hilarity. António supported her, looking at her sidewise with his little black eyes that glistened naughtily from under the enormous brim of his hat.

When they got to the house, António started fumbling distractedly with his papers. His attention drifted at every turn to Maria. *Why wait?* he thought. *Why wait? Maybe she doesn't feel any great passion for me, though who knows? But she certainly feels something for me and enjoys my company. I can read it clearly in her eyes and her gestures.* He recalled how often lately, when walking with him, she'd touch his shoulder, or give him her arm, adjust his tie or collar, and even sometimes lean on him smiling. Just a little while before, when they passed Elvas, António felt on his arm not only the weight of his comrade hanging on him as she laughed hysterically but also the tender heft of her breasts that touched him fleetingly. He saw her gain color from the long walk, the excitement and the breeze. *Don't be shy*, António counseled himself. *What more do you need to convince yourself that she accepts you and who knows maybe has even started loving you? And then, doesn't it look for sure like they'd be living together for years? Isn't he free, and isn't she free? They'd be happy together. Why wait?*

As António was thinking, Maria let out a laugh in the hallway. Laughing by herself was not her usual way. Curious, António listened carefully. A long silence fell over the whole house. Then Maria laughed again, now near the door. António was just getting set to go see, when he heard the unfamiliar tapping of heels, and Maria entered. With short little steps, her heels hammering the floor, she imitated the lawyer's wife by posing and strutting her figure.

"What do you think?" she asked, pointing to the new stockings she was wearing. And hardly moving her feet, she spun around, aping the pirouette the lawyer's wife made in front of her husband's desk. How gracefully Maria did that!

In a flash, António rose and grabbed Maria by the shoulder blades, kissing her ardently. Maria didn't struggle harshly. She placed her hands against his chest and patiently pushed him away, almost gently, but pushing steadily. António expected the pressure of her hands to slacken, and that Maria's mouth would yield to his, and that he would feel her body giving up its cold resistance. But the vigor of those hands only increased, and her mouth resolutely avoided his. For an instant, António pulled his head back to take a good look at Maria. Her eyes were wide open and saw everything, but nothing could be seen in them nor in any other part of her, no excitement, no repugnance, no hatred. Maria's hands pushed back a little more, and she spoke, slightly reprovingly but as disinterestedly as her face and her gaze.

"This isn't right, friend. Behave yourself."

That night they had a long, difficult and baffling talk. António insisted that Maria be his companion, saying he was in love with her—and he was, to a much greater extent than he realized— and, possessed by a sudden abundance of words, rolled out arguments and reasons without end. Later, after Maria obstinately refused, he asked, or rather insisted that she explain why. Maria heard him out patiently, perhaps even with curiosity and sympathy. But to his question why, asked and repeated over and over, she answered always the same way, at once indeterminate and to the point: "Because. No."

The next morning, António seemed worried and had few words. He launched into his work frenetically. He was writing a report on mass struggles that he'd be presenting in a few days.

Maria interrupted him, holding her shoes in her hands. "You see how they are?" she asked. "We're at the beginning of the month. Maybe it would be a good time to have them repaired." With their long walks of the previous day, the heels had been worn down by half. "If we don't have them fixed and if I have to go out, I won't have shoes. I don't have any others."

António glared at her with a neutral, indecipherable expression, as if his thoughts were elsewhere. "It's not just you who lacks shoes.

All the women comrades complain about the same thing. Just a few days ago Ramos said his companion was without shoes."

"Whose companion?" Maria asked.

António laughed rather unpleasantly. "Ramos's companion, who else?" And he stared at her hard, with cold malice in his eyes.

Maria took her shoes and left him there without saying another word. António lit a cigarette and puffed on it hungrily, breathing the smoke in deeply, then crushed a sheet of paper with rage.

It's not good enough, he justified himself. *I'll have to try again.*

Shortly after, Maria reappeared. She sat at the table and with a book in front of her and paper beside her, began quietly studying.

"I don't know why you're not saying anything," António lobbed at her after a minute or two. "Doesn't seem to me I did anything wrong to you."

Maria raised her eyes from her work and looked at him accusingly.

"You can have your shoes fixed," António continued. "I never said I disagreed."

Maria shrugged her shoulders and continued reading.

But António was not satisfied yet. He grabbed his papers, rearranged papers and organized papers. He started reading, started writing, started one thing after another, and in the end left the room, whistling. That story about Ramos's companion lacking shoes was a complete invention. Not only had Ramos not spoken with António about anyone lacking shoes, he didn't even know if Ramos had a companion at all.

Chapter *VII*

1

One sunny morning the woman from the water wheels arrived breathless in Vale da Égua. She came running uphill on the trail, dragging her heavy body, moving her arms to facilitate her breathing, and from time to time pushing her hair, that kept trying to escape as she ran, back under her dark kerchief.

She didn't stamp her feet or give a shout or even knock on anyone's door. But in a tiny village eyes are forever looking, observing the road, watching who's coming and who's going. As soon as she stopped in front of the first few houses, neighbors immediately came out to meet her.

"They're going after Elias's pine trees," she reported, still panting.

Two women helped her to sit down, tired and gasping for air, on some mossy rocks. Someone offered her a container of water.

After a few minutes, a stocky man with a tired old hat tucked down to his ears walked by, from the direction of the water wheels, in a hurry and troubled.

"He fell into unfortunate circumstances," said one of the women tenderly. "He never had any luck in life."

"The misfortune isn't only for him," said another anxiously. "Now it's hitting everyone. They're starting with Elias's pines, but others will follow."

That afternoon, Manuel Rato gathered more information. The Guild's assault on the pine groves in the area had begun. Valadinhas himself, in Elias's forest, had crudely threatened, "Our generous offer is not just for other people. Everyone will have their chance."

Manuel Rato returned home at nightfall. As the soup was cooking on the fire, he spoke with his wife and daughter. They couldn't lose any time. They had to distribute the manifesto immediately. The manifesto had been written to call the peasants to concentrate that day in the village of Mato to resist the selection and decimation of

143

the pine forests. This was the moment. Waiting another day would be too late.

"Father," Isabel asked, her face flushed. "Can I go too?"

"You're going."

"And mother?"

"Your mother?" Joana's ebony eyes glistened eagerly in the red glow of the flames. Her thin face looked more beautiful now, younger and so similar to Isabel's that from a certain angle and in the shadow, they could have been mistaken for her daughter's.

"Your mother's going too," Manuel Rato answered gravely.

As they ate their soup, they decided to go out in the middle of the night when people would be asleep. They stirred up the flames with dry firewood and snuggled around it to pass the time.

"I'd like to be arrested," Isabel said unexpectedly, piercing the silence as though she were talking to herself.

"Oh, this girl! How silly she is!" Joana reacted.

Manuel Rato grabbed a stick and pushed a few loose coals back into the fire.

"Father," Isabel continued. "If I were arrested and I behaved well, I could join the Party, couldn't I?"

"Yes, you could, but even without getting arrested," Manuel Rato answered her, and he stood up, opened the door and went out.

He leaned against the wall of the house, and his daughter came out to be with him. The night had closed in darkly. Only above the faraway horizon could you still see a faint, fading strip of sunset. The silent, calm night was cooling. In a nearby house, a door creaked open into the night, its rectangular doorway lit. A figure filled it for a few moments, the rectangle reappeared and then another figure occupied it.

"It always has to be as you want," said a man gently, as clearly as though he had been standing right next to Manuel Rato.

There was the sound of water being poured, a barely audible woman's voice, wooden clogs shuffling over stone steps.

"I wish it was true," the man continued in the same gentle voice.

The illuminated rectangle reappeared for a few moments, as clear as the voices, a shadow once again occupied it, it reappeared once more, and then the night burrowed in, black and silent.

Manuel Rato and Isabel went back inside. Manuel Rato sat on the bench and Isabel nestled close to her mother. There they remained, mute and sleepy in the flickering glow of the fire until Joana fell asleep. Though she wanted to stave off sleep, Isabel too ended up falling asleep, with her head in her mother's bosom. His face somber and fraught, Manuel Rato continued toying with his little stick, tire-lessly pushing stray coals back into the fire. Every once in a while he would toss in a little kindling branch, amusing himself watching as the fire valiantly caught the dry wood until it broke into a brighter flame that convulsively excited the shadows on the wall. Thus he killed time. Then he rose, warmly contemplated his wife and daugh-ter, crossed the small room, opened the door, went out and carefully closed the door behind him.

2

The air had chilled considerably. Bundling the stacks of manifestos in his pockets, Manuel Rato set out for the fields and pine forests until he reached a sandy path he could barely see in the dark. A lit-tle farther on he halted and listened. After determining for certain his location, he carefully affixed a flyer on the branch of a bush, returning to the path, which he followed for a long time. Then, crossing a pine grove, he stopped in front of a little isolated house tucked away in a clearing. He put a flyer on the step and to secure it, placed a stone he had picked up on the path. Cutting through the local trails, following the edges of furrowed, planted fields, making the rounds of little wells that opened like hatches in the night, Man-uel Rato stopped again in front of a gate whose bright new wood he could make out in the dark. He was trying to post a manifesto when a dog growled nervously and then appeared on the other side of the gate, jumping powerfully and barking furiously. He finished attaching the flyer and retreated into the night. The dog's barking only rose in volume. Manuel Rato guessed it had jumped on top of the wall. A door squeaked. Certainly someone was peering out into the darkness. Manuel Rato fled farther into the forest and brush.

"Douro!" It was a man's strong, commanding voice. The dog did not growl, and the snap of dry branches under heavy steps could be heard.

Manuel Rato got away quickly. No one could see him. But he pictured himself moving furtively, dimly through the tranquil, shad-owed night like some vagabond or thief. He wound up in the olive orchard, which he crossed directly to home. Arriving at the door, he could still hear the loud barking of the dog in the distance.

Isabel woke up shortly after her father had left. Seeing he was gone, she assumed he had gone to the bedroom. She waited a few moments listening for any sound indicating her father's presence in the next room. As she heard nothing, she leapt to her feet.

"Father," she whispered. She scurried to the street door and went out. "Father!" she repeated in a low voice, which could be heard clearly and alarmingly. "Father!" she said yet again, and she shivered, her body warm from the fire shocked by the still, cold night.

She went back inside. Her mother had not awakened, and Isabel again cuddled up with her. She was angry and disappointed. How was it possible that her father had done that? How is it possible that he had promised to take her and had gone out alone, leaving her sleeping? She expected anything and everything, but not this. And of all people, from her father. What to do now? Wake her mother up and then go lie down, both of them? Really, what were they doing now next to the fireside? But no, she couldn't wake her mother. She didn't have the courage to tell her that father had tricked them and gone out by himself to distribute the manifestos. She felt shame—for her father, for her mother and for herself. The weak flames in the hearth were dying out, leaving only the blurry glow of the coals. Tormented with anger, suffering every minute and second waiting and waiting, Isabel repressed her urge to cry, and prepared herself to spend the night there. Much later she heard footsteps outside and without moving, she saw the shadowy figure of her father in the doorway. How was Manuel Rato going to explain himself? What self-defense would he give her? She pretended to be asleep. She felt her father approaching and passing close to them. Then, his bony hand touched her forehead and he gave her a cautious little tap on her face. Manuel Rato's serious, deliberate words made her heart skip a beat.

"Isabel, let's go!"

3

Outside at the door, in the dark, in the cold, still air, the three stood together a few moments. Manuel Rato had gone out to leave flyers at isolated cottages and returned now to distribute them in Vale da Égua with his wife and daughter. Trekking over uneven land in the olive orchard and zigzagging between the trees, they came out in front of the last house, on a slope so much in the shadow that they couldn't distinguish the shape of anything in the night. They stayed together, leaning on one another next to a brier patch, with their ears pricked and eyes wide open to guess what they could not see.

No sound could be heard other than Joana's breath. And although they knew the place almost by feel, they couldn't make out or identify anything.

"Go," Manuel Rato whispered, and handed Isabel a manifesto.

The young woman took the paper gingerly and disappeared. The two remaining drew even closer to each other, trying, uselessly and anxiously, to follow their daughter with their eyes. The door was only ten steps away, but Isabel was taking too long to come back. What was happening? The sudden crack of a tree at some indeterminate place startled them. Maybe it was an isolated cold blast of wind. Then darkness and silence. Did anything happen? But then the figure of the young woman appeared as though it had risen from the earth itself. Restraining her panting breath, she leaned once more against her parents, her face turned toward the dark. Manuel Rato placed his hand on her shoulder and thought he felt the fast beating of her heart.

Sneaking amongst the trees and the stone walls, they stopped again. Now they could see the outline of another house in profile, slightly set back from the street, so peaceful in the still atmosphere it looked like no one lived there.

It was Joana's turn. She took a paper and approached. Crossing a small yard, skirting a pile of brush and lightly stepping on wood spread all over the ground, she soon saw the gleam of a stone stairway half a dozen steps away. At that moment, a dry branch broke underfoot. In the silence, the sound seemed like a shout-out to wake up the inhabitants of the house, echoing through the roads, fields and pine groves to frighten the night. Joana stood stock still. Had they woken up? Would the owner jump out to investigate? She stood there waiting for a time that seemed an eternity, imagining how her own presence would look to someone with a hunting rifle seeing her from the door. She made a quick decision and in three more steps she reached the stone stairs. It was a cascade of bad luck. Her foot struck an empty can, making a loud, reverberating sound. But she couldn't retreat now. With no time to lose, she was determined to slip the paper under the door. Maybe she was too nervous, or maybe because the clearance under the door was scant, she made two, three unsuccessful attempts to slide the manifesto under. She tried to work in silence, but with every gesture she made, grains of sand grated on the stairs and the paper wrinkled against the wood doorframe.

From inside she heard the whispering voice of a woman, then a low monotone of a man, and then the woman again, but louder. Joana tried once more and this time the paper slid through the crack. She got onto her feet, crossed the yard and ran. She was ready to round the house and go back to the road to join her husband and daughter, when they appeared before her, waiting, the two figures close together and standing stiff like sentinels.

And so they made the rounds of the cottages in the village. One by one, they went all over putting the manifestos under the doors. Now there were only a couple of houses left way at the edge of the settlement. At the first one they decided against placing a flyer because the dog, a mastiff that was the terror of any beggar, would certainly sound the alarm.

The second house fell to Isabel. Not surrounded by pine trees, the profile of the roof loomed against its dark background. The front of the house disappeared behind the blurry masses of dung heaps and wood piles. It was hard to move without making noise and without tripping, for the entire front yard of the house was a carpet of branches and logs. Slowly, feeling out each step, now swallowed between two enormous piles of wood, Isabel gradually approached the house. All of a sudden, a horrible thing happened. A figure rose up right beside her, sprang into action, letting out three strident shouts and scraping rashly against her legs, and in a rustle of wings and feathers moved a few meters away and went silent in the dark. Taken by surprise, Isabel let out a cry. The dog from the neighboring house broke out barking. She barely had time to consider if she should or shouldn't insist on leaving the flyer under the door, when Manuel Rato and Joana were right next to her. Manuel Rato took her gently by the arm and led her away. Better to call it a night.

One more time they crossed the olive grove to return home.

They opened the door and the three stood at the entrance. Manuel Rato still wanted to go out and distribute manifestos in the farther-off village of Mato and the surrounding houses. He would be back only at dawn. He searched out his wife's face and felt her soft lips searching for his. He then turned to his daughter's face, felt her cold nose and perceived she was trying to stifle her laughter. He rearranged the stack of manifestos in his pockets and went out to the road. Gravel crunched under his boots. Wife and daughter stayed by the door, eyes peering into the night, and listening until the ever diminishing sound of a man's heavy footsteps on an uneven path disappeared completely. Only then did they enter, closing the door behind them, trying not to make noise.

4

Dancing in immense rotation, the tree-filled countryside surrounds the train. Nearest to the train, the trees fly by, soon peacefully left behind. Farther on, they double around in circles, passing and repassing one type of tree after another, and intersect each other on long curves with no destination. On the horizon, as the pine groves roll by, lazy and melancholic, individual pine trees close to the tracks reveal the black profile of their trunks, delineating a dense, vibrant train-window quadrangle against the background of a clear sky.

Paulo gazes out distractedly. Over everything he sees still looms the tragic vision of the dog he saw a few hours before on the side of the road. He saw him lying immobile some meters from the asphalt, a beautiful golden chestnut animal, his noble proud snout pointing forward. What called Paulo's attention was not so much the immobility but the rigidity. In the dog's pose, gently lying down but arrogantly raised on his front paws, there was something uncommon and disturbing. It looked as though it had been formed with two halves of different creatures grafted together by mistake. What the forward half had in power, vigor and nobility, the posterior half had in vulgarity and laziness.

Paulo stopped on the street to look. A short, quick-witted peasant whose approach Paulo had not seen, also stopped a few steps ahead. "Poor animal!" he exclaimed softly, almost singing.

Leaving the roadbed, the man walked over to the dog and pointed to it with the stick he was carrying. Paulo followed him and could then see the animal's expression: his terrified fixed eyes that, by all evidence, no longer saw anything. Something had captured the animal and kept it completely stiff. The peasant touched it lightly on the back. Then the dog made a sudden, rough roar and, as though making a great effort to bring its gaze forward, glared at the peasant with hatred. Then, opening his mouth, he showed his strong, sharp canine teeth. Paulo stepped back in horror. The mouth was a mass of blood that now ran out in thick ropes. The animal's body remained completely stiff.

"Poor animal!" the peasant said again, turning back to the street. "His hindquarters were crushed."

Paulo also returned to the road and continued his walk. The image of the dog, with his eyes shocked in pain and impotence, his mouth full of blood, did not leave him so soon. Paulo had been a Party member for many years, but one vestige of his childhood he never was completely able to get rid of: his superstitious nature. He feels sad and unsettled. When he would shortly receive the bad news that awaits him, he won't be able to dissociate it from the image of the crushed and rigid dog with his eyes full of hate and powerlessness.

5

The train slowed down. There was the shed where Manuel Rato introduced him to Zé Cavalinho. With an unfriendly look, Manuel Rato stood at the door. With his cap pulled down on the back of his head, Zé Cavalinho raised his glass in the air and repeated three times the last words he had just spoken to the barkeep: "...not worth a plugged nickel...not worth a plugged nickel...not worth a plugged nickel."

Beyond the graying eyebrows, the comrade's attentive eyes reflected both an astute nature and annoyance. He knew all too well the opinion Manuel Rato had of him, and it bothered him that Manuel should find him drinking. His hesitation was short-lived, however: He drank his glass and left. Next to the cement barrier along the railway line, they joined Paulo. A few paces away, Isabel, with her head tall, her face framed by the arch of her braids, observed the group and smiled. Precisely there, at that spot in the half-ruined barrier, a hole opened onto the track. There, too, a few days later, he had given them the manifestos.

The carriage in which Paulo rode, the last one of the train, stopped well short of the platform. The ground was so far down that the car appeared to have been left hanging in the air by some mysterious force. With difficulty, stretching his short legs to reach the boarding step, Paulo jumped.

Loaded with baskets and sacks, other passengers proceeded in small groups toward the exit. Right in front of Paulo, a woman crippled by deformed hips was transporting a heavy hamper. With each step she took, the shoe on her misshapen foot slapping the ground, she lowered her arm that held the hamper and with an awkward contortion shifted her hips in the opposite direction. She repeated this challenging movement with every step. Paulo's attention was riveted for a few moments on this woman's progress, and then he noticed the station exit up ahead.

Something out of the ordinary was happening. Although they weren't many, the passengers strangely remained standing, forming into groups near the exit door. A GNR patrol with a helmet and rifle was watching something in the middle of the group as a woman, standing slightly apart, opened her arms in a gesture of annoyance.

Black market, Paulo figured. In front of him, with the regularity of a machine, the crippled woman continued, foot slapping the ground, arm lowered, hip swung around, with no apparent fatigue. Two other passengers stopped next to the exit door. Paulo found himself just steps away from the door when he felt his arm violently grabbed.

Holding him with both hands, Zé Cavalinho laughed gruffly and artificially. "Hey, partner! So, you think there's an issue with the weight? Come and see for yourself."

Paulo didn't understand what Zé Cavalinho was trying to say with these words. His cap yanked down onto his neck, the ironic tone of his voice, the lively little eyes peeking out from under his gray eyebrows, this was Zé Cavalinho all right. But an almost imperceptible roughness about him and his darting, uneasy glances told him something was up.

"Come see with your own eyes and you'll forget all about it," the railwayman continued with another little forced guffaw, and steered Paulo around toward the baggage claim.

Though he didn't understand the reason for the comrade's attitude, Paulo followed him. Zé Cavalinho had him enter the building, led him through stacks of boxes and luggage and exited with him out onto the square in front of the station, right near the village center. On the sly, Paulo noticed that outside the entrance door another GNR patrol was posted.

In a rapid hike that took a few unexpected twists, the railway worker led him down the length of the cement barrier and, rounding the shed where Vaz had seen him for the first time, squeezed himself through a crevice in the wood, and only stopped there.

Facing Paulo, he grabbed his arms and stared at him deeply. Now there was nothing ironic and amusing about his expression. With moistened eyes, suddenly become an old man, he tried to speak three times, and three times he could only bite his quivering lips. The cap brashly tipped toward his nape only accentuated by contrast the emotion in his thin face. Still biting his lips, he nodded his head a few times in such a quick and constant shaking it looked like he had a nervous tic. Finally he was able to speak. What he told Paulo left him choked with bitterness, so sad, sadder than he had ever felt in his life.

6

The first trees fell. They tilted, slow and hesitant, then lowered fast, tearing limbs on their descent, until their crowns amassed mutely on the forest floor of pine needles. Laid out, enormous, they looked like cadavers of giants mowed down by a volley of gunshot. The cool breeze carried the smell of pine out from the cracked, wounded branches, and the earsplitting sound as each tree tumbled muffled for a few moments the rasp of the lumbermen's saws. Later, here and there, the back and forth of the saws continued like islands of noise in the vast silence of the pines.

Valadinhas and his acolyte with the field jacket circled all about, inscribing on the chosen trunks their death sentence. They were in a good mood and from time to time broke out laughing. Then came the surprise. They had barely just noticed footsteps in the forest, when they saw themselves surrounded by peasants, men and women who stood a few steps away, looking bewildered. Perceiving their puzzlement, Valadinhas did not lose his composure.

"Good afternoon, folks!" he greeted them ironically, as if he had no idea what they were doing there.

Casting his glance around, to take the measure of his adversaries, he felt uncomfortable. Slightly in front of his companions, one peasant with a blond beard, tall and skeletal, glared at him with a dull, illegible expression. He wore his big, unbelted shirt outside of his pants, and his long arms drooped down his body. Valadinhas followed those arms until his gaze stopped, his nervousness newly aroused: In the huge, bony and restless hand covered with reddish hair, the peasant with the blond beard carried a hatchet, which extended his arm until almost touching the ground. Right away Valadinhas recognized him as the owner of the pine grove where he was now standing.

"Have you come to see and learn?" Valadinhas spoke in the same tone as before. "It's not hard. I can teach you." And like a professor going to the blackboard to explain an exercise, he approached a pine tree and earmarked it for cutting.

Immediately, from behind him, he heard a raw, deliberate voice. "Leave it alone!"

Valadinhas looked askance at the peasant, and for a moment his eye fell on a blue blouse filled out with the healthy breasts of a young woman. He approached another pine tree and again stamped it for cutting.

He had barely done it when he felt his arm grabbed in the grip of long, bony fingers, and saw at his side, a little above him, the stern face of the peasant with the blond beard.

"You destroyed my other grove," the peasant said in the same rough, compelling voice. "This one you're not touching, you scoundrel."

Valadinhas was still inclined to smile and make light. But his eye turned to that bony hand covered with blond hair that grasped the hatchet. Looking around to find his buddy with the field jacket, he didn't see him. His ears on high alert, he was surprised not to hear the woodsmen sawing. Furtively, he cast his glance about and only then, it seemed, did he calculate his situation. His expression was clearly pitiful, for a chorus of hoots and howling laughter rose up in the forest.

"So you're not going to teach us?" asked the young voice of a girl.

Cautiously, for he was not looking to provoke a swipe of the hatchet, Valadinhas tried to free himself from the bony hand. The peasant with the blond beard let him go. Valadinhas nimbly slipped away. The crowd let him pass. And he would have gone away without any further trouble if it weren't for his pride. Valadinhas, an officer of the Guild, holder of an identification card that instilled terror among the peasants, all-powerful authority who decided the fate of tens of thousands of pine trees, confident of the power he possessed that he would reveal very shortly, did not gladly retreat, beaten, without response. Some distance from the group, he turned back toward them and made an obscene threat with his angry face.

He saw a woman bend down and then right beside him a pine cone fell, hopping two or three times on the fluffy bed of pine needles. He couldn't tell if the cone had fallen from a tree or if it had been thrown by the woman, but others soon followed that one. One, thick and heavy, hit him on the arm.

"So you won't teach us?" that same young girl's voice insisted.

Valadinhas turned his back and began to run away quickly, when a well-aimed cone knocked his hat off.

"Look at the stupid ox!" a man yelled.

Valadinhas once again turned around amidst peals of laughter. Confused, he saw the peasants facing him, the blue blouse, an arm hoisting a pine cone, the peasant with the blond beard standing stiff, and quickly estimating the distance, he guessed his fallen hat was closer to the peasants than to him. He made one more motion to go back and pick it up, recalling in that instant that he had just bought it a few days before for ninety *escudos*, and he really loved that beautiful green hat. A pine cone, hitting him forcefully on the shoulder, stopped him in his tracks. Then he turned around and fled.

"Stupid ox! Stupid ox!" they shouted after him.

The cold air broadcast a new chorus of laughter throughout the pine forest.

One of the farmworkers approached the hat and gave it a kick with his boot. Valadinhas's green hat, purchased just days before for ninety *escudos*, took flight and fell a few meters away. The farmer attacked it with fury, stomped on it over and over again, crushing it with his hobnail soles and only rested when he saw it reduced to a shapeless mass. Then, with disgust, he gave it another kick and the hat, skimming the pine needle floor, disappeared under some berry bushes.

But now the peasants were not laughing.

7

By the middle of the day the situation remained much the same. Dispersed throughout the pine forest, peasants and loggers, either seated or standing in groups, had friendly talks. The lumbermen had not taken up their work again, but on instruction from their employers, they stayed there awaiting orders. Conversing here and there with different groups, Manuel Rato tried to persuade them to leave their work and go away. But there weren't so many of them and they feared losing their livelihood. They felt compromised and ashamed, but didn't have the courage to join the peasants' struggle. Scratching out little clearings on the pine-needle floor, they lit fires and cooked potatoes in cans blackened by the smoke.

"All this here is finished, boys," said an old woman to two of the lumberjacks. "There's nothing for you here. They took fright and won't come back."

One of the cutters, a thin man with a pockmarked face, shook his head. "You're wrong, auntie. They will return and they won't return alone."

The log cutter was right. Not long afterward, Valadinhas's second man appeared with two soldiers from the GNR, with helmets and rifles across their chests. They stood still at some distance from the groups. Then Valadinhas's adjutant looked right and left to select trees, approached one beautiful pine, brought out his seal and with one, two, three sharp hammerings marked its bark and stripped nude a band of shining yellow wood. The three powerful pounding sounds echoed menacingly throughout the forest, silencing conversations.

With his field jacket open, the adjutant looked crazed. He marked trees one after another, almost at random, ignoring the choices his practiced professional eye would involuntarily have made. With his back protected by the two guards, he had just about convinced himself that nothing would impede him from this attack, when once more he saw himself surrounded by peasants cursing at him. Searching out the guards with his glances, he found them dawdling around complaisantly.

"Let the man work," one of them advised apathetically. "Orders are orders, and we must comply with them."

But saying which, he showed no disposition to employ force. His companion, with a pale, insipid face, appeared to show much more interest in staring at the generous bosom of the young woman in the blue blouse than in answering to the man from the Guild. Valadinhas's aide once again had to suspend his work. But in his expression no one could read disappointment or defeat. An evil smile played on his angry face, and casting his eye around him in a disturbing look, he threatened, "Wait for a beating!"

They didn't have to wait long.

8

Led by Valadinhas, the Republican National Guard burst through the pines and quickly lined up in formation against the peasants. In their demeanor they exhibited nothing of the slack disinterest of the first two soldiers who seemed so disengaged from Valadinhas's aide. Their heavy black boots firmly planted on the ground, their helmets covering their faces down to the eyes, their leather straps and ammunition belts tightly pulled, weapons in hand, they displayed power, determination and brutality. Strangely enough, though soldiers of the GNR were not picked for their faces, all their mugs imparted evil and violence. Even the two who had come earlier, meek and feckless, now integrated into the larger unit, acquired the same monstrous expression.

Protected by the guard, Valadinhas and his second ran from one end of the grove to another, and soon the sound of sawing and the rough hacking of hatchets filled the air. A pine tree fell, swiping adjacent branches on the way down. Then another.

Perfectly appointed in his well-fitting uniform, with his fine-featured almost childlike face, the lieutenant fisted his automatic pistol. He stood at the front of the soldiers with his legs spread in a studied, provocative attitude. In a clear, severe voice, which resonated with a high falsetto all through the pine forest, he shouted to the peasants: "DIS-PERSE NOW!"

With weapons cocked, the guards advanced in slow steps. The peasants backed off, separating out into small, forlorn groups looking upon the loggers' work from afar. The lieutenant displayed a victory smile, the guards placed their weapons back across their chests and also separated out, some here, others there, next to the cutters and men marking trees. His composure regained, and laughing again, Valadinhas taunted the peasants with his mocking glances and cracked jokes with his adjutant. Far too elegant in this forest environment, the lieutenant watched the work disinterestedly. He moved leisurely, bothered and annoyed, as though he were wandering around his own property killing time. Rocked by the cadence of the saws and the hatchets, certainly he was thinking of other things.

Raised voices drew him out of his distraction. Looking in the direction of the voices, he saw to his surprise, a hundred meters away, a new throng of the peasants in a compact mass. The saws went quiet in that area of the forest. Summoning his troops, the Lieutenant ran there. The pack of peasants moved uncertainly but gathered into formation to once more directly face the threatening line of soldiers with weapons ready against the wide half-circle of men and women standing silent and solemn.

In a rage, the lieutenant cast his gaze around and saw the tall, straight figure of the peasant with the blond beard, the wrinkled, determined visage of an old woman, the blue blouse packed with healthy breasts, many dark, anxious eyes, a man with a black mustache with a fraught expression, and the sweet face of a young woman in braids who was smiling at his side.

"Are we just going to stand here?" a young woman's voice rang out.

Was it real or imagined? The semicircle tightened and slowly began to encircle the guard.

"Stop it!" called out a secure, strong voice. It was the man with the fraught expression and the black mustache speaking, now a couple of paces in front of the others. Not far off, the lumbermen—possibly they too were surrounded by the peasants—stopped sawing.

His black eyes glinting from his childlike face, the lieutenant looked around: Faces, bodies, clothes. But again and again, irresistibly drawing his attention, he fixed on that graceful figure and sweet face of the smiling girl in braids.

A cool breeze gently swayed the tops of the pine trees under the bright blue sky. All of a sudden a thunderclap exploded in the air, echoing in waves all though the forest.

Trra-ta-ta-trra-ta-ta-trra-trra-ta-tra-ta-ta-ta!!!

An eruption of shouting broke out. Then a great, awful silence. In a couple of seconds, everything had changed. One part of the human semicircle broke away in smaller groups. Having charged the crowd with the butts of their rifles, the guards stood still, pointing their weapons in several directions. Like the surviving tree after a tornado, the tall, rigid figure of the peasant with the blond beard looked planted in the earth. Another peasant grabbed his arm over his bloody shirt. With difficulty, a young boy tried to support a heavy woman dressed in black, on her knees with her hands on her stomach, moaning softly. Paralyzed by the shock of it all, Manuel Rato and Joana looked to the ground. At their feet, face down in the pine needles, disjointed as a rag doll, lay Isabel, dead.

9

All the people from the surrounding area came to the distant cemetery for Isabel's funeral. At the fore, the poor wooden casket proceeded, lined with white material, carried by six arms which people took up in rotation. The people opted to leave the casket open.

Isabel's face was surrounded by flowers, the tender face of a child felled by death. Augmented by little groups in dark clothing, who waited for her along the trails and roads, the sad cortege filed through the silent fields. When they arrived at the village where the cemetery was, the narrow untidy lines of staggering women cloaked in their great shawls, the men with uncovered heads and children of all ages walking with their families, extended for half a kilometer. Neither the GNR nor the police appeared, and all unfolded without incident. At the end of the funeral, little clutches of people assembled in the streets and bars to comment on what happened, with moderated voices and contrite emotions. Then people retuned to the villages they had come from, and the night fell heavy and bitter in hundreds of homes.

In the following days, the Guild men did not return, and life in the countryside resumed its habitual course. But people's faces remained solemn, and nowhere was open laughter to be heard. The rumor spread that people would be arrested, but days passed and nothing happened.

Until one week later, when three unknown men knocked on the door of the house at the water wheels in Vale da Égua.

Just as when Vaz had gone there the first time, a child's crying inside could be heard, and just as then, the stocky, dark woman opened the door. In the shadow of the doorway and the mother's skirts, the curious child with its naked belly appeared.

"Can you tell us where Manuel Rato lives?"

The women kept her silence, looking closely at the unfamiliar men. The three men looked like many others, but better dressed than usual in those parts. Perhaps they could be friends of Manuel Rato, seeking him out to offer their condolences. Maybe. But without knowing exactly why, the woman acted as though she were hard of hearing. The men had to repeat the question louder.

"Ah!" the woman exclaimed, giving herself time to think. Pointing in the wrong direction, she told them, "Follow this straight ahead. On the road, you'll find it." As soon as the men disappeared around the first curve, she grabbed her son and ran panting to Vale da Égua, as she had done a few days before to warn about the logging in Elias's pine grove.

The following day the three men returned. They accused her of having tricked them to give Manuel Rato time to escape, and told her to come with them. She continued to play deaf and contradicted them vigorously.

"I don't understand anything about these conversations. You men didn't ask for any Rato. You asked for the way to the village of Mato and that's what I showed you. What we have to put up with!"

Two of the men looked at the third, who had a scornful smile that showed his long yellow teeth like a horse's.

"Close up shop and come with us, senhora—"

The woman continued to play dumb, threw her headscarf back and protested excitedly. "So what do you guys want? You ask about the village of Mato and I showed you the way. What more do you want? Do you think I'm afraid of you because I'm a woman and I'm alone? I'm not afraid of thieves, fellas! Get out of my door and get on with your life!"

The men's expressions hardened. "Enough of this nonsense!" said the one with the horse teeth. "Pack your things and let's march!"

"Aaaah!" the woman went, finally showing she understood what they wanted of her. "Who would have thought from these three dandies? Because there's no GNR around here you think you can do what you want. Go with them? Me, go with them?"—and after letting out a threatening peal of laughter, she stopped talking and started to yell loudly enough to spread the alarm all through the valley.

She called them thieves, rapists, bums, pickpockets, scoundrels. Con men, black marketeers and contrabandists. She threatened they'd be beaten to a pulp with a club, cut up with a scythe and attacked with a pitchfork. She gesticulated and waved her arms about, tore her hair and went out of control. The more she shouted, her dark, flushed face took on an ever more violent, angry look, to which her strong mustache lent an air of outright ferocity.

Eyeing one another in surprise, the men tried to calm her down, but with every one of their words and gestures, she responded screaming and acting in ever more desperate ways. Because they did not have mandatory orders to arrest her, and because they concluded the woman had no idea even to whom she was talking, and fearing what could come out of all of this, the three PIDE agents, from the International and State Defense Police, wound up leaving her be. When they departed, the one with the horse teeth exclaimed, "What a witch!"

The woman continued yelling until they disappeared. Only then did she quiet down and, holding the child and straightening her hair under the kerchief, break into a wide, long-lasting smile that lit up her dusky face with innocence.

10

Paulo is seated at the table, staring at the blank paper. His thick fingers hold the familiar pen unsteadily. He's been there a long time without being able to write, nor able to think.

Everything Zé Cavalinho told him passes helter-skelter through his brain, embittered, confused, disordered. Only one image is clear: the gentle figure of Isabel, gently leaning back, her face framed by the arc of her braids, and smiling her innocent, confident smile. And he sees Isabel walking ahead of them in the pine forest, stopping and turning around every once in a while to wait for them, that time Vaz came to introduce him. And he sees her ironically and without malice observing his first meeting with José Cavalinho next to the cement barrier on the railway line. And he sees her when he was sharing the salt pork with cornbread, stifling her laughter in her mother's shoulder until she broke out laughing uncontrollably. And he hears Joana's musical voice: *She's crazy, this girl.* And those images now are so mournful that Paulo can only shake his head and try to chase them away. He attempts to concentrate on the blank sheet in front of him and on the thick fingers holding his old pen and makes frustrated efforts to focus and write.

He will write: *Victory of the Smallholders in the Pine Forest.* Yes, he will write *Victory,* and he'll be right to say it. But why that attack? Why Isabel? Why such a high price? And Paulo's hand, that he forced for a moment to write, stops again. And again that gentle, fine-looking little figure appears before him, the hair so beautifully arranged, and that smiling face: *I'm a young woman, one of your comrades, what do you think? You can trust me.* And just as mournful—or more—the image of Manuel Rato and Joana looms before him, regarding their daughter with pride and love. And now—. *Oh, those shameless criminals! Those bastards!*

Rita comes in, quietly. She looks at Paulo and for once doesn't demand anything. She stands quietly at his side and waits. Paulo runs his fingers through the little girl's hair, and she sighs, "Nice cousin."

Paulo pushes the chair away from the table, sits Rita in his lap, turned toward the table, and lightly rests his chin on the back of her neck. "Nice cousin," she repeats softly and tenderly.

Paulo tries to say something, but can't. His eyes have turned to pools of water. He can't see, his lips tremble, and it's all he can do not to break up into sobs.

Chapter *VIII*

1

As he habitually does, Vítor supports his chin on his closed fist as he slowly exhales smoke. As always, he looks at one and the other ironically. No note of impatience or restlessness could be seen in him.

This calm does not pacify Vaz. The more he recalls the scene at the cheap café door, the more he registers the attitude of Vítor and the other unknown man, the more he's convinced that those two were not there by chance and that Vítor had pointed him out to the other. Certain looks and gestures don't deceive. Precisely for being nearly imperceptible, they strongly suggest compromise and intention. Thus the quick, simultaneous turning away of the two men's glance. He could not be mistaken. They were certainly speaking about him. *You think I didn't notice, but soon I want to see how you explain yourself,* he thought.

Just as they had all sat down, however, Vítor turned to Vaz and spoke. "You should take more care on your trips to the city, friend. Your presence is becoming known." He lazily exhaled more cigarette smoke before resuming. "The other day I saw you walk by with your bicycle in hand and they asked me if I knew who you were."

"Who asked you that?" Vaz shot back. He stared at Vítor sternly and directly.

Without shifting position, Vítor took another puff. "It was Meireles. You all know him," he said calmly, turning to his comrades. "He's not a bad sort. The bad part is Vaz being seen."

"Right, he's not a bad sort," Cesário confirmed.

Eyes glinting behind his thick lenses, Marques made an effort not to intervene. The transparent lack of trust in Vaz's rapid-fire question did not escape him. "It's important not to mistake a stick for a snake," he commented irritably. "If you did things more naturally, none of this would have happened."

Vaz contained himself and kept quiet. He sensed that once again Vítor was slipping through his fingers. That rush to raise that point right at the beginning of the meeting before Vaz could even say a word, seemed to indicate not security and tranquility, but merely calculation. Vítor's explanation only raised his suspicion.

At the end of the meeting, he let Vítor and Marques leave and spoke separately with Cesário and Afonso. Both of them agreed that Meireles was not a bad guy. Afonso knew him well and was even a friend of the family. Though not a comrade, no one could doubt his honesty.

Unexpectedly, Vaz asked, "And who says it was Meireles?"

"Vítor said it," Afonso and Cesário both answered at the same time.

Vaz did not let up. He asked that Afonso inquire of Meireles if he had had such a conversation with Vítor. Distracted and distant from the beginning of the meeting, Afonso disagreed. He considered the distrust excessive and the inquiry inappropriate.

"It would be strange," he began. "If I speak to him about this, he'll conclude right away that there's some connection between me and Vítor, and it wouldn't be hard for him to assume it had to do with Party work."

"I also don't consider it necessary," said Cesário, softly supporting Afonso.

Vaz was still not persuaded. All right, so don't ask about the conversation with Vítor. But at least ask if he knows him. Or else tell him you saw him that day at the café door and observe his reaction.

The comrades were displeased and maintained their own view. Impatiently, Afonso said it did not seem right to talk this way without Vítor present.

"It's a matter of Party security and revolutionary vigilance," Vaz insisted coldly.

Afonso ended by accepting, with a nod of the head, not because he agreed with it, but because the discussion had gone on much too long and he was anxiously awaiting the end of the meeting to discuss his own situation alone with Vaz. The comrade would surely have an answer.

"So?" he asked finally, growing slightly pale.

Vaz assumed Afonso was still speaking about Vítor. "So, it's decided," he said pointedly. "You'll talk with Meireles and then you'll report the result."

"Not about that," Afonso retorted. "About my situation?"

"We're getting to that now."

In the next couple of minutes, Vaz learned from Afonso that Sagarra had finally been given the contact with the biggest peasant organization overseen by the Regional Committee. And Vaz told him that it had been agreed for Afonso to become a Party worker. He even had the exact date.

Why did he wait until now to tell this to me in two words? Afonso asked himself. *Or doesn't he realize what this represents for me?*

"You're not paying attention," Vaz said after several times repeating the locale of the meet-up and the way to get there.

How could Afonso pay attention? At that moment he was seeing before him, looking at him from under those thick eyelashes, a pair of black eyes brimming with tears, and he saw Maria quickly running home to her father after their farewell.

"I'm sorry, comrade, say it once more," he mumbled.

With the meet-up set, Vaz got ready to leave.

"I'd like to talk some more with you," Afonso said.

"Is it important and urgent?" Vaz asked.

"Important and urgent?" Afonso repeated. "Never mind—"

"I'm already late, friend," Vaz explained himself. "I must hurry."

2

Vaz had told him which jitney to take, but Afonso thought it more comfortable to take the train. Because of that, he arrived too early. As he had been instructed, he left his suitcase for safekeeping in a tavern in the town. Then, not knowing what to do, justifying himself with the idea that it's always better to show up early than late, he walked to the locale for the appointed meet-up.

There's no one who hasn't at some time in their life departed late for somewhere they were bound for that they did not want to miss. Then the smallest unanticipated delay along the way creates anxiety, irritation, even suffering. Those who leave and arrive early enjoy total serenity of mind. Arriving early is restful, good for your health, calms the nerves.

Philosophizing thus, Afonso arrived well ahead of the appointed hour at the fountain that Vaz had told him about. He decided to continue down the street, enjoying the fresh air bearing aromas of the forest.

Suddenly, looking up a side street, he noticed two men who were staring at him intently. One was tall with glasses, elegantly dressed. The other, of medium stature, had a full head of hair black and shiny like a crow's wings and small, penetrating eyes that shifted rapidly under the visor of his thick eyebrows. They certainly didn't look as though they came from these parts, and their presence in such an isolated place, their attitude, their glances of mistrust and antipathy, could only raise suspicions.

Farther on Afonso found, positioned on the side of the road and glistening in the sun, a green late-model automobile. A man with dark glasses got out, looked at Afonso directly and disappeared behind some bushes. Ever more suspicious, and desirous of more clarity, Afonso approached the car, peered inside and read the calling card resting on the dashboard.

A few hundred meters ahead, having seated himself down alongside the road to look in the direction of the town at the fields, he seemed to spot two figures turned toward him amongst the bushes. Then they quickly went away, however.

When he figured it was about time, he got up, now somewhat nervous, and turned back. The green car was no longer there. The two unknown men had also disappeared. Arriving at the fountain, he drank and waited a bit. Finally Vaz came.

"The comrade will be here soon," said Vaz.

"It's best not to wait here," Afonso remarked. "Up ahead I saw some strange things." And he referred to the two guys on the side road and the car with someone in dark glasses.

He didn't have more time to expand upon his worries. On the curve of the road a man appeared walking toward them. He had a firm, purposeful stride but, somewhat in contrast with his walking rhythm, his head moved slowly back and forth from right to left, as if he wanted to take in everything happening around him. As he approached, Afonso recognized him: The unknown guy with the shiny black hair he had seen with the well-dressed man on the secondary road. So he was a comrade! The look he gave Afonso from underneath those thick black eyebrows was still untrusting and unfriendly. Vaz introduced him: Comrade Fialho, who would direct and supervise Afonso.

Fialho lost no time. He asked Afonso what means of transportation he had used, why he hadn't come by the jitney, and why was he sniffing around the fountain for more than an hour before the meet-up. He spoke tersely, casting new questions as though they were stones, Afonso answering after each one. When he judged the confusion all cleared up, he commented to Vaz, in words he seemed to have difficulty saying between clenched teeth, "A bad beginning."

In this first meeting as an underground Party worker, Afonso had cause to feel discouraged with the reception he got. Vaz and Fialho seemed like two judges, serious, severe, rigorous, implacable. *A comrade's duty*, Afonso thought, *is not to judge but to help*. Besides, there are bads that turn into goods. Like maybe Fialho had not noticed the green automobile with the guy in dark glasses. Who knows if he wasn't being followed? He mentioned the car and the name he had read on the calling card.

Fialho and Vaz looked at one another and had no opinion about it.

"You've begun badly, comrade," Fialho repeated, drily.

"Let's go here," said Vaz, indicating the edge of a vineyard. "I'll get into town all the same and it's the way I must go."

3

Afonso had spoken with Meireles. Vaz's suspicions were confirmed. Meireles did not know Vítor, had never spoken with him, and never could have been there that day at the café door for the simple reason that at the time he had been outside the city for two weeks.

Vaz heard Afonso's account coolly. In his disinterest in asking for any further details, one could only guess that conclusions had been made, and decisions taken. *You won't escape now, my precious Vítor!* he was thinking, in fact. *Neither Marques, nor Ramos, nor anyone else who's protecting you can save you now from being unmasked.*

Satisfied with this information, Vaz stopped alongside the ruins of an old stone wall and held out his hand to Afonso. "Until I see you again, friend."

Afonso seemed surprised, almost alarmed, by such a speedy good-bye. He had decided, as soon as he transitioned into clandestinity, to ask for a meeting with Maria. When she had gone underground, he acted like a child. Now he didn't want to lose a single day, and he had wanted to get Vaz to set the date for it. "There's one important thing I need to talk about," he said resolutely. "I won't detain you for very long."

"We'll be meeting again to give you contacts for distribution of the paper," said Vaz. "For anything else I'm not the one you'll deal with. For everything else you want to put to the Party, you'll deal with Fialho."

And without noticing Afonso's eager gesture to hold him, he shook Fialho's hand vigorously, hopped over the stone wall ruins, and disappeared over the other side.

Stepping quickly, Fialho led the way. Between a bramble-covered fence on one side and a field of cultivated earth on the other, the narrow path didn't allow them to walk side by side. Sad, disconsolate, Afonso followed his companion. He observed his manner of walking—decisive, energetic and flexible—that suggested the fierce agility of a tiger. He recalled the way he had interrogated him about his arrival when they met, the cutting comment he had made, and felt he would have great difficulty placing the issue of Maria before that practically unknown comrade who almost certainly had no information on the subject. Once again, Afonso felt the Party machine riding herd on human problems, dismissing them on the pretext of the primacy of the tasks, to crush, bend, submit and attempt to deform and mold the rich personality of the human being to schematic formulations. He saw Maria's sweet eyes focusing on him between those long eyelashes, he felt an immediate need to be close to her, believed she also felt the same way, and there was the Party machine lodging itself between the two of them and blocking their happiness.

He was so absorbed in his thoughts that he didn't realize they had arrived in the town.

"Where did you leave your suitcase?" Fialho suddenly asked.

They agreed to meet in another half hour and separated. Afonso went to pick up the suitcase at the tavern where he'd left it. It wasn't large, but after a few hundred meters, his arm was aching, and he sat down to rest.

At the precise hour, also carrying a suitcase, Fialho appeared. When he got to his comrade's side, he indicated with a yank of his head the direction they'd be going.

After a kilometer, having switched the suitcase various times from one hand to the other, Afonso stopped and placed his bag on the ground. He had to rest a little once more.

Fialho stopped also, without comment. But as if to express that their rest could not be very long, he did not put his suitcase down and stood right in front of Afonso.

"It's heavy," Afonso defended himself.

From under his black eyebrows, Fialho's quick glance searched out Afonso's eyes. "Do you want to swap?"

Afonso smiled and, as he truly felt tired, accepted. He soon understood the prank. Fialho's suit-case weighed like lead!

"Papers—" Fialho explained simply. And as though he had not noticed how tired Afonso was, he picked up his suitcase, incomparably lighter, and resumed the march.

Furious with his comrade, Afonso did not wish to play the part of a weakling. But some hundred meters on, drenched in sweat, congested and panting, he had to stop. "I can't—" he groaned in defeat.

Fialho didn't say a word. Without letting go of Afonso's suitcase, he grabbed the other one too and continued walking with the same firm, confident stride. Only his straight, stiff arms showed his effort. *This is how you carry two suitcases*, he seemed to be saying.

Afonso followed, a few meters behind. Expecting that Fialho at any moment would stop to rest or to give him one of the suitcases, he was happy to walk behind. Now it was he who was paying back the prank. Finally, when he thought Fialho had been punished enough, he quickened his pace and caught up with him with the idea of taking back his own suitcase.

"What did you want to talk to Vaz about?" Fialho asked.

"It can wait till later," Afonso answered.

And concluding that his companion was a swaggering blowhard, he didn't offer anything and went on walking with his arms swinging freely.

4

Although still firmly holding the two suitcases and not altering his propulsive stride, Fialho now did start slowing down. *Before long you're going to collapse*, Afonso thought. After the way his comrade had treated him, he couldn't help but feel a certain pleasure in watching him get tired.

As if guessing Afonso's thoughts, Fialho explained, "It's not advisable waiting in the station. The train is at ten and we have too much time," and he slowed down even more.

When they got to the first houses of the village, he stopped, handed Afonso his suitcase and, removing a wrinkled handkerchief from his pocket, slowly wiped off the sweat running down his face, into his ears and down his neck.

It was clear that Fialho knew this terrain like the back of his hand. They left the road, got onto a footpath that would lead them directly to the station. Afonso noticed it was already five minutes past ten. Had they missed the train?

"Don't worry," Fialho spoke before his comrade even said anything. "We'll still have to wait. No train on this line ever arrives less than ten minutes late."

They purchased their tickets and walked onto the platform. After several long minutes, the train came and it was jammed. They settled themselves as best they could in the corridor of a third-class car. With a whistle and a hiss from the locomotive up front, a brusque lurch that could be felt from one end of the carriage to the other, and a morbid clatter of iron against iron, the train left the station rattling down the track.

Combining with the noise of the heavy vibration, the passengers' voices filled the carriage. On all sides people were talking, laughing, arguing. It could have been an open marketplace. Sitting next to the two comrades, almost shouting to make himself heard, a strong man with a flushed face was holding the attention of his neighbors. Right away, the contrast was evident between the narrator's chastened expression and the enjoyment on his listeners' faces.

"The doctor tapped me on the arm," he recounted, "and here's what he told me: 'This is a serious case. I can treat he, but I can't promise to cure her.' What could I say? 'Do what you can, doctor. And may it be God's will.' The guy answered me very peeved: 'You people are all the same. If the patient dies, it's the doctor's fault; if the patient is saved, you give thanks to God.' I wanted to tell him there are cases where the opposite happens: if the patient dies, people thank God, and if the patient is saved, the fault is the doctor's." At this point the passengers laughed, and he continued. "Since I don't like arguing, I shut up. But I couldn't stop thinking about it. After all, the doctor was a serious guy, and the next day he turns to me and he goes like this: 'Why do you have to spend a fortune in cures? I cannot do anything. Your wife is too far gone.' 'If the doctor can't do anything,' I told him, 'then what can I do?'"

The narrator paused a bit, then suddenly switched to a profoundly heavy-hearted tone. "In the end," he reflected, "to save my wife I would have spent fifty *escudos*—. I would even have gone up to a hundred *escudos*," he added with a sigh.

A young farmworker who had followed every detail of the story broke out in a fit of conniptions. An old lady shook her head indignantly. Others continued arguing excitedly, for no one could tell if the narrator had been speaking seriously or if he was just joking.

A nervous thin man said something, but because he had a muffled voice, no one understood him amidst all the noise in the carriage. Leaning forward and gesticulating, the man made an effort to make himself understood and for the others to give him their attention. To no avail. "Listen up, friend," he could be heard finally.

If he was able to make those words be heard, it's because at that moment, for some mysterious reason, as though a mute had muffled the entire carriage, all conversation died out.

"Listen up, friend—" he said again. But no one paid him any attention. The passengers were looking curiously now at the other end of the carriage where something truly out of the ordinary was happening.

5

Afonso and Fialho looked too. At the end of the corridor were two well-dressed men who had not been there a few minutes before, and were acting peculiarly. One said nothing but was standing in such a way as to block the corridor from anyone passing. The other stooped over the passengers and without ceremony rustled through one woman's basket.

From one end of the car to the other, in a sudden ripple, passengers grabbed hold of their baggage as if they had all decided to get off at the next station.

Afonso looked at his companion in shock, wondering what Fialho's suitcase contained. Without having shifted his position, Fialho was also looking toward the far end of the car. *Doesn't he understand what's happening?* Afonso thought, and elbowed him discreetly. Fialho answered with a quick, judgmental glare. *Yes, it's a raid*, the look confirmed. *Did you need to ask?*

The agents moved along slowly, searching suitcases, bags and baskets, interrogating, checking the racks above and the space under the seats. This or that passenger showed some sign of anger, others shrugged their shoulders, and still others took on a shrewdly submissive attitude. But everyone opened their baggage without resisting.

As the agents got closer, moving from one compartment to the next, Afonso felt his discomfort and anxiety rise. He foresaw the moment when the agents would open Fialho's suitcase and find the underground newspapers. *Will this guy fail to do anything?* Afonso thought, eyeing Fialho. But Fialho seemed to have forgotten all about his comrade and displayed no interest whatsoever in the raid as it progressed. His elbow braced on the back of the seat, Fialho peered out the window at the fields with a tired, sleepy demeanor.

"It was my daughter who gave it to me," the soft voice of a woman could be heard. Where she was seated, Afonso couldn't see. But he did see the commanding gestures of one of the agents, who was writing something on a piece of yellow paper. "My daughter gave it to me!" the woman repeated. "What business is it of yours?"

The agent performing the search then handed a large bottle to the agent doing guard, who passed it to a modestly dressed little man Afonso had taken for another passenger.

Then the irritated voice of an agent could be heard: "Who does this bag belong to?" Then the other chimed in, but louder: "Who does this bag belong to?"

At first Afonso didn't see any bag. But the little man with the modest air who received the bottle moved, lowering himself until he disappeared, then reemerging dragging a heavy sack into the corridor.

The agents didn't press the question, and no one answered for the sack or showed any consternation. In those times, black marketeers set their luggage down in the carriage at some distance away and, to avoid problems, kept their eye on it from afar. If the agents didn't examine the sacks, fine, and at the end of the trip the smugglers would pick them up. If they did find them, the agents surely would take them away, the rice or the oil, and as far as the smugglers were concerned, they only observed from a distance but weren't arrested or slapped with fines to pay.

Afonso again discreetly elbowed his companion, who pretended not to be paying attention to anything. Mixed in now with his discomfort, Afonso felt an intense and growing aggravation over Fialho's complete passivity, waiting for the fatal moment without any response or plan. At first Fialho had seemed like a tiger; now he was no more than a common house cat.

Afonso hoped that the train would pull into some station before the agents got to them. Surely they wouldn't prevent them from getting off. So he studied the train's rhythm to guess if it might start braking, but to no effect. Rattling along, throwing the passengers one against another at every sharp curve, the train gave no sign of stopping any time soon. At that speed, neither would it be possible to try and throw themselves off. But then again, who knows? He figured it would only be by some miracle that they'd escape, and what was better? To go rot in prison or, jumping from the train, to risk tumbling over three or four tomes? With such ruminations, Afonso looked out the carriage window calculating the speed.

"That one's mine." Suddenly he heard Fialho's voice beside him. He turned to look. There were the agents. It was Afonso's suitcase they wanted to check first. With his heart pounding as if it were his own suitcase that carried the newspapers, with slightly shaking hands Afonso opened it. The agent put his hands into the clothes and, with eyes semi-closed, trusting his feel, carefully searched every corner of it.

Meanwhile, moving quickly, Fialho placed one foot on the edge of the seat, took hold of his suitcase heavy with printed material, and put it on his flexed knee. He reached for his key ring and unlocked the locks. *He's crazy!* Afonso thought, looking at him sideways, as he placed his own suitcase on the floor. Exaggerating the awkwardness of his position, Fialho touched the agent's elbow to call his attention and deal with him without delay.

"Books!" he said, when the agent turned toward him. And then Fialho opened the top of the suitcase.

He's crazy! Afonso thought again, feeling his undershirt sticking to his body with sweat. The agent didn't even look, and himself closed the top.

At once relieved and stupefied, Afonso expected that—as it would seem natural after the danger had passed—his comrade would turn to look at him. Fialho, however, seemed to completely ignore Afonso's existence. Once more watching through the window as the fields floated by, he yawned, bored and sleepy.

6

Fialho paused at the side of the road, put his suitcase down, wiped off his sweat once again, and to Afonso's surprise proceeded with several weird exercises. He began by spitting into his handkerchief and with it scrupulously cleaned off his shoes. Then it was the turn for his pants. Vigorously grabbing and scratching the cloth, he removed some specks of mud. Then he took out a mirror and looked at himself from side to side, straightened his tie and, removing from his pocket a half-sized comb, he combed himself leisurely, pulling and shaping his black hair which seemed to gain more shine with each pass of the comb.

Done with these operations, he turned to Afonso and without a word handed him the handkerchief, comb and mirror. Afonso shrugged his shoulders and smiled. *Quit joking around with me*, he seemed to be saying. *What do I care about such vanity?*

But when Fialho glared at him, he realized this was no joke. "Clean yourself off and fix yourself up the best you can," he said coldly. "It's a matter of defense of the Party."

Unwillingly, Afonso cleaned his shoes and pulled a speck or two of dirt off his pants. But redoing his tie and combing his hair in the mirror seemed too much. Fialho didn't insist. Closely looking him over from under his dense eyebrows, he retrieved the comb, the mirror and the handkerchief. Still, before he took hold of his suitcase and setting on his way, he approached Afonso, adjusted the knot of his tie to fit neatly under his collar in a reserved, deliberate gesture, which if not seen as simply done to achieve a precise result, could also have been a gesture of discontent and censure.

From there they entered the town, crossed several streets and entered a fabric store. At the counter, a bald little man with an extremely pale face was smiling and humbly attending to a lady customer. "I'll be with you in a moment," he said to the newcomers.

Fialho put his suitcase down, telling Afonso to do the same, and started to studiously examine the material on display. He fingered the quality, looked at the selvage, checked the prices and made comments that from the start left Afonso rather baffled.

"You think she'd like this one? The other one we saw maybe wasn't as nice, but it was a lot cheaper." And before another fabric, "I already know it's not to your taste. But you know, perhaps you do everything your wife wants, and in my house I'm the one who decides—."

Only after a few minutes of this routine did Afonso get that Fialho was just marking time waiting for the customer to leave the store.

That was in fact the case. The woman paid and received her package. Friendly, smiling, almost servile, the tradesman accompanied her to the door, where he remained for a few more seconds looking out at the street. Then he returned inside. His physiognomy changed instantly. Now with a serious, furrowed face, a penetrating glance and rapid movements, he himself grabbed Fialho's suitcase and, opening a door to the back of the store, led the comrades to an interior storeroom annex, where he turned on the electric light.

He exchanged a few words in a low voice with Fialho and left, closing the door. Afonso felt the closure of the lock.

Fialho removed his jacket, went to a cabinet to find wrapping paper and rolls of twine, and placed everything on top of a table. He asked Afonso to uncoil the twine and in the meantime divided the newspapers into small bundles that he wrapped carefully and marked with a letter or number.

The businessman returned with the same serious expression on his extremely wan face. He stowed away a pile of the little packages.

"We unloaded a good bit of ballast," Fialho said.

After a few more minutes they left. The businessman went with them to the door. His expression was so amiable and formal, his smile and obeisance so self-effacing, that a passerby remarked to his wife, "To do business, types like that would lick the boots of the Devil himself—"

"Hunh?" went the woman. And taking advantage of her husband's inconvenient observation, she forced him to stop and look at the fabrics.

7

Arriving in Lisbon, Fialho led Afonso to a room he had already rented. Only then did he explain what his tasks would be. On assigned dates he would go get the papers at the fabric store which they had visited. There he would make up the packets for the various sectors and would deliver them to the places or the comrades he would be instructed to. Just that.

"What's needed is staying calm, being careful, and punctuality," Fialho advised. "Your legs will get a workout, but your head won't get tired."

Vaz had already told Afonso he would work in the distribution system. But in truth, Afonso imagined something else.

"There's not a lot to learn," he commented with a dismayed smile.

"That's what you think!" Fialho answered.

Those words echoed as aggressively as the quick glare he cast from under the visor of his black eyebrows.

To clarify what he had just said, he started explaining. He spoke to him of train and jitney schedules, the best places to get off, the routes to choose, the way to construct and transport packages, the care one must take at meet-ups, ways to bluff a patrol or guard, and the thousand and one tricks to assure the security of the distribution.

"In this work nothing can be done by chance. The underground rules have to be strictly adhered to."

Afonso smiled to himself: Fialho was quite presumptuous. Afonso remembered the scene on the train and the daring with which Fialho opened his suitcase to the agent. True, his audacity saved him. But hadn't Fialho taken a dangerous, adventuresome chance? Wanting to see him embarrassed, he asked Fialho that question.

Fialho didn't get upset. He rose, went over to a chest and pulled out two bundles that he handed to Afonso. They were two packs of religious propaganda tracts. As Afonso didn't understand what they signified, Fialho explained that in the suitcase he was carrying, the Party press had been covered by such pamphlets. The agent didn't look, but if he had, that's all he would have seen.

"It's not any particular formula," he added. "In this work there aren't exact prescriptions. You have to use your imagination and choose in each situation the solution that will work the best."

Everything Fialho explained sounded artificial to him, overly picky and of dubious value. The extraordinary thing is that the comrade obviously gave enormous importance to all this childishness, because he was talking about them for two solid hours.

Finally, he set their next meeting date and said goodbye. As he was heading for the door, Afonso blocked his way in a sudden decision. Earlier he had resolved not to speak to Fialho about Maria. But at the last minute, without thinking, he forged ahead anyway. In but a half dozen words he said he wanted a meeting with her at the soonest possible time.

"You should have taken that up with Vaz," Fialho said. "That comrade is not in my sector."

Afonso reminded him that he had wanted to do that, but that Vaz told him he was to go to Fialho for everything. Fialho explained, "He didn't know for sure what you wanted to talk about. Talk about this issue the next time you see him. For my part, I'll raise the problem at the first opportunity."

Contrary to Afonso's expectation, Fialho seemed understanding. But what did that "at the first opportunity" mean? The way the Party worked, that could be days, weeks, months or years.

8

As it turned out, he did not wait long. A week later they met so that Vaz could tell him where to deliver the paper in the region. He asked for the meeting with Maria.

"It's not up to me," Vaz answered. "I can't set up or authorize meetings of this kind."

Seeing Afonso's desolate expression, he added, somewhat by way of consolation, the same words Fialho had used: "I'll raise the problem at the first opportunity."

The first opportunity, the first opportunity, Afonso repeated to himself. He saw that this form of speech meant infinite postponement, a badly disguised disinterest, a bureaucratic complacency toward cadres' needs. Accepting that the issue would be dealt with that way was the same as giving up. And giving up would be to defeat the entire dream he had invented when he decided to go underground.

No, he could not passively accept that the issue would be settled like that. With unanticipated vehemence he insisted on the importance and urgency of the meeting. "The Party has the responsibility of paying attention to issues of a personal nature that the cadres bring up," he argued. "The personal happiness of each comrade is not only of concern to them but is also in the interest of the Party."

Vaz was not flustered by such a sudden outburst. Did he agree with Afonso? Did he find his rant out of order? Did he know something about Maria that he didn't care to say?

"Later today I'm supposed to meet with Ramos," he said calmly when Afonso stopped speaking. "All I can do is to set up a meeting between you and him. He'll decide." And thus it was left.

*   *   *

Good-natured as always, Ramos greeted him with a clap on the back and showed interest in knowing how things were going with his new life. In his usual manner, laughing and joking, he encouraged him. When Afonso brought up the meeting with Maria, Ramos responded in the same tone: "You know we're not running a recreational society here, where everyone meets to shoot the breeze. I'd like to help you find a way to do it, but meetings between Party workers only take place for work reasons."

Afonso was driven to press his campaign, however, and insisted on the importance of the meeting. Shortly he saw a shadow of annoyance cross the comrade's face.

"But what's the objective of this meeting anyway?" Ramos asked coldly.

"I believe you know there was a situation that existed between us before she went into the underground—"

"A situation? What situation? Were you sleeping with her?"

Embarrassed and blushing, Afonso wanted to explain. But how to explain, and what to explain to Ramos, when he put things so brutally? And, really, what situation did exist? Now, like a lightning bolt, Afonso saw there never existed any commitment between himself and Maria, nothing he could cite to Ramos to convince him.

"We loved each other—" he tried to explain.

Ramos started laughing again, enjoying himself, but his laughter now sounded bitter and cruel to Afonso.

"As lovers?"

How could Afonso, without making himself look ridiculous, speak of the depth of his feelings? If loving one another wasn't reason enough, what reason could he summon? A part of him told him to shut up and let it go. Yet he had the clear feeling that if he gave up now on seeing Maria, he'd never again be able to make the request. Besides which, Ramos's lack of seriousness, deprecating manner and crudeness reinforced his own will to fight even more.

"The issue is clear, friend," he said in a such a self-assured tone that it surprised even himself. "I love the friend, she loves me, and I want to marry her. And being amongst the ranks of Party workers, I believe it's possible the Party can find a solution."

"Well!" Ramos exclaimed. "It's not easy, but we'll see. And she wants to marry you?"

He has no intention of dealing with or resolving a problem, Afonso thought. *He just wants to destroy me.* And impatiently he explained that it was precisely to talk about that with her that he was asking for the meeting, and to him that seemed justification enough. In the end, either because he was tired of making his comrade suffer, or because he never had that intention, Ramos promised to transmit the request.

"But it'll take a while, understand? Don't think later on it's my fault."

Whoever's waited as long as I've waited can wait a little more, Afonso thought. *The important thing is to get to be with her.*

That perspective lent him such joy that he immediately forgot the unpleasant way Ramos had spoken and took hold of his arm amicably: "Thank you, friend. From the bottom of my heart."

"It's nothing, old man, nothing!" Ramos snorted.

9

And so Afonso began his life as a Party worker. Receiving suitcases and packages. Sorting newspapers. Making packets. Taking responsibility for suitcases. Unspooling twine. Receiving new packages. Waiting for trains, waiting for jitneys. Killing time in isolated places. Taking the train. Receiving bundles. Delivering bundles. Spending entire days without doing anything. Exhausting himself other days hustling from one dawn to the next. Not sleeping some nights. Then sleeping whole days. Always the same thing, monotonous, boring, lacking interest. But Afonso did his job. He never failed to appear at a meet-up, never made a mistake dividing up the papers.

Just one thing he didn't understand and considered absurd and stupid: That which the comrades so solemnly called the "conspiratorial rules," or the underground rules. Some, of course, he could understand. Arriving on time, for example. Others were laughable. For example, what did it have to do with Party work, this obligation to shave every day? Was this a matter that warranted being passed as a resolution of the Central Committee Secretariat? It was ridiculous.

But Fialho thought otherwise and one day called it to his attention. "You didn't shave today, comrade. What kept you from doing it?"

"Nothing," Afonso replied. "I don't need to."

"It's a resolution, as you well know."

"For you it's all right, because you have a heavy beard. But I, as you see, hardly have a beard at all."

"The resolution does not apply only to people with a heavy beard. It applies to all Party workers."

"Very well, comrade. But if I don't need to, why do I have to do it?"

So the argument began. Fialho explained that the decision had been taken because there had been a widespread relaxation in that regard, and comrades had become suspect for not taking that measure.

Afonso answered that resolutions could not be applied schematically and, irritated by Fialho's obstinacy, retorted, "Listen. Suppose there was a resolution to cut your hair. And suppose you were completely bald. How would you comply with the resolution?"

Fialho did not bend to such a puny argument. "What you don't want, comrade, is to understand. You don't have much of a beard, that's true. But do you think no one see it? So don't call it a beard, just call it hairs. But do you believe that people don't see when you don't mow those hairs for two weeks? You don't even realize what kind of a figure you present. And even if people didn't notice. There's another aspect to the question: The habit of discipline, the habit of complying. And the habit of thinking that if there's some resolution that passed that we don't understand, many experiences, many instances, many reasons weighed—"

"You mean," Afonso interrupted, "there are never incorrect resolutions? The militants can't think. The Secretariat thinks and it's for the others to comply with their eyes closed."

Fialho's eyes fixed on him squarely and aggressively. And he went on, hammering out his words. "If you have an opposing opinion, oppose! If you want to make criticisms, make them! If you believe some resolution should be changed, say so or write it! But as long as it stands, you have to comply with it."

"So we're back to the beard," Afonso sighed.

"No, we're not going back to the beard today. But certainly, and sadly, we will. I just want to add one more point. What trust can you have that a comrade will fulfill the big things if he falls short on the small ones?"

"He could fall short on the small ones and comply on the big ones—"

"He might. But who is the judge of what is important and what is not? Of what should be done and what doesn't have to be done? Everyone for themselves? You? Me? For that you wouldn't need any standards for work or any Party direction. And the Party wouldn't exist, you can be quite sure."

Returning to his room, Afonso looked in the mirror. He put a blade in the razor and picked up the shaving brush. But then he changed his mind.

"To hell with it," he mumbled.

He put everything back in place, lay back on the bed, picked up a book and began to read.

Chapter IX

1

Night had already set in when Vaz took leave of his comrades and got on the road. Exiting the city, a family of peasants burdened with baskets and farm tools passed him by, soon to be lost in the dark. A while later a bicycle, which instead of a headlight had a candle protected by a slender paper tube and that squeaked with each cycle of its rusty wheels, gained ground on him little by little, passed him and moved into the distance until the weak glimmer from the improvised lantern suddenly disappeared, swallowed up in a curve of the road. He didn't see anyone else.

Night contracted around him in a tight circle around whose periphery he could barely see the shapes of the trees and shrubbery along the roadside.

A light fog turned the shadows even more diffuse. Worn out, insignificant and covert like any nocturnal beast, Vaz had been walking for more than an hour in a rhythmic cadence muffled by the asphalt when the light of two bright eyes glowed a little ahead of him on the right, followed by a figure crawling across the road and wandering off in no apparent hurry. The little bitch of the Pim-Pa-Pum sprang to Vaz's mind, almost dragging its swollen teats along the ground.

Miss Ermelinda came around with her usual mysterious air and whispered the big news: The ladies had given the bitch to a passing shepherd, who took it far away.

"They did that so he'd kill it!" she complained indignantly.

"That can't be!" Rosa protested.

"You don't know those ladies. They were making themselves crazy just with the notion that the bitch was spending her days here. It couldn't have been for any other reason."

When Ermelinda left, Rosa called for Vaz and told him the story. Wouldn't it still be possible to try and catch the shepherd? But then she realized it was a foolish idea. In truth there was nothing to be done, and Vaz went back to his work.

An hour later, returning outdoors, he saw Rosa silent and still, peering out toward the road. She didn't even see him approaching.

"It's not worth upsetting yourself over," he said to console her.

"Hunh?" Rosa jumped. For sure, she had not heard what he said.

"It's not worth upsetting yourself about it," he repeated.

"What isn't?" Rosa asked, and her gloomy eyes that had been focused far off now stared at her companion, still not understanding.

"Sorry, it's nothing," said Vaz, as he returned to his work.

No, he did not care to think about it. They had agreed not to speak about the past. Agreed and accepted. And that was no problem for him. But now, in the dark of night, unable to focus on the immediate task at hand, not even on the meeting he was preparing for, the face of his companion came to his mind and that indecipherable something from the past that constantly called and took hold of her.

2

It was almost midnight. Vaz arrived at the intersection where José Sagarra was to meet him. From one side of the road to the other, you could hardly descry the vague blurs of canebrake and standalone trees. He halted; no one showed. He turned the corner and took a few steps on that road. No one. Retreating to the side of the road to wait, he thought he heard a light snap of dry branches and, looking back toward the road from which he had come, he saw a figure also hugging the roadside.

He returned to the middle of the road and stood observing him. Although he could barely make him out in the damp shadows, he seemed to Vaz a tall man with an elegant posture and dark clothing. Sure of himself, he considered for a few seconds—to approach him and ask the time or the road to someplace? Or ask him straight out what he was doing there? He didn't have time to decide. The figure came off the curb toward the middle of the road and approached him.

It was Sagarra after all, unmistakable now in his short, modest stature.

"I didn't recognize you when you passed me," said Sagarra.

"I also didn't recognize you," said Vaz. "Well, it's true—in the dark all cats are black."

It was odd. If for some reason the figure had disappeared, he could have sworn he had seen a tall, tastefully dressed man.

They left the paved road and started walking on the cross road, a narrow little lane with a rough surface that led off in an unknown direction. In a few hundred meters Sagarra whispered, "There's Tomé."

Vaz still hadn't seen anything amidst the opaque night haze until a figure emerged on the lane waiting for them. The white of his shirt stood out against his dark vest.

"Over here!" he said, his voice distinctly breaking the night silence. Clearly, he trusted that no one was in the vicinity who could hear them.

They walked up an incline in single file. But then, as if a trapdoor had opened under his feet, Tomé disappeared. Sagarra disappeared too. Vaz was still trying to find his way when the white of Tomé's shirt appeared again a little to his left on a lower level. The same clear voice repeated, "Over here!"

Walking over heavy clods of earth, Vaz joined his comrades whom he could hardly see now on the path carved out between two hillsides like a trench. With Tomé as their guide, they walked in silence, snaking across the fields. Then they hopped over a gully, left the path and proceeded along a bare slope. After a good half hour of hiking, they made out a few isolated trees, then a wall, and suddenly the black volume of a house. After the hard-packed trail along the slope they started treading soft, damp ground and marched on without a sound. A sweet, acrid odor from nearby stables filled the air.

Tomé left his comrades to themselves and returned shortly with a lantern. His legs dancing grotesquely in the reddish light, he led them to another building. He opened the door and they entered. Turning around, the reddish light illuminated piles of hay, a pail and farm implements, and sharply brought into view a man who rose, screened his eyes and settled into a corner.

"This is Comrade da Barrosa. He was the first to arrive," Tomé explained. "You can lie down over there." It was not clear if da Barrosa was his name or if he was from someplace called Barrosa, but that's how people referred to him.

Da Barrosa mumbled something. Tomé left. The hayloft was left submerged in complete darkness. The smell of hay mixed with that of the neighboring stables. Every once in a while, in the silence, you could hear the jerky bodily movements of the heavy animals.

3

Drenched in a cold sweat, Vaz awoke with a start. Tomé had returned and the light from his oil lamp fell on the sleeping José Sagarra.

"It's time," Tomé said softly.

They had to shake the comrade for him to awaken. Sagarra yawned noisily and stood up, shaking off the hay that had stuck to his clothes. The reddish lantern light once again danced alongside Tomé's legs until it disappeared when the two men went out. From the stable beside them came the gentle sound of animal hooves stepping on the wet ground. Vaz coughed.

"Who are you?" da Barrosa asked in the dark.

"A comrade," Vaz answered.

"A comrade, a comrade," da Barrosa repeated. "I too am a comrade."

Silence reigned again. Chilly, Vaz raised the collar of his jacket, adjusted it around his neck, covered his legs with hay and went back to sleep. He woke up again to the infernal sound of a sudden downpour of hailstones on the tile roof of the hayloft.

"Are you awake, partner?" asked da Barrosa, almost shouting to make himself heard.

"Yes, I am," Vaz answered sleepily.

"Do you know what this is going to cause?"

"This what?"

"This what?!" da Barrosa repeated, and muttered something else that Vaz didn't understand.

A little later, with the same furious speed with which it started, the fusillade ended. The tumult gone, only the sweet, limpid murmur of water falling from the eaves remained, and the nervous squirming of the animals in the stable.

Through the cracks in the roof and the door the day was starting to brighten. Vaz now saw the figure of his comrade before him, seated on the hay and leaning against the wall.

To the sound of approaching steps, the door opened, and s few men gathered uncertainly at the entrance.

"Take a place inside, you guys," said Tomé, who guided them. "The others won't be long."

"Don't worry, comrade," a fine, suave voice responded. "We'll be okay."

Slowly, searching out a place, the men sat down.

Outside Tomé could still be heard, speaking to someone far off. Her words swallowed by the distance, a woman answered. Someone entered the stable to the side and poured water into a basin, speaking tenderly to the animals.

"The day begins," that same fine, suave voice commented, coming from a corner of the hayloft. The peasant's face was hidden under an enormous hat, but from the voice one could imagine a friendly, calm expression.

Da Barrosa was about to say something, but a new, equally noisy fusillade of hail, unleashed upon the tile roof, didn't allow him to continue.

4

Filtered through the narrow window and the cracks in the walls and roof, the pale light of dawn now allowed everyone to see each other's faces.

In all they were eleven. Seated on the hay and forming a wide circle, they looked at each other with curiosity. Everyone stared with special interest at those they had never seen, instinctively wondering where they were from. Some vaguely recalled seeing this one or the other in the city, or at a market, or on some street. But all of that was distant and uncertain. Although they had come from nearby villages, they all felt the purposefulness of their meeting—to bring into being a world far vaster than they had ever imagined. Each one felt strengthened by the presence of the others, and by the simple fact that, coming from different parts, there they were, in a dim hayloft in an underground encounter that seemed a revelation of the power of the working class and its Party. Only eleven, they were conscious of doing something risky and important, and you could see it in their serious, almost anxious faces.

Adjusting themselves on the hay, they moved a little closer and tightened the circle. Only one young man, with a brown Arabic-looking face, remained a bit apart, regarding the *companheiros* with visible reserve, apprehension, with even a somewhat haughty air.

At Vaz's insistence, Sagarra opened the meeting. In a few words he laid out its objective: to see how to coordinate the struggles of the rural workforce in the region and discuss how to better organize the Party.

Then a thin, nervous peasant took the floor. "For our part, things are going well. The marketplace committee is still functioning with very hardworking people. They have everyone's support and it's with them that the bosses have to deal—"

"It's as Alfredo says," another added, wearing a fur-collar jacket. He was crouching at his comrade's side and was from the same village. "Last week we won a raise of two *escudos*."

"Not much," the fine, suave voice of the peasant with the big hat interrupted.

"What do you mean?" the thin, nervous peasant protested.

The discussion heated up. People spoke at the same time, and the general conversation split up into separate arguments of each one with their neighbor or their opponent. Vaz tried to listen to everything people said, but as he paid attention to some, he lost what the others were saying. José Sagarra did not try to prevent it. In the middle of the noise and confusion, the clear, well-modulated voice of the fellow with the Arabic face rose above the rest: "I ask for the floor!"

Surprised by the grandeur of the statement, almost everyone quieted down. "What of it?" the thin, nervous peasant could still be heard. "By next week, you'll see!"

"Shhhh," went da Barrosa.

"If the comrades will permit me," the youngster with the Arabic face began, "I would like to offer my opinion. The arbitration committees posted wage tables, but many of the bosses didn't abide by them and paid higher wages. With the result that those bosses were fined and will continue to be if the government learns they're paying day rates higher than the table. If working conditions are delineated in the market, that's what will continue happening. For that reason the bosses are now proposing to do away with the market and start contracting each one for himself. To me that seems like a reasonable proposal because they'll be able to pay more without being fined."

"Ha, ha, ha!" da Barrosa broke out laughing.

"In the opinion of the Local Committee that I'm part of," the young man went on undisturbed, raising his harmonious voice, "we have to accept such a proposal. For the first time there'll be the possibility of uniting in the struggle against fascism both the workers and the bosses—"

"Ha, ha, ha!" da Barrosa erupted in laughter again. Throughout the hayloft people let out their own exclamations either of approval or protest.

Several of the rural workers then intervened, speaking all at the same time, contradicting the young man's view.

"You people can't see what's right in front of your noses," da Barrosa shot out, still laughing. "What those guys want is to do away with the market only to screw you all later one by one."

"That's not really correct," the young man persisted. "The fact is they're paying higher than the table. It's also a fact that they've been fined. Things are not so simple. And if the comrades are surprised by the unity of the workers with the bosses, it's because you don't understand the Party's policy of national unity."

"Ridiculous!" Alfredo exclaimed, truly agitated by now.

"Let Comrade Belmiro have his say," someone proposed.

"Listen, comrade," said the fine, suave voice of the big-hatted peasant. "Do you have a marketplace committee?"

"For what?" retorted the man with the Arabic face. "So we can legitimize the labor market as the slave market that it is?"

Everyone at once piled on top of him, recounting their own experiences, their gains in the dayworker markets and the raises they had won.

"Just look at this!" Alfredo said emphatically, looking about from one to the other in a state of excitement. "These guys have a market and want to end it. And we here in this area didn't have one and it was us who created it!"

"I don't know where he's been, but certainly not in Portugal," a strong, ruddy peasant of few words commented aggressively.

"Where is he from?" Vaz whispered into Sagarra's ear.

It was the comrade whom Afonso had made contact with only a few days earlier. He was a member of the local committee where the largest number of rural wage earners in the region were concentrated. Until then it had been under the direct control of the Regional Committee.

Vaz said nothing, but his facial muscles contracted visibly. Another one! The Regional Committee—and Afonso himself—despite all the discussions and decisions, continued conveying their own opinions to the peasants under their supervision.

Speaking in the face of so much comment from the others, the young man never lost his calm, speaking well and defending himself point by point.

Finally Vaz decided to say something. "In reality there are two different ways of looking at things. You're not at fault," he said, turning to the man with the Arabic face. "Your organization has lost sight of reality, at the margins of the struggle, the experience and the victories that are meanwhile taking place every day in the region. Forgive me if I repeat, but I'm in accord with what a comrade said a few moments ago: It seems like you've been abroad—"

"The approach is the approach of the Party," the young man said with utter conviction.

"It was the approach of the Regional Committee, you mean to say," Vaz countered, "but that's a thing of the past. The meeting is not over yet, and you will hear what the other comrades are saying, and I feel sure that you will be persuaded."

5

The longer the meeting progressed, the more the fellow with the Arab face stumbled on surprise after surprise. Everything said there was different from what he had heard before. To him, it all seemed contrary to the Party approach that he had always gotten from the Regional Committee. Everything seemed out of order, outside the set formulas, outside the discipline of meetings that he had always attended. At times he even admitted feeling he'd fallen into some anti-Party group. At the same time, the facts cited and the enthusiasm of the reports revealed to him a new situation in the fields in his own region that he had never witnessed. The surprise was so great that for some hours he frankly doubted the truth of what was said there. It almost seemed to him like a convention of storytellers talking about peasant struggles the way hunters and fishermen boasted of their own triumphs on land and sea.

They spoke of mass assemblies of peasant workers on the large estates and in the villages, of elections of marketplace committees, of struggles in the marketplace, of setting higher wages, the demand for bosses to give work to older and sicker day laborers, of gatherings at the People's House, of work stoppages and even small strikes.

They elaborated a whole new theory, based on experience, always starting from concrete cases to arrive at more general conclusions. And despite the successes and victories they celebrated, everyone showed profound dissatisfaction with the results obtained, and spoke of broadening and uniting the struggles that to the young man's eyes appeared like dreams or fantasies.

"Did we get higher wages? We certainly did," said Alfredo. "But what good are higher wages if prices rise and staples aren't available? If we fight for higher wages we also have to fight against the lack of foodstuffs and above all the lack of bread—"

"This is what Comrade Belmiro told us," the peasant with the big hat interrupted. "And that's exactly what we did. Just last week we forced them to distribute three sacks of flour."

In the course of the discussion, Vaz heard the comrades several times respectfully quoting the opinions of Comrade Belmiro. When they spoke of that comrade, their voices took on a more solemn tone. It was doubtlessly someone well-known and esteemed among the workers. But why? Who was it? Was it one of them? Earlier, at a certain point when someone proposed that Comrade Belmiro have his say in answer to the fellow with the Arabic face, and then the peasant with the big hat spoke, Vaz supposed that was Comrade Belmiro. Now, from what people were saying, he concluded that couldn't have been him. So which one of them was it?

He asked José Sagarra in a discreet whisper, but Sagarra, maybe because he was paying attention to the discussion, didn't answer.

6

At midday, Tomé brought a huge bottle of wine, bread and a long *chouriço*. On the break in the meeting, each person pulled out his knife and one by one carved off small slices of *chouriço* and hunks of bread cut on the bias. Passing the bottle around from hand to hand, they began eating and drinking in silence. But shortly the conversation started up again. Taking advantage of the quiet, the strong, ruddy peasant of few words spoke to Vaz in the combative manner that was apparently his style.

"Now, you listen to what I want to say and tell it to the Party. I never wanted to know anything about politics, and I don't know anything about politics. But I learned more in three months than I ever did in my whole life. I'm forty years old and I admit I was walking around for more than thirty-nine of them in the dark. The Party showed me the light, now I see the road ahead and believe I'm on the way. Up to now what the Party has said has rung true. I believe in the Party because it has been right about things. We've been talking here about how we have to move things forward. But the Party should take heed. Just as it has gained the people's trust, it can also lose it."

"Here!" the *companheiro* next to him said as he passed him the bottle.

He took the bottle but, before drinking, finished his speech, still looking at Vaz. "The Party will make its decisions, and I agree. But watch out! It's not enough to decide, it has to decide well."

"Trust the Party, comrade. We're doing everything to get it right," Vaz answered.

The answer surely did not satisfy Sagarra because, addressing himself to the peasant who had just spoken, he added, "The Party is sizable and has a lot of experience, friend. But what is the Party? Here, in our region, the Party is us. The Central Committee is the Party, but you are the Party too. Making decisions, good or bad, is in our hands, and also in yours."

"Well said!" da Barrosa mumbled with his mouth full.

"I agree," the peasant insisted. "Let's go forward. Just remember, as we gain trust, we also can lose it."

"To lose trust in the Party," said the fine, sweet voice of the farmworker with the big hat, "we'd first need to lose trust in ourselves."

7

The young man with the Arab face stumbled on revelation after revelation as they spoke about the struggle for better wages, the marketplace committees, and all that had happened over the past few months. The biggest surprises, however, which left him not just confused but angry, came when they touched on problems of Party organization.

"We've talked about struggles, comrades," said Vaz. "Now we need to talk about the Party. Without the Party what has been accomplished would not have happened. On that we all agree. It's the Party that unites us and teaches us. It's when we're organized in the Party that we can lead the workers' struggles. So we need to look at how the Party is organized and how we can organize it better. Every comrade here at this meeting is an affiliate of the Party. So we can speak openly."

Other than occasional interjections, da Barrosa, his legs spread open as his strong torso leaned against the wall, had kept his silence until now. On hearing those words, he interrupted in anger. "Wait a minute, friend. It's not as you put it. I, for example, am not an affiliate of the Party."

"What?" Vaz asked bewildered. "What are you saying?" Since da Barrosa didn't address his comrades familiarly, Vaz kept his address correct as well.

"I'm saying what I just said: that I am not an affiliate of the Party."

Sagarra didn't show that he was ruffled in any way and patiently asked da Barrosa, "Are you in accord with the Party?"

"Of course I am."

"Are you part of the Party organization?"

"Yes, I am."

"Do you pay your dues?"

"Yes, I do."

"Well, then," Sagarra said, "that is what is called a Party member."

"That's hardly news, Comrade Belmiro," da Barrosa shouted— revealing with that utterance that the mysterious Comrade Belmiro was Sagarra himself. "You've told me that many times."

"Here's someone," the dark fellow with the Arab face remarked, "who's a member of the Party and doesn't know it!"

Da Barrosa didn't give up so easily. "I don't know why you're making a joke of it," he replied sourly. "I didn't say I wasn't a member of the Party. I said I wasn't an affiliate. Member of the Party? Yes. But an affiliate? No."

"Excuse me for saying so, friend," the young man persisted, "but it's obvious you don't know the ABCs—"

The others looked at him reprovingly. A militant for several years now and very sure of his opinions, the young man only shrugged his shoulders in disdain of the general ignorance.

8

Vaz asked how many Party members they could count in the area. The peasant with the big hat answered in his delicate, sweet voice. "For my part, comrade, I can give you two responses. I can say that in my village there are fifty Party members, and I can say there are only five. In both cases, I'm speaking the pure truth."

As if to recover from the awkwardness of just a few minutes before, da Barrosa let out another of his loud bursts of raw laughter.

Looking over at Sagarra, Vaz again noticed no sign of surprise. In his earnest, freckled face, his bright blue eyes expressed a deep contentment.

"The pure truth," the peasant repeated in an even sweeter tone. "If you ask me how many comrades are with the Party, how many follow what the Party says and recommends, how many want to go to meetings, how many are prepared to help the Party, I'd answer: all except half a dozen jerks. Now if you ask me how many were invited to enlist in the Party, then I'd say only four or five."

And searching around him, maliciously enjoying the effect of his words, he added, as though wishing to embarrass the others with his little game, "That's how things are in my area."

Vaz was honestly somewhat embarrassed. The neat boundaries in workers' organizations between Party members and sympathizers appeared in that case hard to determine. At the same time, by way of contradiction, both of the peasant's responses seemed correct and incorrect. But he said nothing, waiting for others to speak up.

"Alfredo, what do you say?" asked Sagarra, turning to the thin, nervous peasant who had so well described the work of the market-place committees.

Without hesitation, Alfredo blurted out, "Maybe twenty, maybe thirty!"

"Okay, that's not quite right," the comrade with the fur-collared jacket corrected him. "They're all good comrades, but actual Party members are just the two of us—"

"That's rich!" Alfredo disagreed. "Do you think we're better than the others?"

The conversation livened up to the point where almost everyone was talking, but found it hard to understand one another.

Only the dark young man with the Arab face showed no restraint. Speaking now about the Party organization, he felt completely at home, finding some ground on which he would certainly pull far ahead of the others. "In our corner, things are well organized," he began. "We have the Local Committee with three comrades, and two cells with two each. The rest of the men don't yet have much political consciousness. We meet every week and everyone pays their regular dues plus the press. I know that in the struggle for better wages we may be behind, but with respect to the organization, we can say we are well organized."

The young man concluded proudly. After all the confusion that had arisen concerning Party organization, it seemed to him that his Local Committee could be a real example for the others. He even expected that the report he had just given would lead the others to reconsider the opinions they had expressed when he spoke earlier. The comment that ensued, however, left him perplexed once again.

"Great work!" Alfredo protested. "You have everything well organized, but you don't know what's going on with the workers, you don't have a marketplace committee, and you let the bosses push you around. Is that what the Party is good for?"

9

Is *that what the Party is good for?* As Vaz walks back to the city in the twilight, this question constantly comes to mind. Yes, Alfredo was right. It's all right there: Is that what the Party is good for? What is its mission? And is it fulfilling it or not? The Party is not an end in itself. If its organisms exist and don't know about the current problems of the workers, if they are removed from the masses, if they don't educate them and guide them, if they don't know how to find forms of organizing that lead to struggle, what purpose does it serve in fact? It's of little value to be oh-so-organized, with everything in its proper place, everything corresponding to the prescribed plan, if those organizations and those comrades live with their eyes focused inward, internalizing the Party within themselves. No, this not what the Party is good for.

Vaz is coming from a meeting of men who only recently found the Party. He feels exalted by all that he heard. He admits that as a cadre he gave much less to those young peasant organizations than the Party, through its involvement, will receive from them.

He recalls every moment of the comrades' discussions and opinions. He sees before him those faces yesterday unknown and today so familiar they seem like old friends from childhood. Again he pictures Alfredo, thin and nervous, cocky and combative, the guy with the big hat and the voice so suave, sly and sharp, and da Barrosa as insolent as he is trusting, the strong ruddy man of few, but demanding and imperative words, and Tomé lending his house, guiding the comrades, offering them food and drink. He recalls the way José Sagarra framed his comments, his calm and assured manner, his style of dealing with everyone, indicating a profound knowledge of human beings and their problems. He himself, Vaz, who came to appreciate him ever since he had first met him, feels agreeably impressed with the capacity and prestige of that nearly illiterate comrade. He remembers, too, their meeting the night before, at the road crossing, when in the dark, standing still and silent on the side of the road, the comrade's figure looked like a tall and elegantly dressed man.

It's true, Comrade Belmiro, Vaz thinks, *in the dark I was already swearing you were a fine gentleman.*

Chapter X

1

Maria tore the rod out of António's hands, mussed his hair with a quick gesture and escaped into the fields. And thus, by an extreme measure, she cut short the question of who owned the rod, because both of them claimed to have discovered it just minutes before in the heather. António ran after her. Rushing ahead like a wild goat, showing her surprisingly white and healthy legs, discarding her shoes along the way, dodging and cutting back and forth, Maria did not allow herself to be captured. Tired and begging for relief, António stopped chasing her. Then, huffing and puffing herself, Maria approached him and handed him the rod.

"Let's make peace, dear friend. I don't want you to kill yourself running."

Exhausted, she lay down on the grass in the shadow of some bushes, her hands folded as a pillow behind her neck, her eyes closed, her breath deep and rhythmic. António sat beside her and watched her closely and affectionately. Then he went to search for her shoes, which he found only with difficulty, and when he came back again, Maria looked at him with a fixation and a smile that he couldn't figure out. The image came to him from some time back when they returned from the lawyer's house. And in a sad tone he said, "Shall we go back? It's time."

In no hurry, Maria got up and shook off her clothing. "It was nice here," she mumbled.

Not far from the village they came across Elvas spying on them. That morning in town he had offered them kerosene to purchase and Maria gave him a few *escudos*. There he was now, his chest exposed to the sun, his black beard fluttering in the breeze, leaning insolently against a wall. *He may already have gone to the house to deliver the kerosene*, Maria thought.

On a street in the village they ran into the young ruddy-faced woman who, on the first day, had offered to go fetch water from the fountain. Whenever she encountered Maria she always demanded a few minutes of conversation, generally to air her little discontents. She asked neither for an opinion nor understanding. She just wanted someone to hear her. This time, she had left her soup to burn. But there was no way that such a simple thing could be expressed in but a couple of words. She had to explain it was a bean soup with kale, not forgetting the details of where she got the kale, where she bought the beans, how she lit the fire, how she prepared the broth and what she did while the soup was cooking and what she was doing when the soup got scorched. All that took a certain amount of time.

"Look!" Maria said suddenly, elbowing António. Turned toward them, leaning lazily by the tavern door, Elvas was holding a glass. It almost looked as though he were waiting to be seen before deciding whether to drink or not. Then he disappeared inside, reappearing with another glass, which he also gulped down. Having finished, he wiped his chin with his hairy forearm, sighing noisily.

Maria stopped listening to what the woman was saying. ""Hey, my friend," she claimed, "it looks like you're drinking up our kerosene!"

Right there on the street António couldn't chastise Maria for having given Elvas money. "It certainly isn't kerosene" was all he could say, somberly.

Maria surely did not pick up on his tone because, after Elvas came back to the doorway with a third glass, she forgot the money and found him amusing. "What a character, huh?" And she laughed.

The young woman was still talking a blue streak and wound up her story of the burnt soup. "I never had anything like that happen to me!" she exclaimed. "Disasters, tragedies and affliction, that's all. It is truly worth living like this?" And with that, they said their goodbyes.

Returning to the house, an overheated Maria sat on the edge of the bed, her legs extended, looking at António with that same smile he couldn't decipher.

"It's a shame you're such a sourpuss," she observed. "You have no idea what I'm thinking—."

Various possibilities came to António's mind, but they all seemed so preposterous that he didn't answer and started working.

A few minutes later, raising his eyes from his papers, he saw Maria eyeing him from the door.

"What's up?" he asked.

"I just wanted to see you," Maria said. "You look handsome today."

2

A few days later the comrades arrived early in the morning. Wan and silent, Maria prepared their coffee, and shortly the meeting began.

Forcing himself to overcome his emotions, Paulo began to relate what happened in Vale da Égua. But when he spoke of the death of Manuel Rato's daughter, he couldn't hold back his tears and had to interrupt his story.

Without any comment, Ramos proposed that they continue the discussion on that point later, and that Vaz should take the floor and report on his sector.

Vaz had sought out Marques. Gliding silently through the narrow corridor, the carpenter's mother had led him to her son's room. She looked at him apprehensively for a moment before retiring without further word.

Marques received the comrade with manifest frigidity, and Vaz went directly to the subject. He informed him of what Afonso had said about Meireles and asked Marques a series of questions.

Marques interrupted impatiently. "It's terrible to be so distrusting of comrades. And even worse to handle matters furtively, outside the established organisms. If you have something to say, it's at the Regional Committee that you should say it. And if you want my opinion, I'll tell it to you. This is all about women."

"I wish it were," Vaz said, unruffled. "But it's a serious matter that forces us to be vigilant. I came to see you because you know Vítor better than anyone."

"I know him perfectly," Marques started. "I'll speak with him."

"No, no. I didn't come here so you could go talk to him. That would only tip him off."

The carpenter's eyes shot bullets through his lenses. He let off a dry laugh. "So you mistrust me too?"

"It's not a question of that, comrade. It's only a matter of gathering as much information as we can, before our meeting, about Vítor and Meireles. Later, as you say, it's at the proper body that the issue would be raised."

"We understand things quite differently." By now Marques was shouting excitedly. "If there's something unclear about a comrade's activity, it's with the comrade himself that you should clear it up. To go looking for someone else to dig up information seems more like intrigue and police interrogation. These are not our methods of work. I'm not onboard with you, friend. Don't count on me for this ride."

The questioning thin face of the carpenter's mother appeared at the door.

Vaz stood up and looked directly at the comrade, extending his hand to say goodbye. "Leave it for the meeting, then," he said in his same calm tone, in which one could infer an icy determination.

In the corridor, Marques repeated, "I can talk with him—"

"No, you're not to talk with him, comrade," Vaz cut him off. "It's good this is settled—as an order, or as a decision, however you want. Don't talk with him."

Marques laughed once again, quick and dry. "You command, I obey! Is that the way it is?"

"Those are not the appropriate words, but I'll answer anyway. Yes, it is!" And once again grasping his comrade's hand, he left.

Ramos seemed entertained listening to Vaz. At the end he limited himself to saying, "Very well. Put your cards on the table and then we'll see."

His words indicated approval of Vaz's ideas. But the airy tone with which they were spoken seemed to say, *Let's see if you go looking for wool and it's you who gets sheared.*

Vaz appeared not to notice that tone and returned to the necessity of profoundly reorganizing the regional work, which was now needed because Afonso had left and because of the predictable removal of Vítor. But right away, significant differences of opinion emerged. Ramos proposed that Sagarra join the Regional Committee alongside Marques and Cesário.

Vaz insisted that a solution like that would throw away all the work with the peasants. "That would mean effectively giving Marques control over the peasant sector, which he's long wanted. It would confuse, derail, and even sabotage Sagarra's work. What did we see at the cadres' meeting that I called? Everywhere, under Sagarra's leadership, the peasant struggles and the reorganization of the Party are developing. Only in the sector controlled by the Regional Committee—and it's their own fault—the comrades see everything backward, they're paralyzed, they do practically nothing, to such a degree that the others asked if they had been in Portugal all this time. Marques might be a good comrade. At present, in my opinion, he's a hindrance to the local leadership, and even more to the regional."

"Sounds like you're pissed at him," Ramos remarked.

Vaz did not reply to that observation. They did not reach agreement and decided to return to the problem at a later point in the meeting.

3

More in control now, but still mournful, Paulo recounted his work, and they could then discuss the peasants' struggle in Vale da Égua. As they were now not describing facts, but evaluating them, it was easier to bypass emotions and express opinions. Like the other comrades, Paulo offered his. As much effort as it cost him, however, to consider the facts alone in a political light, there, always in front of him, was Isabel's face, with her braids in an arch, looking at him and smiling upon him. As much as he tried to resist it, a vague sense of responsibility berated him, as if he could have prevented the girl's death, or even that in some way he had contributed to it. So he felt relieved when they finished with this item and moved on to reports about the rest of the sector.

As he did not supervise big organizations, he gave special attention to small events. He reported that in the sawmill, for example, a young cadre had appeared, a young, bony-faced fellow with an unkempt beard and lots of enthusiasm, desirous of more meetings, asking for books, distributing the Party press. He also related how pleased the lawyer was to have Maria in his house and was now always offering whatever was needed.

"In the end," he commented, turning toward Vaz, "he's not as bad as you thought."

"Don't lose this opportunity!" said Ramos, though it was not certain if he was faking the happiness to discharge the heavy atmosphere of the meeting, or if he genuinely was feeling it.

And directing himself to Paulo, he repeated what he had always told him: "You turned the lawyer around, but now the one you won't be able to turn around is the cobbler!" He was referring to the shoemaker who for months had been promising and was always postponing the Local Committee meeting.

He was wrong. Paulo had already turned him around. Paulo had gone up to see him one more time. In his dark cubicle, the shoemaker gestured him to sit on a bench.

"So?" Paulo asked.

"Nothing doing," the shoemaker replied. "These guys don't want to be bothered."

How to get out of this? Paulo wondered. If he, Paulo, spoke with the comrades, maybe he could manage to persuade them. Should he make such a proposal? For some instinctive reason that he would be incapable of explaining, he didn't do that. For the same reason, he felt unable to be sincere with the shoemaker, and words came out of him with no forethought.

"You're right," he agreed. "It's better if we don't think about calling a meeting any more. Keep passing out the paper, help where you can, and that's not so bad."

The shoemaker was visibly pleased by those words. So pleased that for the first time he gave Paulo some specifics about the other comrades. One was a small farmer who, according to him, was only interested in cows and milk. Another worked in a distant factory, leaving early in the morning and returning well into the night, with no time for anything else. Another was a blacksmith, unfortunately so sick his only thoughts were of death.

"Do you hear that?" he asked.

Paulo pricked up his ears. Not far away, he heard the intermittent sound of a mallet pounding iron.

"He doesn't have the energy for much more," the shoemaker commented.

Paulo agreed that under such circumstances, there was little to expect from these comrades. But once again, by the same ill-defined intuition that he himself could not explain, he added that maybe the blacksmith could at least provide an explanation about the placement of the plate on a printing press.

"If you want, I'll ask him," the shoemaker offered.

Paulo answered that it wasn't worth the trouble, but then he suggested the two of them could go over and see him. "You can introduce me and I'll take it from there. It's nearby, and it won't take long."

Skeptically, the shoemaker raised his eyes from his labor. "I can't leave my work." He pointed to his miserable bench and toward the mountain of old shoes.

"It'll just be a minute," Paulo said as he rose.

Annoyed, the shoemaker finally also stood up. "Ask what you want, and we'll come back right away. I can't leave my work for very long, as you can see."

4

Mallet and tongs in hand, the blacksmith barely suspended his labor when they arrived. He was a skinny man dressed in rags, his face covered with grime and lips surprisingly pale.

"Are you alone?" asked the shoemaker, looking into the corners of the shed. The man nodded yes.

"This is a comrade," the shoemaker said, pointing to Paulo.

The blacksmith regarded him indifferently and started beating the glowing iron again.

"Our friend is in a hurry," the shoemaker said after a few moments. "He wants to ask some advice from you."

"It's all right, it can wait," said Paulo. And the idea struck him now, clean and neat: *If I can talk with him, I'll convince him.*

So when the nervous shoemaker remembered he had left his workshop abandoned, Paulo answered him softly. "Go on, I'll see you shortly."

Angrily, the shoemaker stayed. "Our friend is in a hurry. He wants some advice from you," the shoemaker repeated after a while.

The sooty, skeletal arm, its veins filled with a bright blue, stayed in the air for an instant. Out of the black, sooty face, a steady glance turned sideways toward the visitors. And in an unexpectedly thick, majestic voice, which seemingly came out of another body, he rudely fired back, "If he's in a hurry, then he can get on his way."

"Let's go!" said the shoemaker, pulling on Paulo's arm.

"I can wait," said Paulo stubbornly, not feeling hurt by the blacksmith's crude response.

Anxiously eyeing the shed door as if from there he could see the abandoned workshop, the shoemaker still did not leave. He imposed on the blacksmith to interrupt his work and on Paulo to stop waiting. Finally, fed up, he left the shed almost at a run.

Paulo sat down on a large packing crate and waited patiently. Finally the blacksmith turned to him expectantly. Paulo struggled to recall the pretext he had given the shoemaker, and spoke of the need to repair a printing press. Since he knew nothing about the subject, he had trouble saying any more.

"You guys are funny," the blacksmith said, with his mighty bass voice that rolled out of his pallid lips. "When you need them, you seek out your comrades. When you don't need them, you don't even remember they exist. What the Party is even trying to do is beyond me."

Taken aback, Paulo did not immediately understand the import of these words.

The more the blacksmith spoke, the more Paulo's shock. From what the blacksmith said, for a long time the Local Committee comrades were insisting that a Party worker should come. The Party promised and promised, but never sent anyone.

"How can that be?" Paulo asked, stupefied. "The Local Committee refuses to meet, a Party worker comes around month after month and now you say the committee wants to meet, but no one shows up."

Each one held fast to his view. Finally, although neither one believed what the other was saying, they did agree to try a litmus test: They themselves would set the date for a Local Committee meeting.

"And Esteves?" the blacksmith asked. Esteves was the shoemaker. "I'll tell him," Paulo responded.

Which he did, as soon as he returned to the shoemaker's shop. Esteves showed no surprise. He didn't even lift his eyes from his work. He only said, "You are luckier than me. You achieved in one hour what I couldn't in a whole year."

"Where did you acquire such cunning?" Ramos said when Paulo stopped talking.

"The Local Committee meeting is in a week," Paulo answered. "Let's see what comes out of it."

Yes, good work would come out of it, but the mysteries would not end. Paulo would long reflect on it. He would minutely recall words, attitudes and expressions. Finally he would come to a certain conclusion. For months the shoemaker answered to the Party worker saying that the Local Committee members never showed up, and he answered the Local Committee saying that no one from the Party showed up. Many explanations would later be given for this practice. What for years no one knew or even imagined is that the shoemaker acted that way because he had spent the comrades' dues on himself and was afraid it would all come out one day.

5

That morning António acted strangely. With various excuses, every time the discussion of a given topic ended, he asked for a minute's break and left the room for a few moments. Unlike his customary pattern, he asked no questions about any issue, and his comments had been brief and obscure. Ramos began to think António had been affected—discouraged and anxious—by Paulo's report on the struggle in Vale da Égua and the death of Manuel Rato's daughter. Observing him closely, however, he concluded that António was in a good mood and actually was trying to hide it. So when António returned after one of his short absences, Ramos addressed him face to face before they resumed the discussion.

"You make me remember a classmate I had in school. He also would frequently ask to leave the room. You know what the teacher told him one day? *Son, this business of always running out has to stop. If your belly bursts open, I'll reimburse your daddy for the repair, but stop—*"

"You got it wrong!" António interrupted him, his eyes burning lividly.

In fact he did not continue to ask for breaks, although as before, he remained somewhat withdrawn from the conversation.

When the meeting broke for lunch, Ramos and Vaz had already stood up. Rather than showing any rush to go out, António asked that they stay a bit longer.

"What is it?" asked Ramos.

"A matter about cadres that I wish to report," António said with unusual solemnity.

"So urgent it can't wait till later?" Ramos asked.

"I'd prefer to raise it now," António answered.

"All right," Ramos gave in. And they seated themselves again.

"Comrades—" said António, his voice trembling slightly before he went on quickly and flustered. "I wish to communicate to the Party that Comrade Maria is my companion."

If with this declaration António expected an effusive reception from his comrades, he would have reason to be disappointed.

Ramos just shrugged his shoulders. "Okay, now we know," he said. "It's your business."

"G-good," Paulo stammered. "What can I say? Be happy!"

Impassive Vaz said nothing.

"Has the discussion on the matter of cadres concluded?" Ramos asked. "Concluded?" he repeated. "The meeting is adjourned and we proceed to the next point on the agenda—lunch."

Wasting no time, before any of the others, António ran to the kitchen to assist Maria.

6

Turning toward the table with the pan in her hand, Maria placed a big cooked mackerel on each comrade's plate. Then she retrieved a pottery bowl and similarly gave each one a serving of steaming hot potatoes. She moved without speaking, only casting a questioning eye to one and the other. A couple of times she blushed noticing everyone's unusual silence.

Holding a sharp-pointed knife, Ramos quickly cut onion circles. Unlike his usual self, he wasn't joking around. He seemed upset, still immersed in the issues they had just been discussing. Securing the cork to check the flow out of the bottle, Vaz made a controlled circular motion to let out a thin wire of oil. Smiling, and constantly lifting his eyes to follow Maria's movements, António carefully arranged his plate with the fish on one side and the potatoes on the other. Finally, with a sigh, Maria sat down. Only then did she spot Paulo scrutinizing her over the top of his glasses, with a disapproving face.

"It isn't right," Paulo said softly. "You took the smallest one for yourself—."

Without responding, Maria offered Ramos the bottle of vinegar. She had to repeat it three times. As if waking up, Ramos adjusted himself on his chair, energetically rubbed his hands together, took the bottle, sprinkled his potatoes with vinegar and began to speak.

"The mackerel is a great fish," he began. "Bourgeois people don't eat it because, since it's cheap, they see in it a class enemy. But it's fully the equal of any other. The head of a grouper looks as stupid as a banker with a cigar. Just seeing it, you lose your taste for it. Fried fish makes you think of an old lady covered with face powder. Robalo—snook—is tasteless and insipid like some wealthy kid. And red mullet grilled with butter makes you think of a student who greases his hair with vaseline—and saying this, Ramos looked at António as if wisecracking provocatively.

Smiling, with his mouth full, António looked sideways at Maria, admiring her long black eyelashes falling like a curtain. Holding the mackerel's head with his fingers, Paulo sucked on the delicacy. Slowly wiping his mouth with the back of his hand, his face unmoving and his eyes fixed, Vaz observed Ramos. In the way the comrade had begun speaking, with a relative absence of jokes, he missed Ramos's natural spontaneity and guessed he was making an effort to conceal his bad mood.

"Ramos is going to write a book on fish and the class struggle," António remarked with a smile.

"I could do it, old man," Ramos responded. "The existence of class struggle shows itself in everything, even in the most trivial things. Even in the way a mackerel is eaten."

Only then did the comrades notice the bizarre way António was eating. Fork in his left hand, knife in his right, he separated the skin from the flesh as though he were performing a delicate operation. He was not bothered by his comrade's allusion to his class origin and with maliciously twinkling eyes placed another forkful in his mouth. Maria recalled that dinner at the lawyer's house and flushed in disgust. Paulo looked at Ramos reprovingly.

"Where did you buy them? Vaz asked Maria.

Maria answered promptly, to change the conversational direction. Everyone then told their difficulties obtaining foodstuffs, and António related how Elvas wound up with their money for kerosene and went to the tavern to spend it ostentatiously. António bitterly lamented the amount lost. Maria also was bothered by that incident, but she judged it in a different manner.

"It's not so much about the kerosene, nor even the money, dear friends," she said now with disproportionate passion. "It's about trust. Trust. There's nothing that hurts more than when we trust someone and we're duped."

They noticed other changes in the vagabond. Soon after that scene at the tavern, he appeared greatly transformed. He mended, or had someone mend, his miserable shreds of clothing which before looked like he had purposely made that way. And how strange! All buttoned up, his body covered, hair combed, he had lost his arrogant, imposing, insulting demeanor and now seemed small, even more miserable and profoundly destitute. He had begun speaking in an even more extravagant fashion.

"You hear?" he'd shout to the heavens. "Don't forget what I asked for. Tomorrow I want sun in the morning and rain in the afternoon. Don't forget, you hear?"

The meal ended.

"The despair of the afflicted!" Ramos exclaimed, laughing and talking at the same time. "The poor guy feels he's lost the game. That's what it is!" And for the first time making reference to the new situation between Maria and António, he turned to him and added, "And you're the one responsible!"

António laughed heartily. Without a word, Maria rose from the table and left.

7

Lying face down, her head buried in her arms, her black hair tumbling across the pillow, Maria didn't move when Paulo timidly entered the room. Paulo immediately guessed she had been crying. Actually, when he saw her leave the kitchen, he guessed right then that she was about to cry. He stood for a few moments, hesitant and ambivalent, and then gently sat on the edge of the bed as if he were afraid it might not support his weight. Without knowing what he was doing, he posed his stocky hand on the comrade's head and his short, awkward fingers searched amongst the thick hair, for the hard cranium in a protective caress.

"There, there, my friend—" he stumbled for words.

So still it seemed she didn't notice his presence, Maria didn't respond.

Paulo wants to give her a comforting word, but nothing occurs to him. An ill-defined sense of pity, sadness and tenderness overcomes him and, constrained and choked, tangles his words in his throat. "There, there, my friend—" he says again.

Maria breathed deeply. Then, slowly, she sat up gently, nestled herself on the bed and swept her black hair off her face.

The big eyes, long-lashed, moist and reddened, stared sadly at the comrade. Above her knee, her white, shapely thigh could be seen, but she felt no need to adjust her skirt.

"Thanks, dear uncle," she said in a surprisingly composed voice, using the term she had lately adopted for Paulo. "Thanks for coming in."

She placed her delicate hand on her comrade's heavy-set hand and kept it there a few moments, resting naturally.

"I'm so unhappy. So unhappy," she added as she started crying again. "You can't imagine how unhappy I am."

Paulo remained silent. What could he say? He knows only to speak about the struggle and the Party, and what good is that now? "You're young, my friend," finally he said, slowly and with difficulty. "You have many years of life ahead of you. You'll live, you'll realize all your dreams, believe me."

Maria shook her head, disconsolate.

"You'll live. You'll realize all your dreams, believe me," Paulo repeated as if he wanted to convince himself of what he assured her.

They remained silent and motionless for long minutes. Now, with two fingers of one hand, Maria started stroking a finger on her other hand. With her eyelids lowered, her eyes stared at her own gesture.

"Our life is hard—" Paulo finally sighed. After another pause he continued. "So hard that, because we accept it and choose it, some folks consider us special people who like hardship, people cold and indifferent to pain, pleasure and affection, people who act and don't dream."

Surprised, Maria raised her gaze to her comrade. His glasses having slipped, he looked at her directly. He maintained his usual timid, supplicating expression, but in it was now something new and serious that he hadn't shown before. His words came out in a sad, covered breath, as though he had never thought them nor was even thinking them now, as though he hadn't the need to articulate them, as if he was just opening his inside to outside view.

"Many things differentiate the human being," Paulo continued. "Above all, we are different because of our ability to dream. At the genesis of every beautiful thing ever done in history, of everything beautiful that we can do, at the genesis of all achievements and deeds, always—always—we find that marvelous ability to dream. We all dream, friend, all of us. We dream of a better world where some will not live off the suffering of others, where they don't kill children with machine guns, where you can breathe the air of freedom. That's the dream that gives us the strength to struggle and to suffer, to say we are happy in our hard life, even when we lose much of what is most dear to us. But that is not our only dream. We'd be lying to others and to ourselves if we denied dreaming also of our personal happiness, if we didn't yearn for burning love, for children the enemy wouldn't kill, for peace and a minimum of comfort. Our militants give everything, friend, but they should not renounce anything. If we killed our dream, we'd also kill ourselves as the very human beings we are."

Maria looks at her comrade with growing admiration, this man ordinarily so frugal with words and now so eloquent. And what most surprises her are not so much the words she hears but something else, deeply felt, dramatic and passionate that shines through them. Paulo's controlled voice gets softer and softer, now is almost a whisper, but the lower it goes, the more covered, the more uttered in secret, the more intimate elation it reveals.

"Today we have to give everything, all we've got without restrictions or limits, give our lives perhaps, and surely, give things that cost more to sacrifice than life itself. If the struggle robs parents of a beloved daughter, what greater sacrifice can be imposed on them? We have to give it all, friend, without lamenting how much we lose. And believe me, this is easier to say when injury touches us personally than when it touches those to whom we're showing the road to struggle. But it has to be said and has to be felt." And after another pause he added, "We already can see our desired goal shining before us. Some will fall, others will live."

Paulo paused again, sensing he had strayed far from the conversation. He concluded, "You will achieve our dreams. Believe it and trust me."

Finally he stopped, humbly gazing at his comrade. In the contrast between his expression and the conviction of all he had just said, Maria guessed a tremendous, unshakable inner force, that no one had ever revealed to her so vividly. Now she also feels the need to speak. But now it's not about her problems that she needs to speak, but about this man before her about whom, in the end, she knows nothing.

"So, dear uncle, do you have children?" she asked.

"Me?" Paulo asked in surprise, because in everything he had said nothing seemed to involve him personally. "No, I don't have children."

"And do you have a companion?"

"I don't have a companion either."

Maria balked. "And you never had a companion?"

"No, never had a companion."

Maria grabbed her comrade's hand. "Your family?"

"Family? My family is the Party. It's you. It's the comrades. I have no other family."

Maria feels the need to pronounce a word of comfort and speaks with a commanding tone as if to erase the sense of doubt that tinges what she is about to say: "Listen, dear uncle. You too will realize your dreams. You will, believe it."

"Me?" Paulo asked once again. But his voice conveyed not any doubt about the future, for in truth he was not thinking of it, but his shock that Maria would speak in that way.

Vaz appeared at the door. His face implacable, eyes fixed, he appeared not to notice the two comrades' surprising attitude and expression. "We've already washed the dishes," he said calmly. "We have to continue."

8

In António's sector, things were going fast and well. The movement for demands, that the committees led in the shops, came together under the local Party leadership. The number of Party members continued to grow. Manuel Rato, now working in the village, was already connected with other comrades. Despite all the attempts by the fascist union leaders to impede the workers' participation in the elections, despite the provocations in the general assembly, the opposition list was elected, and Gaspar was now president of the union.

"It's even a pleasure to work like this!" commented António, glowing.

Vaz and Paulo asked for some clarifications and expressed their opinion about various aspects of the Party and the ongoing struggles. Given Gaspar's new responsibilities in the union, and the need to protect him, they agreed that Manuel Rato should replace him on the Local Committee. It appeared as though the general discussion was over when Ramos pointedly inquired what was happening with the small groupings and contacts in the sector.

"A person can't go everywhere at the same time," António explained. "I preferred to latch onto the basics and set the ancillary activity aside."

"Poor judgment, friend," said Ramos, as if, expecting precisely that response, he had already prepared his criticism. "The Local

Committee is running smoothly on its own two feet. It doesn't need a lot of help. What's lacking in initiative and support are the smaller Party groups and isolated comrades. That's why they're flailing and aren't making any progress. You should certainly have given more time and attention to those folks. You have no cause to celebrate."

"Maybe you're right," António answered. "Still, it seems to me that the decisive importance of the local organization in the struggles being waged and in the overall progress of work requires the presence and assistance of the Party organizer. It also seems to me that the successes already achieved demonstrate that such presence and assistance were not in vain."

Ramos smiled condescendingly. But he spoke with irritation that, though he tried to control it, in the end controlled him. "With Gaspar, with Pereira, with a Jerónimo and a Manuel Rato, with a well-ordered organization and such dedicated, capable cadres, it would be amazing if they didn't mark progress. It's not hard to show off your good work by the work of others."

Paulo tried to defend António. "I don't fully understand," he said, peering at Ramos over his eyeglasses. "Any number of times, I believe, I heard you express exactly the same view as António—that considering the difficulty of grasping everything, it's best to get ahold of the fundamental thing and put the small stuff to one side."

"And was there difficulty grasping everything?" Ramos broke in. It was clear he was trying to justify some reasoning that he felt slipping away. And the effort to do so showed the more excitable he got.

His arms crossed, his face long and angular, pale and composed, his eyes placidly taking in both of his comrades, Vaz did not enter the argument. It was only when a confused António recognized his fault that Vaz calmly said, "Proceed with your work happily, comrade. Try to strengthen the other contacts, as Ramos says, but also continue to help the local organization the best you can. Right now that is very necessary."

Turning his head toward Vaz, annoyed and almost aggressively, Ramos faced his steady gaze. "We'll come back to this subject," he said in a threatening and wholly disproportionate tone.

"Yes, we will," Vaz replied, not altering his position.

9

Late that night, when they concluded their meeting, they pushed the table to one corner, placed the bed against the wall and spread the straw mattresses on the floor. Paulo sat down and started taking off his shoes. By the light of an oil lamp, a white, freckled foot emerged, heavy as a mallet. Vaz carefully folded his trousers. Yawning loudly, Ramos hung his jacket on the back of a chair and, after placing a bullet in its chamber, placed his pistol on the floor next to the wall. António's voice then came to them, friendly and contented: "Sleep well, comrades."

They looked at him. António stood at the door, his left hand on the latch and his right holding an oil lamp. He was smiling. His little black mustache accentuated his youthfulness. An expression of complete happiness shone from his eyes. "Sleep well," he repeated.

Only at that point did the other three seem to understand what perhaps they had already forgotten. António would not remain there on the improvised bunks like the other times. Now he had his own room and his companion waiting.

"Good night," Vaz answered.

Curved over, Paulo took a few more moments to remove his other sock. Only then did his eyes appear through his glasses and between strands of his white hair. "Good night," he said quietly.

"Sleep well," a smiling António repeated once more.

"Sweet dreams, sweet dreams!" Ramos called out without turning around. In his blue flannel long johns, with his shirttails hanging out, he feebly searched out his tobacco amongst his papers.

António disappeared down the corridor.

With slow, deliberate movements, as though he were performing a chore, Vaz covered himself up to his ears with the blankets.

Making heavy footfall on the floor, Ramos got up to go to the kitchen to drink water. Paulo heard him collide against a bench, the porringer hitting the heavy earthen jug, and the gurgling of water running down his throat. Then he saw him return, noisily wiping his mouth on the back of his hand and heading toward the table, where he started fussing with his papers without seeing what he was looking for. He adjusted the flame on the oil lamp, carefully folded a newspaper, scratched his right foot, and then started rolling a cigarette, spilling so much tobacco onto the paper that he had to remove some of it and return it to the pack. He lit the cigarette with a turn of the wheel on the cigarette lighter, and inhaled two drafts in a row. Finally he returned to the bunks. But before Ramos blew out the oil lamp, Paulo saw that he had placed his tobacco and lighter underneath the pile of newspapers that served as his pillow. Then, heavily and boisterously, he slumped onto the straw mattress next to Paulo, remaining with his back against the wall. The red glow from the cigarette diffused through the room. For a moment, a corner of the table, the legs of a chair and the iron bed which, seen from below and without the mattress, resembled the skeleton of a prehistoric animal.

Through the night silence, Paulo heard low, broken voices in the other room. When he fell asleep quite a bit later, Ramos was smoking again.

10

António undressed in silence, not losing sight of Maria's figure, her back toward him, her black hair splayed across the white pillow. Underneath the cover, he made out the body at once so delicate and brimming inner frayed chemise. For the first time in his life, António knew, in Maria, the beauty of a woman as only complete intimacy could reveal. Like other students, he had frequented houses of prostitution and he had had casual relations with a servant in his home. All that seemed nauseating and almost monstrous to him now. Maria was truly the first woman he knew. And how beautiful she was! Never, never in his youthful imagination had he believed a woman could be so lovely. Not only in form, but in the softness and heat of her skin, in her poses and movements, in that certain allure that called him, that grabbed him, that made him think he would never desire any other and never would stop desiring her.

António entered the underground life prepared for sacrifices and thinking only of sacrifices. At the time, he figured that the struggle itself would grant him happiness. He never dreamed that such a life would bring him a different and unexpected joy. Now he desired nothing more in life, truly nothing more. He had the struggle and the Party and he had that beloved young woman there, tucked under the blanket, who would shortly be nestled in his arms.

"Maria," he murmured softly into her nape, his hand poised on her tender, sculptured shoulder. "Are you sleeping?" She didn't respond or even stir.

"Maria," he repeated. Surely she was in a deep slumber, because generally she awakened readily. But strangely enough, instead of her usual deep breathing, rhythmic and gentle, she now seemed gripped by absolute immobility.

"Maria," he whispered for the third time, now a little concerned.

He was getting ready to shake her when she spoke. "What do you want?" she said in a tone so calm and clear that it was obvious she had not been asleep and was completely alert. Her inflection and her attitude were out of character.

Appearing not to have noticed that, getting into bed, António cuddled her hungrily. Still with her back to him, inert and stoic, Maria allowed him to embrace her. But when António sought to turn her around, Maria spoke again, now imploring and distressed. "Leave me alone, *amiguinho*, leave me alone."

"What's the matter? Don't you feel well?"

"Nothing's the matter, my friend, just stop."

"What do you mean nothing's the matter? Are you sick?"

Maria didn't answer. Once again António wrapped her in his arms, now tenderly, inclined against her shoulder, whispering sweet nothings into her ear. Unmoving and not reacting at all, once again she accepted his caresses. But as António continued, she shook him off with an ill-tempered, brusque shove. "Leave me alone, I told you!"

"What's wrong? What's going on?" he pressed further.

Maria broke free of him in an exasperated rebuff. "Leave me alone, don't you hear?" Although she contained her voice, it was rough and disagreeable, such as he had never heard.

He lay beside her, hurt and infinitely sad, with one arm still entwined with his companion. But with a gruff, unforgiving hand, she removed his arm from her and then separated herself from even the most minimal contact between their two bodies.

In the other room, one of the comrades began to snore.

11

Maria bundled the pot in newspaper so the rice wouldn't get cold and, reading by the oil lamp light, waited patiently for the meeting, which had gone on all day, to end. Finally, it was already night when she heard the scrape of chairs and the comrades appeared. She noticed an expression at once serious and satisfied on all of them, and concluded from it that some important decision had been reached and that they were feeling confident about it. She was not wrong. It had been decided to prepare for a strike in the region in the very near future. Everyone understood that such a decision corresponded to positive conditions as a result of their work, and everyone saw in it the very reason for the Party to undertake its activity. They all felt the new responsibilities and all shared the clear idea that from there, from that humble house, from that small group comprising four exhausted, persecuted men hunted down as if they were wild animals, would emerge the first impulse that would lead thousands of workers into the struggle.

After their meager meal, they remained to shoot the breeze some more, since they couldn't really leave until dawn. António, after what had happened the night before, was less expansive than usual.

From time to time, looking in Maria's direction, a cloud of apprehension and sorrow darkened his face. Later, seeing her in a good mood, speaking with gusto and turning toward him lovingly and attentively, he became a little more relaxed.

Ramos seemed to be touched by the same aura of amiability that had affected all of them that night. Avoiding his snide jokes and impertinent allusions, he showed special friendliness toward Maria and António, as though he wanted to compensate them for some harm he had done them.

The conversation flowed and circled spontaneously. At a certain point they spoke about age. They admired how young Ramos seemed and asked how old he was.

"As old as I look," he answered with a chuckle.

Paulo noticed Maria looking at him. He guessed she was comparing his awkward, ponderous, aging affect to Ramos's vigor and visible boyishness, although Ramos was in fact a few years older. He guessed that someone would also ask his age. A response came to mind and at the moment he thought it would be clever: *Young enough to love the struggle, old enough to not fear death.* When Maria actually did pose the question, that response struck him as possibly arrogant, pretentious and ridiculous.

"Forty-nine," he answered, flushing lightly, not because he felt it a crime to be that age, but because he felt it as a failure on his part to have arrived at that age without having realized any of his personal aspirations in life.

From Ramos, ordinarily, some kind of witticism could be expected, even if deprecating. That night, he spoke in another mood. "Looking at him there," he addressed Maria, "you'd never know the quality of that man. You'd never be able to imagine what our comrade is capable of."

And he told about Paulo's audacious escape some years back. He sawed jail bars, walked across a drainspout suspended across the façade some fifteen meters off the ground, let himself down to the street on a rope of sheets and, refusing to halt when a guard ordered him to, fled under fire.

Surprised, Maria looked closely at Paulo's reddening face, the white wisps of hair on his head, the imploring gaze toward Ramos.

"Weren't you afraid of dying?" she asked in wonder.

Afraid of dying? Paulo's eyes repeated the phrase. That same answer came back to mind: *I'm young enough to love the struggle, old enough to not fear death.* But he sat there embarrassed, not knowing what to say.

It was Ramos who answered for him: "If he was afraid of dying he wouldn't still be alive!"

On Vaz's long, angular face, always so serious and impassive, a wide smile opened up, showing his white, beveled teeth.

"It's a shame you laugh so little," Maria told him. "A laugh looks good on you, you know?"

Chapter XI

1

Conceição asked António into the kitchen and told him, smiling, "He won't be long. He went to take care of something but he'll be right back."

Approaching the wicker basket sitting on the floor, she looked inside and once again looked at António with a happy smile. "Go look."

So he did. To be civil, not out of interest. Babies of that age were not of interest to him. When they were still in other people's arms he found a certain charm in them. But if they screamed or fussed, honestly, he didn't have the patience. Lowering himself over the basket and holding out his hand toward the sleeping boy, he took hold of the most solid thing he found: a medal attached to a fine chain. He fingered the medal as if he might have touched a ringlet of hair, an ear or a tiny hand.

Conceição interpreted his gesture in her own way. "Does it seem bad to you?" she asked.

"No, friend. You're the mother," António answered, pursuing the thread of his thinking, and assuming that Conceição was asking if it seemed bad to indulge in such enchantment with little beings with no graces.

"Vaz was here the other day and I asked him what I just asked you. And he told me, *No, friend, everyone has their belief. We don't believe in those things, but if you do, we respect your belief.* Those were the exact words he said, I memorized them well. What do you want? I like having the boy wear a medal around his neck. I think he's more protected that way."

Only then did António get what Conceição was referring to. He let go of the medal. "Anyway, friend, that's your belief, right? You well know we don't judge you for that."

The words were respectful but, on saying them, a naughty smile glinted from his wrinkled eyes.

Conceição slowly adjusted the side combs on the bun that gathered up her voluminous head of black hair. Now she stared at the boy with a grave, melancholy expression. "You asked if that's my belief. Yes, it's my belief. But you know? I feel my belief is not as strong as it once was, and that thought gives me no peace. I've learned many things from you folks, and what before were great mysteries for me, where I only saw the power of God, are now simple facts of nature and the simple lives of human beings, and the glory of God has nothing to do with it."

She crossed her weighty arms across her bosom. "Just now we were talking about the medal, and I told you I felt my boy more protected with it. Before, I would have surrendered protection of my child over to God. And now I trust more in cleanliness, in baths, fresh air, and all those things my companion talks to me about and explains. God forgive me for what I've just said," she added, shocked by her own words.

António listened quietly. He accepted and followed the direction of the Party but, when it came to speaking about religious subjects, he could barely conceal his complacent or even ironic attitude.

"I still pray," Conceição went on. Bending over the basket, she straightened her son's clothing. Once again, as she paused in her talking, that tender, caressing expression spread across her face that only mothers have for their little babies. "I still pray. I ask God to watch over my son and my companion, to defend the freedom of the comrades, that he allow our movement to triumph, and that he protect the Party."

She stopped there, with a satisfied smile of victory that seemed to say: *If God comes to our side, isn't that important?*

"If we work hard," António said with a smirk, "he will surely listen to your plea."

"He will, won't he?" Conceição's voice was ecstatic.

At that moment, steps were heard at the door, and immediately Pereira entered, swinging jauntily. "Everything is ready," he said, vigorously shaking António's hand, without any other formalities. "It'll be smooth sailing."

Hearing Pereira's warm, enthusiastic voice, António felt shocked by his cold green eyes popping nervously out of his skin darkened by the air and sun.

"Is it right away?"

"Have lunch with us first," Pereira answered him. "There's time."

2

The meeting took place in Jerónimo's little roadside house just out-side of town. Under the shade of the grape leaves in the back, they placed a table, and on it a bottle of wine and several glasses, not so much to drink but to justify their presence on a late April afternoon with a bright sun and no breeze.

The owner of the house had a sizable family. Sons and daugh-ters of all ages, at the windows and doorway, circling up and down the street and through the surrounding fields, were assigned to run and warn their father in case someone suspicious or simply some visitor appeared. One nine-year-old boy was propped a few meters away from the table where the men were meeting. Seated on the ground, not moving and with his face in a scowl, he remained there the whole afternoon. When the father told him, two or three times, that he should get up and join his siblings, the boy only shrugged his shoulders. When his mother wanted to pull him away, he threw her off him angrily. Even when his favorite bird, a warbler, all black with a red cone, arrived with its uniquely disorderly flight pattern and landed on the highest branch of a bush, he hardly looked at it.

Aside from Pereira, who had come with him, and Gaspar and Jerónimo, António met Túlio there, from Gaspar's factory, and an unfamiliar comrade who looked younger than thirty. His blond hair cut short and stiff like a brush gave him a military look. Antó-nio mistook him at first for Manuel Rato, whom he hadn't met yet, because it had been agreed that he would come to the meeting. But the comrades introduced him as "Vicente." He did not belong to the Local Committee but was responsible for one of the biggest factor-ies and belonged to the Coordination Committee of the workers' movement.

"We had agreed on something else," António said.

The comrades looked at one another. "Speak," Gaspar said to Pereira, "you speak."

"Yes, we had agreed on something else," Pereira said confidently. "But, thinking it through, we saw it was too early to substitute Gas-par, especially at this moment. Besides that, Comrade Rato has done a few things, for sure, but he's still new in the area and we don't know him well enough to bring him onto the Local Committee so soon."

António spoke of the importance of Gaspar's work in the union leadership, the legal nature of that work that counseled against his participation in the clandestine work of the Local Committee. And as for Manuel Rato, he remembered that the information about his virtues came from the Party leadership, and about the positive work he'd recently done from the Local Committee itself.

"Yes, it looks that way to me too," Jerónimo sighed, glancing at his son with tired eyes. "But the comrades are of another opinion."

Túlio spoke up: "If Comrade Gaspar leaves us, what are we gonna do? He's the one with his hands on the wheel, not us. Besides, he's Gaspar, after all."

Gaspar said little, but António got the impression that it was his influence behind the others' opinions. In fact that was the case. Gaspar believed he should stay on the Local Committee and only out of modesty refrained from expressing his thought. At heart he was convinced that without him the Local Committee could not fulfill its tasks and all its work would suffer for it.

"It'd be best," he ended saying, "to put that off until after the movement."

"That's precisely what we wanted to avoid," António insisted. "The movement is one of the reasons for Gaspar to leave the Local Committee."

António did not succeed. He could not or did not wish to impose his view, and the question was decided according to the Local Committee.

Everyone then recounted the magnificent attitude of the workers toward the struggle, the sharpening of the movement in progress, and not only the possibility but the necessity to heighten the struggle, independently of what was happening in the rest of the region.

"If the Party doesn't speak up at the right time," said Vicente, "the working class will move ahead of the Party." And he told how in one section of the factory there had been a spontaneous work stoppage for half an hour, despite the opinion and intervention of the comrades in that very section.

"In that case we were trailing behind," Vicente continued. "And it was a warning of what could happen throughout the factory. The workers want to fight. Our job is to place ourselves at the fore, not at the rear, and guide them and show them the path."

"The comrade is too optimistic about his factory," Gaspar explained, turning to António. And he went on to relate what was happening at Cicol with the workers: The movement he personally led was truly important. But the tone of his words left no room for doubt that he considered the importance of his work by comparison to the relative insignificance of other comrades' work. His evenly modulated voice and fluent speech underlined his facts. His whole speech said, *Isn't it self-evident?* In the insistence with which he described his personal role in the movement, in the careful way he emphasized his own experiences at work as a kind of apprenticeship for the other comrades, one could read a deep satisfaction with himself.

Túlio nodded affirmatively. Pereira corroborated with a short phrase every so often. Vicente listened with all ears, his hand supported on top of his hair as if he wanted to control it. Only Jerónimo seemed distracted, watching his son and extending his lower lip.

3

The argument heated up when it came to the composition of the Strike Committee and Gaspar's participation. António again cited the incongruence of his participation given his work in the union and the fact that he was so well known to so many people. Gaspar did not agree to be put aside. He recalled that he had been the spark behind the first big movement for demands in the area, that at Cicol he had led the communists' and workers' activity step by step down to every detail, that all the union work that ended with the election of an honest leadership that he chaired had happened on his initiative, that it was he who first observed the sharpening of the struggle and the potential for a work stoppage; and he felt that if he were removed from effective, direct and constant leadership of the movement, the other comrades would not be prepared to assure success. For all this he ferociously opposed António's opinion.

Pereira and Túlio supported Gaspar; Jerónimo and Vicente supported António. But after a long discussion, Vicente came around to support Gaspar and they wound up agreeing that the Strike Committee should remain in its present hands, that is, of the Local Committee plus Túlio and Vicente. Seeing himself incapable of convincing his comrades of the higher directives he was conveying, and lacking the arguments, while himself frequently swayed by the others' arguments, António refrained from proposed that Manuel Rato become a member of the Strike Committee, despite the recommendation of the Party leadership. He found himself before a nucleus of capable, active comrades, all industrial workers with ties to the masses, with more experience than he had and, little by little, he reduced his intervention and role in the discussion. The effective leadership of the meeting shifted to Gaspar.

"Cicol is the key industry around here," Gaspar said, referring to his own factory after explosively unsealing his lips, as though it had been like pulling teeth to get him to speak. "It's the most important factory, not only in terms of production but because of the number of workers. That's where we have the cell with the most members, and committees with the most experience for labor unity and union work. In my view, the call for a strike should be made by Cicol. Cicol is to be the first to call a stoppage. In the other places, workers won't initiate anything, but they'll wait for Cicol to stop and as soon as they stop, they will too."

"And if Cicol doesn't stop?" Vicente asked.

"It will stop, for sure," Gaspar said, challenging the impertinence with a severe look of disdain. "If we're unable to stop Cicol, we won't be able to stop anything."

Jerónimo kept his silence, sticking his lower lip out scornfully.

"Gaspar is right," Pereira said excitedly. "You just have to look at the cell at Cicol. We have 24 comrades and they distribute 52 copies of *Avante!* While at Vicente's factory there's just seven comrades who distribute 20 papers. In mine there's only six comrades and we pass out 15 papers. And in public construction, where Jerónimo works, there's nine comrades who pass out only 12 papers."

"Comrade Rato says he's recruited four more comrades," Jerónimo interrupted, the whole time watching his quiet little boy on the ground, "and he needs ten more papers."

"Good," Pereira continued. "That's not everything in public construction, but whatever, the difference is still very big in relation to Cicol. Just Cicol alone has almost as many Party members as the rest of the district and hands out as many papers as all the others."

Visibly contented for having demonstrated his perfect familiarity with the organization, Pereira looked around at each of the other comrades, with his cold green eyes that so contrasted with the warmth and enthusiasm in his voice.

Vicente din't give up. He stroked the brush of his haircut and insisted, "We are, in fact, only seven in my factory. But we have a good Unity Committee—and it is really a Unity Committee. That is, not just Party members who take part in it, but honest non-party workers, and it carries a lot of influence in the workplace. There are also women and youth in it. Similar committees exist in every department. The factory has 280 workers, and 34 of them are part of the committees. After the spontaneous work stoppage that I told you about, when we discussed the incident, those workers agreed that, with the proper preparation for it, they'd do a work stoppage throughout the whole factory. We can form a strike committee not only of comrades, but with non-party workers too, which is good not only for broader influence but for the security of our organization.

In that sense, I believe, we are not behind Cicol. Even if Cicol didn't strike, we would."

"You certainly won't have any need to prove it," said Gaspar with a smile. "But if Cicol unfortunately doesn't strike, then we'll see."

"We'll see!" Vicente responded coldly. The stern face beneath the blond brush hair took on a rigid, hostile look, as though he were threatening an enemy.

Gaspar still had more to say about the role of his factory. Just as he understood that it should be Cicol to sound the call for a local strike, he also saw the local strike as the call for the regional movement. But on this point Gaspar's opinion went so far against what had been discussed with Ramos, Vaz and Paulo that António countered it with a forcefulness he had not shown since the start of the meeting. The more he spoke, the more he sensed that he owed that forcefulness to the decisive way Vicente, just the guy responsible for his cell, presented himself before better known and more highly placed comrades, defending his ideas openly and strongly.

"We're talking about a regional movement, comrades," António concluded. "The date and the moment have to be decided on a higher level, also on a regional level, not on a local level."

Gaspar replied that, without the timing chosen and decided there in the region, and particularly not at Cicol, in that case he would not be answerable for what might happen. "Ask Pereira, or Jerónimo, or Túlio," he said, without naming Vicente in his support. "You'll see they share my opinion."

But they didn't. "No," said Pereira, "I don't see things the way Comrade Gaspar sees them. I'm sorry," and he turned toward Gaspar, "but I just don't see it. We do need to proceed at the proper time. But given the importance of the regional movement and especially the farmworkers' action, I think we can organize things so we can declare a strike when it's been decided on a higher level."

"Of course we can!" Vicente said in support.

Jerónimo also expressed support for Pereira. Túlio paused, and with a flushed face, looking at Gaspar, softly said, "I also think things should be coordinated and be left to the comrades at a higher level to set the date. Though obviously Comrade Gaspar also knows very well what he's saying."

During these statements, Gaspar's face indicated, by the obvious expression of annoyance and the way he was anxiously biting his lips, his displeasure at not being supported by any comrade on this point. It looked like a new and unexpected phenomenon for him.

"Then I wash my hands of it," he concluded. "If the move-ment flops, it won't be that I didn't point out the danger." His ears grew red and his eyes filmed over. He suddenly seemed sad and offended.

4

The meeting took place on a mountain situated on a high plain bris-tling with broom and gorse, whose bright golden yellow flowers glowed in the hot sheet of the sun. All that could be seen there were the wild brush and the pure blue sky. From time to time, someone got up to take a walk around the area, peering into the slopes of all the mountains around, returning silently to rejoin the others. Directly exposed to the broiling sun, the men sweated.

The peasants explained how the landowners were refusing to pay the required daily rates. In various marketplaces the National Guard had appeared, trying to intimidate the workers with their presence. Nevertheless, the moment was favorable to the rural wage workers. If they stayed united and solid, the owners would finally give in. Here and there, faint signs appeared of conflicts, delays in finishing work and postponements in beginning it, tardiness in the market. The lack of foodstuffs was becoming more aggravated—sometimes so scarce that despite the meager wages, even at price control rates, there wasn't enough to spend it on. Everything turned up on the black market, but there you could spend a week's wages for what you needed just that day.

"I've been saying this for a long time," said Alfredo, "and Com-rades Vaz and Belmiro will recall I said it at the other meeting. If we don't force them to bring more bread and food to market, us fighting for better wages is of little use."

Everyone was agreed on the need and possibility of a work stop-page in the fields for one or two days, pulling the population out to march on the two towns in the region, joining up with the striking workers and demanding bread and food from the authorities. What they needed was to set the day.

"People will come out, yes, they'll certainly go," said the peasant from under the shade of his big hat—he had also attended the meet-ing in Tomé's hayloft. "But if we just show up and say 'Now' they won't come out, they certainly won't."

He looked about and rather enjoyed the surprise over his appar-ently contradictory opinion, adding, in his fine, smooth voice, "In my area that's the way it is."

"Let the comrade tell us," someone proposed.

"The day? I can't tell you now," Vaz explained. "We need to coordinate it with the factories. What I would ask of the comrades is, if the set day is communicated to you one week before, if that's enough."

Everyone said yes, some verbally, others silently nodding their heads.

"Are you sure?" Vaz insisted.

"Our word is our word," said a thin old man, his face shining with sweat.

"You don't have to keep asking," da Barrosa muttered.

The issue could have been considered settled, when Sagarra spoke up. He squeezed one hand with the other and his voice trembled when he first began speaking. But the ideas came out as clear and pure as his blue eyes that he raised toward the comrades and lit up his whole freckled, dark, wrinkled face.

"We can't just leave it at that," he started in his nasal voice. "For us, all days are not the same. If, for example, the comrades order a strike on a Thursday or Friday, for what demand are people going to leave their work when it's the end of the week they already contracted on Monday?"

"That, my friend," said a young peasant sitting next to him, "is up to the person—if they want to, they will, if they don't want to, they won't."

"The best day is a Monday," Sagarra went on. "Monday is the market day, and then if the owners don't pay the required wage—and they surely won't, as they haven't been doing—that's when we walk out. On Tuesday or Wednesday they'll be forced to raise the wage because they won't have workers for the week, and we're in the season now when the fields can't wait."

"Right," many agreed. "Monday is best."

Vaz then remembered what the workers had told him the day before at a ceramics factory. *The worst day is Monday,* they said. *'Cause Sunday is too late to properly prepare the people, and from Saturday to Monday a lot of people would cool off.*

"Comrades," Vaz said, "for you Monday is the best day of the week, but for the factories it's the worst. We have to work together the best way possible. So I ask you, What if it was some other day? Could we count on people to leave their work?"

"If it was agreed that the best day is Monday, and if Comrade Belmiro already clearly showed why, why are we now asking if it could be some other day?" da Barrosa asked, shrugging his shoulders and turning to face everyone one by one.

"When the comrades say to strike, that's when we strike," said the thin old guy.

"Sure, you can strike," said the peasant with the big hat. "But think about it. If it's Monday, it's the labor market day. Everyone is all together—they'll make the strike at the market because the owners won't pay what you ask. If it's any other day, people are out in the fields, scattered here and there. Those who were contracted for the week have to find the owner or the manager and make a new demand about their wage, saying they want more. So almost certainly, some will stop work, but not all will."

"Exactly," Sagarra confirmed.

One dark strapping boy with his shirt open got up to do the rounds searching the surroundings. The conversation came to a halt and everyone shifted position, looking at the blue sky and the sunlight and then blinking as if seeking the shade of a tree they well knew didn't exist.

Seen from below, the mountain looked naked and even drier. In that sun, the last thing anyone would be looking for would be human beings.

5

As for the business with Vítor, it had been decided to put all the cards on the table. But this wasn't possible. Marques explained that Vítor had to leave the city, called to his village by his dying mother. He had asked for leave from his job and expected to be away about a month.

The problem of Vítor's participation in the Regional Committee's work was thus simplified. Vaz sensed, uncomfortably however, that once again Vítor had escaped through his fingers like an eel. Every time Vaz believed he had finally been able to uncover Vítor's true character, by one fluke or another he watched as Vítor got away. Now he felt particularly disturbed because he remembered his conversation with Marques, at whose insistence he would personally reveal to Vítor the incident of the conversation at the cheap café door with an unknown person who, contrary to what Vítor had said, was now known not to be Meireles. Vaz could not dismiss his suspicion that Marques was somehow implicated in Vítor's sudden departure.

"Did you talk with him?" Vaz asked.

"What are you implying by that?" an irritated Marques responded, not to the words but to the thinking he imagined. "If there's something you need to say, say it."

"Nothing," Vaz answered calmly, though a hint of emotion could be noted. "Just that you could have found this out talking personally with him or his having sent you a message."

"No, he didn't send a message. He came to my house to tell me."

Sure, sure. Two and two add up to four, Vaz thought. *You went and told him the suspicions about him, and right away he invented that story about his mother being sick.*

With Vítor absent, together with Afonso's departure, what was a Regional Committee—and what was regional about it was now only the name—was now reduced to two comrades, Marques and Cesário, and required urgent reconstitution. Even before Vaz broached the issue, Marques spoke up about it. The proposal he offered was another surprise.

"You've often referred to the fine qualities of Comrade José Sagarra. I admit that at first I didn't think much of those qualities, but fortunately I was wrong. I believe the best solution for the Regional Committee, as it enters a new phase of truly regional work, and giving due importance to the peasant organizations, would be to bring José Sagarra onto the Regional Committee. As I make this proposal I feel certain that it conforms with the views you have expressed so many times."

Marques's intelligent eyes observed Vaz from behind his thick lenses and seemed to say, *This time we're in agreement, eh?* No reaction appeared on Vaz's face. Staring at his comrade, he held his tongue for some time. He recalled that Ramos had made the same suggestion and on the same basis. However, he could not tell Marques what he had told Ramos: That he had changed his opinion because he no longer viewed Marques as he had seen him before, and because he now believed Marques to be a hindrance in the local leadership, and even more so the regional.

"The issue now," he said at last, "is to constitute a Local Committee that without losing any time will study the possibilities of struggle in the city, in coordination with the regional movement. The peasant sector is prepared and has its own organisms. It's not the right time to place it under the direction of a Regional Committee put together in a hurry."

Taking note of Marques's contrary, disaffected nature that he knew so well, Vaz thought to himself, *The fewer words, the better. Not worth casting pearls before swine.*

"As far as the local organism is concerned," he continued quickly and drily, "I have higher instructions as to its constitution. You two will remain, plus Comrade Henriques."

On hearing these words, Marques broke out in a mocking laugh. And Vaz remembered absolutely the same outburst that he had heard a few months before, when in the Regional Committee meeting he said he was bearing directives to speak with José Sagarra.

"Like it or not," Vaz continued, his voice even drier and more aus-
tere. "Like it or not, that's how it'll be constituted."

Marques's eyes shot through his lenses, but he was still laughing
when he said, "Bad system of work, friend, bad system. How can
the higher-up comrades resolve issues of local cadres without hearing the concerned local comrades themselves? This looks like it's got
Cesário's fingerprints," he added, turning to Cesário and laughing
as though to excuse his jibe.

Cesário's face flushed, but he answered with control. "You know
as well as I do that Henriques is a serious, trustworthy man, and no
one here in the city has done better work than him. Vaz didn't talk
with me about including Henriques, but I'd like to say my opinion
is in favor. It's a good choice. I don't know anyone better in the city."
And after a pause as he crossed his brown arms, he added, "I don't
know any better, among the men—"

Marques moved his lips getting ready to make some comment
on Cesário's last statement. Cesário thought he guessed what he
would ask: *And which woman are you talking about now?* But Marques
went another way. Still laughing, a deceptive laugh to disguise
his deep anger and the potential for a sudden explosion of fury,
he placed his pencil behind his ear and said, "Come! Let Henriques come! We'll have a Regional Committee you can tip your
hat to!"

"It's not about the Regional Committee, comrade," said Vaz.
"Henriques, in my view, would be good on the Regional Committee, but that's not what this is about now. It's about the organism
that can immediately confront and lead the movement here in the
city."

"And what movement is that, if I may dare to ask?"

"Dealing with you takes a lot of patience," Vaz answered. "But
rest assured, we'll do it."

Once more he reviewed the movement in preparation, which
Marques knew perfectly well about, and the need to win support
for it in the city. Cesário indicated his agreement. In his opinion, in
Henriques's shop as well as in the jute factory the conditions were
ripe for a small work stoppage. When he spoke of the Jute, Marques
shot him a quick, amused look, and though he didn't say anything,
Cesário figured he was thinking, *That woman, huh?*

"We're going to destroy the little we have," said Marques darkly.

At Vaz's urging that he elaborate further on this thought, Marques
said only, "The leadership decided it, isn't that true? So, it will be
done. I know what discipline is."

6

Paulo made the rounds throughout his sector. Now he was aware of the criteria which determined the distribution of responsibility for the organizations after he and António had gone to work with Vaz. Vaz rightly kept a few of the most important ones. But while António had been given developed organizations with many comrades and movements on the go, he, Paulo, had only been given isolated contacts without broad horizons. In the preparation stage of the movement this had become clear. While Vaz and António work feverishly and anticipate strikes and demonstrations, he, Paulo, much as he tries, could secure nothing but a vague promise of work suspension at a sawmill and a tentative gathering in front of the City Hall in one town. But what could he do with the lawyer, or with the local committee that was now meeting secretly from the shoemaker, its former leader, or with Zé Cavalinho, or with various other contacts with artisans, employees and small businessmen? What could he do if, in his sector, there were hardly any factories or rural proletarians?

His hope is the sawing factory, the only industrial cell in the sector he controls. If at least the comrades there could respond to the regional struggle.

The young thin-faced comrade with the scraggly, unkempt beard led him silently to a slope in the pine forest. Meeting there were six members of the Unity Committee, of whom only two were Party members. He introduced Paulo as a worker from another locale, and Paulo informed them about the preparations for the regional day of action.

"Regional unity," he concluded, "will give greater power to our demands and will make it easier later to continue the separate struggles in each place and enterprise."

The workers asked a number of questions, and Paulo answered cautiously. It was understood he would not present himself as a Communist because in the young man's opinion, if the factory workers smelled the Party, they were capable of running away in shock. One of those present, a lame guy, asked an embarrassing question: "And what role is the Communist Party playing in all this?"

The query was all the more embarrassing insofar as Paulo for sure only knew the young man who had brought him there, didn't even know which one was the other Party member, and couldn't know from the others who weren't Party members what their attitudes were in relation to it.

Paulo hesitated. "That's not what I came to discuss with you, friends," he said finally. "The issue is to prepare for a strike in the region. That is why I came here to talk with you."

"That's fine," said another, wearing a yellow corduroy cap over his eyes. "Fine. But who is leading the movement? Certainly someone is leading it?"

From the way the two men pose their questions, Paulo sees they are not Party members and, warned in advance by the young man, he guesses at some lack of trust around the explanation given for his presence there, and even hostility toward the Party. This thought was reinforced by the young man's response.

"These questions are of secondary interest," he said. "What's important is that we've fought in our factory, obtained some success, and that we now face the need to suspend work if things continue as they've been going. Preparing, as is being done now, a movement in other locales, it's in our interest to go forward with our own. Isn't that right? What importance is there of the role of the Communist Party?"

"Maybe none for you," said the lame man. "But for me, yes." He adjusted his crutch, filling his jowls with air with an indignant face as his eyes searched the other friends for their approval.

Paulo began feeling in an awkward position. And in truth he was, but for reasons opposite to what he assumed. The young man had implanted the idea that introducing himself as a Communist could shock or drive away the non-Party workers who formed part of the committee. In fact, the workers wanted to verify the leadership of the Party as a guarantee of seriousness and success.

"Just so there's no confusion," said the corduroy cap, "I want to express my opinion. If it's the Party guiding and leading the regional struggle, I think we should join the struggle. Otherwise, the best we can do is continue our own fight here with no other help."

The lame man vigorously nodded his head as a sign of approval.

"You told it like a preacher," a third one said, short and fat with the wide smile of a child.

Paulo eyed each one of them in turn above his tortoise shell glasses. "All right, comrades, I see we can speak like men."

7

Ramos met Vaz on an empty, open, dusty road. They continued on to Vaz's house, arriving at nightfall. Miss Ermelinda, hearing footsteps, came outside to have a look.

"Good evening, Ermelindinha"—Ramos always called her by that endearing diminutive in a combination of friendliness and joking that she greatly appreciated. "How's the health? How are you doing?"

Her mind at ease, as always whenever she saw Ramos, the woman responded. The two comrades entered the house.

"So?" Rosa asked, kissing her companion and straightening out the stray hairs on his sweaty head with her fingertips.

"Coming along," Vaz answered.

Ramos understood that the question and answer had to do with previous conversations and didn't quite know how to interpret them. He simply noticed Rosa's more attentive and caring attitude toward her partner, taking his cap and jacket, placing his briefcase on top of the work table, touching his sweaty shirt and insisting that he change it. Ramos didn't waste time thinking about it. He sat at the table and, drawing a pile of papers out of his briefcase, began leafing through them, reading some, underlining others, setting some aside, putting others in envelopes. Meanwhile, Vaz washed his feet, shaved, and got ready to wash his torso in cold water.

"What if it makes you sick?" Rosa asked. She had stood next to him, observing how thin his body had gotten, especially his prominent shoulder blades, and thinking, *How could he have lost so much weight in such little time?* "Do you want me to heat up some water for you?" she asked. "It'll just take a minute."

"No, I'm okay," Vaz said.

Pouring the water into the red bowl, he washed his sweaty body with gusto and wiped himself dry. Rosa helped him into a cool clean shirt, and Vaz combed his hair fastidiously.

"You look like another man," said Rosa, gently cradling his face between her fingers. "But you are thin! Thin, thin! You have to take care of yourself, José"—whenever she raised some serious subject she reverted to his real name. "Why don't you put the question to our friends? Do you want me to talk with them?"

Vaz pulled her toward him, drawing her face to his. Hers was as thin as his.

"You won't be able to go on like this," Rosa added.

After night had closed in, António arrived. As always, when he entered, he kissed Rosa on her cheek. He had come on foot and seemed quite fatigued. Shortly, a comrade arrived whom António had never seen, a modest man of 40 or so, evidently at ease with himself and of a gentle mien. At first sight his face had no special features: it was a long face with a broad forehead and straight hair badly combed. But when he spoke, that face came alive with personality, his expressiveness speaking alongside his words and reinforcing his meaning. Paulo was the last to show up. He came in shirt sleeves with his jacket under his arm and, in place of his usual hat, he wore a Spanish-style beret that lent him a completely different look.

"Are you coming from the beach?" Ramos asked with a cackle.

"You guessed it," Paulo said, smiling. But since they spoke no more about it, they didn't find out if he was talking seriously or kidding around.

Even before eating the dish of soup Rosa served them, they began the meeting. They had no time to lose. Each reported the work in his sector, with little discussion, only now and then a question or observation from someone. When António related how Gaspar had remained on the Strike Committee, Vaz remarked, "I hope they won't regret it."

When Vaz reported the meeting with Marques and Cesário, it was Ramos who observed, "He grouches and growls, but in the end he gets things done."

And when Paulo, as though begging forgiveness for his poor work, mentioned he had only been able to count on the sawmill, it was the unknown comrade who said, "You achieved more than could be expected."

What they had to deal with now were to set the date and the duration of the action, write a manifesto, get it printed and distributed quickly, and make sure the contacts were active. The only point on which there was prolonged discussion was setting the date and the duration. That's where the unknown comrade posed a number of questions, and Paulo as much as António wondered how he knew their sectors in such detail, with the names of comrades, the number of cells and movements in progress. The questions he asked could only have been raised by someone who knew those sectors like the back of their hand. It was clear not only that Ramos had kept the higher organisms well informed but that the new comrade had closely followed and studied all the reports of recent months. At one point, when António was flummoxed by a question, Ramos laughed and said, "It seems he knows your sector better than you, hey? But don't be upset, old man."

In the end they agreed to launch the call for a one-day strike, with gatherings and demonstrations that same day. As for the date, after a long discussion, they consented it should be a Monday, and proceeded to deliberate the time required to publish and circulate the manifesto and complete the preparations for the cells and contacts. The unknown comrade pulled a datebook out of his pocket and searching with his finger, said, "Today's Thursday the 7th. How about Monday the 18th? Agreed?"

Silently, and full of emotion, they looked back and forth at one another before starting work. The determination of that date was the result of a tedious, complex process, of long, tiring effort, of countless considerations, analyses, arguments and hopes. For a few instants, the awesomeness of the responsibility cast a shadow over the five comrades' countenances.

While Vaz, Ramos, António and Paulo remained at the table deciding how their contacts should work and their meetings take place during the movement, the other comrade retired to the kitchen to write a draft of the manifesto because, despite his insistence that it be Ramos to do it, everyone answered that no, he should do it. Rosa was seated at the kitchen table.

"Are you happy?" the comrade asked quietly but sincerely, as he sat down to start writing.

"I'm concerned about just one thing," Rosa replied.

The comrade began, writing, *Workers! Factory hands and peasants!*

"Tell me," he said in that same steady voice.

Rosa remained silent for a moment, observing the comrade's hand scurrying across the page.

"Tell me," he repeated.

"All these important struggles are being waged, and you guys are going around so exhausted, while I'm here sitting idle."

The comrade's hand continued rushing across the paper as he inscribed another line in fancy capital letters: *Monday, May 18th....* And he underlined these words with a long, firm stroke, then another. When he finished, he raised his eyes from the page and looked into Rosa's thin, serious and sad face.

"You make a good point, friend. Not that you're sitting idle, because you well know the use and need for your presence in this house. But the truth is we haven't given due regard to the work of our comrade women Party workers, whose job has almost exclusively been to ensure the integrity of the Party houses. There are women Party workers we seriously need to draw into the work of the organization, and we're now confronting that problem in earnest. It's not just your situation, it's many."

"I well know," Rosa said.

The comrade returned his glance to the page and went on writing, as if he were paying no further notice to Rosa's presence. Rosa didn't interrupt him again. She sat there for an hour, watching his pen race over the paper, go back, cross out, change a word, hesitate, fly ahead once more, all reflecting as in a mirror what was passing through the comrade's mind.

8

One morning, before checking in to work, Gaspar met with the Party leaders at Cicol. At lunchtime he spoke with comrades from one section and the Party person from another. During his afternoon shift, on one pretext or another, he managed more than once to approach other workers and exchange a few words with them. In the evening he went with Pereira to a cell meeting from Pereira's factory. That night he met with Vicente, sought out some comrade tradesmen, and met the comrade assigned to distribution. After all this, he left town and met up with Jerónimo.

Jerónimo had just arrived and was drinking a big glass of water in the kitchen.

"Are you meeting tomorrow?" Gaspar asked.

Jerónimo looked at him with his cheerless, ashen eyes and before answering, calmly drank his water and wiped his snowy chin masked by his shapeless, grown-out beard.

"Yes, I am."

"Then tell me where we have to meet."

Jerónimo stared at him in silence for a few moments. He wiped his chin once more, with the handkerchief he slowly extracted from his pocket and then passed through his sparse white hair.

"Do you want to attend?" he asked deliberately, in such a tone where it was hard to say whether he wanted an affirmative or negative response.

"Yes, I do."

Taking his time, with his lower lip dropped unhappily, Jerónimo put away the water jug, adjusted the wick on the oil lamp, and sat down at the table. "You have a seat, too, friend. I think we'd better talk."

Jerónimo is nervous about Gaspar's extraordinary activity. He recognizes he possesses a dynamism greater than that of any of the other comrades in the area, and he sees that his personal influence and popularity will unquestionably help to bring many workers to the movement. Nevertheless, one thing worries him, and another upsets him. The fact that Gaspar's frenzied activity will inevitably become noticed worries him—running everywhere, talking with one group after another, even in public settings taking comrades aside by the arm to whisper with them, and thereby at the very least compromising his highly important position in the union. He's upset by the fact that Gaspar steps over organisms, wanting to do everything without trusting anything to others and even—even in his own case, being in the Party as a member of the Local Committee like himself, wanting to attend the meeting of the sector for which he, Jerónimo, is responsible. If he, Jerónimo, told Gaspar he'd like to attend a meeting of the Cicol cell to give it guidance, what kind of reaction would Gaspar have? He'd doubtless consider such a desire a completely absurd, unjustifiable and rude interference in his activity. It's apparent that Gaspar considers himself superior to everyone else on the Local Committee, and this causes Jerónimo a certain irritability that he has to force himself not to show.

"I believe you're going around exposing yourself too much," Jerónimo said, looking at him across the table. "Remember the recommendations from our higher comrades, and don't forget the vacuum you'd cause if anything should happen to you."

"Someone has to do these things," Gaspar answered coolly.

Jerónimo once more leisurely adjusted the wick. Without a funnel, the lamp spread a dusky yellow light that lent a funereal expression to his pale face.

"The work is the obligation of everyone," Jerónimo said. "If you do it all, the others will see in that an excuse for them not to do anything. Without having anyone to do things for them, they will be forced to do them on their own."

"There's doing and there's doing," Gaspar answered, smiling indulgently, meaning: *Surely now you're not comparing my work with other people's work.*

Jerónimo got up to get another glass of water and drank a few gulps. "No question, with you doing things, they are done better." His voice grew slower and darker as he proceeded, all the while peering curiously at the bottom of the glass. "It remains to be seen if the benefits compensate for the drawbacks. The way I see it, they don't."

He uttered the last words with unexpected haste. When Gaspar contemplated their implications, his face turned red.

"You mean you think it a bad idea that I attend the civil construction meeting. That's it, right?"

Jerónimo drank another swallow of water. "It's not only that, but it's that too. What I think is bad is you going around exposing yourself the way you've been doing. You want to do everything and don't trust other people."

Jerónimo had already said more than he wanted to say. He read it in Gaspar's expression. To undo the effect of his words a little, he added, "I repeat, friend, if anything happens to you, you'd leave a big hole. You tell me: who's out there that could take your place?"

Gaspar took a while to respond. He opened his thin lips from time to time, then spoke in a measured, sure voice, his tone one of authority and self-confidence.

"There are battles where you have to throw yourself in body and soul. If you see that your effort is needed, if it's indispensable, you'd give a poor accounting for yourself if you refused to make that effort. I know I've exposed myself, comrade, and I know what this could mean. I'm not unaware of the mistakes I make, and don't think this is false modesty. (*No, I don't think so,* says Jerónimo's slack lower lip.) But in this first big test of our local organization, we cannot fail. Have I gone to lots of places? Yes, I have. Have I spoken with comrades who've avoided knowing who I am? Yes, I have. Have I directly tried to attract workers, some of whom probably don't deserve it? That's also true. But I am certain, my friend, that my effort is useful and—why shouldn't I say it?—indispensable. (*No doubt of it, no doubt,* Jerónimo's lower lip confirmed.) For this movement to take place, if it requires my sacrifice, you won't see me trying to haggle my way out of it. Wouldn't that be right?"

"All this is right," Jerónimo said in an even-keeled manner that could be heard as praise or derision. "It would even be good if you could go around to still more places than you've gone already. Your presence at tomorrow's meeting with the comrades in civil construction would be extremely valuable. Extremely. Unfortunately we have to do without it."

Jerónimo paused. With his tired, ashen eyes, he focused on Gaspar. "So, let's agree then: You won't go to the meeting, right?"

"If it need be, then so be it," Gaspar answered, as if at one point it had been envisioned that he go to Jerónimo's sector and now it was required to go back on that decision.

"It's good you've come around," said Jerónimo in that same ponderous, monotonous voice. "Rest assured. We'll do everything we can and know how to do. And maybe we'll find a way."

Gaspar left in a hurry, because despite the late hour of the night, he still had to meet with some comrades. After Gaspar left, Jerónimo drank the rest of the water in his glass and distractedly watching the oil lamp, slowly wiped his wet chin with his handkerchief.

9

The comrades in civil construction meeting took place near the river. Little white clouds raced like wild horses across the blue sky. A soothing breeze made the cane reed leaves dance and whisper.

Apart from Jerónimo and Manuel Rato, four other comrades sat on the cool ground, each of whom oversaw another two or three Party members and a few sympathizers. Manuel Rato removed his hat, and the broad arch of his head, generally protected from the sun, stood out from his face, where his black, close-cropped mustache accentuated his dark complexion. With a fraught expression, his eyebrows united in a single deep fold, he scratched the ground with a little stick as Jerónimo spoke. He allowed the others to comment and limited himself simply to say that Jerónimo had said all that was necessary. The movement was approved in principle, as well as the demands to be presented.

"I'd only like to focus in on one other aspect here," Rato said finally, his features bearing even greater weight as he continued raking the earth with the stick. "In our class, in these parts, we're all divided by our little jobs, and some even do individual piece work or work at home. To withhold our labor, presenting ourselves before the bosses to demand better wages, is a simple thing for us and, in the end, a very insignificant movement. We can and we must help in another way. As we are more at liberty than the comrades in the factories, we can help bring the people out to the street, and especially the women. But for that to happen we need all of us, and every one of us, not to wait for others to act."

Listening to Manuel Rato, Jerónimo reflected on the great difference between Manuel Rato's and Gaspar's process. In the last few weeks, Manuel Rato had recruited several new members to the Party, had established committees, created a cell of the river workers (something the Local Committee had never achieved), introduced two seamstresses to the youth league (who knows how he found them), but by contrast to Gaspar, he did it all quietly, unobserved, without anyone paying attention to him, neither friends nor the authorities. Jerónimo took note further of his pragmatic organizing sense, finding tasks for each one and encouraging each one to assign tasks to those they oversaw.

Other comrades spoke, and Manuel Rato went on toying with his little stick.

Beyond the canebrake the men heard the slap of oars in the water, and went silent. The boat was now close to the shore, because the boatmen's distinct voices could be heard.

"Yes, he's got a new boat," said one strong, rough voice.

"It's his second one already," said the other, more meekly and amazed.

The boat passed. With their ears pricked, the comrades remained still for a few minutes watching the blue sky, where isolated clouds continued their gallop south, always to the south, as the timid breeze made the cane leaves sing.

10

During a meeting with Cesário and Henriques that took place without Vaz present, Marques laid out a vast plan for the movement in the city. Everything was accounted for: strike committees in formation, the distribution apparatus under construction, a diagram of the contacts, security detail for the demonstration, slogans to publicize, women's and youth actions. It even anticipated the first reactions from the authorities and provided a response to each of the several eventualities. For almost an hour that Marques spoke, Cesário almost always held his arms crossed, leaning back and glancing from time to time up to a shelf where an alarm clock sat. Henriques, thrown across the table, his chin in his hands, his mouth hanging open and his eyes blinking even more than usual, looked like a scrawny chicken that had just been offered something to drink.

"So, friends," Marques summed up. "Now tell me what you think."

Cesário looked again at the alarm clock and before speaking lay his strong brown arms on the table. "What do you want me to say, friend? Everything you explained is very well thought out and very well said, but not for our organization in the state it's in. All that is beautiful on paper, but too complicated. Besides, it would be better to share it when Vaz is here. Day after tomorrow he'll be here."

The carpenter's eyes shone, but behind his lenses. "Vaz, Vaz. Always waiting for the higher-up comrades, always the same lack of initiative," he replied bitterly.

"I think all that is very complicated," Cesário repeated.

"And you, comrade?" Marques asked, turning to Henriques.

"Hunh?" Henriques grunted, as if awakening from a dream, as he was still looking at Marques with the same shocked expression.

"What's your opinion?" Marques asked again in a tone somewhere between protective and ironic. "Surely you have an opinion."

"Opinion?" Henriques answered in his high-pitched voice. "The comrade gave us a big lollipop to suck on! Yes, sir, a big lollipop!" And with his wide-open eyes blinking on his pointed face, he turned toward Cesário. *Yes, sir, a big lollipop!* his expression seemed to repeat.

Cesário couldn't help but smile. He knew Henriques all too well and knew his artificial ingenuousness concealed cartloads of experience and craftiness.

"Concrete points, friend, concrete points!" an impatient Marques pleaded.

Henriques looked at him, blinking his eyes, still with his chin in hand. "I know nothing, comrade," finally he said in his singing voice. "And anyway, I didn't get everything you explained. Yes, I got a little, very little. If they tell me we have to stop the workshop that day at such-and-such a time, maybe the workshop will stop. But if they tell me to do what you've just indicated in your speech—your important speech—I confess I wouldn't know what to do." And he looked at Cesário again with the same expression as before: *Big lollipop, yes, sir!*

The carpenter's eyes shone even brighter. The facts were once again proving him right, and showing how Vaz's decisions, and those of the higher comrades concerning the cadre, without listening to their opinions, led to true dead ends. But, summoning all his patience, he explained one more time everything he considered necessary for the movement to be a success. He spoke at great length, and now Henriques no longer evinced the same sense of shock. He only watched attentively, blinking his eyes.

"If it's necessary to do everything the comrade indicates to create a movement," he said when Marques finished talking, "we're still not going to get there from here."

Marques turned questioningly to Cesário, who again had his arms crossed and sat back on his chair. *What do you want me to say?* he seemed to be asking.

11

Lisete came to speak with Cesário, her brother-in-law, that night. The young woman looked a lot like her sister, similarly tall and slender, with the same shy and sweet affect. Her hair was lighter, blond and wavy, gathered in the back with a ribbon and bangs in the front. Her hair lent her a jauntiness in contrast to her figure.

"I spoke with Bela and with Isolda. They're both of the same mind. The workers are fed up with promises and the time is right. Now you just have to tell us the day."

In recent months, under the influence of Vaz on the one hand and events on the other, Cesário greatly changed his opinion about the fundamental merits and qualities of his comrades. Earlier, Marques had seemed to him like the indisputable leader of the city, a real role model, and even before Vítor he, Cesário, felt shy and insignificant. His whole ambition at that time consisted in being able to expound upon a problem and to speak and reason with Marques's or Vítor's ease and brilliance. Later, life in the Party organization taught him something else. That words are important, but more important are acts. Words that don't correspond to action and ideas with no intention of being realized were losing all enchantment and traction for him. And in the heated arguments between Vaz and Marques and Vítor, he was slowly but surely acquiring a real sense of boredom and disgust with the blowhards. At the same time, he was getting used to appreciating, respecting and admiring those people who, saying little, do much, who appear personally disinterested, pure in their devotion, simple and modest over their success. Time was, for him, that Marques was the model of a militant and Lisete a nice girl and nothing more. Now, imagining a great scale weighing merits against defects, with Marques on one pan and Lisete on the other, it was most certainly Lisete's side that weighed more, that Lisete he had before him, tall and slender, shy and sweet, tidy blond hair, and saying in half a dozen words that she would do what Marques swore up and down in long speeches couldn't be done.

"And the others?" Cesário asked.

"I told you," Lisete answered: "People on the Committee are agreed, and the rest of the workers trust us. We just can't wait too long. Of course, I'm only speaking about now. A month from now I can't say. Do you know the day yet?"

"Tomorrow or the day after we'll know," said Cesário.

They both kept silent thinking about the great moment that was coming. *Just as well that Vítor left her*, Cesário thought.

Cesário's wife came and sat down beside the two of them.

"Listen," Cesário said, resting his big brown hands on her thighs. "If I have to go underground, you'll go with me, right?"

The young woman laughed. How could he doubt it?

12

Sitting at the side of the road, resting his hand on a brown paper package and looking at a lonely medlar tree, Afonso felt hungry, thirsty and tired. Since he began his new life he'd enjoyed few days of repose. All the rest were hikes, loading packages, nights of poor sleep, missed meals, grueling, uncomfortable trips, and more hikes and packages, hikes and packages. He'd often arrive home in the middle of the night, sweaty and downcast, having to unpack and pack in a hurry, always watching the clock until dawn, without having rested even a little on his bed, only to set out on the road again, running to catch some means of transportation. Up until now he had always completed the work that he had been given. He barely thought, but over time grew ever more convinced about it, that many of the directives he had received under the rubric of caution and conspiratorial rules were absurd and unbearable demands. With what right and for what reason did they insist that he shave every day? Or that he should walk a league on foot just so as not to enter the rail or bus station of a town where supposedly— but only supposedly—there was surveillance? And that he should not accept meals a comrade someplace might offer him because that comrade was already "hot"—too well known to the police. No. Afonso fulfilled the work assigned to him without fault (and with the distribution of the May 18th manifesto he was demonstrating it well), but submitting to those putative rules would in the end reduce the range for his work, impair the easiest execution of his tasks, atrophy—visibly to the naked eye—as was happening, and thus ruin the health of a Party cadre. All things considered, not following the "conspiratorial rules" was to defend the Party, and to follow them would hurt it.

These were Afonso's thoughts as he sat at the side of the road looking at the gangling boughs of the medlar tree with its shiny yellow fruit. Fialho had told him that after an incident occurred with two comrades, resulting in their almost being sent to prison, it was expressly prohibited for Party workers to pick any fruit without the owner's permission. This is easier to say, however, or order, when you aren't hungry or if you have exceptional resistance. And then (as in the present case) what kind of danger could there be in this isolated place without houses or hiding places, where not a living soul could be seen, what danger could there be in reaching a hand out and gathering a few fruits?

By the time Afonso had arrived at this point in his thinking, he had already raised and extended his hand to the medlar. Tall as he was, he quickly filled his pockets and returned to his position at the curbside, spitting out the seeds, discarding the skin, and eating the deliciously refreshing, sweet juicy fruits. In the meantime, he prudently looks down the road, not out of fear that the medlar's owner might appear, as in some fairytale, but because Fialho is about to arrive and it's always better to avoid being seen eating the fruit. Not that he wasn't capable of saying something himself, because he was, but because that way they'd not have to engage in a futile argument from which nothing useful would emerge and which would only spoil someone's day. Afonso checks his watch, sees there are three minutes left before the designated hour, and now wishes Fialho would come a little late to give him time to empty his pockets.

Fortunately, medlars are eaten quickly, the whole fruit at once, and in an instant Afonso felt restored and fortified.

He arrived on time. Around the curve of the road, some hundred meters away, Fialho's figure appeared, in his rapid, determined stride. Afonso stood up and walked to meet him.

"Are you starved?" Fialho fired as his first question, giving a quick glance at his comrade's face and then closely eyeing the surroundings and the other end of the road.

Afonso heard Fialho's words as a chastisement. Could his comrade have observed him from afar? Had he insufficiently wiped his mouth? Was his chin smeared?

"Yes, I'm starved," he answered tenuously.

"You're in luck," Fialho said, as he continued to look about. "I brought something."

And having studied the dry, naked fields surrounding them, he ended up choosing the shady spot where Afonso had been waiting next to the medlar tree as the most agreeable place to encamp. So the two sat down, and Fialho unwrapped a loaf of bread with fried fish that he divided evenly in two, giving half to Afonso and starting to eat his half in huge bites.

"Someone was already here today with more luck than us," he sputtered with his mouth full, pointing to the medlar seeds and skins right at their feet. "Did you deliver them all?"

Confounded by the observation about the medlars, Afonso had to make an effort to understand Fialho's question.

"No, I haven't delivered them all," he answered, pointing to the brown paper package. "These are left."

Fialho swallowed with difficulty and then bit into the bread again, reducing it now by half. "Not too many," he said, once again with his mouth full. "Let's see the others first and then we'll deliver them. It makes you thirsty!" he added pointing to the bread and fish and then gazing at the medlar.

Afonso ate in silence, nervously scanning the skins and seeds strewn over the ground, still fresh, with signs of being bitten and chewed.

"Did you read it already?" Fialho asked after his last gulp, with the big movement of the neck that only hungry people make. And seeing Afonso's affirmative nod, he added, "Everything will stop, you'll see."

For the first time, in that moment, Afonso felt the purpose and importance of his job. And without knowing why, alongside that feeling, arose another, of sadness and annoyance with himself.

13

Whoever, as an ordinary traveler, might ramble through the region in those days, wouldn't notice anything extraordinary. In the factories, in the fields, in workshops, offices, small jobs, work carried on as usual. On the streets, roads and paths, the usual people appeared with the usual faces. The spring sun lit everything with gold, lending its ample serenity and glee to the landscape as well as to humankind. Meanwhile the fire was already being stoked and was ready to break out. There were those who were feverishly preparing the events. Not in exciting rallies with lots of people, but rather in quick little encounters of only two or three, where but a few brief words were exchanged.

In the city, in the towns, in villages, in factories or at their exit gates, near busy railway stations or in peaceful fields, and when night fell, in humble houses or on quiet streets, last-minute orders were given, final details were agreed upon, people expressed their doubts and their hopes.

Not everyone was so confident. What was in preparation was no easy, simple thing. In a fascist state, to call thousands of workers out to the struggle on the same day at the same hour is truly the work of giants. How could those few dozen exhausted men pull this off, forced into silence and discretion as they were, their freedom threatened by the smallest imprudent word? That was the carpenter Marques's thinking, for example. For that reason he sought out Cesário again, and as he was unable to convince him, he sought out Henriques.

"If things are this badly prepared," he said, "they're bound to fail. It's better to do less and do it well than wanting to do more without the proper preparation." And observing his comrade with his intelligent eyes, he repeated a phrase he had already restated innumerable times during those days: We'll lose the little we have."

Henriques appeared to be indecisive.

"And the manifesto?" Marques pushed on. "Who came up with the idea of calling the population out to the struggle with only one manifesto, when the truth forces us to recognize that we don't have an organization at that level, nor true influence? Wishing for things is not enough for them to happen. Failures like this only discredit us."

Where Marques saw insuperable difficulties, others envisioned an action of sublime simplicity. In the same city, Lisete, for example. She asked several women in her factory, "If everyone goes out, will you too?"

Almost all of them answered, "If the others go out, I will too."

When she told Bela the date of the strike, Bela asked, "Are you sure the workers will stop everything?"

"Why wouldn't they?" Lisete responded.

Yes, there were many different ways each person approached the movement. Opposing opinions, discordant feelings. Optimism, faith, distrust, fear, whim, calm, the idea of duty, spirit, doubt, apprehension, all of it coursed through people's hearts.

One of those days, in late afternoon, on an empty street next to a pale-colored lumber factory, a couple of men were peacefully conversing.

"It's just three days away," one limping man said as he leaned on his crutch. "Can you believe it? Only now do I feel like I've just started living."

"Damn! You're right!" responded the other, short and heavy-set with a child's smile.

Whoever could have heard them and then run a few leagues away to hear what others were saying at that same instant outside a tavern would have difficulty believing they were all talking about the same thing.

"Something needed doing, in fact, but isn't this going too far?" asked one worker black with coal dust.

"The worst of it is it'll be us that have to pay for it," responded another, looking all around him.

"Necessary is necessary. But we'll pay for it."

"Wouldn't it be possible to issue a counter-directive?" asked the nervous one.

"The machine is already running. No one can stop it."

That man called it a "machine" and he had good reason. Admitting it could be seen as a machine, however, it was a very special machine. It had nothing to do with mechanics, because it was not built of inert parts with no will, with controls and adjustments, but by men and women, complex and diverse beings. It's like what Gaspar said and what Manuel Rato said.

Speaking of the stoppage at Cicol, one member of the committee reassured Gaspar, "Keep calm, friend, I'm responsible for my section."

"I'm going there," said Gaspar. "You guys, don't do anything until I get there. It's safer."

"It's not necessary for you to go. You can trust us. And stay calm."

"No, friend," Gaspar insisted. "I'm going there, otherwise things could end up badly. Wait for me."

Manuel Rato spoke completely differently to two railway workers at a crossing. "Don't wait for me. Just count on yourselves. If you guys don't do it, no one will do it for you."

Mere situational differences? Or differences of nature?

Differences of human nature are a factor in differences of situation. For people who do not understand this, surprising failure can result. José Sagarra understood that.

He met da Barrosa at nightfall on a narrow by-road, surrounded by undeveloped terrain and thick brambles. The gathering birds filled the air with their chirping.

"Have they agreed on the price?" Sagarra asked.

"It's still the same," da Barrosa answered.

"Everyone agreed?"

"Of course they are, needless to say," da Barrosa muttered.

"And distribution?"

"To be done Sunday night."

José Sagarra raised his bright eyes toward the other, looking even purer in his dark, worried face.

"You're not participating in the distribution, agreed?"

Da Barros nodded affirmatively.

"Agreed?" José Sagarra repeated.

"I just said."

"Agreed?"

"Agreed," da Barrosa gave in moodily.

A brief silence ensued.

"Give me your word of honor."

"Why are you pressing me so hard?" da Barrosa demanded, clearly irritated. "I already told you I won't participate. Agreed is agreed."

"Your word of honor."

Unhappy, da Barrosa delayed his response. "All right, I give my word of honor."

"Swear by the health of your children."

And da Barrosa had to swear by the health of his children, and had to say again that agreed is agreed and once more give his word of honor. Only then did Sagarra leave, but still not without saying, "Now let's see what you do."

Chapter *XII*

1

Although many days had passed since the incident with Maria, António hadn't yet found time for an explanation. The day after, he left with his comrades and spent several days working to prepare the movement. Now, returning to the house, he felt so enervated that not only did he not pursue such a conversation but would have evaded her if Maria had wanted it.

Maria allowed him to kiss her, spoke to him in a good mood, poured water into the basin for him, and placed dinner on the table. But during the dinner she was constantly reading—which was frequently the case in recent weeks—and after dinner, when she asked a few questions about the movement preparations, she immediately turned back to her studies, writing energetically and from time to time placing the tip of the pencil in her mouth. Silently seated, his arms propped on the table, António picked up a newspaper to pass the time, but that was not his desire.

"Maria," he said, putting the newspaper aside, "I'm going to bed. I'm tired, you know?"

"Hunh? she grunted, continuing to write and paying no attention to António's words.

"I'm going to bed. Don't you want to come?"

Maria placed the pencil on the table and suspended her study. António thought he saw her blush. He read in her eyes a shadow of annoyance.

"So soon? I have to study a while longer. This has to be ready," she added, shuffling the papers as though António could appreciate from this gesture the task that awaited her.

António went back to his newspaper and read a few more articles with effort.

"Maria," he repeated after a bit. "I have to leave early in the morning and I'm tired. I'm going to bed. Aren't you coming?"

243

Maria stared at him now. "It's early still, and this has to be ready today, dear friend. Work comes first."

António recalled once more that strange attitude of rejection and distancing on Maria's part that last night he had slept with her, when the comrades met at the house. He attributed this mood to her displeasure about the lack of news of her father. Now, in this zeal for study, he saw a new, indirect form of rejecting him again.

Practically collapsing from sleepiness, António got up and approached her. Again, Maria allowed him to kiss her and caress her, but when António hoped he'd be able to take her with him, she disengaged from him gently and told him, calmly and indifferently, "Go ahead, dear friend, I'll see you later."

It was the same calm and neutral voice that António had heard from her the first time he kissed her, against her will. Offended and despondent, he went to bed and waited. The dry rot creaked in the wooden framework, and in the quiet of the small house he could hear Maria's hands turning pages from time to time.

"Aren't you coming?" António asked once again, this time from the room.

"I'll be there," Maria answered.

António fell asleep. Only late, very late, Maria lay down beside him, cautiously so as not to wake him. All night, António had a vague notion of her presence. When he woke up early the next morning, Maria was already up and about, shoeless and her hair uncombed, fanning the stove.

2

He returned two days later as night fell, and found Maria in the patio, talking with a woman neighbor and with Elvas. Elvas kept up his new look, his clothes sewn up and buttoned properly. To António, as to Maria days before, it was jolting to realize that his new aspect gave the vagabond an even more miserable and piteous impression than what he had when he was semi-naked, barely covered by the purposefully ripped scraps of rags.

"You want to hear something, Senhor Lemos?" the neighbor asked. "Elvas here says he's going to go laughing into the world to come."

Pulling tobacco out to roll into a cigarette, António offered it to the vagabond. He declined it with a gesture, but after attentively watching how António rolled his cigarette, asked if he could borrow a few grams.

António went in to find a small packet. Elvas looked at Maria with a contented air, perhaps the result of his new look, but with a hovering, melancholy smile.

"Remember our conversation the other day?"

"What conversation?" Maria inquired.

"About how if I don't meet my creditors in the next world, I can't pay them my debts."

"What nonsense comes out of that man's mouth!" the neighbor laughed. "Now I see he's obsessed by one thing, and tomorrow it'll be something else."

António returned with the small packet and gave it to the vagabond, who thanked him and said goodbye. After he'd walked a few paces, he stopped and turned to the sky. "Are you listening?" he demanded dramatically. "Send another beautiful day like this tomorrow, which my sister will appreciate a lot. Don't forget, you hear? And always send her our daily bread and send her laughter and flowers."

The neighbor laughed again. Maria blushed, following Elvas with her eyes until he disappeared just up ahead. As if daydreaming, with her eyelids half-closed, her big black eyebrows almost meeting, she sat there a few more seconds staring at the brush behind which Elvas had vanished.

They conversed a little more with the neighbor, and soon after retreated into the house. António sat down and pulled Maria toward him. Standing with her arms hanging at her sides, she allowed herself to be held.

"Didn't you miss me?" António asked. His gaze was at the same time satisfied and saddened. Putting her fingers through his wavy hair, Maria mussed it up and drew herself closer to him, looking at him deeply.

How António feels happy again! As if it had all been just his imagination and passing gloom. Maria is truly his companion and there she is again, gentle, tender, throbbing, still smashing and graceful. Oh, beloved companion! Beloved companion!

After dinner, António, who had to catch a train at two in the morning, asked Maria if she would lie down with him. Dodging him again, she declined and remained working at the table. At half-past midnight she stood up and went in to wake him. She spoke coldly, as if wanting to avoid any intimacy.

3

Jerónimo was with Manuel Rato to organize the distribution of the manifesto and handed him an envelope as he left. "The comrade who was there left this for you. I almost forgot."

Manuel Rato placed the envelope in his pocket and without removing his hand from it, headed home. His nervous fingers felt the thickness of the paper as though they could divine what it contained by touch. News from his wife? No, surely not. Just a few days before, he had received a letter, and she hadn't written in care of the Party. What could it be then? Manuel had no other personal ties. His wife was all he had left. Everything. With lowered head, trying to chase away terrible memories—always the same, forever the same, always that pine forest, always those guards, always that beloved smiling face, always that poor dead body—Manuel Rato entered the house where he was living in a rented room. His hostesses, two middle-aged sisters, both dressed in black, both with brass-framed eyeglasses, were still sewing in the little entrance parlor by the weak light of a 25-watt lamp. As always when he returned home, they were ready to chat a little while because they believed, in their innocence, they could distract their guest from his somber temperament.

"Maybe you still don't know!" said the older one, raising her glasses to her forehead. "They say on Monday everything's stopping."

"What's stopping?" Manuel Rato asked.

"Everything's stopping, there's going to be a strike," said the other, peering above her glasses and continuing her stitching. "Seriously, you didn't hear anything about it?"

"Yes, I did hear something," Manuel Rato answered, his fingers squeezing the envelope in his pocket. "But it's probably a rumor. People say all kinds of things."

"It's serious. Serious," one of them insisted. "The person who told me heard it from Gaspar Oliveira, and that guy knows what he's talking about."

It was the third time that day that different individuals had spoken to him about the strike, tying it with Gaspar's name.

Manuel Rato removed his hat. By the light of the lamp, the pink of his receding hairline and the curve of his scalp stood out like an actor's makeup in contrast with his grimy, worried face.

"I have to get up early," he said, retreating to his room. "Have a good night."

The envelope had nothing written on it and contained one large sheet of paper with verses printed out on a copy machine. *Verses?* Manuel Rato thought. *This isn't for me.* The title read simply, "Tale of the Peasant Girl." *There's some mistake.* And placing the envelope and the paper on a chair, he got ready for bed. He had to get up early to meet before work with his comrades charged with promoting the movement, and he was behind on his sleep. He had already turned down the covers, when he suddenly turned around, picked up the verses and read:

> The fields of wheat are weeping
> And the red poppies.

With growing agitation, Manuel Rato read the verses on both sides of the paper. When he got to the end, with trembling hands and lips, he went back and anxiously read them again as if he hadn't understood. Once again he arrived at the point that read

> They killed our dear friend,
> Isabel, cherished bloom,
> The bravest and most lovely of all.

He lay down on the bed with his head nestled in a knotty fist that violently crumpled the sheet of paper.

In the room next to him, the two sisters heard a strange noise coming from their guest's room and, pricking up their ears, they thought at first there was a yelping dog there. Looking at each other, one from above her glasses, the other from below them, they silently asked, *Did you notice anything he was carrying? I didn't.*

4

Ernesto and his wife had left for the fields, leaving Anica alone in the house. Anica walked down the path and ambled up the olive grove slope to visit her friend. Seated on the doorstep, Rosa was sewing as she conversed with her neighbor Ermelinda. Wordlessly, she took the little girl's hand and pulled her back between her knees. Miss Ermelinda was telling another story about the Pim-Pa-Pum, her favorite subject when she wanted to talk trash about someone, which was a lot of the time. Her eyes glistened impishly in her plain, mannish face. Her flutey voice seemed to lash into her pet targets.

"The oldest one of them went to study nursing and she knew quite a bit, there's no denying it. She was scrupulously clean—no one was like her. One day her late husband read aloud a notice that said, *Senhora, very sick with contagious disease, seeks help from generous souls.* And she yelled at him, *Ay, man, contagious disease! Put that newspaper down right now and go disinfect your hands!*

And Ermelinda let out a metallic blast of laughter which coursed down through the olive trees to her husband's ears and made him shake his head with displeasure.

"Have you ever looked at her hairdo?" Ermelinda continued. "Because of that hair of hers she wanted to kill herself once. She was so vain about her hair. Even the very night of their marriage, at every move or turn, she warned her husband strictly, *Don't touch my hair!* That went on after the marriage too. The poor guy could do anything else but if it looked like he was going for that mop of hers, she'd immediately shout, *Get away! Don't touch my hair!* She told him that so many times, the poor man in desperation dropped some concoction in the water where she was going to wash her head, and her hair came out all stiff like palm fiber. It's then she wanted to kill herself and decided to do it with an injection. I mean, she was serious. Her husband found her having just sterilized the needle and disinfected her skin—"

And with that Ermelinda burst out with another shriek of laughter, so high and cutting that Anica was shocked and drew closer to Rosa, while downhill, at the neighboring house, the husband suspended his cobbler's awl in the air with his ears cocked.

"So, my darling," Rosa said to Anica, "were you all alone?" Anica nodded.

"You like this Senhora so much," Miss Ermelinda said. "You get to eat a little muffin, a sugar cube—"

Anica's mood turned suddenly sulky. And since Ermelinda persisted in wanting to know why she liked the Senhora so much, Anica finally explained with a challenge: "She calls me 'my darling!' That's why!"

Pulling the little girl's head to her bosom, Rosa distractedly scanned the big curve in the road. If Vaz had seen her there, he wouldn't fail to ruminate once again about that part of Rosa's life and character that escaped him, that mysterious memory whose presence he sensed so often.

Miss Ermelinda went home, and so did Anica. After watching the girl until she disappeared from sight, Rosa kept on sewing pensively. She needed to go inside for something and when she came back she halted in the door frame and shouted, "Francisco! Come right away!"

In front of the door lay the inert bitch the Pim-Pa-Pum had given to a distant shepherd to take away and kill. The white fur even dirtier, the body more skeletal, the huge, even heavier, more misshapen teats even more prominent against the animal's scrawniness, her eyes looked red and teary.

"Where did you come from? Where've you been roaming?" Vaz asked, interrupting his work in response to Rosa's call.

The dog's ears trembled, her eyes roused under bloodied eyelids without eyebrows. She breathed with difficulty, shook her head and snorted as though trying to expel something from her nostrils. Rosa found a piece of bread for her, but she didn't want to eat. She brought a saucer of water: the dog tried to drink, but couldn't. She lay there the whole afternoon looking at her friends when they came to the door, shaking her head and whimpering. At night, Rosa laid out some old clothes in the usual place and the bitch lay down there. The next morning, when Vaz opened the door, she was dead.

5

Seated on a garden bench in front of the church, Ramos and Paulo were waiting for Vaz. It was a bright sunny afternoon with a gentle breeze, and a few other people seated on benches there were enjoying the weather.

"Beautiful towers on the church!" said a young priest on the next bench to his companion.

"I like the main altar in the chapel more," the other responded.

The church before them stood deaf to such praise.

"At least these guys are interested in works of art," Paulo whispered quietly.

Ramos laughed. "Hey, old man, I don't know where you've been all your life. Look! Look over at that bench and you'll see the works of art sitting there."

Paulo turned to the indicated bench and saw three girls conversing and laughing excitedly. Church towers, main altar of the chapel, how was it possible? Paulo blushed up to his ears over his naïveté and over the shamelessness of the two young men in cassocks.

Soon Vaz appeared. The three left the garden, walked across the town and followed a road. Ramos told Vaz that he, Vaz, had been coopted to the Central Committee. Impassively, Vaz asked only, "They're removing me from this sector?"

"For now you'll continue," Ramos answered, and he informed him of a meeting the next day with a comrade from the Secretariat.

They exchanged thoughts about the latest news of the preparation for the strike and agreed that the three of them should definitely meet with António on the 18th at 1 o'clock. The place was carefully chosen so as to be at the shortest possible distance from the main points in the region and served by means of transportation. By that time, Vaz, António and Paulo should already have met with the leaders of the most important sectors they supervised and would bring the first reports about the movement in order to coordinate the regional action.

Paulo separated from the two other comrades, who continued walking on the same road. A little farther, Ramos said he needed to buy tobacco and asked Vaz to accompany him on a side street. They hiked quite a distance and Vaz asked himself why they needed to go so far to buy tobacco when, on the other street below, there was a store that certainly had some. Finally Ramos found a little bar where no one was about. He clapped his hands, and after a few moments a pretty young woman appeared, with her black hair in curls and a pair of bright shining eyes. Vaz saw the girl smiling embarrassedly at Ramos, and that later they repaired to the end of the counter where they spoke in low voices. It was at the very least rather unusual behavior between a customer and a tavernkeep. The woman laughed, and Ramos, before parting from her, grabbed her arm with familiarity. Only then did he ask for the tobacco. He received it and paid.

The two left and on the way back by the same road, Vaz asked Ramos if he was also going to be catching the train. Ramos stared at him naughtily. "Today I'm remaining here!" he answered.

They proceeded in silence. "Friend," Vaz said at last in his calm, serious tone, "I don't know if I I'm wrong saying this, but if I am, you'll let me know. Do you have some secure place of support, of trust, in these places here? Or are you intending to spend the night in any random place?"

Ramos looked at his comrade and his tightened face suddenly took on an expression of irritation and animosity. "I believe you have no business in my personal life, comrade."

"Yes, I have no business in your personal life," Vaz said in that same calm voice. "But any one of us has something to do with the security and activity of the others. Many bad things have happened to the Party out of suppressing opinions and warnings from modest, humble comrades, and from considering authority as a kind of all-purpose pass."

"Did I just hire a tutor?" Ramos exploded. "Or are you saying this because you've been a Central Committee member for a week?"

They stayed quiet for several minutes. Then Vaz spoke again, with his familiar serenity. "Look, comrade. In the Party we don't have big lords and poor peons. Members of the Central Committee or of any organization at the base level, all without exception have the same duty to defend the security of the Party and its members, and all have equal duty to submit to the discipline and norms of work. I repeat, friend: All without exception."

Making a visible effort to control his bad temper, Ramos pulled himself together a bit. "That's not the issue. The issue is that you insinuated that I, for some less than appropriate motives, was paying no attention to my personal security."

"I'm not your tutor," Vaz sallied back after another pause, "and I'm not forgetting that you're at a higher level than me. But I want to frankly tell you that tomorrow I will report this little incident, because vigilance is an obligation for all of us. Our personal life does not belong to us alone. Everything is permitted to us that's not prejudicial to the Party. But nothing that is prejudicial is authorized."

"Alright, alright," Ramos said, angry again. "Let's get to the important stuff," and he quickly raised the last items they had to deal with.

6

The next afternoon, Ramos met with the comrade from the Secretariat, who had already spoken with Vaz. He asked Ramos where he had spent the night. Ramos related that in fact he had an arrangement with the tavern lady where he'd bought the tobacco. The woman lived apart from her husband and had already spent three nights with Ramos in her house. As for the husband, according to Ramos, he was a legionnaire and had already created some scenes at the bar, but with Ramos there he wouldn't do such a thing, the comrade could rest assured.

"Tell me frankly, you wouldn't be talking about this if Vaz hadn't raised the question."

"Probably not," Ramos agreed in a heavy voice. "I didn't think it was of any interest to talk about it. Besides, you know my personal situation, and I'm completely free."

"Yes, we know of your personal situation. We know the companion you had didn't want to join you in the underground and that the comrade you're living with now has a very specific situation which neither she nor you wants in the end. But all those are not reasons to give yourself up to amorous adventures that sooner or later are bound to end badly."

"I like women, friend," Ramos interrupted. "I don't know, maybe the others don't."

The comrade appeared not to take note of the offensive tone of that remark. "No one is criticizing you, or has criticized you, for having a woman, or even for the various connections you've had in your uncertain life on the move. What's being criticized is your lascivious spirit, which in truth is the issue here. What we're criticizing are liaisons in circumstances inappropriate for a Communist, which affects the standing of the militants and puts their security in danger. Look, comrade. At a moment when you are leading a sector involved in a very important struggle, when we're two days out from a strike with far-reaching consequences for the life of the Party, you're taking risky liberties with an adventure of this kind. Sadly, it's not the first time we've dealt with you in similar cases. As you well know, friend, we don't stop at criticizing."

Ramos went silent. His expression contrite, he stared at the ground a few steps ahead. Finally he sighed and his gleeful, spontaneous voice returned. "I see I've screwed things up again. Tell them it won't happen again."

After a pause he added, "I know it's not the first time I've said it won't happen again. But this time it won't be the same."

They continued a few more steps without speaking.

"What?" Ramos asked suddenly.

"I didn't say anything," the comrade responded.

He hadn't said anything. But immersed in his thoughts, Ramos imagined hearing the same words from that same comrade the last time they'd raised a similar question: *We'll see.*

7

No one ever learned how it happened. Could the wind have lifted a spark from the fire burning in the patio onto the storage shed? Was one of the children carrying a lighted stick? Délia later said that Rita brought a live coal inside, but Rita always denied it. The fact is that the fire erupted with an unexpected fury. The grape arbor crackled in a bonfire of bright flames, rising angrily and rapidly escaping onto the roof, wrapped in lethargic, milky white smoke. The children fled in terror. Rita remained inside, behind the woodpile.

"In the corner, she stayed in the corner!" the older sister shouted.

Attracted by the screaming, Paulo went out to the patio. At the shed door Madalena, suffocating from the smoke, was coughing and yelling for help and for her daughter. *How can she stay by the door?* Paulo thought. Out of the shed came only the snapping of fire, while from the roof a dark smoke from the pine branches started to rise. Without knowing why, Paulo took off his eyeglasses, handed them to one of the kids, and pushed into the shed, slightly limping and slow. He felt a hot wind lick his face and eyes and tried not to breathe, cast away flaming logs with his hands and feet and walked in the direction where they said Rita had stayed back. In the depth of the shed the hot lashes seemed to ease, and in the middle of the smoke he heard a weak coughing and the faint crying of a child. Now out of the flames, he could barely see a small figure holding its arms out to him. Then he felt those tender little arms holding onto him with unimagined strength, and one thought, one single urge took hold of him. To go back, cross through the fire once more, cover the little girl in the concave of his body and arms, defend the flesh of that imploring, trusting child.

In a flash, a number of people had gathered in the patio. In the midst of a barrage of strident shouting, they ran with pails of water to fight the fire. When they saw that smoky figure curved into itself emerging from the shed, as if wrapping something with his own body, they spilled buckets of water on him and stared at Paulo. With his red and blackened face, without eyebrows, covered with soot, he looked like a wild animal. At his side, Rita, hardly singed but with a slight burn on one leg which she didn't notice hurting her yet, put her hand on her mouth and opened her shocked, guilt-ridden eyes as though now she needed to defend herself against a deserved punishment. The curious thing is that Paulo, awkwardly putting his glasses back on, demonstrated with his entire attitude an expression similar to Rita's. He also looked as if he were asking pardon for what he had done.

They brought Paulo and Rita to the pharmacy and both were treated with a yellow solution. Only on the backs of his hands, one cheek and a leg did Paulo suffer burns requiring treatment. In any case, he was mostly concerned with his burned pants. There were reasons for that, for he would miss them dearly, and Evaristo, though having several pairs, likely wouldn't think to offer him one.

With his hands bandaged and a dressing on his face, Paulo had to leave that same day. His meetings to prepare the movement would not allow for delay. During this trip, despite the importance and interest in the issues under discussion, a memory constantly came to mind that would occupy his thoughts for long days and that he would never forget the rest of his life: those tender little arms force-fully holding onto him and begging to be saved.

"How's Rita?" he asked as soon as he returned to the house.

Oh, that Rita! Seated in her bed, with her leg bandaged, she was laughing with her older sister, who held out, then retracted a little box, saying, "Don't grab it! Don't grab it!"

Rita suddenly gained such importance that Elsa and Zeca looked upon her with a kind of envy for not having remained inside the shed instead of her.

There's no one like children to take advantage of situations! That day Rita achieved what she never had before, despite many attempts. Slowly, still dubious of succeeding, she gave Paulo's face a caress. Then she touched him on the nose with two fingers. Finally she moved decisively. She grabbed hold of Paulo's glasses and sus-pended her gesture as if to ask, *May I?* Filled with happiness, Paulo said nothing, but the lack of response indicated, *You may!* Then the little girl lifted the comrade's glasses and suavely basked in her triumph.

8

On Sunday the 17th, Pereira had just left the house when someone knocked on the door. Conceição hesitated for a moment at the doorway, staring at the tall man in front of her, certain she had seen that face, but unable to identify him. Suddenly she stepped back into the house and opened the door wide. "It's you! Come in, come in. I hardly recognized you."

Her face flushed from surprise and emotion. It was The Friend, the first comrade she had met, who had stayed five days in her house two years before and connected the Pereiras permanently to the Party. But how different he looked! His beard had grown out, the lines and wrinkles in his cheeks as if carved in iron, his face even longer and thinner, and all of him—clothes, hands, face, and especially eyebrows and eyelashes—covered with a thick ashy dust. He looked as though he'd just been rolling around in a pile of cement.

"Did you come because of the strike?" Conceição asked.

"Strike?"

The Friend knew nothing about it. *How could this be?* Conceição asked herself. And she looked at him with a new clarity, almost fearing she was mistaken. But no. It was definitely him. Still eyeing him, surprised by his appearance, she explained to him what she knew of the movement that was set to break out the next day.

"I came at a bad time," The Friend said in a voice so low and grave that it removed all her remaining doubt that it was really him. "Did you notice anything in front of your house?"

No, she hadn't seen anything, nor did it appear that any suspicion or surveillance of the Pereiras existed.

"I want to ask you three things," The Friend said finally, still standing. "First, if you can give me some water so I can wash. Second, can you give me a bite to eat? And finally, if you'll let me sleep a little—anywhere will do. I have to be leaving here around noon. Alright?"

Conceição led him into the kitchen. "But this way you won't get to see my husband. He'll only be back later today."

She filled a large basin with water, placed a fresh towel on the back of a chair and lit the oil stove. The Friend indicated no sign of hurriedness. He remained quiet and still, in his old habit of deep tranquility, watching Conceição busy herself in the quick movements of her rounded figure and the sharpened breathing as she always worked. When she looked at him again, he seemed even taller, his face even thinner, his figure fuller and older, terribly older, his wrinkled skin lined with dust and his affect blurry and tired.

But after a short time The Friend opened the kitchen door to let Conceição in, and once more he looked the same as she had remembered him from two years earlier. Shaven and combed, in shirt sleeves, he was tying a bulky parcel. *He wasn't carrying anything in his hands when he came in*, Conceição thought, taking the earthenware pot off the fire. Was it his jacket? No, it wasn't his jacket.

"Later, when you can," said The Friend in his subdued voice, pointing to his jacket hanging on the chair back, "could you do me the favor of shaking it out outside? But don't let the neighbors see, because you'll surely set loose clouds of powder."

Conceição filled a bowl with the previous night's soup, and placed a piece of bread alongside it. "That's all I can give you now. Never mind, you'll get your fill at lunch."

While The Friend washed, Conceição made the bed and covered it with a new, brightly covered bedspread pulled from a chest and smelling of mothballs. The things we have should be used, right? And if not with your comrades, then with whom?

"You can sleep there as long as you like," she said, bringing him to the room.

"Thank you," The Friend said, beginning to walk with her to the door to shut it.

Conceição got all indignant. "Wait! You're gong to lie down without seeing my little boy?"

The two carefully approached the ornate wicker basket, and Conceição bent over placing a finger to her nose, as if to say, *Be quiet and just look*. She was right. Never in this world was there a more beautiful boy. Slightly turned to his side, he leaned his cheek lightly on his closed hand. His other little hand, puffy and rosy, two fingers curled and another two sticking out, rested gracefully on the pillow. He was sweating and in a deep sleep.

"Have you observed that all children are born Communists?" Conceição asked. "Look at that closed fist! It's only with age that some get corrupted."

A few hours later, when Conceição opened the door to call The Friend in for lunch, she saw him stretched out on the floor still asleep.

"No, friend," he explained himself. "I wasn't going to get your bed dirty. My clothes are so filthy that anywhere I lay down would have gotten like this. Look!"

Indeed, looking at the spot on the floor where he had been lying, Conceição saw a wide shadow of that same ashen dust. *Holy God!*

she thought. *Where has this man been?* And not knowing why, the idea came to her that immediately seemed absurd: *He's coming from abroad.*

When she returned to the front of the house, the boy was no longer where Conceição had left him. On his feet, on his fat bow legs, holding onto a chair, he dragged himself toward the kitchen door, obviously with the intention of escaping. If at that moment she had grabbed him, it would inevitably have turned into a terrible scene—his determined willfulness showed it. But no. The mother waits, and he advances more resolutely. When he reaches the door and sees that he can leave before the mother intervenes, he accelerates his movements, with an expression at the same time desperate and triumphal, as if to say, *Now you can't catch me!* Audaciously he extends his little arm toward the threshold, lets go of the chair, makes one quick, nervous, shaky step forward, rebalances himself, and there he is in the kitchen. Conceição runs, draws him to her, and as she kisses and scolds him, the boy frees himself and laughs uninhibitedly. *See, I won!* he seems to say, and continues laughing over his successful victory as his mother smothers him with kisses.

During lunch, The Friend asked further questions about the next day's movement, and from all these questions Conceição concludes for sure that he has not been working for quite some time. *He's coming from abroad* occurs to her again, however absurd the thought. After lunch, before he took his leave, Conceição brought him to her boy, who was now playing on the floor, and told him, "Go on, give my son a kiss."

After the Friend left, she held the boy and started talking to him in a low, halting and singing tone: "You're going to become a brave man, as brave as The Friend, like Vaz, like António, like your dear papa."

One more thought, new and sad, occurs to her, because she suddenly holds the boy close to her breast and starts kissing him repeatedly on his curly hair, his ears, his neck. "My beloved son, beloved, beloved, beloved—"

The boy was ticklish and laughed even more hysterically.

Chapter XIII

1

On the morning of the 18th, crowds of Cicol workers massed at the gates. On the way to the factory, many had found manifestos affixed to the walls, buildings and trees. They found others on the ground, along the roadsides and footpaths, in stacks topped by a stone, as if inviting everyone to take just one and leave the rest. For days the talk was of a work stoppage, and as this conformed to the general sentiment, the most convinced were awaiting the order to halt, the more timid ones who agreed with that perspective would go along, and only a few weaker men, slipping out in small groups into interior courtyards, were waiting for their chance to start working.

Several questions circulated about: "Has Gaspar come yet?" "Did you see Gaspar?" "Where's Gaspar?" And they searched with their eyes for the companion's tall, well-known figure, waiting for his decision or advice.

Beside the main gate, his thin face channeled with ruts, Túlio looks anxiously to the street. The work sirens sounded once, then again, sinister, alarming whistles. The comrades in the factory seek out their Party leaders and ask, "So?" And the leaders say, "Wait." They then go up to Túlio and ask him too: "So?" And Túlio answers the same: "Wait." From one pair of lips to another, Gaspar's name continues to he heard. "Where is he?" "Why doesn't he come?" "Why doesn't he speak?"

"This won't succeed!" cries a strong voice dominating the whispered conversation.

As if responding to this call, a group of workers stirs from their standing position at the gate and heads for the courtyard. In front of Túlio, a short, heavy man, the brim of his cap over his eyes, shows impatience. "It's less than five minutes away," he shouts in Túlio's face. "We have to do something."

257

"Gaspar should be here any minute. He recommended we do nothing until he arrives."

"And if he doesn't come?" the fat man asks.

"Why wouldn't he come?" Túlio wants to be sure of what he says, but the pallor of his face and the tremor in his voice betray him.

A few workers huddled in a group laughed. "There you go, my friend," says one of them, "it was always that way and always will be."

The number of workers gathered at the gate is now considerably smaller. Most of them had already passed through to the interior courtyards. A few minutes before, a foreman entering the factory, seeing the crowd, thought it wise to duck through unobserved. Now another foreman insolently teased a few of the workers in his department, grouped sadly out on the street. "Well, boys, what are you waiting for? Until Joe the Locksmith gets here?"

One more cluster of workers deserts the gate and enters the factory.

At that moment the worker with the cap over his eyes jumped on top of the wall. "Comrades!" he shouted in a sharp appeal. "Today no one in the region is working! Are we going to betray our fellow workers?"

But it was too late. The siren silenced his voice.

"Now!" a shout came from a hopeless, disillusioned worker. He filed into the factory with effusive gestures.

The motors started howling. And Cicol, the biggest factory in town, the one with the best Party organization, the one on which the work stoppage of all the others depended, began its workday. Túlio, the heavy-set comrade, and a few others, barely a dozen in all, hesitated for a few minutes by the gate, still counting on Gaspar. But finally that group entered the factory too. When they punched their time cards, the guy in charge smiled as he checked the hour on the clock, but did not make an issue of it as he normally would.

Only Jaime, the heavy comrade with the brim over his eyes, and one young, baby-faced apprentice, did not enter for work. After all their other comrades and workmates had disappeared into the factory, these two exchanged a few comments and ran out to the street.

2

At the last meeting on Sunday, Gaspar, followed by Pereira and Túlio, had prevailed with his point of view which earlier, with António, had been rejected. Thus it was agreed that all through the town they should wait for the shutdown at Cicol, and that when Cicol stopped, they should stop as well. In case the others did not strike on their own initiative, workers from Cicol would go there and make them go out. Jerónimo and Vicente opposed this strategy but, in the minority, they had to submit.

"Remember this, comrades," Gaspar had said as his final argument. "If Cicol doesn't strike, even if there are other small work stoppages, it'll be a complete failure."

On entering his factory in the morning, Pereira stated they should begin working and wait. As soon as the news came from Cicol, which a comrade on outside duty would bring, they would walk off too. The first electrician was a comrade. If the workers didn't walk out, he would unplug the motors.

Pereira's instructions traveled through the cell and through the unity committee and, as the workday began, the workers had a glowing expression on their faces, at once happy and focused, it being evident that the majority were waiting enthusiastically for the moment to suspend work.

A few minutes passed. On one pretext or another, two workers made it a point to remain by a window opening onto the side street where the outside comrade would come to bring the news. Continuing at their jobs, the workers kept eyeing one another as if to say, *They're about to see the whirlwind that's gonna kick up*. And the foremen, who had also read the manifesto and were on to the rumors that had been floating around for days, look at the workers' faces and do not feel at ease. From their expressions, from a few words exchanged in whispers, from the quick glances seen, they perceive that something is about to happen and they're nervous.

The outside comrade appeared all out of breath by the agreed-upon window, and with his words, the workers froze: "Cicol is working!"

They went to tell Pereira, who ran to the window. "Liar!"

"They're working, I just said so," the messenger said.

"Did you see them yourself?" and Pereira's feline eyes pierced him almost with rage.

3

On the construction job outside of town only ten men were working. That morning, Manuel Rato spoke with the two other comrades he had there, the three of them spoke with the rest, showed the manifesto to those who hadn't read it, and decided not to start working. Only one stonemason, a sad-faced, middle-aged man, asked if they were sure they also wouldn't be working in the other factories and construction projects.

"No, friend, how can we be sure?" Manuel Rato answered him. "But if we all thought like you and always waited for the others, nothing would ever happen."

Except for the mason, who paced in confusion in front of his workplace, the other men went out to the road heading for the main town in the area. At the first factory they passed they found a strange thing happening. Outside, the street was deserted, and nothing unusual seemed to have taken place. The workers remained inside the factory. But the machines were quiet and, as you'd hear at the entrance to a market, the sound coming from inside was that of many voices talking at once.

With his eight companions, Manuel Rato crossed through the gate and entered. The porter tried to prevent them from going in, but the attempt was so faint-hearted it was obvious he made it only so the owner the next day couldn't say he hadn't done it. Passing through empty corridors, Manuel Rato led his friends toward the sound of the talking. Having hiked the whole length of the building, they came upon the workers massed in front of the offices.

"Have you gone out too?" one worker asked with a smile.

Immediately, those who were nearest to them became excited to see the newcomers, not because they were so many but because in some circumstances where the smallest gestures of support have tremendous value, even the fact that they were few, but of good will, can be worth more than many who are insincere.

"The committees are here," one of the men explained. "The bosses wanted to receive only three of us, but they had to receive thirty!"

He had just finished speaking when the comrades appeared on the stairway landing in front of the offices. Vicente, with his short crewcut and no hat, raised his hands to ask for quiet, and a man with a long face and white hair standing beside him spoke. He addressed them in a natural speaking tone, but in the profound silence that suddenly fell over the courtyard, his voice resounded as clearly as if in a small auditorium.

"Companions. We presented the demands you all approved. Despite the promises made, week after week, once again they refuse to give us a raise and once again resort to promises. Now I've decided."

A hurrah of exclamations and shouts rose in the courtyard. From the landing, Vicente again opened his arms to ask for silence, and when the silence came it was he who spoke next: "It's decided, comrades, isn't it?"

Just then a heavy-set man with a brimmed cap over his eyes and a young man with a childlike face, coming in from outside the factory, cut a path through the workers and headed for the landing. The fat one approached Vicente and whispered to him, "Gaspar was arrested last night. Cicol went to work."

To the comrade's astonishment, Vicente showed neither panic nor surprise. "Of course!" he mumbled with a wry smile.

At that same moment Manuel Rato had also opened a path to the landing and he heard the words of the fat comrade from Cicol. While Vicente was talking with people from the worker and the unity committees, Manuel began shouting in a voice that surprised even himself for its toughness and power:

"Comrades, comrades!" And when the men quieted down, he continued. "In civil construction they also didn't listen to our demands and we also struck. We're here to greet you and join you."

Amidst the shouts of approval, Manuel Rato heard behind him the angry voice of one of the committee members, "We don't have anything to do with civil construction. Those guys will ruin everything."

Vicente again raised his arms. "The opinion of the committees," he said, "is that we should call a work stoppage today and go back to work tomorrow. Do you agree?"

More applause and shouting in support. But then a strong, red-faced man excitedly walked a few steps up toward the landing, As the workers blocked his way, he turned halfway up the stairs toward the mass of workers and bellowed roughly:

"Comrades, don't let yourselves be taken in. All this is the handiwork of the Communists. Do you want the proof? Here's the proof right here!" And saying that, he held up a copy of the manifesto and waved it high into the air.

Laughter broke out.

"Here's another one just like yours!" a worker shouted in reply, waving his hand in the air.

As the man tried to continue speaking, another worker who was a few steps above him on the stairway threw him a kick on his back, which sent him flat onto the floor below. The man got up with his shoulders raised, arms spread in an arc and head cocked like a bull, and leapt up the first few steps in a rage. The workers standing farther off saw a whirl of people, like a tornado, moving in to pacify the guy, then come back to life and finally dissolve into the crowd.

At that moment, from the landing, Vicente shouted, "Everyone to Cicol!"

"To Cicol!" came the penetrating voice of a young woman in a red blouse.

"To Cicol! To Cicol!" shouts came from all sides.

Some members of the committees, among them the one who expressed disagreement with Manuel Rato's intervention, looked glumly out over the general enthusiasm. Obviously they did not share it.

4

Three hundred workers from Vicente's factory, in part reinforced by Manuel Rato's small contingent, joined up farther on with another group of workers, among whom Jerónimo could be seen. Like Manuel Rato, right after arriving at work he and his comrades decided to stop working, and joining them were workers from a locksmith shop where they had read the manifesto. Through the streets and alleys, the residents came to their windows and doors, looking on curiously. Here and there a woman would call out a word of support. Children attached themselves to the cortège, at the front and alongside the first rows, as though it were the village band on a festival day. Cicol was a little away from the center of town, but they would arrive there in a few minutes. They had already turned onto the road leading directly there when a man dressed in ashen gray passed by them in a hurried pace, pretending not to look at the demonstrators and rapidly moving ahead of them. They could still see him from a distance entering Cicol and when they got there a few moments later, the heavy, high factory gates were closed. At the other end of the courtyard the man in gray disappeared into the darkness of a door.

Somewhat disoriented, the new arrivals on the scene formed into groups in front of the factory gates. In the courtyard, some fifteen meters away, the porter, a foreman and an office employee, the three of them standing still and close together, looked sideways now out to the street and now toward the factory buildings. From outside, the shout rose up to open the gate, threatening and provoking them, but the three men stayed unmoving in the same position as if they heard nothing.

The workers from Vicente's factory surrounded their committees, but the committee members shrugged their shoulders as if to say, *What do you want us to do? This isn't our business now.* Some even responded with impatient gestures when asked questions, as if protesting, *This isn't what we were asked to do, and we came only so people wouldn't say we didn't.* A little apart, next to the factory wall, Vicente, Jerónimo, Manuel Rato and the young woman in the red blouse were talking with the heavy-set Jaime and the young apprentice with the childlike face. These two, the only Cicol workers who didn't go in to work, are now telling their companions they can easily enter the factory via a small gate that leads onto some fields. Jaime and the young man offer to enter there with another dozen committed workers, go in and open the gates. Vicente agreed with the idea and went off to find the other workers and leave with the comrades. But Jerónimo gestured him solemnly, that he should wait. With his tired, gray eyes looking absentmindedly over to the masses of fellow workers gathered in front of the gates, he spoke slowly and dispassionately:

"No, comrade, you shouldn't go. Your place is there, with the comrades from your factory, whom you shouldn't abandon even for a minute, much less right now when they're hesitating and need your presence. And these two friends should show the back gate, but shouldn't open the front gate. Being from Cicol, they'd be branded."

Shortly, Jaime, the young apprentice, Manuel Rato, Jerónimo, the woman in the red blouse and a few more workers disappeared some hundred meters away around a corner of the factory wall. Seeing them vanish from view, some of the workers concluded the game was not yet lost and stopped threatening the three men standing on the other side of the gate, and started peppering them with jeers and insults.

Meanwhile, Vicente was talking with his committee members, yielding a development that he hardly expected.

"No, friend, don't ask me to go along with this," said the man with the white hair, who half an hour before had reported the result of the session in the bosses' offices. "I am part of a factory committee to defend the interests of the workers. I am not part, nor want to be, of any revolutionary actions."

Upon which, he removed himself, taking half a dozen of his companions with him. Vicente assumed he was standing apart only to underline his disagreement about the assault on Cicol. But no. He crossed through the groupings of workers, and continued walking, walking in the direction toward town, followed by a few more. *It's only half a dozen*, Vicente thought, *and on the committees alone there are more than thirty involved.* But many looked on indecisively without knowing what to do, for the man with the white hair was one of the most highly regarded workers and a longtime committee member. And, after all, what were they doing there? Cicol was working, the gates were shut, so what could they do? Some workers started saying goodbye to their companions and set off for home. Vicente passed his hand over his brush haircut as if trying to tame it, then remembered Jerónimo's words: *Your place is there, with the comrades from your factory. They need your presence.* Climbing onto a slope on the other side of the street, he shouted with all his force:

"Comrades! Our fellow workers at Cicol are being held as prisoners inside. Will we abandon them?"

The workers turned to hear, and Vicente continued speaking. More than instruct his companions, his fundamental concern was to hold them for a few more minutes and keep a great number of them from going home, giving time to those who had entered the factory to open the gates.

He didn't need to wait long. Shouts and cries and exclamations went up near the main gate. Inside the courtyard there was a commotion. While Manuel Rato and the other companions restrained the resistance from the porter and the two other guards, Jerónimo and Jaime—who, like the young apprentice, could not contain himself from joining the others out of fear that they'd get lost inside the factory—opened the gates wide.

The first person who could readily be seen by those outside was the young woman with the blood-red blouse. Turning to them with her arms raised, she was yelling something over and over again. But the sound of all the voices and shouting was so great that no one understood what she was saying.

5

It wasn't as easy as it looked. Only some workers at Cicol, once they noticed workers from the outside entering the interior courtyards, left their work and went to meet them. Inexplicably, as though disinterested in what was happening, Túlio continued working.

The workmates in his section stared at him questioningly because he was well known as Gaspar's right-hand man. Túlio evaded those glances and tried, with a pale face, trembling hands and sweat bathing his forehead and chest, to concentrate only on his work. Meanwhile, the foremen and an employee from the office dressed in gray—the same man who had passed in front of the workers to warn the factory about shutting the gates—quickly lined up men they trusted, armed them with heavy sticks and iron pipes, and posted them in groups near the entrances.

To Túlio it seemed like a fog had taken possession of his senses and that he was another person there, living a nightmare and trying in vain to shake it off and wake up. He heard shouts and voices in the courtyard, running footsteps of the section foremen, shattering glass, more yelling and voices, and enveloping all those sounds, the rhythmic, monotonous, soothing noise of the machines in operation. Túlio looks only at his workbench, but he feels upon him, nailing him like arrows of fire, the glares of his section comrades, and from beyond the barriers and walls, the stares of all the workers in the factory and of the whole working class in the town. He sees Vicente's fixed eyes under that brush that was his blond hair; and Jerónimo's ashen, tired eyes; and Pereira's cold, green eyes; and António's smiling eyes surrounded by wrinkles. And all of them fused together in the same censure, the same condemnation. The noise of voices grows, more glass is broken, more shouts and deafening, indecipherable noises of things and bodies colliding, and everything still wrapped in the steady, soothing sound of working machines. Túlio wants, he so wants to lift his eyes and look at what's going on, at least right around him, but they are fixed with horror on the now accentuated tremor at the tips of his own fingers.

The scrimmages that had taken place at the entrances did not resolve things. The workers who invaded the factory maintained their determination to bring it to a halt. But the foremen and their trusties unflinchingly cut off their path. Inside the factory, confused, without organization, habituated to wait for all their directions from one man, Gaspar, the workers continued working, feeling a sense of guilt but powerless to react.

Maybe that's how things would have remained if an unforeseen occurrence had not arisen: Inside the factory, a huge new contingent of unfamiliar workers streamed in. At their helm, his cold green eyes like a cat's, Pereira was quickly advancing, swaggering with his broad-shouldered body.

It was only then that the manager, for so long trapped in an outbuilding and peeking at what was happening, felt suddenly filled with dread and, courting ruin and damage, gave the order to disconnect the motors.

6

When Paulo boarded the jitney heading toward the meeting place, he met face to face with Ramos, who had lowered his newspaper to see who was entering. The eyes of the two comrades locked for a brief instant, only to quickly divert away as though out of disinterest. Paulo chose a space farther back, next to a fat old lady dressed in black who practically took up the two places on the seat. Seeing that Paulo was intending to sit down, she looked closely at him and made every gesture of kindly accommodating herself to the remaining space. She raised herself slightly, shook out her body, and sat down again with her eyes pointing to the space she left for her new neighbor, readjusted the folds of her skirt and breathed deeply, like someone who's just completed a great effort for someone else's benefit. In truth, she did not give up a centimeter of her former position. Half-seated, Paulo looked back at the woman over his eyeglasses. With her prominent double chin, she looked sideways at him too, smiling: *You don't have to thank me*, the smile said. *We're here for one another*.

Paulo thought of changing seats, but the other passengers who boarded with him had taken them all. The route was full of curves and potholes, the jitney was moving along at a good pace, and Paulo constantly fought to balance himself on the edge of the seat that his neighbor had left him. In this awkward position, his burnt leg aggravated him more. *I'm going to arrive more tired than if I'd walked*, he thought. *Doesn't this woman realize she's taking up my space?* Once again he looked sideways toward her. Imposing in her avoirdupois, with her neck gently twisted, the woman continued to look at him askance and, when she saw him turn toward her, she smiled at him with that same look of someone who's performing a great favor and possesses the generosity to dispense with gratitude. One especially tight curve threw Paulo, and he practically landed sprawled in the aisle. The woman didn't budge. *I really need to say something to her*, Paulo thought indignantly. *If I was Ramos I would already have said it*. But in the end, the trip was short and not worth the bother. And then, who knows, maybe the woman would cause a scandal, calling attention to him from all the riders. Paulo bore up with his uncomfortable position until the end, but worse than that were his irritation at the unknown woman's behavior and his own bashfulness.

The two men got off at a crossroads. They let the jitney proceed on its route, both started up a narrow and equally potholed little street, and only then began to talk.

"What happened?" Ramos asked, looking at Paulo's bandaged hand, his burnt face and his singed eyelashes and eyebrows.

"The lumber factory struck," Paulo answered, "and they're considering a march this afternoon. I don't know about the rest yet."

"No, *that!*" Ramos said, pointing to the comrade's burns, but Paulo didn't respond.

The tiny, bending road snaked though pine forests and fields of yellow stubble. Seasonal crickets pulsed in the warm, heavy air. Farther on they cut through a path in the pines, and after a hundred meters or so they stopped. Ramos looked around, stared closely at the treetops and finally chose a site on the ground with soft pine needles and little brush.

"Choosing a site in a pine grove," he said, removing his tie, "is an art. If you don't pay good attention to the treetops and the path of the sun, you'll be changing your site from minute to minute. We're good here," he added, looking about and taking his jacket off.

Hatless and in shirtsleeves, relieved and comfortable, they sat in the shade. Paulo checked his watch: A quarter to one.

"The train must have come by now, but from the station to here will take António a good quarter of an hour."

"Yes, it will," Ramos agreed, stretching out on his back and looking at his comrade.

Paulo searched in his jacket for a railway schedule and started leafing through it.

"You didn't have lunch, clearly," Ramos said.

"No, I didn't."

"Me neither, old man. But this air feeds you too." And to feed himself, he breathed in deeply, filling his broad chest.

"We're in the sun already," said Paulo with audible intent.

"Damn! Looks like I didn't choose so well." Ramos stood up and peered into the upper story of the pine trees with an air of profound understanding. "Here, this place will do. We'll have shade here until sundown."

After a quarter of an hour, and after running from the sun two more times, they heard footsteps and saw a thin, pale man approaching with a bicycle in his hands.

"I didn't recognize you," Ramos said as the man walked toward them. "You're thin!"

"I was here a good half hour ago," said Vaz. "I figured you'd be coming later." And he briefly recounted what he knew about his sector. He had been with José Sagarra and with two other peasants in the lead organization. In all the villages that he'd heard from, the rural workers left work and—something no one expected—some small artisans also struck. They were going to hold hunger marches this afternoon in two towns that they chose. He had also been with comrades from two places where they confirmed strikes. Aside from the comrades' reports, Vaz could see, from the bicycle ride he took, that the strike was far more extensive in the fields than the organization predicted. On account of the manifestos, certainly thousands of workers went out, and it was expected that the hunger marches and demonstrations would be on the same scale. As for the Regional Committee of Marques and Cesário, Vaz hadn't been with them, but Sagarra spoke with one person heading out of the city who said life there was completely normal. About the repression, it's still too soon to know anything for sure.

"Let's see what news António has," Ramos said. "That's the only industrial center in the region and maybe the best organization. Between that and your peasants the movement may be roaring."

António was a few minutes late. He arrived, sweaty and over-heated, and gave some disconcerting news: He knew nothing, because Gaspar missed the meeting.

"And what did you do to reconnect the contact?" Ramos asked, as if to say, *I'm asking, but I see already you didn't do anything.*

António was embarrassed. The truth is he had done nothing. He had waited for Gaspar more than half an hour, which seemed like too long already, killed some time and finally went to catch the train. But the worst of it was that he didn't see how he could reestablish the contact that day because he had a meeting scheduled with a com-rade somewhere else.

"What?!" Ramos exploded in anger.

The comrades looked at one another. All their work was com-promised by the lack of information from the most important sector.

Ramos continued to glare at António aggressively. *There's no time now,* his look seemed to suggest, *but later you'll see how I feel about it.*

Then he turned to Vaz. "You shouldn't go," he told him. "If you go we could wind up being disconnected from everything. But the truth is—"

Without completing his sentence, Ramos looked at Paulo and everyone guessed what he wanted to say: *But the truth is, if you, Vaz, don't go, surely Paulo is not the man to go.*

"I'll go," Paulo said, so calm and composed that Ramos looked at him in surprise. And in further surprise, because Paulo, as though his proposal was already an agreed-upon thing, started right away consulting his railway guide.

"I think it's good if he goes," Vaz offered, as though fearful of any other solution.

Looking at them all one by one, abashed and confused, António perceived the haste of Vaz's intervention. What Vaz dreaded was evidently that he, António, offer himself and persuade the others to send him, and to have Paulo replace him at the meeting later that afternoon.

"Comrades," António said with some hesitation. "I recognize I should have gone into town and established a contact before I came here. I don't know why I didn't. But I think that if someone goes there, it's right that it be me, because I'm responsible for the sector and because I know more comrades."

"Did you see anything?" Ramos asked Paulo.

"There's a train at 2:15," Paulo answered. "If I take Vaz's bicycle to the station, I can still catch it."

Even more confused because no one even reacted to his proposal, António then told Paulo where Manuel Rato lived. As Paulo knew Jerónimo and his family, one way or another he'd be able to reconnect the contact.

Ramos would go on to Vaz's house. The other comrades would go there as soon as they could.

Paulo folded his jacket, placed it on the luggage rack and took hold of the bicycle. Short in stature, ungainly, a lock of his white hair hanging out from under his Spanish beret, his tortoise-shell eyeglasses halfway down his nose, the burn on his face, his hand in a bandage, he looked like some poor maladroit incapable of doing anything serious.

"Do you know how to ride a bicycle?" Ramos suddenly asked in his upbeat voice, amused by the comrade's figure but at the same time, without knowing why, rather moved.

Paulo carried the bicycle out to the path. There he placed one foot on the pedal, made two, three, four hops with the other foot—"He knows! He knows!" Ramos shouted with a hearty laugh—and there he was sitting on the saddle. The bicycle coasted down the path, leaning perilously to the right, then to the left—"He's falling! He's falling!" Ramos exclaimed, rising to his feet—and then again straightening up. The bicycle returned to the middle of the path, now balanced and silent, carrying Paulo's figure with his head so buried between his shoulders you could only see the Spanish beret. Together with the road itself, he gradually disappeared.

7

In the region Vaz supervised, the work stoppage in the fields was absolute. In places where there was some organization they offered up their demands. Wherever the manifesto reached, rural workers followed the call to refrain from work on the 18th and not even show up at the farms. Where there was no organization, and where the manifesto had not reached, the work stoppage broke out all day long as news arrived of what was happening in other places. Since rural wage earners predominated in the region, it could be said that all the agricultural workers struck on the 18th.

In the villages, the strikers gathered in groups, and artisans and housewives joined them. Even the small farmers ended up leaving their little plots and, either out of sympathy or mere curiosity, came to join up with the workers. A strange spectacle could be seen throughout the region: Units of men, women and children marched down the roads, paths and byways in long, irregular lines. Only on a few of them did people converse. The great majority walked in silence, with a peaceful, solemn demeanor. Here and there, in the settlements and houses they passed, curious faces appeared. They asked questions, and more men, women and children joined the processions. Like rivulets of water trickling down the slopes toward the valley, that fuse together timidly at first, then form ever denser cascades until they are transformed into an unstoppable torrent, these strands of human beings, flowing from all directions toward the two main towns of the region, met up, mixed in, getting ever larger and more animated. When they arrived at their destination via different access roads, they were already compact groupings of hundreds of people.

In both towns, the demonstrators concentrated in front of City Hall. The two concentrations took on distinct aspects, however. In one town, the peasants gathered on the main square preserved their patient silence. Some of the town residents came out to join them. Windows were crowded with people eager to watch. As the day was warm and bright, it was almost like a festival day in town. The president of City Hall, who at the first warning locked himself in his office to telephone for "troops to crush the revolt," ended up listening to his subordinates and going to look out the window. Seeing that throng of peaceful folk showing no sign of rebellion, and noticing the high number of women and children, he ordered the Guard to make them disperse.

"There's only six of us, sir," said the sergeant. "It's better to let them be. They'll eventually go away."

The softness of others turns cowards into warriors. In a sudden decision that even he couldn't say had any particular purpose, the City Hall president appeared with his subordinates on the balcony overlooking the square. All the people focused on him then and, still in complete silence, a few demonstrators initiated a weird gesture that he took as an obscenity: They raised their hands to the level of their mouth and appeared to be pointing at it with their fingers. Only a handful started the gesture, then dozens picked it up, until in short order everyone in the square was doing it. What a grotesque, tragic and threatening thing for him to see—the silent multitude all pointing to their own mouths. *Bread! Bread!* Finally the president understood that silent gesture.

In the other town things went quite differently. Thousands of men, women and children entered from the access roads. Shouts echoed across the plaza. And at the tip of sticks or canes, black kerchiefs, black rags, even a black skirt, people unfurled their flags of hunger. In shock, business owners shut their doors, and the Guard came running to protect City Hall, stationing themselves at the top of the outside stairway. Out of the crowd of demonstrators a small group of peasants, five men and two women, climbed the stairs with determined steps.

"We want to be received by the president of City Hall," said to the sergeant of the Guard one peasant with a dark, freckled face with shining clear eyes, in one of which was a visible little white cloud.

Meanwhile, hundreds of voices clamored in rhythm, "Bread, bread. Bread, bread—"

Around two in the afternoon, forces sent from the capital fell on the demonstrators. Hundreds of steel-helmeted guards, armed with rifles and submachine guns, jumped from their trucks and, led by plainclothes agents arriving in wagons and cars, surrounded the town center. All afternoon, in the midst of shouting, protests and minor scuffles, police vans or simple freight trucks, in a constant flow, carted both men and women peasants, helter-skelter with artisans and mere bystanders, off to the capital. There they were crammed in the barracks of a military base hurriedly transformed into a concentration camp.

The City Hall president, an imposing, ruddy-faced man flushed with rage over the humiliation he'd suffered, described to the plainclothes agents the features of the peasant committee members whom he'd tremblingly received in his office just hours before. He did not know their names, however, nor where they were from, and this infuriated him even more.

"Their leader has a cloudy eye and freckles on his face!" he shouted at them. "Freckles! Do you understand?"

From all that had taken place, that's all he could say.

"Freckles, for God's sake!" he repeated. "Freckles!"

8

At dawn Marques the carpenter woke extremely anxious. The night before, reflecting on the preparation for the movement, he concluded that because of the dangers it represented for the local organization, he would not have the manifestos circulated in the city. Except for those reserved for the factories and workshops under Cesário's supervision, it was he, Marques, who was charged with organizing and directing the nighttime distribution. To that effect he had chosen some comrades and sympathizers with the idea from the beginning that they would either refuse, or wouldn't show up, or would appear only so as not to be called cowards. To his surprise, of the five he chose, four cheerfully expressed themselves as willing. And to his greater surprise, they all turned out for the meetup set for 11 that night.

"The comrade never showed up," Marques invented to explain his not having brought the manifestos. "You'll have to excuse me, but some other time—"

Marques justified this behavior to himself by the need to defend the local organization from an adventurist action involving tremendous dangers which the comrades on a higher level, unfamiliar with the concrete local circumstances, did not recognize. But having promised Cesário and Henriques to complete the distribution and deliberately not doing so, seeing the enthusiasm of comrades and sympathizers that he considered "worthless" and deflating their enthusiasm with a lie, caused him a painful restlessness that the higher reasons he invoked would not overcome. The few hours he spent in his bed he tossed from one side to the other, trying to reinforce in his own mind the reasons for such conduct, mentally repeating over and over again that only the interests of the Party determined it, but tormented because stating it did not succeed in restoring either his peace of mind or his sleep.

He left in the half-light of the new day and went to find Henriques at home. Henriques was surprised, almost frightened by the visit, by the unusual hour, and by the fact that it was the first time Marques had ever sought him out.

"Wait a minute," he said when he came to the door. "I'll be right out."

There was in fact nowhere in the house where Marques could have been received. Henriques's companion and two youngest children were sleeping in the bedroom, and in the kitchen were the mother-in-law and the two older children.

"I decided to come talk with you, comrade," Marques began when Henriques emerged to meet him, chilled by the cool of dawn and blinking his eyes even more than usual, "because the situation we're in is especially serious. There's supposed to be a strike today in your shop, at the Jute and other workplaces. But what will come of it? If we issue the call to strike and the workers don't strike, it would be tremendously damaging to the Party. If we go through with it there will be a fierce repression without a doubt."

Marques paused in the street and faced Henriques so that he would better hear and understand him. In the weak dawn's light,

Henriques saw only the eyeglass lenses obscuring the rest of his comrade's face.

"It's a well-known teaching of Lenin that the vanguard should never throw itself alone into battle. But that is precisely what's about to happen here. We—the vanguard, the Communists—are throwing ourselves into the battle, and not being joined by the masses, we expose ourselves to getting destroyed by the enemy."

Marques went on talking, and Henriques, his thin, diminutive body contracting against the wind, heard him attentively. When Marques finished, saying he considered the strike there in the city a piece of nonsense with tragic consequences for the Party, Henriques asked him, in his lilting voice, "Did you speak to Cesário?"

No, he hadn't. He had decided to speak directly to Henriques because there was no time to lose.

"Obviously," Henriques said in his high-pitched manner, blinking his eyes. "Well, thank you so much for the lesson, friend. He who doesn't know learns, right?"

And taking his leave of Marques, he added, incidentally, "If I have the time, I'll talk with Cesário. If I have time. It's okay with you, I'm sure."

Henriques immediately ran to Cesário's house and told him of his talk with Marques.

"What the hell's that guy doing?!" Cesário spurted, with an expression of deep frustration.

"I can't repeat his exact words," Henriques said. "But it seems to me that on some things he may be right. If we, the Party, rush to the front and we're not followed, we'll be washed up without question."

Cesário interrupted him excitably, in a tone Henriques had never heard from him. "Meaning: the organization decides on something, gives instructions to all the comrades, prepares everything that's needed, and at the last minute some little comrade"—and using this deprecatory term for the first time in relation to Marques, Cesário repeated it—"some little comrade, deeming himself a great leader of the Party, goes around, on his own, giving counter-orders. If I didn't know Marques as well as I do, I'd say he was doing the work of disruption and provocation."

Henriques shook his head. "Listen, I also think it was wrong for him to come see me and that's why I came to you. But to deny that he's right on some things? That I can't do."

"Friend!" Cesário broke in again, with the same excitability. "Look. Under the influence of Marques, you're saying that the Party comrades, if they're not followed, will expose themselves to repression. Obviously they're exposing themselves, above all if they didn't do their work correctly. But just yesterday you told me we would be followed, that the workers without a party and the committee members were also in agreement with the strike. To what end now are the little comrade's lessons? Only confusion and misguidance. There are no more excuses, not even half-excuses. Now we just have to carry out what's been decided and do whatever is possible—and impossible—to pull off the strike."

Henriques left resolved to follow Cesário's advice. But when he spoke with the workers committee at his shop, he found they had completely changed their opinions from the previous day. Except for one, all the others were pessimistic and reluctant, stating their view that they should go back on the idea of shutting down the shop. *So you see, in the end Marques always was right about some things*, Henriques thought.

What Henriques did not know is that Marques, after leaving him earlier, went to speak with these same people who now were acting so discouraged.

9

Having received directions the previous evening and having read the manifesto, the workers were waiting for the order to strike. No one gave it. Party leaders and members of the committee tried to fade unseen into the woodwork, as if they had no knowledge of anything.

"So what kind of people do we have leading us?" yelled one strapping fellow so worked up in anger that the veins in his neck looked like ropes. "Are they men or are they Borralhas?" His listeners got the reference: Borralha was a pathetic drunk, a servant in the shop who was the butt of ridicule from his coworkers.

Henriques began talking with people here and there, advising them not to start work. Unsupported by the committee members— all of them disaffected thanks to Marques's intervention—he ended up, with the worker who called the committee members "Borralhas" and three others who agreed on the spur of the moment, taking the demands to the manager, as had been decided. It did not escape the manager's notice that Henriques showed up without his former *companheiros*.

"A new committee, Senhor Henriques?" the manager asked. "Very well. For now I can't decide anything because just a few weeks ago I gave you a raise." And eyeing Henriques with a malicious smile, he added, "I know people out there are saying certain things. Your most sensible colleagues have already abandoned you. You need to watch what you do. Whatever happens is going to be your responsibility."

Henriques looked back at him, blinking his eyes innocently. "But are you considering it or not? Giving a raise or not?"

The strapping young man interrupted, setting his closed fist on the desk. "You, sir, are threatening my coworker Henriques, but I want to say to you that I and my *companheiros* are with him. What he will be 'responsible' of, I'll be 'responsible" too."

The manager began toying with a letter opener and gazed at him with that same diabolical smile. "Very well, very well. Now I know and I won't forget. I like real men who speak up."

"But are you giving a raise or not?" Henriques insisted. "It's always good to know."

"I have given my answer!" the manager said as he rose to his feet, signaling the end of the meeting. "If you guys do anything crazy, it's you going to get harmed, not me. If anything bad happens, you asked for it."

Henriques and his coworkers left the office and reported the result of their effort. The strong young man who accompanied Henriques—whom the comrades in the shop had never noticed—spoke with such passion, and his speech corresponded so neatly with the general sentiment that the workers applauded him several times. Following Henriques's recommendation, the workers decided to go on strike for 24 hours, just as the manifesto said. But two members of the formerly constituted committee, feeling personally drawn to Marques's view, counseled against such a move and, under their influence, many workers took up their work posts.

At the same hour, Cesário's small shop went out, also several public construction jobs, a warehouse and the jute factory. There, many women, already committed the day before, didn't even show up for work, and those who did unhesitatingly decided not to start their workday. Tall and thin, with her blond hair cut in bangs over her forehead and the rest tied with a ribbon in back (a red ribbon that day), Lisete went from group to group, quietly and patiently talking with the other women. One strong brunette took hold of Lisete's arm: "Oh, if Maria could only see us now, how happy she'd be, eh?" And she smiled remembering her former factory coworker who had left months before.

"She'll know about it!" Lisete told her, smiling too with her sweet, bashful expression.

10

Paulo left the bicycle for safekeeping in a tavern, took the train and got off one stop ahead of his destination. He would have to walk several kilometers, but the station would be under such surveillance that Paulo thought it good prudence to do it. He realized his good sense when he exited the train: Although it was a depressing little station in a rural area with no industry, a Guard patrol on the platform next to the gray wooden sheltered area was attentively observing the passengers. The guards neither asked nor said anything, but Paulo felt their eyes scanning him from head to foot in a rude and hostile manner. Outside the crossing stood another patrol. But they seemed not to be paying any attention to the new arrivals. One of the guards, with an open collar, was wiping his sweaty neck with a kerchief.

Paulo crossed the station grounds and started on the road. He had barely gone a few hundred meters when, by surprise, at the first fork in the road, he encountered a roadblock. Four helmeted guards formed a group next to the road signs marking directions and distances. Another two were talking with some women in the middle of the road that Paulo intended to follow. Along the edge of the road and near the guards, various groups of civilians, mostly peasants, hovered silent and thoughtful.

It was too late to go back and find another way through the fields. Paulo continued straight ahead and stopped a short distance away from the two guards talking with the women.

"I understand very well, no need for more talking," one of the guards, with a big red nose, was saying. "What you wanted is to join up with them. There's enough people screaming there already."

"It's obvious that's what she wanted," another guard reinforced the other with importance.

"You have no idea the inconvenience you're causing me," the woman said slowly and patiently. "If I don't go there today, I don't know when I'll be able to return, and I'm the one listening to my husband, not you guys."

"Even if we let you through, it's a lost cause," said the red-nosed guard. "All business is closed." And looking around with a sudden insecurity, he added, "I've already told you more than I should have."

Contracting his eyebrows, he then assumed a hard, cruel expression, chastising the others for the revelation he himself had committed. He eyed Paulo, as though noticing his presence only now and asking what he was doing there.

"So are you saying there's some kind of disturbance there?" Paulo asked in a voice as diffident as the rest of him.

The guard continued to stare at him with his pinched face. It seemed he wanted to take the measure of the newcomer's resistance to the guard's threatening look, and read any forbidden intentions in signs of impatience or resentment,. "Why?" he asked. "Do you want to go there too?"

"If there's no disturbance, yes, because I live there and my whole family's there. Now, if there is a disturbance, let them fend for themselves, I'll stay at my kid's godmother's. I've already got enough headaches," Paulo said, holding up his bandaged hand.

The phrases came out of Paulo as naturally as if that were truly his situation. With no intention of playacting, he put on a sly smile that perfectly matched his words.

With annoyance, the red-nosed guard took his gaze off Paulo and looked toward his companion. "This guy is leaving his family to the fire and it doesn't bother him. And surely he loves them."

The other guard nodded affirmatively, with the same air of approval and importance.

"You said it well, sir," Paulo continued in an inflection somewhere between humble and shrewd. "But three dead people are worth less than two dead and one living, and I only have one life."

"Yes, well, that's your business," the red-nosed guard said depreciatively, feeling himself as great a defender of good morality as a defender of public order. Turning toward his companion, he added, "It takes all kinds these days—"

Not yet knowing what requirements they demanded from those who wanted to pass, Paulo stepped back a few paces and joined other people at the side of the road. Meanwhile, an old lady with a basket came up to the guards and spoke with them, and after examining her basket, they let her continue on her way.

Paulo approached them once again, pointing to the old lady walking through. "So, you can get there without incident?" he asked.

The one with the red nose stood for a few moments sizing up that short little man in shirtsleeves, with his jacket across his arm, with the Spanish beret under which a tuft of white hair poked out, with unimposing eyes behind his glasses, with charred eyebrows and bandaged face and hands. Then he shrugged his shoulders. "A coward! That's what you are!"

"I'll be going, then," Paulo said, in a voice the guards heard as submissive and resigned. "But I'd like to know, right?"

And passing the guards, he continued on the road, expecting at any moment they would call him back to ask him something or check his pockets. But no. The two guards followed him with their eyes, and the red-nosed one said, "If it wasn't for me, he wouldn't be going, you can be sure of that."

"He sure wouldn't," the other confirmed, importantly.

11

On his way, Paulo met a man coming from the opposite direction and leading a burro. The man appeared to be crazed with fear, talking in unconnected sentences. He told the story of a plane which flew overnight dropping papers, and Paulo understood by what he was saying that the factories had gone out, with troops everywhere. He also said that just ahead, at a crossroads, uniformed guards and others in plainclothes were searching everyone as well as vehicles that were trying to pass from one side to the other.

"The only thing they missed were the burro's ears," he said with wide open eyes.

The man continued on his way, and Paulo, leaving the road, decided to cut through the fields. He did not know the region well, but the distance was not great and it wouldn't be hard to find his way. He chose the first white houses of a town as his objective, figuring that once there he'd be at close range with his destination point and could obtain more specific information. One thing that surprised him as he walked was to find, on a beautiful day like that and at this season of intense agricultural work, the fields completely deserted. He saw shocks of hay and blond sheaves of harvested cereal grain, but no one following through on the work. Paulo's goal was to reach the industrial center, establish contact with the comrades, obtain correct information, and give instructions appropriate to the situation and to secure the future contact. From the guards he met, and from the news the man with the burro shared, he already believed the workers' strike had been a success. But given that there was no peasant organization there, nor had any peasant strike been prepared similar to that in Vaz's sector, Paulo didn't analyze the strange phenomenon of the empty fields, nor did he tie it to the movement that day.

As he neared the little village he had set as his first goal, he wondered if he would meet anyone on the streets who could give him information, or if he would enter a village abandoned like the fields. The path by which he walked into the village, and the first byways he saw were in fact deserted. But suddenly he came upon a spot with tremendous animation and movement. A numerous crowd had gathered around an open, uncovered truck there. In it were some twenty-odd peasants, men and women, who talked and laughed, and whose words and laughter answered the others in the gathering. At first sight, Paulo thought it was some festive celebration, but right away he was surprised to see several armed guards surrounding the truck. There was no doubt: The peasants laughing on the back of that truck had been seized and were to be taken away. By the looks of it, this did not detract from their high spirits.

"Mariana!" someone shouted. "Put today's dinner together with tomorrow's for when I return. At least I'll have a full plate!"

The others on the truck laughed, and people on the ground responded in kind.

The truck clearly had some motor problem, because a military man was having a hard time with it. In the meantime the peasants continued to laugh and make mocking jokes.

"Go ahead, laugh, laugh! Maybe you'll be crying soon!" the corporal of the Guard shouted. From the tone he employed it was evident this was not his first attempt to put a stop to this impudence.

As though they had been rehearsed, the peasants promptly obeyed the corporal's suggestion and started wailing and pretending to cry.

"How sad now that we can't laugh...woe is me, we're not allowed to laugh!"

New rounds of loud guffawing resounded from the crowd.

"Stop with this insulting act!" the corporal yelled, red-faced with ire and impotence.

It's as though they had been given the order for a new scene. The apprehended peasants, with great moaning and redoubled sobbing, started shouting, "Ay, how unfortunate that now we can't even cry! How sad we're not allowed to cry! Ay, they won't let us cry!"

And the people went on laughing. Even a teenage boy was laughing who, with an enormous rag, was tirelessly wiping blood flowing from his nose and forehead from being beaten with a rifle butt hours before.

They repeated to Paulo the story of the plane flying at night and distributing "orders." He learned that all of the industries had struck in the town where he was headed, that in the surrounding fields many workers had stopped first thing in the morning, that no one had worked past noontime, that many peasants had come in to join the factory workers. But also that now the troops were not allowing anyone through because there was a hell of a commotion going on and they were arresting and beating people everywhere.

12

The peasant who gave these reports to Paulo was a short, skinny old man with a pinched, wrinkled face and sunken, observant eyes that practically disappeared under the shade of his hat. As they talked, Paulo was steering him toward the sidelines of the square. He asked him the best path to take to his destination without passing through the line of troops. He explained this need with the same story he had told the guards on the road—that he was from there and had his family there.

While Paulo spoke, the old man didn't take his sharp eyes off him. After reflecting a few moments, he told him, in a calm, lowered voice, "What you need is to get there without incident, and you will. I will show you the way myself, and my grandson will do the rest."

The old man told Paulo to wait just outside the square, hidden in the shade of a wall, and he returned shortly with a young boy some nine or ten years old, shoeless, hatless, and dressed in rags. At a sluggish pace, for the old man only walked with difficulty, the three cut through the fields, around a hill, all the time out of view of the road because of the contours of the land and vegetation. Thus they ambled for ten minutes. All of a sudden, only a few hundred meters ahead, there arose the clear, happy outlines of a row of houses in bright sunlight. And right past them the heavy, clumsy yellow buildings of a factory stood out; and farther away the enormous red bulk of a bullring.

"Continue on to the farm," the old man said to the boy, "and if your godfather is around, or anyone from his house, tell them it's on my behalf."

And turning to Paulo, he added, "That way you'll get to the middle of town and avoid any bad encounters on the roads."

Paulo extended his hand to the old man, who squeezed it with unexpected warmth, even as his eyes welled up. *I understood right away that you don't have any family over there, my son*, that warmth and emotion conveyed. *If I didn't understand that, I wouldn't have done what I'm doing.*

"Thank you, comrade," Paulo said, sensing what was coursing through the old man's soul.

On hearing those surprising words, the old man held out his left hand too, held Paulo's hand between both of his own bony, gnarled and trembling hands, and paused there movingly a few more moments.

"This is a great day," he said finally in a voice tremulous like his hands, and separating from Paulo, pushed him along with a deliberate gesture. "Go. Go on, my son."

This is a great day, Paulo thought, walking a little behind the youngster through the trees of an orchard. *A great, great day.*

The young boy kept silent. With the steady, noiseless steps of his shoeless feet, he led Paulo through the farm, and without anyone about, brought him to a gate that opened onto a wholly deserted town alley. There he stopped, turned toward Paulo and smiled.

Only then did Paulo clearly see his face, narrow and tanned, with the delicate nose and mouth of a child, and small, watchful and understanding eyes like those of his grandfather. Paulo reached his hand out, and the boy awkwardly did the same, for it was the first time in his life that he had ever shaken hands with anyone.

This is a great day, thought both of them.

13

Since Jerónimo's house lay on the main road well away from the center, it would be hard for someone like Paulo, who was not that familiar with the town and the surroundings, to get there without stumbling on the troops, so Paulo decided to first go to Manuel Rato's house. He knew it was across from an abandoned building called the Old Factory, and António had said that, asking for the Old Factory, anyone in town could show him the way to it.

The route Paulo followed was a mixture of road, trail and street, where houses alternated with walls and rough garden fences. No one could be seen, and all the windows and doors of the houses were closed.

The road came to an end at a long, narrow street with a line of houses on each side, where several groups of people could be seen standing around. Only much farther away could Paulo discern the greenish blur of a patrol. Otherwise all was tranquil, and the people standing on the street appeared completely at ease. Paulo sought out two women conversing on the other side of the street, just beyond where he had entered it, to ask them about the Old Factory. But when he was but a few steps away from them, they suddenly turned with excitement to face the top of the street, and following their gaze, Paulo saw, some fifty meters away, a large number of people rushing headlong toward him. In a few seconds he saw that mass fill up the whole width of the street and thicken in a torrent of humanity gushing in from two side streets.

"Here they come! Here they come!" the women shouted, stepping up onto the stone steps of a nearby house.

The excitement possessed the other groups there, and everyone quickly found a place in the doorways. Looking again out on the mass of people approaching to occupy the street from one side to the other, Paulo did as the others and found a spot next to the women. Meanwhile, from the opposite direction, a little farther down, at the mouth of the deserted alley from which he had come a few moments before, now came several armed guards who had surely come by that alley, and even farther down, other guards appeared from a cross street, marching hurriedly but then disappearing again.

At the fore of the demonstrators came a row of young people hand in hand. One girl with a bright red blouse marched a little in front of her two neighbors and not satisfied with their pace, seemed to be pulling them. In that first row also one young man with short hair like a brush and a willful demeanor stood out. He was saying something to the people at his side and more than once turned his head around to speak with the people following behind him. After that hand-in-hand row came a large group slightly differentiated from the mass, and Paulo recognized Jerónimo among them. He seemed paler and older, but it was definitely him, and close enough that Paulo could see the gray of his tired eyes, and the irregular, unshaved beard. If he could only say two words to him, just a couple of words to set a meeting time.... But the front end of the demonstration had passed already, and Jerónimo disappeared behind the others.

The multitude of men and women became dense and compact, seeming to glide more than walk along the streets. Here and there, like debris floating atop the current, a black rag at the end of a stick. Factory workers were the majority, but broad swaths of the white shirts and blouses of field workers could be seen. And there were also men and women who, by their hats, their hair styles, their collars, the makeup on the faces, were obviously neither factory nor field workers. Amongst the mass of marchers, Paulo's attention was drawn to one strong brunette woman. With one arm she was holding a quiet, bored little boy perched on her shoulder, and with her free arm she was raising the black kerchief she had removed from her head and waving it as high and as energetically as she could into the air. Her loose hair swept over her face, some over her eyes, but she seemed not to notice. She shouted endlessly, congested and hoarse, tirelessly continuing to wave her black kerchief. Paulo could not understand the words the woman was shouting. But in the strength with which she held the little one, in the vigor of her raised arm, in the violent passion etched on her face, Paulo read the determination and courage of people on the march, and he couldn't take his eyes off her until she disappeared from view.

The river of people stopped for a few minutes, compacting even more. Certainly up front they had stopped also. Then it started up again. Now a big banner appeared across the street, held up by two sticks in the grasp of a strong woman and a hatless young fellow.

At that point in the cortege, unlike the rest of the marchers, demonstrators walked in formation, and from one side to the other came cordons of people hand-in-hand. The human river stopped once more at that moment, and Paulo saw Manuel Rato just a couple of steps away from him.

He had his head uncovered, and his forehead, generally spared the sun's rays, shone out whitely from his darkish face, even blacker for the ebony of his close-cropped mustache. With his eyebrows furrowed, his face determined, Manuel Rato looked straight ahead toward some indefinite point.

Paulo came off the two steps where he was standing and called to his comrade. Manuel Rato did not hear him, but someone else beside him called his attention.

"You?!" Manuel Rato blurted out, in even greater surprise because of Paulo's singed and burnt appearance.

Then the cordon of hands-in-hands broke to let him through.

"Where can I meet you when this is over?" Paulo asked.

"When this is over?!" Manuel Rato repeated, seemingly perplexed and confused, and coming up with no response.

Just then the cortege started up again, and Paulo, after helplessly trying to exit the human stream, was dragged along by it.

14

At the mouth of that alley over which Paulo had walked, the clutch of guards was still there, holding back with no attempt to intervene. Ahead, at another crossing, on one side and the other, other groups of guards also made no moves to intervene. More than once, Paulo tried to exit the parade, but to no avail. The demonstrators on that narrow funnel of a street literally scraped the walls.

"This is not wise, my friend," Manuel Rato kept saying, shaking his head in displeasure, his broad white forehead swollen, his dark face focused in gloom.

Despite the attention he paid to Paulo and to all that was happening around them, he seemed swamped and dominated by the memory of some distant nightmare. But at another crossing, when they again saw the guards standing there without moving in, Manuel Rato appeared to awaken from his daydream.

"They're going to trap us in," he told Paulo. "You must get out of here somehow."

As if giving proof to these words, they heard loud voices and shouting from the front of the march. The cortege stopped again. At that moment, they also heard cries and clamoring from the rear, and after a few more moments, sudden waves of pressure on the mass of people indicated something abnormal happening back there.

"You have to leave," Manuel Rato repeated. "You cannot get caught."

The other demonstrators also gradually understood the situation: The march was being surrounded by the troops.

"Don't separate yourself from me," Manuel Rato warned, and he said a few words to a couple of the people next to him, a young man with the blue shirt of a fisherman and a man with a black hat. These two, on their part, tried to break through toward the center of the cortege and in an instant disappeared from sight. Meanwhile, the march slowly started again. Up at the front the constant shouting continued. The boy with the blue shirt and the man with the black hat reappeared, and a whirlpool in the cortege took shape. The cordons of people hand-in-hand melted, the banner held by the hatless young man and the strong woman went waving away from where Paulo was, and he found himself surrounded by new faces.

"Don't separate yourself from me," Manuel Rato insisted. "We have to break away."

As they walked, he spoke with people around them and was guiding Paulo toward the outer edge of the cortege. Then everything happened at lightning speed. Passing by a small street, Manuel Rato, the boy with the blue shirt, the man with the black hat, and another, numerous bunch of demonstrators threw themselves on the guards. Paulo did, too, sensing that the comrades before him had opened the way for him, scrambling well past the place where the guards had been a few seconds before. But then, to his surprise, he saw before him a gray uniform and a hesitant young face staring at him from under his helmet. He held onto an arm from a comrade next to him and tried to knee the enemy, but both he and his comrade were brutally pushed on their sides, and he received a violent blow on his head. Knocked silly, he saw another guard going for him. He tried to break away again and raised his fist, but another hit, this time on the back of his neck, felled him and all went black for some time. Then he had the vague notion of people running by his side, of shouting that sounded very distant, and of someone who lifted him up by the armpits to support him.

And of a breathless, whispering voice panting into his face: "Come on, friend, keep trying, keep trying."

15

Paulo leaned on the arms offered him on each side and, stepping uncertainly, allowed himself to be led, unable to see anything more through the hot, red humidity that covered his eyelids than the intense, painful light of the sun. A profound silence seemed to encase the terrain through which they passed, broken only by the huffing and puffing next to him from whoever carried him.

"Come on, friend, try to get up," a voice told him into his hair.

They helped him over a stone rampart, and he felt pushed, grabbed by the wrists, suspended in air, while other hands touched him on his legs and feet. Looking up, he saw for the first time the face of the person holding him, an unfamiliar visage drenched with sweat.

"Let go!" a voice from below ordered.

The face remained above him, growing ever farther beyond him until it disappeared. New arms supported him, and he heard Manuel Rato's well-known voice right next to him: "Hold him by this side."

So they carried him, tripping on rubble and stopping from time to time to rest under the cool shadows. Finally they carefully laid him down in a thicket of cane, and Paulo heard steps that went away and returned, and he felt a damp cloth wiping his head, his eyes and face. The steps came and went, and someone washed his face and eyes again. Only then did Paulo feel a sharp pain at one temple and he shuddered, recoiling from the wet cloth. Two men mumbled something in a low voice. Then they placed the wet cloth on his forehead, adjusting it neatly, and suddenly the hands that were doing it went still and suspended.

"Did you hear?" the voice of Manuel Rato asked.

The men halted all their movement, and for a few moments all that could be heard was a brief rustle of leaves. Then, far off, some clear, spaced-out cracks could be heard. *Pow!... Pow!... Pow!*

The men held their breath. Again, all that could be heard was the slight, irregular ruffle of leaves. They whispered something more and Manuel Rato ran off.

How many hours passed? Paulo felt overtaken by an all-powerful weakness that kept him from thinking and speaking. He drifted off into brief patches of heavy sleep, both depressing and restful at the same time. He was aware of having been wounded, but he couldn't say how or where he'd been hurt. When he opened his eyes, he saw beside him, sitting on the ground, an unknown man wearing a black hat, delicately planing a stalk of green cane with a pocket knife. Every once in a while this stranger removed the cloth from his forehead, stepped away and returned shortly with the cloth newly wetted with fresh water. At times, Paulo woke up with a start, trying to raise himself up. And then he saw the man stop his work with the knife and gently look at him sideways. One time, when he woke, the air seemed more shadowed and cooler. The comrade wasn't there. That absence gave him a jolt of insecurity, and he raised himself with effort. Then he remembered the demonstration in all its detail, and finding Manuel Rato, the fight with the Guard and running. Meanwhile, the comrade with the black hat returned and, seeing him sitting up and leaning against the cane stalks, looked at him curiously.

"We have to wait," he said in a quite distinct voice.

"Where is Manuel Rato?" Paulo asked.

"He's coming—" the man in the black hat responded, but Paulo heard the voice grow quieter until it disappeared.

He wanted to ask something else, but that invincible fatigue forced hm to shut his eyes.

It was night already when he was awakened by a new sound, but a nice and peaceful one. Standing quietly, the comrade listened. The sound of oars gently stirring the water could be heard, and only then did Paulo realize he was burning with thirst. There were two cautious whistles.

"Here!" said the guy with the black hat, moving the cane aside with a swish.

Paulo distinctly heard Manuel Rato's voice but couldn't make out what he was saying. They then placed him in the boat, settling him into the hull. For a long time all he heard was the timid, sweet *slap, slap* of the oars chopping the water.

Chapter *XIV*

1

The mobilization surprised everyone. It surprised even the organizers, who did not expect such a quick and widespread acceptance of their demands and directions. And it surprised the authorities, who didn't believe the rumors of a strike that came in from every side through their network of informers. If on the night of the 17th they had arrested Gaspar in his own house, it was not so much out of fear of the strike but to put a stop to such rumors, which various sources attributed to Gaspar himself. Then, on the 18th, the same people who the night before had pooh-poohed the potential for a strike decided from the outset this was an insurrection. Thus the frightened local authorities' appeal to the government and the impressive forces deployed across the region.

Wanting to punish all those who participated in the movement as an example, the fascists arrested thousands of people on the afternoon of the 18th. They arrested people randomly, without selection, like a furious monster pawing the dark. Men, women and children, workers and peasants, the self-employed and small business owners, all who were found in the locales of the demonstrations were surrounded, closed into circles of rifles and machine guns, and held, while a constant traffic of trucks carted them off to the capital. At the biggest demonstration, the one Paulo was dragged into, the troops, once they had enclosed the demonstrators and after a few clashes involving shots and swords, forced them into the bullring and from there transferred them out all night and into the next morning.

Then on the 19th, the authorities realized their error. The prisoners were so many that the police felt themselves incapable of differentiating the leaders from the mass, which in some cases took in practically the whole population of small villages, and in other cases, almost all the workers in factories and shops. And to aggravate the situation, in several places in the region there were protest demonstrations against the repression. So on the night of the 19th and into the 20th, the great majority of those arrested were let go. Only about three hundred remained, whom the police identified as being the "suspects," though in fact they were as suspect as the rest. So poor was their aim that among those freed were almost all the Party leaders in the region: Vicente, Pereira, Cesário, Sagarra, da Barrosa, Lisete and many others.

Manuel Rato and Marques escaped being taken. Manuel Rato because, when he opened up the way for Paulo to run through, the Guard did not pursue him, seeing right away the mistake of chasing one bird while leaving the cage open where all the rest were held. And Marques because that afternoon he stayed home, closed up in his room, nervously pacing from one wall to the other. He decided not to go out in order to completely distance himself from the events and take no part, either direct or indirect, of the responsibility for what he imagined would be a tragic failure. It was only later in the day that his mother, returning home, told him there'd been a strike at the Jute and other companies and that lots of people had assembled in the city center.

"And Mother went to check it out?" Marques bellowed, suddenly excited.

The old woman stared at her son with her two big distrusting eyes, crossed herself three times and left his room. She came back to the door to look at her son once more, and crossed herself again. Marques well understood that his mother believed she was bringing him great news and that she did not understand why he remained at home nor why he so demonstratively disapproved of the movement. As night fell, contrary to what he had planned, Marques left the house. He learned of the strikes, the demonstrations and the dozens of arrests in the city. Concerning what had actually happened in the region, the reports were very confused. Someone spoke of a revolution, and many people believed a movement had broken out in Lisbon.

Only on the night of the 20th did Paulo manage to get to Vaz's house, where they believed he had been arrested. On top of his burn marks, Paulo appeared with his head all bandaged, feverish and still in shock from the beating he had taken. That same night António arrived with his good news, and on the 21st Vaz returned after having been with Cesário and José Sagarra, who'd already been released. And so the comrades were able to maintain leadership of the struggle.

A week after the mobilization, new manifestos appeared in various factories throughout the region. Committees called on the employers to convey to the authorities the workers' demands that their still detained companions be set free, and the same was done in towns and villages appealing to the local authorities. Under such conditions, keeping 300 "suspects" prisoner, against whom nothing in particular could be proven, was becoming meaningless, serving only to ferment new fights. The government understood this, and on June 11, all the "suspects" were freed. Among them were Henriques, the young woman with the red blouse, and Jaime, the heavyset comrade from Cicol. From the thousands taken prisoner, only three remained: Gaspar, in whose house the police had found clandestine printed material, and for that he was sentenced to several years; someone else for whom there'd been an arrest warrant out for some crime; and Jerónimo, considering his previous arrests. In the search of Jerónimo's house, nothing was found. At all his interrogations, Jerónimo looked at the agents with his serene, tired eyes, and always answered, "I just went along with the others." When Gaspar was questioned about Jerónimo, he declined to make any statement about his Party activity, saying that in fact he only knew Jerónimo by sight but had never spoke with him and didn't even know he had ever been arrested for political reasons.

Early one morning they came for Jerónimo in the cell where he had been held incommunicado and brought him to the police headquarters in a prisoner transport vehicle.

"You're getting out this morning," an investigator told him rapidly and unemotionally. "But don't think for a minute you got away with anything. You can tell your comrades out there it's the last one who laughs the most."

His lower lip dropped, his gray eyes distractedly staring at the investigator's hands moving across the top of his desk, Jerónimo seemed unmoved by the threats.

"Is today the third?" he asked when the agent stopped talking.

"Yes, it's the third. Do you have an appointment today?" asked the agent with a joking chuckle as dry as his normal speaking voice.

"No," Jerónimo answered in his drawl. "But on the third, a kid of mine's having a birthday so I'll use my time in Lisbon to buy something for him. So it worked out well."

2

On the 19th, all who were available presented themselves for work, but in many cases, both in factories and workshops, as well as in the fields, the crews were reduced owing to the high number of arrests. On the 20th, despite there still being 300 workers held, work recommenced normally everywhere. Only Cicol remained closed. Not because workers didn't show up, but because the government decided to shut the factory to punish the manager who had ordered the motors unplugged, "thus collaborating with elements disturbing the order and giving a bad example to the meaning of managerial responsibility." But neither could that measure be sustained. With the factory closed and the workers wanting to work, gathering every morning at the gates—where a substantial force from the GNR was present—and then dispersing through the streets, where they ambled about all day, a new spur to agitation was created, which the authorities were interested in tamping down. So when in Vicente's and Pereira's factories the workers suspended their labor for ten minutes as a protest against the Cicol closure, the authorities finally grasped that they had to cut off such pretexts for agitation and ordered the reopening of the factory. The workers considered this one more victory: One enthusiast set off three firecrackers in the courtyard, right under the Guard's noses. He was fired for this but, as it happened a few days later with Jaime, his companions' pressure forced management to rehire him.

Before the month of May was over, in the fields as well as in the factories and shops, significant raises in wages were recorded, and throughout the region foodstuffs that had not been seen for a long time reappeared. In all instances it was said that such measures were only possible with order in the streets and with a spirit of cooperation between classes and between the people and the government—and that in the event of further disorders such as that of May 18th, these improvements could not take place or be guaranteed. The workers, and the people overall, scoffed at those explanations because it was plain to see that such concessions had been achieved only by virtue of the 18th of May.

Did this mean that the authorities had resigned themselves to such a complete defeat? Certainly not. The fascists and the bosses in general well understood the 18th of May as a serious warning, and considered it an imperative necessity to uncover and liquidate the Party organization in the region. The organization had acquitted itself capably as the general staff that blended in with its own soldiers. The mass arrests had completely rounded up all the leaders. But they would not escape a deep-seated investigation that caught them unprepared.

A deluge of plainclothes police fell over the region, spying on individuals, making nighttime rounds to hunt down distributors of manifestos, searching out information about unfolding events in workplaces, directing systematic investigations brought to fruition by the local bosses and authorities themselves, into all manner and means of transportation to catch members of the underground apparatus.

3

Manuel led Paulo to the hut of some fishermen on the river. The family was too large for that small space—an old woman, a married couple some years on, three adult children and a child—but they all welcomed the wounded man, whom one of the adult sons transported in his own boat. It was Renato, to be precise, the young man with the blue shirt who had helped break through the GNR barrier.

Alongside the water, in that untamed place linked to the world by the river, there were half a dozen huts, leaning against one another as if supporting each other in mutual solitary misery. No secrets could be hidden there. The next morning all the neighbors came to see the wounded man and what it was all about, then left the hut with grand gestures, exclamations and comment. Naturally they attributed to the Guard not only the wounds on his head, but the bandaged hand and the scorch marks still visible on Paulo's face. They surrounded Renato, making him describe the demonstrations over and over again, the struggle with the Guard, and the way they transported Paulo. And from the approving nods from the oldest ones, to the excited interjections from the women, to the young girls' smiles and the solemn faces of the children, it was clear that the little community hailed Renato's action and looked upon him as a suddenly unmasked hero. Renato returned to the town to get more news and when he returned, saying the people had been corralled into the bullring and later taken to Lisbon, there came further exclamations and comments.

On the morning of the next day, Paulo tried to get up from his improvised bed because in the middle of his slumbers, he recalled how worried his comrades must be and how damaging his own absence could be from the continuing fight. Blinded by a giddy dizziness as he stood up, he had to lie down again. Manuel Rato did not leave his side. He changed the panels of cloth soaked with cold water and vinegar on Paulo's beaten scalp, and he personally served him the soup or coffee that the owners of the house or the neighbors brought, asked how he was feeling from time to time, and just sat, silently watching with an anxious expression.

Since the Vale da Égua tragedy, Paulo could not think comfortably about a future encounter with Manuel Rato. It was he who had instigated the struggle by the smallholders in the pine forest, explicitly mobilized Manuel Rato, his wife and daughter, and for whatever good reasons he tried to conjure, he couldn't dismiss a vague but painful feeling of guilt over the death of Isabel. Thinking about meeting Manuel Rato again, he always imagined Manuel would eye him with a certain reserve and judgment.

But the opposite occurred. Not only had Manuel Rato saved him from certain arrest, he was now beside him with fraternal concern. During the long hours of silence that day and for the two nights that he remained at his side, Manuel Rato never for a moment stopped thinking about Vale da Égua, his little house, preparing for the mobilization, distributing the manifestos with his wife and daughter, and the terrible, nightmarish day when he was robbed of his beloved daughter. At the feverish, beaten Paulo's bedside, Manuel Rato remembers all that, and the memories are so heartbreaking that at times he has to get up, violently and forcefully, to distance himself, thinking that if he doesn't, his head and chest are going to explode. But never for an instant does any recrimination against Paulo come to mind. In Manuel Rato's heart, Paulo and Vaz are two especially beloved comrades, for both of them knew *her* and admired *her*. For some unfounded and inexplicable reason, Manuel Rato even thinks it was Paulo who wrote those verses of homage to his dead daughter, and feels touched by that assumption.

At nightfall on the 19th, Paulo, who had slept off and on all day, managed to stand up and walk a few steps. That vise that had gripped his head had slackened, and the cloud that weighed on his eyes almost disappeared. He wanted to leave immediately, but Manuel Rato dissuaded him. It would do little good to leave. At that hour they wouldn't be able to snag any transportation, and Paulo was surely not in good enough shape to walk many kilometers on his own.

The next morning, when they headed for the boat on which Renato would take them, everyone in the huts saw them off. That sojourn of Paulo and Manuel Rato was an important event in those people's stagnant, miserable life with no exit. The fishing community learned during those days that across the world, and very near to them, the struggle was on for a better world. One fisherman among them, Renato, with his friends there, showed them the possibility of a new way of life. The menfolk said goodbye with earnestness to the two unknown men, and several women raised their fingers or the hem of their skirt to their eyes.

Manuel Rato walked alongside Paulo to the jitney and took the train to return to his place. He was worried about the situation he was going to face, with the near certainty of arrest of the Party leaders, and he visualized what he could do to establish contact with the remaining Party groups so as to give accurate information to Paulo in the meeting they set for two days hence. But when he arrived home, Pereira and Vicente had already been freed, and Pereira had already sent a message to the house asking him to contact him.

Aside from that, Manuel Rato found another bit of news: a letter from his wife written in a strained handwriting. She said she was in good health, she complained about the harvest, and ended with these extraordinary words:

For many years, even when you were not here, I wouldn't abandon our house and out belongings for anything in the world. Now what am I doing here? Take me to be beside you for good. I want to help you in everything. The one who had the least responsibility gave her life for the good of others. For what she died, we must live.

4

In the improvised concentration camp where he was placed on the 19th, Sagarra found himself with almost all the comrades in his organization. He also found many peasants from various other villages and right away agreed to visit them. So when he was freed the next night, he left with meetings set in all the sectors, and broad new possibilities for the organization. But to attend to it all, how could he hold down a job all day long? And not working, how could he contribute his share toward the house and how to sustain it? Earlier, by agreement with his older brother, he would frequently take some time off so he could move about here and there. Now this wasn't sufficient. Now, with the necessary traveling, to get to all the dates he had set up that day under arrest would take him a whole week. This was an embarrassing situation, made all the more so as he felt timid about placing it before his brother and even before Vaz himself. He didn't have time to appear at the meeting with Vaz on the 20th, set up to be a supposedly chance encounter in the open. But by the rules of underground activity, a second alternative date would be set in case someone missed the first time. He would get to Vaz on the 21st.

On the 21st, Vaz appeared. Noticing how remarkably skinny his comrade had become, Sagarra gave him a detailed report about the movement and spoke of new potential for work. "Within a month," he concluded, "we'll have twice the number of Party members than we had before the mobilization."

Explaining all this to Vaz, it did not occur to him to mention the hardships in his personal life, the impossibility of at the same time working as a day laborer and going every which way wherever he was needed. But what did not occur to Sagarra now did occur to Vaz. All too well did he know there are tasks that only someone who devotes all his time to can do—and even then with the greatest of effort that would exhaust a man of iron.

"If the Party were interested in your becoming a Party worker, would you be ready for that?"

José Sagarra remained quiet a few moments, as though confused. "I don't know that much," he said, finally. "Surely there are comrades with more background than I have."

"That's not what I'm asking," Vaz pushed. "What I'm asking is if you're prepared to leave your whole present life behind, leave your land and family and become someone who lives exclusively for the Party."

José Sagarra still hesitated. "Well, friend. The problem is that I wouldn't be capable. I don't have your experience or that of the other comrades. As far as my intentions are concerned, well, you know me." And in his burdened, freckled face, the clear eyes he turned toward his comrade confirmed his words.

They separated. And only then did it once again come to José Sagarra's mind that, to perform his immediate tasks in the next few days, he could not go to work, nor did he know what he'd say at home or how he'd eat. The more he thought, he couldn't see how to overcome these problems, for the idea hardly struck him that he could desist from going wherever the interests of the Party should call him.

That night, when he arrived home, he spoke with his older brother and told him he had things to take care of the next day and couldn't go to work. His brother was also a man of a serious appearance and little talk. He looked at the floor and nodded his head as he listened. In the end, he made no comment.

Early the next morning, as the two men left the house—the brother for his work in the fields, José for a faraway meeting—the brother said to him, "Come and eat with us all the same, hear?"

José Sagarra did not go to eat. He returned late that night and left again when it was still dark, to avoid talking with his brother. He didn't eat anything that day, and another day like that awaited him.

5

When he found out that the comrades arrested on the strike day had been released, Marques went to see Cesário. He found him glowing, having dinner with his wife and Lisete. The in-laws and a few neighbors were also there, and everyone was talking excitedly about the day's success.

"Sit down, sit down," Cesário said, offering a chair to the carpenter. "It's good you came. We feared you'd been arrested."

Words spoken without irony, though Marques felt them as an allusion to his disinterest in the mobilization. He sat down, quietly scowling.

"That's exactly it!" exclaimed Cesário's father-in-law, continuing the conversation. "If you do nothing, nothing happens. I've always said it."

He had not always said it. To the contrary. In the days before the strike, gathering that something was in the works and that his son-in-law and youngest daughter were involved in it, he did everything to dissuade them. Now, after the success, and in the joy over the release of both of them, he forgot his earlier judgments.

"I've always told you," he added, eyeing Lisete with self-satisfaction, "I've always told you that these guys will not be appeased lightly. Now they'll be taking stock of the warning."

Marques listened silently to the conversation for some time. Everyone spoke freely in front of him, for they knew who he was. But because of the stance he had taken toward the movement, and above all for neither having taken part in it nor been arrested, he felt incapable of joining the conversation and the general happy mood. Besides which, it seemed a little ridiculous to make such a fuss over such a small thing. They had spent two days under arrest and now wanted to pass themselves off as heroes. He wound up feeling like a fifth wheel there, and given his absolute silence and funereal mood, so in contrast with the others, they too started to feel it.

Marques stood up. "I just came to see if it was true that they'd released you," he told Cesário somberly. And coolly taking his leave of everyone, he left.

Cesário walked him to the door, smiling and in a hearty mood. *As you see*, Cesário's smile and attitude said, *things went better than you thought*.

"They're still holding Henriques," Cesário said as Marques left. "We'll do something to get him out. Tomorrow or soon we have to talk, don't you think?"

They agreed that Cesário would meet Marques at lunch time, but he didn't show up. Marques went to wait for him at the exit from his shop and saw from his friend's face there was news.

"Vaz was here," said Cesário. "He'll come back someday soon and will talk with you then."

"What day? When?" Marques asked, his intelligent eyes fixed on his friend seeking to guess some meaning behind those words.

"He didn't say," Cesário said in a voice that Marques found self-conscious. "When he comes, I'll tell you right away."

The fact is that after learning of Marques's attitude toward the mobilization and in particular his behavior with respect to Henriques on the very morning of the 18th, Vaz told Cesário that when he returned the next Saturday night, he would only see Cesário himself, and that in the meantime he would report the Marques case to the Party's higher body.

That Saturday night he returned and, joined by Cesário, went to see Marques.

Marques was studying, seated at his little table. He was visibly delighted to see Vaz and even more satisfied that the comrades, coming by surprise, had caught him studying at night. *You can see how I use my time usefully*, his expression said. But very soon, in just a few minutes, his satisfaction vanished. Vaz sat down in exhaustion, his nostrils dilated and breathing with difficulty, and he handed a paper to Marques.

Marques read. It was a resolution. Considering Marques's undisciplined action and the sabotage he had committed in the lead-up to the mobilization—citing only the conversation with Henriques—it censured Marques and declared that he was removed from regional and local leadership.

Drained of color, his hands trembling slightly, his eyes glistening through his lenses, Marques handed the paper back. Twice he tried to speak, but held back as if he might regret the words he would say. Finally, in a voice he struggled to control, but which came out of his sallow lips hurt and emotional, he said, "I want to say that I consider this decision unfair—and completely abnormal that such a decision would be made without first hearing out the person concerned."

He paused, starting to add something else, but only said, "That's all."

Cesário was also moved. He had agreed with the decision when Vaz had told him of it. But at that moment he recalled that Marques was the oldest and best known comrade in the city, that he had already served time in prison and conducted himself admirably, and that it had been Marques himself who had drawn him into the struggle and signed him up with the Party. And wasn't he right that they should have heard him out first?

Vaz maintained his impassive front and spoke with restraint. "If you want to write to the Central Committee, you can do so. Meanwhile, it won't be hard to find another assignment for you."

An angry explosion of rage could have been expected of the carpenter. But he kept his peace, evidently afraid of what he might say. Vaz and Cesário got up to leave.

"Comrade," Vaz addressed him, "your future in the Party is in your own hands."

An ironic smile passed through Marques's knowing eyes and across his wan, furrowed face. Once again he moved his lips and then closed them in silence. Only when they said good-night did he say to Vaz, "You have good reason to feel contented. You achieved what you wanted."

6

Vaz spent the night at Cesário's house and left early in the morning to meet Afonso at the first train station past the city. Afonso had been prohibited from going into the town and for this meeting with Vaz had been instructed by Fialho which train he should take. Recently Vaz was incapable of rapid commutes by bicycle and on almost all the hills he had to get off and walk. But he had left Cesário's house in plenty of time and arrived at the station before the train arrived.

The morning was foggy and tepid, the station plaza deserted. Vaz sat down on a pile of wood to wait. After a few minutes, the train clattered in with a rumble of old iron. In the weird silence that followed, Vaz saw a couple of peasants exiting the station—her with a basket, him with two sacks made of colored fabric patches. They weren't happy with the distribution of baggage, because the man grabbed the basket and gave one sack to the woman, and then stopped to trade sacks, only right away to go back to the original deployment— him with the sacks and her with the basket. At that moment the train whistled and departed. A railway worker appeared at the station door, looked to one side and then the other and returned inside. *Afonso must be waiting until everyone is gone*, Vaz thought. More minutes passed, and no one else came out of the station. Then Vaz glanced over to the other side of the square and saw the peasant couple now propped against their things and a young man with a package coming down the street. He decided to go onto the platform and see for himself whether Afonso had come, but when he stood up and looked again down the street he saw, some twenty paces away, the young man with the package and immediately recognized him. It was Afonso.

"Didn't Fialho tell you to come by train?" he asked.

"I came," Afonso replied in tones of impatience and irony that Vaz had noted for the first time a few days before when Vaz told him to let go of his feeling for Maria. "I left through the rail crossing gate."

Vaz's bright eyes stared harshly at his comrade for an instant, but he said nothing more about the subject as they continued the conversation along the road leading out of the city. They had walked a good kilometer when a dark van passed them headed for the city.

"Just now that van passed us in the other direction," said Vaz.

"It's not the same one," Afonso answered.

Farther ahead, they separated. Afonso was to take a jitney on that same road and Vaz would go off in another direction on his bicycle.

"Just watch that no one's following you," Vaz warned.

"Don't worry."

Vaz continued on by bicycle. Many kilometers ahead, a dark van passed in front to him that looked the same as the one before. He got off his wheels and wrote down the van's license number. After another hour, now fairly close to home, some three leagues away, he saw it again in a little settlement, parked and with no one there.

At that point Vaz did not take a direct route home. He detoured at the first cross street, shifted onto paths and secondary roads, and made such a wide berth that on arriving home he headed straight to his room and threw himself on the bed, without the energy to say even a single word to his companion.

7

Seated at the edge of the bed, Rosa looked at him seriously worried. Despite the warmth of the day, Vaz complained of the cold and, disturbed by the light and noise, went to his room to lie down in the shade. More than once she saw him close his eyes, and when she figured he had finally fallen asleep, she saw him open them again suddenly with a shocking expression, convulsive and painful, sometimes with his whole body shaking violently, and asking, *Huh?* or *What?* as if some horrifying fact or some infernal sound had entered his ear in that sepulchral room. Rosa placed her fingers on his face or on his damp, cold forehead.

"What's wrong? What are you feeling?"

Vaz then lost his shocked, suffering expression and, staring at Rosa with his usual serenity, answered, "It's strange. The very moment I fall asleep I seem to hear a huge blast and I'm free-falling."

"See if you can sleep, friend. You're totally wiped out, that's what it is."

Before Vaz managed to sleep, the scene repeated itself several times. Now, when he regained consciousness after opening his astonished eyes from another frightful episode, he looked at his companion and smiled weakly and sadly, which was something new for him. *Will you take a look at this craziness?* his smile seemed to say by way of excusing himself. He was suffering for sure.

He woke up as the day grew dark, with a waxy pallor and drenched in sweat. During dinner they spoke of the state of his health, and Rosa insisted that he should rest a few days or at least reduce his activity for a time until he recovered.

"It's a bad time for that," Vaz answered. "The strike opened up new possibilities for our work and we have to act on them."

"And if you collapse on your bed?" Rosa asked. "Then you won't do much, or even little, and the Party will have to go on without you."

Vaz stared at her with his steady, impassive eyes, not revealing if he was thanking her for her care, or censuring her for her incomprehension.

"I know there are those who believe," he said slowly and gravely, "that militants should save their good health with an eye toward the future, with their vista set on the great struggles ahead. But if we all thought that way we'd never arrive at those grand fights that we aspire to, because to get there, the indispensable precondition is victory in the smaller struggles that we go through today."

"Moderation! Not too much and not too little," Rosa said. "No one's denying that great efforts are called for today. And that we need to sacrifice. But some fights demand more than others. The complete sacrifice of life is the maximum sacrifice. But the big insurrection, not the day-to-day struggles, is the time for that."

"You're wrong," Vaz replied. "That's not the maximum sacrifice. To give your life all at once in the insurrection requires less of a spirit of sacrifice than the slow-burning, patient struggle of today."

They remained quiet a few moments.

"To give your life once," Vaz expanded, "is far easier than giving it little by little, day by day."

Although she insisted that her companion curtail his activity or rest for a while, Rosa fundamentally agreed with him. She always looked upon him with inner happiness and pride when he set himself to work under conditions where many others would have retired to their beds.

Yes, he's giving his life little by little, Rosa thought, *and it's necessary for him and many others to have the courage to do likewise.*

After that conversation, Vaz worked at the table for a few hours and, now in bed, since neither of them was sleepy, they lay awake for a long time. The light was off and the window open, through which a waft of fresh air and a weak lucidity blew in. Remembering the dark van, Vaz thinks he could be arrested, and as a result many years could pass without his seeing Rosa, possibly never seeing her again, separated without them ever having surmounted that barrier raised by their agreement not to speak of the past. Rosa is now at his side, silent and pensive and, who knows, maybe dragged into those thoughts and memories that divide her from him, maybe prisoner to that mysterious presence that Vaz does not know about.

"Rosa—" Vaz murmurs.

He considered saying, *Why don't we dismantle that little thing that still keeps us apart? Why do we have to allow, not the past as such but the not knowing about the past, to place itself between us and keep that constant distance between our lives?* Something keeps him from putting it quite that way, however, and if you asked him, he wouldn't be able to say if that something is the fear that Rosa would find it so hard to speak of her past, or the fear that this past would come to position itself between them even more powerfully than the not knowing.

The words they exchanged veered away in other directions in the quiet, cool atmosphere of the room in semi-darkness.

"It's funny," Rosa said softly after a few minutes feeling the pulse in Vaz's wrist between her fingers. "It beats slowly, slowly—and then sometimes it skips a beat."

8

After a few days, Vaz arrived in the city. It was already night. With his bicycle in hand, he headed for Cesário's house via the back streets and trails he usually took. The night was dark, and his route was even darker, in contrast to the bright lights of the city splayed out like stars a few hundred meters away. Although he knew the way well, Vaz paused for a few moments at the entrance to an empty field, trying to discern the only barely visible narrow pathway through.

Suddenly he retreated a few steps, attempting to fade into the shadow of an old wall. Coming out of the darkness from the opposite direction, he espied a heavyset figure walking at a silent, incomprehensibly sluggish pace through the deserted field. The figure stopped in the middle of it and stood still for a bit, barely visible in the darkness. He traced a few more steps and stopped again, now closer. And there he stood for some time—to Vaz it seemed like many long minutes—heavy and unmoving. He wasn't doing anything, so it was precisely in that absolute immobility that Vaz could clearly see that the man had a well-defined reason for posting himself there. After a while, he slowly walked away and when he disappeared completely, Vaz left the sheltering wall and continued on, quickening his steps.

When he got to Cesário's house he related the incident, asking if anyone had seen something unusual. They hadn't, and also found it odd.

"At that place and at that hour, he certainly wasn't just out taking a stroll," said Henriques, who had been released a few days earlier and was there.

At Cesário's, two important pieces of news awaited Vaz. The first had to do with Marques. Henriques was in jail with two young men, taken prisoner during the demonstrations, whom Marques had asked to distribute the manifesto on the night of the 17th. They both recounted how they showed up, with some others, in the middle of the night. Marques came to tell them he didn't have the manifestos to give them because the friend who was supposed to have brought them had missed his meeting with him. He had also been with the only workers committee member at his shop who participated in the stoppage, and he told how Marques had spoken with him and with the other committee members the very morning of the 18th trying to dissuade them from the movement—which he achieved, with all the other committee members.

"That's crazy!" Cesário exclaimed. "I was the one who gave him the manifestos, and you can be absolutely positive of that. In fact, two days before!"

He insisted on this, as though anyone could doubt him and believe what Marques had told the young guys.

Although Henriques had known about this strange story for two weeks already, he still spoke of it excitedly, which gave to his voice an unusually sharp edge. "On the 18th, when our friends on the committee seemed completely turned around, I thought to myself, *Marques is right after all. The people are not as favorably disposed as it seemed, and the better ones among them see things the way he sees them.* In the end they were paralyzed, just reciting the Our Father. That is, if only half the shop went out, we owe that to the comrade."

And turning his tapered face and blinking eyes toward Vaz, he added, "And if you could have seen the food they gave me to eat, and Cesário too! This business of knowing too much is worse than knowing too little!"

The contracted muscles on Vaz's face indicated his extreme tension. What was the meaning of all this? Why would Marques have acted that way? Just out of disagreement and lack of discipline?

Marques was an old comrade who had already been put to the test—all the more reason to view his conduct as so strange. If an old comrade behaves the way a provocateur behaves, then isn't he a provocateur? Then Vaz thought about Marques's friendship with Vítor, the constant defenses he made for him, even when Vítor had become more than suspect. Was there some understanding between the two of them?

"Does anyone know if Vítor has returned?" he asked.

According to what Cesário knew, it was reported that Vítor was still in his home village with his sick mother, but someone had said he'd been seen recently in the city.

"Two days ago," Vaz said, "although these facts were still not known, Marques was removed from any leadership work. The little we knew about his stance in relation to the mobilization, and in particular about his talk with comrade Henriques the morning of the 18th, was, together with many other lapses and errors, more than sufficient for such a decision. When it was communicated to him, comrade Marques protested against it, considering it unfair, and saying he should have been heard out beforehand. And all the while he knew perfectly well that aside from the breaches for which he was being sanctioned, he had committed others even more serious. When a new decision is made, as it undoubtedly will, who knows what he'll say then? That's how it is, friends: If someone doesn't correct their mistake, he falls into an even larger one and tumbles from mistake to mistake by increasing degrees."

"And how about the tasks that you've thought about for him?" Cesário asked. "Just yesterday he said he was ready to do whatever was asked of him."

Vaz didn't answer.

The other important piece of news had to do with Afonso. A few days earlier, someone in Henriques's family went to the home of Afonso's parents and found him there.

"There must be some confusion," said Vaz. "That can't be."

But then, as if placing his own words in doubt, the last meeting he had with Afonso came to mind, at the station past the city, when Afonso appeared from the side opposite of the station. And he recalled the dark van that had passed by him several times.

"There must be some confusion," he said again.

"No, comrade," Henriques said, blinking his eyes, "There's no confusion. I don't know what Afonso is doing or not doing, if he's left the city or if he's back already. The only sure thing I can say now is that when my nephew was at the house, he was there too. My nephew is a serious boy. I spoke with him, and there's no possible mistake about it."

9

In fact there was no mistake.

If from the start of his life as a Party worker Afonso considered the rules about conspiratorial work overly fastidious and fussy, and from time to time evaded them, today not shaving, tomorrow picking fruit on a deserted highway, later taking an ill-advised means of transportation, that attitude for some reason turned into his normal pattern of behavior ever since the day Vaz told him to let go of his feeling for Maria.

Afonso so badly wanted to convince himself of Maria's affection that although they were perfectly clear, he did not consider Vaz's first words a final settlement of the subject. For sure, some comrade had his eye on Maria and was trying to block Afonso's approach to her. Could it be Vaz himself? Couldn't that be the source of all the ill will he had shown from the beginning? Afonso did not think he had been vanquished by those first words and obstinately insisted on the meeting he asked for. At that point Vaz delivered these cruel words:

"The meeting was authorized, my friend. It's the comrade herself who said she has no personal relationship with you, nor interest in meeting."

Everything jumbled up in Afonso's spirit. As if it were someone else speaking, he asked if they had told Maria that he was a Party worker, that he continued to think of her as before, and wanted to make her his wife.

"Yes, everything was said," Vaz answered unsparingly. And as though he did not grasp that Afonso still had a thousand questions he wanted to ask, he added, "Can we move on to other matters?"

They had moved on to other matters. To everything that Vaz raised, Afonso responded impatiently, often shrugging his shoulders or smiling ironically and inappropriately. That day, until he returned to his room, Afonso, with delicious pleasure, in every way disregarded the "fussiness" that the comrades called the "conspiratorial rules." When he went to the clothing store he did not habitually take care, as he had been told, to wipe the dust off his shoes, comb his hair and be on his best possible behavior. Later, instead of walking to the station where he met Fialho for the first time, he had taken a jitney, just a few dozen meters away from the clothing store, to the station. Then he traveled on a train arriving on a long route from the border, though advised against it because PIDE agents always rode it. Then he got off at Lisbon's central station. Finally he got onto an electric tram at the station exit and got off at the stop nearest his quarters. When he got to his room, he threw himself onto his bed, breathing deeply and thinking irritatedly, *So, that's it. They make such a fuss, everything so complicated, and in the end everything is easy.*

But that night he slept badly; and the next day, when he had no meetings scheduled, he felt, as he had never felt before, the anguish, the weight and torture of solitude. Only now did he feel that in all the life of a Party worker the hardest part was this personal solitary state, unbroken, in fact reenforced, by all his trips and meetings with comrades on the road and on the street. He observed now for the first time that the comrades only had words for the work, for the execution of assignments, for taking precautions, for speaking about the "fussiness," for criticizing and offending; and hadn't a word, not a single word for his personal problems, for the human being that he was, a young man thirsting for love, for friendship, for caring and understanding. Until that day he was driven by the hope of meeting Maria and making her his wife, and if that happened—ah, if that could have happened!—the life of a Party worker would turn into the best and happiest of lives. In the end the whole dream crashed to the ground. According to Vaz, Maria said she had no personal relationship with him nor was interested in meeting. *No, that's not possible!* Afonso concluded. *She's good and honest, and couldn't have said that.* But then, returning to the earlier thread of his thoughts, he came up with another conclusion: *They're all stupid, that's what these women are.*

Over the next few days after that talk with Vaz, Afonso kept thinking about his family, especially his mother. It surprised him that only now did he think how much suffering his leaving, and the lack of news from him, must have caused her. Stricken with compassion, he called himself a bad son, shocked by the cruelty of which he was capable toward those he most loved.

Some days later, he had to spend the night in his region, and he thought, *I don't have anywhere to stay there at a comrade's house. A room in a pension is not safe. Best would be to go home and stay the night there.* And he went. The tender words, the accusations and supplications made him cry, feeling all the pent-up longing for the house where he was born and raised, for the family, and above all for his mother. After that time, within a short period, there were others.

When Fialho assigned him a meeting with Vaz at the first station past the city, indicating which train he should take, Afonso, instead of going as he was instructed, spent one more night at his family's home and made the trek by foot. He told Vaz he had come by train because, as far as the "fussiness" was concerned and its ridiculous conditions, he was evolving his own personal philosophy: *What's important is not to obey them,* he figured. *What's important is not to bother obeying them without it becoming known to the comrades and without any harm coming from it.* It was this philosophy that now often gave his words an ironic and impatient tone.

When Vaz noticed that Afonso approached from the street and not from the station, Afonso said he had come by train and left through the crossing gate. And when Vaz, noting the dark van passing by and mentioning it, Afonso responded categorically, *It's not the same one.* Such responses came out of Afonso even before he thought them, maybe out of instinct for self-defense. In truth, how could he say he had walked from the city while it was still dark from his parents' house where he slept, and that the van had in fact passed by him before? For the first time, the worry grabbed him not just of the possible consequences of his errors, but that sooner or later, he'd get caught in one of them one day. When he was alone he thought of this, and felt such great disappointment in himself that all he wanted to do was close his eyes and forget everything—dreams, disillusionments, his own personal philosophy, lies to his comrades. And he threw himself with increased vigor into his work, not missing a meeting, appearing at the right time, not sparing himself long walks, not ever complaining about missed meals and nights of no sleep. Except about the "fussiness": he didn't acquiesce. It was beyond his powers.

10

Two days after that encounter with Vaz, Afonso met with Fialho. Standing next to a kilometer mark on the road, Fialho told him to go on a certain night to a nearby liaison point to pick up some material, but he should not go there without checking to see if Fialho had left a signal on that kilometer mark. If the signal was there, he should not go to the point, because Fialho would already have gone. If there was no signal, he should pick up the material. In either case, the two of them would meet that same night at about one league from that site.

They met, and Afonso stated he had gone to the liaison point, but the material wasn't there.

"What!?" Fialho exclaimed. "Did you forget to look for the signal?"

As he'd been doing for some time now, when he was asked about such matters, Afonso defended himself quickly, before even thinking or measuring the implications of his answer. "I didn't see any signal, friend. And look, I went through almost a whole box of matches."

Despite the darkness that night, Afonso saw his comrade's head twist in a sharp turn toward him, and imagined his worried, observant eyes under the visor of his black eyebrows.

Fialho spoke no more about it. But rather than follow the road they usually walked, he dragged Afonso onto another, in a direction for which Afonso had no immediate explanation. He only found it an hour later, when Fialho made him stand next to the kilometer mark where they had agreed on the signal. Fialho took his flashlight out of his pocket.

"See," he said, shining the light on the signal. "It's perfectly visible, seems to me."

"Look, friend, I didn't see it," said Afonso shrugging his shoulders impatiently and walking away to the middle of the road.

Fialho didn't follow right away. He remained next to the mark, directing the ray of light here and there, carefully searching for something on the ground. Then he joined Afonso and going back, walked down the road for a while in silence. Fialho strode at a determined pace and, by the movements of his head, it was clear that he was eagerly looking for something that would stand out in the dark. Taller and slightly bent, Afonso walked with long, easy steps and appeared absorbed in thought.

"You've got yourself deep in the mud up to your knees," Fialho suddenly exploded, in a rapid-fire voice that must have come through clenched teeth. "Errors create more errors, lies create more lies. What kind of story is this about the matches? You went through a box of matches and there isn't a single matchstick to be found. First you didn't go to check the signal because you forgot the arrangement or out of laziness. Then you want to look all innocent, even if you implicate another comrade as guilty."

"I don't understand," Afonso mumbled. "If only—"

"Shut up!" Fialho interrupted in a commanding low voice. "You should be ashamed of yourself!"

They walked farther. Afonso felt the need to react, to defend himself, say something. But what? It was Fialho who spoke:

"Unfortunately this isn't any bigger than the others. It's just one more to add to the collection. On the very first day, what were you doing strolling around the meeting place? The Comrades are in jail, so we can talk about this. Why did you have to go check out that car and see the comrade's name? All because you didn't hear that time, and almost never want to hear instructions you're given. A whole string of errors and lies. That's what your whole life as a Party functionary has been. In everything, comrade. Even in the littlest things, like those stupid medlars you picked. You surely remember those." (Afonso blushed in the dark—so the comrade had seen!)

"You've disrespected Party vigilance, and now look at the situation you've created. I saw Vaz today and he told me you've gone to visit your family." (Afonso's heart started beating wildly.)

"These are real crimes against the Party, comrade. The police are making a ferocious effort right now to catch us. And in this situation you are playing with the safety and lives of our comrades, with the security and work of our print apparatus, all on account of your impulses and your little sentimental problems. Either you're not taking things seriously and behaving like a child, or you are and you're just a good-for-nothing."

Fialho remained quiet for a few moments. He looked closely as a light went on in a house that stood back from the road, then he studied the constellations in the starry sky. That pause was more painful for Afonso than the words Fialho had delivered.

"I don't know what the Parry will decide," Fialho continued. "I wouldn't be surprised if you were fired as a Party cadre. So there you have it. If you are a Communist, which despite everything I believe you are, you should learn something from that lesson. If you don't learn anything, then you're truly a man hurled into the swamp." And after a pause, he repeated it with emphasis: "Into the swamp."

An almost imperceptible change had occurred in the way Afonso walked, the way he swung his arms, the irregularity and uncertainty of his step. Looking at him sidewise, Fialho saw him crying. But he went on castigating him hard.

11

Three days after José Sagarra had been freed, he met with da Barrosa in the shade of an old olive tree. With a pot sitting on his knees, da Barrosa sipped a soup and talked at the same time: An infernal, indecipherable noise came out of his mouth as a result. He ate with such zest that only when he had finished the soup did he see that his comrade, against his will, had been staring at the pot. He cleared his throat, unwrapped a small sheet of paper with a minuscule piece of goat cheese and pulled out a knife. His fingers brought the knife close to the cheese to carve the first slice, but he hesitated indecisively. Da Barrosa figured that if he was here with him at that place and time, coming from other meetings and moving on to others, Sagarra surely ate poorly. The devouring glance directed toward the pot that had surprised him could not have more than one meaning.

Continuing to clear his throat and speak with truncated words, da Barrosa ended up sharing his bread and cheese with Sagarra, and gave him, more liberally, a swig of wine. When the meeting ended, dealing with the increase in dayworker pay in some places, he spoke of the hardships of life.

"Everything is so expensive. You can't manage anything beyond a soup. There's no ham, no cod, and you can only have cheese on holidays. You get to the end of your lunch or your dinner and you're as hungry as you were before."

José Sagarra knew this was the pure truth, and always felt constrained accepting whatever the comrades offered him. Although few offered. He'd be together with them out in the fields and no one would remember to ask if he'd eaten already or if he was hungry. He never went home to eat. He was used to coming home at night, and leaving the next morning when it was still dark. In that way he avoided explanations and potential insistence from his brother and other family members that he eat. For sure, one of these days he would collapse from starvation in some gutter if he hadn't decided that he absolutely needed to eat, even without working to earn money, without having anyone who would give him food and without money.

From the moment he started thinking that way, the only preoccupation he had on his long hikes was to find some bean fields. When he found one, he filled his pockets, sometimes even his hat, and walked off chewing. For one week that's all he ate. During that week, he ran all around the region, walking leagues and leagues without stopping, speaking with all the comrades he was supposed to speak with, holding meetings with the marketplace committees, including in his own town, searched out the peasants he had met that day in jail, and at the end of that week, not only had he given direction to the continuing struggle going beyond the 18th of May but had set the foundation for new Party formations in another eight villages and settlements.

One thing started to worry him: the frequency of seeing GNR patrols and the constant reports from the comrades of the appearance of strange guys arriving in cars or vans and seen sometimes standing right on the road or at the entrances to villages closely and carefully observing the peasants who came and went. Many things were said of them: that they were from the foodstuffs administration, or from the tax division, or that they were petty thieves, or that they were hunting them. But the May 18th struggle and the thousands of arrests were too fresh for the wiser people not to make a connection between one thing and the other. People related how in one village these suspect individuals had spent a long time visiting the priest at his home; in another talking with the local officials; and in yet another with a grocer who had Nazi propaganda photos and posters pinned on his walls.

When they gave him these reports, they were news to José Sagarra, for he himself had only seen the abnormally frequent GNR patrols. But a few days later, walking on a road, he suddenly came upon a parked automobile. Several men were inside it, and one of them, as Sagarra approached, got out to stretch his limbs, almost cutting off his pathway, and as Sagarra passed, stared at him weirdly, as though he wanted to find something in his face or in his expression—maybe the freckles or maybe the color of his eyes. *This is absurd!* he thought as he continued walking on the road. *How would they know?*

At some distance ahead, looking back, he saw the automobile in the same spot. A few kilometers farther ahead, after a long straight section of road, he looked back again, and once more saw the car almost disappearing in the distance. It still looked parked, but certainly it had moved a few kilometers in the same direction Sagarra was walking, and at the same speed as Sagarra on foot.

He then detoured into the fields and didn't see the car any more.

12

The following Monday he went to the laborers' marketplace. Like the other workers, he was hired at the highest rate of recent years, rates imposed by the marketplace committee on the owners and managers. Only one thing called his attention. An unknown man accompanied a manager circulating around the square. There was nothing special about that fact. But unusual was the curious way this individual scrutinized the peasants, as they also scrutinized him. To José Sagarra, it seemed just like a few days before with the automobile guy, that he was trying to find something in his face or his eyes.

For three days, during which he pursued a normal life in his home surroundings, spending the day working in the fields and returning home at sundown, Sagarra saw nothing else out of the ordinary. But on Wednesday at sundown, when he went out for a meeting with Vaz, he saw a parked van with its lights off at the crossroads leading to the village. He told Vaz about it as soon as he arrived. Vaz withdrew some papers from his pocket, asked Sagarra to light a match, and on a little slip of paper copied down the license number of the dark van that had passed by him several times the day of his meeting with Afonso.

"If you see it again, you have to check if this is the number," Vaz said, recounting how it seemed he had been followed by a van with that registration.

José Sagarra reported to Vaz on the suspect men seen in the region, the raises in wages that had been achieved, and the progress of the Party organization. Vaz told him he had not yet received a response concerning Sagarra's acceptance into the cadre of Party workers.

After they separated, José Sagarra passed that crossroads again. The van was still there. He approached it and took note of the number, which, black on a white background, stood out in the semi-darkness of twilight. The van was empty, and Sagarra entered the village and went home.

He had hardly arrived at the house when someone knocked at the front door. To his sister-in-law's question came the voice of a man in response. Sagarra ran to the back door and in the shadows saw a figure opening the patio gate. Like a thunderbolt, Sagarra leapt over the wall as men's voices were heard shouting behind him. At the exact moment when he jumped into the neighbor's yard he heard a shot. *Who's setting off firecrackers at this hour?* he thought, not seeing any relation between the shot, his exit from the house, and the man at the patio gate. He ran and ran, scaled another wall, got onto a trail and disappeared into the fields. When he stopped, huffing and puffing, the peaceful night calmed him, heightened by the chant of the crickets.

13

When he saw Sagarra jump out from behind some bushes along the road, Vaz immediately understood some important news was afoot. Sagarra told how he had submerged underground and was now hidden at Tomé's house, in the same hayloft where some time back a meeting with Vaz had taken place. He confirmed that the license number on the van was the same as Vaz had given him, and went on to say that after they assaulted his house, the police and GNR, and sometimes both together, ordered cyclists to stop at the entrance or in the environs of the village, asking for documents, and interrogating and searching them.

"You can be sure they're looking for you," José Sagarra concluded.

At his suggestion, they took pathways and trails so that Vaz could move onto another route far from the village. Vaz handed Sagarra money, advised him to be prudent, and set a date for another meeting in one week. At that point he was counting on bringing him a decision on the comrade's employment by the Party.

From there Vaz proceeded to several other locales, and in two of them the comrades also said the GNR was ordering cyclists to stop and demanding documents. It was Cesário, however, who gave him a more precise report.

Speaking of the results of the mobilization, of some raises already won in wages and improvement in foodstuff supply, Cesário also mentioned repression against black marketeers.

"Until our movement," Cesário said, "no one was concerned with the black market. Now they've decided to investigate, but just the little guys."

He related how at the gates to the city foodstuffs administration brigades were conducting searches of highway jitneys, stopping cyclists and ransacking packages.

"They told me today," he ended, "they're looking for a black marketeer transporting oil on a blue bicycle."

As soon as he uttered those words, Cesário understood the true meaning behind all this sudden inspection. "My friend!" he blurted, grasping Vaz by the arm.

Vaz's bicycle was blue, in fact, and now it looked very clear that Vaz had been located and they were beating the bushes to nab him. How could Cesário believe it had anything to do with repression of the black market?

Still, on the way back to his house by bicycle, where he would see Ramos, Paulo and António, he didn't see anything unusual. But as António at that meeting also reported that in the area around Cicol the comrades were seeing increased vigilance at the station and as trucks and jitneys arrived, it was decided, in order to throw the police off their trail, that Vaz, Paulo and António should switch some of their contacts among themselves. Vaz would connect with Pereira and Jerónimo, Paulo would go to Sagarra and his region, and António would be Cesário's contact. They also decided not to meet at Vaz's house anymore, and to reinforce their security and defense measures. Concerning Vaz, though, these measures would be only temporary. As a member of the Central Committee to which he'd recently been appointed, he would shortly be assigned to another sector, and another comrade would come to substitute him.

14

Meanwhile, strange things continued to arise. If in normal times some of them might have attracted little attention, now none escaped Vaz's examination. On the day when he went to introduce António to Cesário, on leaving the house, on that same empty field where a few nights earlier he had seen that suspect figure, the two comrades saw a man standing immobile some meters away from the trail and with his back toward it. Peering in the direction in which the man was turned, Vaz saw nothing that would hold his attention for such a long time. It was obvious nevertheless that in such a deserted place the man, hearing steps and voices, would naturally look to see who was coming, but he kept himself utterly still, even when Vaz and António passed him just a few meters' distance away. A few steps farther on, Vaz turned around brusquely and his glance met that of the other man, a watchful glance on a troubled face. In that brief instant, Vaz had no doubt that the man was watching the approach of the two of them with interest and wanted to conceal that interest and hide his face.

"They're searching the city," said Vaz. "When you come here, be careful."

"I will, I will," said António. "I have no desire to be arrested." And with his eyes smiling under the brim of his oversized hat, he added, "For every reason, plus one—"

Vaz understood the "plus one" was Maria, but thought António's self-satisfaction and sly intonation out of place.

That night, after traveling a great part of the distance by jitney, when he walked home, some ten kilometers away, a new incident aggravated his anxiety. It was long past midnight and on the deserted road he heard only the sound of his steps. Low, dense clouds filtered the moonlight. He could make out the clear ribbon of road, the trees along its edges, and the impassive bodies of the surrounding hills. Shapes of everything looked imprecise, muddled in a tenuous cloud of light. Up ahead the road descended in a slow, straight line toward a small bridge among leafy trees embracing in an overhead vault, which put that stretch into deep shadow. It was when Vaz started his descent that he spotted two figures separating in the middle of the road and disappearing into the darkness, one on each side. He remembered being told about thieves attacking isolated travelers in places like this. When he got to the point where the two figures must have been waiting in ambush, he pulled out his pistol and noisily inserted a bullet into the chamber. In the night silence, the crisp, metallic sound echoed far. Whoever was waiting for him in ambush had to have heard it.

Pistol in hand, he crossed the shaded passage, where nothing could be discerned but the massive volume of the huge trees. No noise, and no suspect movement. Yet somewhere there in the dark shadows, two men were certainly spying on his steps. Who were they, and what did they want? When Vaz emerged again onto the clearer part of the road, the glare of two headlights described a semi-circle in the space in front of him and then flashed directly on his face, luridly illuminating the road. Vaz turned backward and saw two men rushing away from the heavily shadowed redoubt, one from each side of the road, pursued by the strong beam of the head-lights. A heavy truck rattling loose pieces of iron and lumber passed Vaz, leaving a cloud of dust in its wake. Once again the road turned silent, quietly submerged in a filmy light filtered through the clouds.

When he got to the house, Rosa told him she had tried to engage the neighbors in conversation to see if any suspect people had been about. No one had seen anything. She further mentioned that a woman with a small child had come to the house begging for alms. Beggars had often appeared at the house, some for the first time, which in and of itself was not remarkable. But Rosa was apprehensive.

"When we're worried and scared, everything looks suspect," she said. "But there was something unnatural about that woman. Her eyes were dry, wandering and purposeful, and you don't see eyes like that on beggars."

15

The next morning, Vaz and Rosa left the house to walk around the neighborhood. It was a lovely sunny day, a light breeze blow-ing, and the neighbors greeted them warmly, especially Vaz, who rarely showed his face outside the house. They conversed with Miss Ermelinda and with her husband, talked with Amélia, and spoke with others. They strolled through the settlement, on the street, and through the nearby pines. No one noticed anything, nor did they, absolutely nothing, that could be considered suspect in any way. Everything appeared as always, and the light-filled atmosphere rein-forced their impression of peace and safety.

That afternoon, by himself, Vaz decided to take a longer walk out to the countryside so as to assess the road. In some places he hung around for a while, observing the occasional traffic of vehicles and pedestrians. All seemed normal.

On his way back, more than a league away from the house, he walked down the asphalt road. Feeling extremely tired, he chose a shady place under a tree to rest a little, sitting alongside a clump of foliage whose bright green gave off a vivid sense of freshness.

His eyes wandered from side to side as he tried to find something of interest in the landscape, in the birds, the insects; and meanwhile, not knowing why, his glance focused irresistibly on the tar surface of the road right in front of him in the tree's shade. Something there drew his attention, not just once but several times. Eventually he stood up and started to study the ground. Distinctly planted into the black tar were the dusty impressions of rubber soles. They were not those of someone casually passing by. The marks appeared pointing in every direction, and sometimes in thick, superimposed patches. Someone with shoes of a type rarely seen in the region, someone who was clearly no peasant, had also been there in that shade. It wasn't only the type of sole that called his attention. Whoever it was had been there a long time, now turned toward one side of the street, then to the other, sometimes walking and standing a little farther on. The coincidence gained Vaz's even greater interest when, as he continued walking down the road, a couple of hundred meters later, in another shady spot now on the other side, he noticed a new set of impressions from the same rubber soles, indicating, as at the first spot, that whoever wore them had also spent a long time there waiting for something.

"My own inclination would be to move to a new house right away," he told Rosa when he got back home. "But seeing things calmly, nothing justifies a precipitous move. If we were to change houses every time we saw a beggar with dry, wandering eyes, or shoe marks in the asphalt a league from the house, or some figures on the street at night, we'd never stay put anywhere. If we're noticing these things now it's only because we've been forewarned by what's happening in other areas, and by the fact that I've possibly been located and followed in the sector I was in charge of. We've redoubled our vigilance, so of course we're seeing more than we saw before. I feel like I've turned into a Sherlock Holmes—"

And as so seldom happened, Vaz laughed out loud in satisfaction, showing his rows of white, chiseled teeth. As Maria had once said, Rosa thought laughter suited her companion well, and that it was such a shame he laughed so infrequently. But now Vaz's serious face closed up again in his usual impassivity.

"Let's increase our vigilance even more. If we need to, we'll take appropriate measures."

Vaz and Rosa did reinforce their vigilance, but in the following days nothing alerted them. Under the blue sky and shining sun, all seemed quiet and happy.

Chapter XV

1

One afternoon the next week, when Vaz was crossing through town about a league from his house, a peasant placed himself in front of his bicycle, and as soon as Vaz braked, the man grabbed the handlebars with the sudden jerks of a drunk.

"Senhor Francisco!" he shouted in a wine-soaked state. To his surprise, Vaz recognized Ernesto. "Come here!"

Ernesto led him onto a quiet little lane. Swaying as he stood, he looked warily one way and then the other, and in a raw voice recounted how that morning some guys had been in the area talking with the Pim-Pa-Pum. Miss Ermelinda, who never missed any bit of gossip and ran to share it, told Ernesto's wife that they were from the foodstuffs administration seeking information about the family occupying the Costa house, Costa being Vaz's landlord. Ernesto intended to ask his wife to go over and warn Senhora Rosa, but hadn't, so as not to scare her. At dinnertime, Sapo, who had gone that morning to town, reported that at the Four Corners, between the town and the settlement, a GNR patrol, along with two plainclothes men, were making cyclists stop, demanding documents, asking where they lived and searching their baggage and pockets. In light of these developments, and knowing from Anica that Francisco was not at home, Ernesto had decided to give up an afternoon work shift and go to the town to catch Vaz on his return trip home. He himself had seen how they forced cyclists to stop at the Four Corners.

"I'll never forget what you did for me one time," he ended in a blubbering voice. "It could just be my craziness, and please forgive me, Senhor Francisco, but who knows, just in case, to prevent something bad happening."

Constantly looking from one side to the other, Ernesto emitted a strong whiff of wine.

"Thank you," Vaz said, shaking his hand. "Probably it has nothing to do with me, but thank you. Thank you, friend."

Though pallid and furrowed, Vaz's face maintained its imperturbability. But from that handshake, from his insistent expressions of gratitude, from the word "friend," which Vaz said to him for the first time, Ernesto understood the importance of the warning he had just given. When that dawned on him, be began trembling all over like someone with malaria and, trying to say another couple of words, he could only babble a few indistinct sounds.

2

Vaz went to a small business asking if they would store his bicycle for a few days in case he didn't come back before nightfall to retrieve it. He then left the town and headed into the fields in the direction toward home.

Despite how tired he felt from his trip, and how great his debility, he ran as long as he had the breath for it, followed that with a brisk walking pace, and then started desperately running again. He had no doubt now that the investigation had him as its objective, and he had to admit that his house had been identified. The only question was at what moment the police would attack. Possibly they were hoping to seize him in the street and only then attack the house so that, as they had done in other cases, they could attribute the denunciation of the safe house to him. Who could know? And what assurance did he have that they hadn't attacked the house already and weren't waiting for him there? Hours before, when Ernesto left the area, they hadn't done that yet. But now? His chest assailed by hooks of fire, Vaz continues running. The only fear he feels is that he'll fall from fatigue and wind up face down on the ground. From behind some bushes he saw the Four Corners from afar. He recognized the blotch of military uniforms, the metallic brilliance of weapons, and two other figures half hidden behind the directional signage.

He turned to run away in little spurts, the fire burning in his chest almost asphyxiating him. *To arrive in time. Arrive in time* is his only thought. Suffocated, pouring sweat, the stings of fire more and more strangling his throat and lungs, he trips through the stones and brush, now hardly keeping his balance, not in control of his steps. Now he's neither running nor marching. He proceeds at a dragging, irregular pace, as though with each tentative, out-of-kilter move, protecting himself from crashing. He feels like a drunkard, his head spinning, everything whirling wildly around him.

When the house appeared in view from a distance, he observed it anxiously. As always, with one window open, the others closed, it stood out white, peaceful and happy amongst the olive trees.

At Ernesto's house, where he decided to go first, the wife regarded him with her black eyes wide open in terror. *The house was raided*, Vaz thought, *I arrived too late*. But what terrified Ernesto's wife had nothing to do with the house. What shocked her was the way Vaz himself looked, his face flushed with fatigue and heat, water pouring out of him as if they had twisted it out of him from the top of his head, his parched mouth hanging open, his lips bloodless, his torso heaving, his burning, staring eyes buried in two bruised, reddened circles. But no, the woman responded, there wasn't anything going on at the house, because not long ago she'd seen the Senhora outside taking in the clothes.

"How long ago?" Vaz asked. His question came out so faint and confused that he had to repeat it.

"A little while ago, just a little while—"

"Good," Vaz exhaled. Even his breathing had become easier.

Nervous and frightened still over Vaz's appearance, Ernesto's wife, after asking if he and her husband had met up, told him that just after noon a van came with four or five plainclothes, stopped near the grocery store, and two of them had been talking privately in the road, right there in front of them, next to Miss Ermelinda's house. Also, half an hour ago, a car had stopped farther down along the big curve in the road, but since from here she couldn't see that spot, she couldn't say if it were still there.

"One day you'll understand all this better," Vaz said, clutching her hand. "You'll understand and you'll appreciate us more."

Leaving Ernesto's wife, moved by the danger she guessed was hanging terribly over her neighbors, Vaz descended that path in long steps and now, not rushing, crossed the road, passed in front of Ermelinda's house, walked up through the olive grove and knocked on the door. Rosa opened.

Vaz didn't even give her the time to look at him. "Put your shoes on and grab your coat," he said, entering.

With calm, centered moves, as if they had been rehearsed for a long time, in profound contrast with the tortured way he looked, he emptied a basket of potatoes onto the floor, took it to his workroom, and in half a dozen quick gestures, threw in it all the papers he had on the table.

"Are you ready?" he asked.

Rosa started to say something, but what she had to say was too much for the time they had. Vaz noticed the glance she cast all around, as if to ask, *And the books? The typewriter? Clothes? Personal things? And all the rest—not much, but all they had?*

"Are you ready?" he repeated.

As if suddenly remembering something very important, Rosa ran back to the bedroom and returned with a small bag in her hand. In less than one minute from the time Vaz had entered the house, the two of them exited. They walked down through the olive orchard, crossed the road, and crept into the pine grove up above Ernesto's house. It seemed no one saw them.

From the distance, in the quiet, declining twilight, from behind an opening between the trees, they could make out the beginning of the path down below from the road up to the house. The house itself could not be seen from there, but they did see a number of dark figures running up the path, certainly men, and certainly dressed in city clothes.

They were in fact police. A minute or two later, five men with weapons in their hands broke through the door into the abandoned house.

3

It was well past midnight when Vaz and Rosa sat down, exhausted, on the side of the pathway. The night was still and tepid, and the stars pricked the deep black sky with lights. The police would surely search the whole region that night, and for that reason they had to evade settlements and roads. The nearest place where Vaz knew he could be taken in safely was almost twenty kilometers away by the road. But as Vaz wanted to get there only on trails and through fields, and would surely be forced to make some circles and detours, they would have to walk all night long. Not used to such long treks, Rosa already had blisters on her feet, her legs almost numb. Fatigued as he was, it was only the urgency of the situation that kept him from falling asleep. Despite the reverse he had suffered, he felt at peace. His hands coddled the heavy basket in which he carried all the documents he had in the house—notes, reports, letters, Party literature—which, as an old habit of his, he always kept on top of the table. He did this thinking of the possibility of a police raid at the house so as to most quickly destroy or, if there were time, to grab and flee with them. He'd done this for years and always maintained the necessary discipline to never fail from doing so. At times his comrades referred ironically to what they called an "excess of organization and caution." The moment had come, however, and the tenacious efforts he'd made for years and years paid off. The police occupied the house, but the papers were smiling there in that basket.

For long minutes they didn't exchange any words. Rosa lightly placed her thin hand on her companion's thigh, and from that gesture Vaz understood that she was going to say something of importance. Rosa gently caressed her companion's leg with her fingertips. She stopped and spoke.

"Listen, José," she said, using his real name, which she had not done for a while. She became quiet again, and when this almost cheeky voice went silent in the grandeur of the night, the night seemed even more spacious, peaceful and solemn. "Do you know I have a daughter?"

At some other time Vaz would have received this news with surprise and disturbance. Right now it seemed to him something distant, meaningless, and irrelevant, something that had nothing to do with the present situation, with his life, or with Rosa's life, with both of their lives insofar as the essence of it was concerned—the struggle and Party activity.

"Yes, I have a daughter," Rosa continued, calm and sad. "A bourgeois daughter, like her father, a daughter who doesn't know and doesn't care to know her mother. They stole her from me. Father, grandmother, judges, they all robbed me of her. First they threatened me, then they offered me money. Money, friend! For a mother to abandon her daughter. They ended up just stealing her from me. They said I was a hindrance to my daughter's happiness and that she'd be in danger living with me. Just for being a worker and a communist."

Rosa went quiet, and once again the silence of the night soothed them. Vaz began to sense that Rosa's words were in the end not indifferent to her life as a militant and to all that had taken place that day. To the contrary, it was those events that led her to speak.

"Personally, I don't hate them," she continued, her voice even more calm, though with an overtone of old, deep emotions. "Their class, yes, I hate, hate, hate them. Extremely! Their morals, their ideas, their ways, their feelings and their words. Everything coming from them is destructive. We have to create the world anew, friend," she added after a pause.

Rosa's hand lay heavily on Vaz's thigh, and he placed his on top of hers. That mysterious presence in Rosa's past—he now had before him. A certain distractedness, certain gestures, certain ways of acting, everything in one moment became clear. And Vaz felt that, of all the possible reasons for it, this in no way lowered Rosa in his eyes, nor added to what he knew of her. Far from driving them apart, it brought them together more.

"We have to create the world anew," she said again.

And briefly squeezing Vaz's hand between hers, she strained to move her beaten, numb body, stood up and put her coat on her shoulders. Vaz got up too, stretched with a shiver of his sweaty, worn-out body, and took hold of the basket.

"We can't take such long rests," he said, roughly coughing up phlegm. "If we cool down too much we won't be able to get going again."

Now the only matter at hand was to walk all night and get to the safe space. He was used to it. But Rosa? He felt great pity for the weak woman he had at his side, denied everything and complaining of nothing.

Rosa stood standing quietly another moment, her head bent to the immensity of the starry skies. Was she thinking about her daughter? Or her seducer? Everything she left behind in the abandoned house? The brutal march imposed on her now? Her feet with open sores? The new sacrifices and dangers that awaited her? Swallowed up by the night, she seemed weak, helpless and sorrowful. Vaz put his arm around her and held her against his side, shoulder to shoulder. Rosa stretched her neck around until she was face to face with him— two thin, tired, worried, sweaty and cold faces that understood and loved each other all the more for that.

It was Rosa again who broke the silence. "If it wasn't for the Party," she said, plain and resigned, "it wouldn't be worth living."

4

It was still daylight when Ramos arrived at António's house. Not per usual, he came by bicycle, a heavy, black bicycle with the handlebars reversed like the horns of a bull.

"What do you think of this bull?" he asked, pushing the bicycle into the corridor.

As Maria was trying to make room for him to pass, Ramos brusquely turned the handlebars toward her. Surprised, but also tickled, Maria leaned against the wall. The bicycle truly did look like a bull.

While Maria was saying that António was running late, as he should have been back in the middle of the afternoon, Ramos put the bicycle away, threw his briefcase and pistol on top of the table, took off his jacket, and headed for the washbasin. Maria remained to watch him, for she liked the way he washed his hands. First he slowly rolled up his sleeves, then picked up the soap, wetted it with a quick squirt of water and ran it first over his palms and then over the backs of his hands. Then he put the soap aside and made lots of lather in a leisurely ritual of his own, fitting the palm of one hand to the back of the other. Finally, he dipped his hands several times in the water until there wasn't even the slightest vestige of a soap bubble. When he finished, Maria handed him the towel, and said without thinking, "See, if I'd gone to live with you, you'd always have someone to hand you the towel."

Ramos ogled her, smiling eagerly, and Maria blushed vividly. Not because of the comrade's cheeky look, but because of the words she had said, whose meaning was only now apparent. She tried to right herself.

"Maybe I'm giving you some bad habits. But if your companion found out, she might get angry."

"My companion?" Ramos laughed somewhere between amused and irritated. "Who told you I have a companion?"

Seeing that Ramos wished to insinuate that he had no companion, Maria suddenly remembered the conversation with António when she rejected his advances and he spoke of Ramos's companion. Maria never questioned those words, which led, as she well knew, to her yielding eventually. Did António lie? Again Maria blushed and lifted her hand to her face.

Ramos put the towel back and they sat down at the table. But the first few minutes of pleasant talk evaporated quickly, as if that brief exchange of words made them pensive and sad. As they waited for António to have dinner, they spoke about this and that, but soon exhausted the conversation. For long pauses they remained looking at one another in silence, each one thinking about something, with the thought that the other was thinking the same thing. Then they spoke of António.

"Is he late?"

"Yes, he's late."

And Maria surprised herself thinking it wouldn't be so bad if António were delayed a little longer, to extend her innocent pleasure at being alone with Ramos for a little while.

By 9:30 that night they both started to get nervous.

"Did you put the signal in the agreed-upon place?" Ramos asked.

"It was for you as much as for him. Didn't you see it?"

For a long time no one spoke, Ramos making a rough drawing, and Maria fussing with her nails. Later they started speaking again about one thing and another, with long pauses in between, but now there wasn't even a hint of lightheartedness in what they said.

At 10:40 Maia put a few more coals on the fire to keep the soup hot and suggested that Ramos eat, for he must be needing it. She would eat with António when he came.

"I'll wait too," said Ramos.

Pulling a stack of newspapers out of his briefcase, he began to read them, making long underlinings with the stub of a red pencil. Maria tried to read also, but could barely do it for two contradictory reasons: She was anxiously expecting António's return. At the same time, she raised her eyes every once in a while from her book and felt a strange comfort seeing Ramos working in the calm of the evening, in the peaceful intimacy of that little room, badly lit by the oil lamp. Looking at him without being seen, she now watched him willingly, without the disruption he sometimes created for her in his overly vivacious gestures and expressions, when he directed them at her.

Ramos looked at the clock: Twenty-five to twelve. He pulled out a calendar. "Isn't today Thursday?" he asked, though he knew perfectly well it was.

There was no mistake. There was no accounting for António's delay. They started making plans in case he should not be home by midnight, when they heard a noise from the street.

"Listen!" said Maria.

It could practically be said they were just waiting to hear Maria's voice before they knocked.

"There he is!" Ramos claimed with relief and happiness.

Maria ran excitedly to the door.

5

It wasn't António, but Vaz. He entered dragging his feet. He sat in the kitchen on the bench they brought for him and stared at the comrades with weak, hollow eyes on his extremely pale face, shining with sweat in the light of the lamp. He took his hat off and his messy hair clung to his scalp.

"Disaster?" Ramos asked.

Vaz nodded lightly and tried to speak. He only coughed, low and muffled. He could barely sip from the glass of water Maria handed him and before he could manage to speak he had to wait a little while longer.

"My house was raided," he could finally say. "My companion and my papers are saved"—and his hands, in an anomalous gesture, seemed to reach for support on the nonexistent arms of a chair.

Not asking any questions, Ramos helped his comrade to stand up from the bench and lie down on the bed. Maria straightened up his pillow. Vaz closed his eyes, his skin the pallor of death, as he breathed haltingly. They sat there for long minutes, Ramos and Maria on the edge of the bed and Vaz unmoving with his eyes shut. Finally he took a deep breath, coughed that same muffled sound, breathed deeply again and sat up in the bed.

"We have to talk," he said in a foggy voice.

Then, in few words, he related what had happened. After leaving Rosa in the house of a comrade where they arrived just at dawn, totally spent, Vaz, not resting even a minute, got on the road again so as not to miss any meetings he had for the day, and walked almost all day long without anything to eat. He only took a jitney for a one-hour stretch, which let him off two leagues from António's house.

"Well, later we'll talk," said Ramos. "Let's eat now."

Holding the lamp., he went to the kitchen, followed by Maria. He himself served the soup. Vaz appeared shortly. His abased figure was so severe, his cheeks so drawn and his eyes so weak, that Ramos and Maria could hardly take their eyes off him until he sat down and started to eat the soup with a tremulous hand.

Ramos told Vaz about António being so late in coming, and asked if he knew where he had gone.

"He's my substitute. He went in my place," Vaz said. "Yesterday he had his first meeting at Cesário's house."

They all stopped to look at one another. One thought occurred to everyone: António had clearly been arrested.

6

After eating, they asked Maria to leave them alone for a few minutes so they could decide what they needed to do. They would leave immediately. Vaz would catch the train at two in the morning, would go find Paulo, taking all precautions, and with him figure out the best way to learn what happened to António, maybe through José Sagarra. In case António had been arrested, he'd deal with moving Maria. Ramos would go to a series of meetings that Vaz would have had, among them one at the Pereiras' house, for Vaz was in no shape to exert himself any further. Vaz and Ramos would meet together with Paulo within a few days, in a pine forest the three of them all knew well.

They called Maria. Appearing out of the darkness, she wrinkled her face to the lamplight.

"We're going to leave," Ramos told her. "It could be there's nothing serious happening with António and maybe he was simply delayed for reasons unknown. If he shows up, so much the better.

We'll find out. If anything happened to him, we'll come looking for you within two or three days. If you see anything suspicious around here, do you have someplace to go?"

Maria remembered the lawyer's house, where she had been that time she went to the dentist.

"Great," Ramos said. "How much money do you have?"

Maria got out a cardboard box, pulled out a twenty *escudos* note, and spilled the coins onto the table. Ramos didn't let her count them.

"Take these," he said, handing her two bills. "You might need them." And he started organizing his briefcase.

Maria stood by him, glued to him, holding him by the arm. For an instant or two, Ramos saw her long-lashed eyes fixed on him, with the same firm and sad sweetness as the fingers squeezing his arm. He imagined that Maria was more nervous about him, Ramos, and by their imminent separation, than she was over António's fate.

"Have courage, girl," he said. "Probably it's all right."

Vaz approached her silently and embraced her, which he had never done before. Also for the first time, Maria kissed him on his cold, wan cheek. Ramos peeled his arm from Maria's hand, retrieved his bicycle and brought it to the door.

"Looks like a bull, huh?" he smiled and pointed to the turned-up handlebars.

Maria smiled too, a sad smile which carried a faint judgment: *Why are you leaving me all alone, friends? / Why?*

7

When they left the village and, at a fork, passed a tiny little road, Vaz and Ramos saw the taillights of a parked car at a few meters' distance. They looked around in the darkness. They knew that that little street, where construction had begun but had never been completed, had no exit. There were no houses there and no reason for any car or truck to be there at that hour. Why, and what for? When they took a few steps, the parked car lit its headlights, advanced, reversed, advanced again, turned around and approached them. It was a Jeep. Huddled at the curb, Vaz and Ramos saw it go toward the village. Following the beam of headlights moving along the horizon, they observed the Jeep crossing through the village without stopping and continuing quite a bit farther until the beam suddenly disappeared in the dark.

"It might be nothing," Vaz said. "But anyway, we shouldn't have left Maria."

Ramos lit his cigarette lighter to see his watch: 35 minutes past midnight. "Yes, it's better to take her," he said, remembering Maria's hand gripping his arm, her big eyes staring at him with a vague hint of censure: *Why are you leaving me all alone, friends? Why?* "You go take the train. I'll go back and get our friend, put her in a safe place, and remove all the papers from the house."

The two comrades shook hands.

"As soon as you can, try to get some sleep," Ramos told him. "And eat, you hear? Eat! In situations like these it's a crime to stop eating just to save the Party a few pennies."

Vaz went on his way, dragging himself along with difficulty. Ramos mounted his bicycle and turned back.

"Did you forget something?" Maria asked when she saw him come in, and her eyes shone appreciatively.

Ramos related what they had seen. It was best to leave the house immediately, taking all the papers. Later, when it were possible, and if nothing else had happened to the house, they'd come back and pick up other things.

Maria accepted this decision with visible contentment. She didn't even ask what would happen if António should return, for like Vaz and Ramos both, she figured for sure António had been arrested. They filled a briefcase with documents and clandestine printed material. Ramos got ready to put all the best books in a big package.

"What can I take?" Maria whispered, holding the suitcase she had carried when she slipped into the underground movement.

Ramos recognized that suitcase well and remembered the first day he met Maria; and Maria also remembered how the comrade had stood on the other side of the ditch, placing the suitcase on the ground and opening his arms for her to jump.

"Pack whatever you want in the bag," Ramos answered. "Your clothes or whatever you like."

While Ramos finished packing up the books, Maria went to the bedroom to get dressed.

First she put on a blouse. Then another on top of that, and still another—all that she had. Though it was summer, she put on a woolen pullover and, after a moment's hesitation, put on another as well. Then she shook her head unhappily, took everything off and put on a second chemise, finally putting on the three blouses and the two pullovers again. More satisfied now, she put António's best clothes in the suitcase—two shirts, a tie, a pair of pants—a few of António's personal items and two of his favorite books. Only then did she pack a few more items of clothing and objects of her own.

When she finished—quickly, because the suitcase could hold only so much—Ramos had already written a note to leave on the table, admitting, though improbable, that António would show up and make use of the key, which normally he didn't. He told Maria to write a letter to the landlady of the house, saying that her husband had returned late, that his mother was sick unto death, and they had decided to leave on the early morning train.

"Put it under her door," Ramos said, "so there won't be anything to be alarmed about in the village."

As Maria wrote, Ramos tied the suitcase to the luggage rack, tied the typewriter on top of that, the packet of papers and books, and on top of the pyramid, António's briefcase.

"Can you take all of that?" Maria asked in shock.

"And I'm taking you too!" Ramos laughed, attaching his own briefcase onto the frame.

With everything set, he checked the tires and gave them a few energetic pumps.

"Shall we go?"

Maria closed the indoor window shutters, locked the kitchen door and grabbed her jacket.

"Put it on, it's quite cool out," Ramos warned.

But after Maria said she already had too many clothes on, Ramos tied the jacket on top of António's briefcase.

"A skyscraper!" he said, looking sideways at her, as he adjusted the ropes near the seat.

They put out the light. Barely able to balance the bicycle with so much cargo, Ramos left the house. Maria closed the street door and joined Ramos in the darkness. Farther up, in the quiet village, they slipped the note under the landlady's door and left the settlement. As they started down the road, Ramos straddled the bicycle with his feet still on the ground.

"Get on," he said. And as Maria didn't understand what he meant, he repeated, "Get on," and helped her sit across the frame.

"Are you able to carry all of this, dear friend?" Maria asked in a voice from which Ramos could guess she was smiling.

With its headlight off, the bicycle glided smoothly along as though it were carrying no weight at all. Maria felt her comrade's face bending into her hair, his chest leaning on her back, and his arms laced around her. *How is this possible*, she thought, as a breeze stirred up by their movement hit her face and sent her hair flying into her comrade's face. *How is this possible? António's been arrested and I'm feeling happy being here with Ramos.*

Without speaking, they traveled for two hours. Several times they got off the bicycle, sometimes on the uphills, sometimes for Maria to rest a little from her awkward position, other times for Ramos to rearrange and better secure the luggage. When they saw the lights of a town, Ramos stopped again.

"Listen, friend," he told her in a tone Maria thought a little uncertain, "when we left the house, I didn't time the trip well. We'll have to wait here for the jitney in the morning. It's best if we spend the rest of the night in a pension."

Ramos then went quiet. In the dark, he couldn't see anything in Maria's face.

"If we present ourselves as brother and sister, it will look weird," he continued. "But I don't know if you'll be uncomfortable sleeping in the same room with me."

Maria didn't answer. Ramos added, his voice slightly irritable, "Don't take what I said in the wrong way. I'm only suggesting it because of underground security."

Maria remained quiet. Ramos tried fruitlessly to see something in her face, but saw only her silhouette. One arm was drooped alongside her body and the other bent, possibly with her head in her hand, a common gesture when Maria was embarrassed.

"Look, friend," Maria said finally, but weakly, in which Ramos thought he detected a glint of happiness, "if you think it's necessary, then let's do it."

8

Briefcase in one hand, typewriter in another, Maria entered the small, poorly lit room. She saw a wooden bed with a red bedspread, a frayed rug next to it, and a night table. She had taken several steps without feeling Ramos's hand on her shoulder as, without knowing quite why, she somehow hoped, and turned toward him. Ramos had just shut and locked the door, placing the suitcase, the other briefcase and the package of books in a corner of the floor. Facing her, he also looked directly at her. Maria did not see the customary good humor in his face, nor his sly, perceptive manner, nor that inviting and nervous expression she'd seen in him on the train the day she met him, and which, again without quite knowing why, she had hoped to see in him now. Ramos had an extremely disturbed expression, regarding her severely, almost with antipathy.

His hat still on, Ramos opened up the bed and saw two thin cotton blankets, one of which he yanked off. "You're in luck," he said fast and nervously. "The two sheets and the pillow are clean. So you can undress and get in bed."

In contrast to how things usually happened between them, it was Ramos now who was frazzled, but considering his nervousness, and as if responding to it, Maria felt calm and in control of herself.

"Where are you going to sleep?" she asked, seeing Ramos spreading the blanket out on the floor next to the bed.

Ramos removed his jacket, which he threw over the foot of the bed, went to the sink and washed his hands, drying them off slapping his palms on the threadbare towel. Sitting on the edge of the bed, on the side opposite to where Ramos had spread his blanket on the floor, Maria watched his movements with her long-lashed eyes wide open, feeling a great sadness rising inside her. *Did I do something wrong to him?* she thought.

In quick moves, Ramos turned away from the bed, sat on the floor on his blanket, undid his tie, took his shoes off, removed his watch from his wrist, wound it and put it on the night table, placed his pistol under the pillow, and adjusting his blanket, lay down, got comfortable and covered himself up to his ears.

"Whenever you want, you can turn off the light and go to bed," he said curtly.

Maria nestled herself on the bed but did not let Ramos out of her sight for an instant. She shook her head slowly in a gesture of surprise and disapproval. "You're not going to get any rest there, friend," she said with caring. "You could lie down on the bed next to me. Nothing wrong with that."

"Go to sleep, go to sleep," Ramos said, without changing position.

"This is ridiculous," Maria insisted. Ramos made no response.

Maria held back for a few minutes. Then she inspected the sheets and pillow and saw that in truth they were clean, so she removed her jacket, the woolen pullover, the three blouses, and her shoes. For a second she looked questioningly at her white, rounded legs and, shaking her head, shut off the light, removed her skirt and stretched out facing Ramos's side.

"Friend," she said after a while, almost whispering. Ramos didn't answer, and she repeated, "Friend."

"Hunh!" Ramos snorted.

"Why don't you lie down on top of the bed? You're not going to get any rest there and you'll get cold."

"Not necessary. Not necessary," Ramos said angrily, his voice muffled by the blanket he had wrapped around him.

His words sounded to Maria as if saying, *Don't demand the impossible of me, friend.* But despite understanding them as such, she insisted once more, nearly begging like a child, "Lie down on the bed, dear friend."

Ramos didn't answer. After a few minutes, Maria heard snoring. *He's faking it*, she thought instinctively.

9

Opening the door, the lawyer's maid felt flustered seeing Maria with an unknown man.

"He's my brother," Maria explained.

"I just brought them their coffee in bed," the maid said, looking through Maria toward Ramos, flattered by the way that nice gentleman eyed her. "I don't know if they're up yet. I'll tell them." And inviting them to enter the parlor, she disappeared down the corridor.

Maria sat down, tired, her hands resting on her lap. By her feet lay the suitcase, the typewriter, the briefcases, the package. She looked like a passenger awaiting the train in a rural rail station. His hands tucked into his pockets, Ramos ironically surveyed the paintings decorating the walls. Nothing showed of his concern for the serious events taking place. His usual disposition returned. He no longer looked at Maria with the severity and antipathy from the previous night; and Maria thought she noticed, when he looked at her, the unveiling of a strange expression of pleasure and mockery, as if he were enjoying the confused sensation of shame and disappointment that Maria was feeling since that night. *Why is he so contrary toward me?* Maria asked herself, though she wasn't able to put her finger on exactly how her comrade was contrary.

The lawyer's wife appeared in a gleaming blue robe, her hair in disarray. It was clear she hadn't yet freshened her face, though she had done her lips up in blood red.

"So, another tooth?" she asked, grasping Maria's hands, her face leaning in to hers and blowing her an air kiss so as not to muss her lipstick.

Maria explained in a few words that she needed to stay there a few days, for she'd had to urgently flee the house she was living in.

"Of course," the lawyer's wife said plainly. First, and skeptically, she looked at the baggage, and then at Ramos with a perplexed and mistrusting bearing. It was beyond her comprehension to see such a young woman, and good-looking at that, in the company of men at all hours of day and night and out on the roads and highways.

The lawyer entered at that point. Dressed in striped pajamas, smiling, he rushed right to them and shook the comrades' hands without question of any kind. He seemed happy to see them there.

"Are your teeth worse now?" he asked, like his wife.

"Nonsense!" the wife answered, having already forgotten that she had asked the same question.

They explained what was happening, and the lawyer suggested they have some breakfast, for surely they hadn't eaten. He himself called the maid and told her to prepare the meal.

In the dining room they started conversing. It was a rich contrast between the lawyer's manner of speech, embellishing his sentences with worldly-minded and somewhat theatrical gestures, and Ramos's, whose frankness and loose talk bordered on insolence, if it weren't for the fact that he felt so sure of himself. Ramos launched into talk as though he were in his own house, or had known his hosts there for years and years. The odd thing is that right away they seemed to enjoy his company. In the middle of the conversation, Ramos split open another bread roll, smeared it with butter and handed it to Maria.

"Go on, eat, I know you like it."

And turning toward the lawyer's wife, he added, "You have to force this girl to eat, otherwise she'd kill herself from hunger." And laughing out loud, he recounted the first time Maria had gone to their house when, once they were outside after lunch, she had to get something to eat with António.

The lawyer was surprised but ended up laughing, showing his yellow, but polished teeth. The wife retracted her chin, annoyed and embarrassed, but smiled politely. Burning with shame, her eyes filling with tears, Maria could have died, as if she had been publicly accused of something ignominious. *Why is he so cruel toward me? What wrong did I ever do him?* she thought.

Ramos got ready to leave. Taking leave of Maria in front of the lawyer and his wife, and as though he didn't note their presence, he took Maria by the shoulders, his hands seizing the roundness of her flesh, and looking at her straight on, he searched her whole face in a fleeting but observant look, her black hair crumpled over her ears, her reddish cheeks, her mouth, and ended fixing his glance on her long-lashed eyes with an expression both inviting and provocative. At that moment, Maria understood Ramos's behavior of the night before and also clearly understood then that she loved Ramos as she had never loved anyone, and could have been his if he had wanted it.

"Stay well, comrade," Ramos said.
"Stay well," answered Maria.

10

As he and Vaz had agreed, Ramos went in his place to a series of encounters. For two days everything ran smoothly. In the areas he went to, nothing extraordinary had occurred. Everywhere people reported success and progress. For his part, in all the movements he made during those two days, by bicycle, train or jitney, neither did he notice anything that could be called exceptional vigilance.

On the second day he met with a married couple of old militants, who for reasons of illness and age could now do very little and had almost been forgotten. At the beginning their faces betrayed a mood of criticism, but they beamed when Ramos asked if he could stay overnight with them from time to time, and even more when Ramos announced that he'd start using the house the very next day. When he left, the old woman handed him some modest provisions, and the old man insisted that he also take the remainder of a packet of cigarettes.

Ramos happily kissed one, then the other, opened the door to leave, turned and went back in to whisper so that people outside shouldn't hear: "Until tomorrow, comrades!"

The old lady made a sign of goodbye, and Ramos left.

It was on the third day, while heading to a meeting in a small rural area, that he encountered the first surprise.

Having gotten off the train at the deserted stop, and retrieved his bicycle from the baggage car, he walked down the platform and exited by the gate to the street. At that moment his attention was alerted, some fifty meters away, by a man in a white jacket who looked back, certainly toward him, and disappeared through the door of a commercial establishment. When Ramos passed by the shop he saw the man clutching a telephone in the shadow of the interior. The man was watching the street but turned his head away as soon as he saw Ramos. *I don't like this*, Ramos thought.

Next to the railway stop there were only a dozen houses along the street. The settlement lay a few hundred meters away. Instead of following the road directly to the entrance to the settlement, where the meeting was to be held, Ramos cut through some stubbled terrain with his bicycle in hand, climbed a hill where he remained hidden by some shocks of hay, and poised himself to observe the road. He hadn't been there two minutes before he saw, coming from the settlement, two well-dressed men walking quickly, one of them short, broad-shouldered and hatless, whose figure looked familiar. Then he saw the man in the white jacket appear, coming from the direction of the station. When they met, the three men halted, and the short, squat man, looking around into the fields, made large gestures, which also looked familiar. Ramos crouched behind the sheaves of hay and saw the three men climb to a small elevation, just as he had done, turning around in all directions. Then the short, stocky man, always with his eye on one end of the road and the other, went with the guy in the white jacket back toward the rail stop, while the other returned in a run toward the village. *So, we're going to have a party!* Ramos thought, beginning unexplainably to humor himself.

His surprise increased even more when he saw an automobile coming from the village stop next to the running guy, and three men got out who also looked all around in every direction. Then the car turned around on the street in a few smart moves and went back, raising clouds of dust. *Very nice, sir!* He had no doubt whatsoever it was the police in a genuine blockade waiting for Vaz, who was supposed to be at the meeting. He also had no doubt at all that the guy in the white jacket had seen him get off the train—the only passenger to get off there and with a bicycle just as Vaz should have arrived—and alerted the others. From the contours of the terrain, he instantly realized it would not be easy to escape without confronting them. Before him, on the other side of the street and stretching from the station to the village, lay a flat field of low stubble where without question he'd be seen immediately from either the rail stop end or the village end. *As fast as I might run*, he thought, *I'd be hunted down like a hare by a pack of dogs*. To the right was the rail stop and the train line. Behind him, more stubbled fields and the tall white walls of two farms. To the left, the village, spreading out right after the first curve in the road. *I can't stay here*, Ramos thought, seeing two workers approaching him and gathering up sheaves. *I only have two choices: either try to jump over the wall into one of those farms and hide until night, except even if I succeeded in jumping the wall and there weren't any dogs, it would be very hard to do without being seen; or try to make a run for it now*. Ramos decided for the latter, hesitating over whether or not he should abandon the bicycle. *No*, he figured, *it could still be useful. If I have to run, I can discard it then*. After surveying the lay of the land with great attention, he decided to cross the road near the entrance to the village and try to get to a swell of land that he saw off to the left. But when he got closer to the first few houses, he spotted two figures standing in the street.

"Yes, sir, everything by the book!" he said softly to himself, more and more amused by the minute.

In a quick decision he turned back, climbed the hill again, descended down to the street once more and, mounting the bicycle, headed in the rail stop direction.

Nearing a hundred meters from the rail gate, he saw the short, broad-shouldered man leaning against it and immediately recognized him: Soares. Yes, it was Soares, the police agent Soares whom he knew well. And who knew him equally well. He was turning his head nervously from one side to the other. When he saw Ramos, he stopped, and didn't move except for his hand slipping farther into his jacket pocket. *Okay, my boy, bring it on, bring it on!* Ramos thought. And dismounting his bicycle and steering it with his left hand, he put his right hand in the outside pocket of his jacket. Without losing sight of the other man for an instant, he continued in the direction of the gates. Now he saw in every detail Soares's round, close-shaven face, his hair loss accentuated by an excess of brilliantine, his evil little eyes staring at him too. Ramos is just a few steps away from him. The two men glare at one another intensely, as if a dizzying current of observations, doubts and questions runs between their two pairs of eyes. With an obvious gesture, Soares moved his hand inside his pocket. Continually staring back at him, Ramos had already opened the gate, and walked onto the platform.

"Good afternoon!" Ramos said, not knowing why he said it, but feeling the absolute need and extreme fun of doing so.

"Good afternoon," Soares responded in a dampened voice.

Ramos broke out into a good laugh—but only internally. Jumping on his bicycle, he pedaled rashly to the end of the platform and, arriving there, followed the line a few dozen meters farther, and then turned back. Just like the guy in the white jacket when he arrived, Soares now ran to that store. *Telephone, boy, call your Daddy!* Ramos was infinitely amused.

If he thought about it, he'd certainly believe his expression was carefree, pleasant and even playful. But no. His expression did not conform to the pleasure he was feeling. For a peasant passing by kept staring at that tall, dark man on a bicycle with an enormous reverse handlebar, whose crinkled face spoke of shock and anxiety and whose eyes flashed with hatred as they concentrated on the road.

11

For several kilometers he followed the railway line by bicycle and then cut through undulating fields tufted with bushes. He decided to approach the Pereiras' area only through virgin, undeveloped land, but after a few hours of it, he saw he hadn't gotten very far, owing to the weight and entanglement of his enormous black bicycle. He wasn't sure what to do, when he came upon an isolated cottage, at whose door stood a man and a young woman who looked at him suspiciously.

"Do you want to earn ten *escudos*, my friend?" Ramos said as he opened the conversation.

As it always happened when he spoke with unfamiliar people, the peasant was reassured by his way of talking and smiled, taking the question as a joke. The young woman smiled too, showing her pretty teeth and making sure Ramos saw them.

"I have to go to S— to see about some firewood," Ramos said, "but going through this terrain with the bicycle, I'll never get there. If you can hold onto it until tomorrow, or a few days if I can't make it back tomorrow, I'll pay you ten *escudos*."

The peasant smiled again, but his shrewd little eyes, surveying Ramos from under the brim of his hat, seemed to say, *I can hold onto your bicycle, but about the ten escudos, are you kidding or serious?*

"I'm serious!" Ramos reassured him, guessing his thought.

The peasant shrugged his shoulders to show that if he held onto the bicycle it wasn't for the money, giving off the impression that he wasn't interested in the money at all. Then he told the woman to step away from the doorway and let Ramos through and into the house with the bicycle. He could hardly imagine that this request, and this bicycle, would for years be the greatest source of mystery and anxiety for him.

It was already getting dark when Ramos arrived at the Pereira house. A few meters from their door, a man in a denim suit looked back at him. *Now I'm seeing police everywhere*, Ramos thought, smiling at himself.

At the top of the stairs he knocked on the door. An unknown woman opened it, with shock in her eyes. In a low, fearful voice she said no one was at home.

"Are they delayed?" Ramos asked, remembering the man in the denim suit.

Her eyes more frightened than ever, the woman mumbled something confusing—isolated, disconnected words—as though she couldn't express what she wanted to say. At that moment Ramos heard the scrape of a chair inside the house.

"See you later!" he told the woman, and ran down the stairs.

When he got to the street he saw two men before him, standing side by side. A little farther off he saw the guy in the denim suit. With a sideways glance he noted the same expression and the same gesture in the two men. He held on tight to the pistol inside his pocket and proceeded in a long stride along the street trying to find a little trail he knew.

"Halt!" they shouted after him.

Before he knew it, he felt a strange, undefinable jolt, as if someone had fired tons of cotton at him. His legs collapsed and he went flying forward face down. His left hand went right to a small pocket in his jacket, from which he pulled out a datebook. Bringing it to his mouth, Ramos desperately started biting and gnashing it with his teeth. His right hand pulled the pistol out, but his arm had fallen extended and inert on impact with the ground. Ramos heard footsteps approaching with a terrifying noise, making the ground tremble as though from the pounding steps of a giant. The paper he's chewing ever more furiously now has the taste of earth and blood.

From a distance of three paces, the chief of the brigade kept firing until he emptied his cartridge.

Chapter XVI

1

Gaspar had been arrested on the eve of the strike. Finding the clandestine printed matter in his house, the PIDE was certain they had nabbed an important seam in the Party net. Gaspar was no ordinary person. The bosses told them this was an uncommonly able worker who commanded great respect among his companions. He had been the instigator of the actions both in the factory and in the working class overall, and recently been elected president of the labor union on a slate that for the first time placed the workers in opposition to the fascist leadership. In the union's general assembly, the first the workers had attended, all the attempts to impede, intervene in or falsify the election had been spurned by the energetic response of the workers.

Apart from the underground printed material, the police found nothing of Gaspar's that would allow them to uncover other Party members. Beaten three nights in a row, Gaspar refused to denounce his companions.

The PIDE then tried to find out, with the help of the factory owners and some informers, who had been closest to Gaspar. All the reports coincided: Gaspar's right arm had been Túlio.

Túlio was followed and observed both within and outside the factory. As they found nothing conclusive about him, and as there was record of his timid behavior on May 18th, they decided to arrest and test him. He was seized at home in the middle of the night, thrown into a van and brought to Lisbon.

The van stopped in front of PIDE headquarters, silent and apparently asleep, on a street intentionally dimmed on that stretch by unlit streetlights. The peephole in the plated door, opening with a faint metallic sound, showed an illuminated rectangle, shortly covered by the shadow of someone's head. The door opened cautiously. The two agents who accompanied Túlio pushed him into the atrium and inside through a large open grate to the clanging of keys and locks.

Only two men were there: the uniformed guard at the door, and another agent in overalls. Both were silent, hands in their pockets, both with a cigarette hanging from their lower lip and their eyes semi-closed, from fatigue and against the smoke. In both figures, their manner and expression were so identical and so repugnant, conveying such insensitivity, cynicism and evil, that you couldn't tell if this presence arose out of these two men's natural character or if it had been assumed to inspire terror. But for sure, when he saw them, Túlio thought he had fallen into a criminal den where there was no hope to be had and where he would be completely at the mercy of such men. His right kneecap started to tremble, and a strange sense of paralysis came to his chin.

One of the agents who brought him reappeared at the grate, summoning him with a finger and a whistle. He told Túlio to come forward and made him climb a narrow, dark staircase up to the third or fourth floor. There he suddenly opened a door, where a sharp beam of light shone directly into Túlio's face, and he found himself in front of a desk at which a strong man in rolled-up shirtsleeves was writing, his hair shining lustrously. Túlio made out that on one side and the other were additional men either seated or standing.

"We want to know," the man at the desk fired, glaring hard at him, "who are the others at Cicol?"

Túlio barely had time to shrug his shoulders to indicate ignorance, when a blow blasted one ear and, as his body rocked, a brutal beating on the other side reestablished his balance. Dizzied, he sat down.

"So?" the man at the desk asked, staring hard at him all the while.

Túlio could hardly see him. In the midst of the shrieking inside his muddled head, everything seemed confused and terrible in that harsh bright light. He felt totally defenseless, at the receiving end of brute force, with no possibility of resistance. In that moment he knew he'd end up talking. He knew it since May 18th when at his workbench he heard his companions joining the struggle and with trembling hands, he failed to raise his eyes from his work. Still, there was something that prevented him from naming names.

"I don't know anything—" he stammered.

Like an explosion, new whacks buffeted him on his head and face. Túlio felt himself pushed into the middle of the room and there, in the center of a circle of agents, he bore a rainstorm of kicks, cuffs, cracks, blows from truncheons. They piled on him, making him stumble from one side to the other, turn around, fall, get up again, while in front of his eyes appeared a strange face shouting at him threateningly, a leg, a green rug, a fist, another face, and he heard indistinct words, insults, screams and the dull sound of the thrashing he was getting.

The man from the desk now stood up in front of him, crossing his naked, hairy arms showing off a handsome watch and a gold bracelet. Breathing with difficulty, bent over, one eye closed and his lips swollen, Túlio tried to swallow the blood that constantly collected in his mouth.

"Just say who they are at Cicol. We don't want anything more from you. Say it and we'll leave you alone."

Túlio still refused to talk and the beating resumed.

At five in the morning, they desisted for a few moments and brought him a glass of water. With a convulsive tremor, and spilling most of it, Túlio drank eagerly and awkwardly. Swallowing the fresh water, it seemed he was returning from a horrible nightmare to a delicious life of breezy delight. He would give up years of his life not to go back to that nightmare and to go on drinking, slowly and peacefully, those gulps of fresh water.

The interrogator was seated again.

"All right," he said in a mild and friendly voice. "To put an end to this, say who they are at Cicol and everything will be over. No one will touch you any more." And picking up a pencil, he prepared to write.

Speaking almost unintelligibly, Túlio mentioned five names, which the man immediately wrote down. But when he believed he could finally sleep and forget, once more they told him to get up and fell on him furiously. The interrogator broke out laughing and shouted directly into his face like a demon: "Do you take us for idiots, or what? Tell us who's on the Local Committee or we'll kill you, you fucking dog!"

That morning and over the succeeding days, Túlio gave the names of Pereira and Jerónimo. And he said Gaspar was also on the Local Committee. He said further that the slate placed before the union vote had been selected by the Party. And he said he had attended a Strike Committee and the man who showed up with the comrade in charge was Pereira. And he understood that comrade had gone to Pereira's house. And he mentioned names of four more comrades at Cicol. Túlio revealed everything he knew. The only one he didn't name was Vicente. Not by way of protecting him. If he didn't, strange as it might seem, it's just that he forgot about him.

Even though he confessed, they didn't spare him. During his questioning he was invariably assaulted and beaten. He could barely see or speak anymore. They had to hold him up bringing him back and forth, and kept at him. When he supplied truthful information he was mistreated if the police had a different view of things. So in the end, they beat him when he didn't talk, beat him for lying, and beat him for telling the truth.

2

"That is not correct," Jerónimo calmly declared to the investigator. "I haven't been engaged in any activity for a very long time."

"It's not us saying so," the investigator said, repeating a favorite expression. "It's your comrades saying it."

"Let them come here and say it to my face," Jerónimo said, his lower lip relaxed, looking distractedly at the PIDE agent's hand, all decked out with ostentatious rings, that flicked the ash off his cigarette. "Then you'll see who's telling the truth."

"No, no. We're not going to give you that pleasure. You're refusing now, but we'll get you to talk."

"Is that a threat?" Jerónimo asked in his same sober voice, without taking his eyes off the hand, the rings and the cigarette.

"No, it's not a threat," the agent said with a little nervous chuckle. "The police don't treat anyone badly, and you well know it. But we have scientific methods of investigation," he said with another little snicker.

Jerónimo's tired glance shifted indifferently toward the investigators's face. He stared into his eyes for an instant and went back to watching the movements of his hands and the cigarette. "Let's be frank," he said, his voice ever more calm and patient. "You're not a kid and neither am I. You know I've already been in prison and both times they employed those scientific methods of which you speak"— and Jerónimo didn't even change his intonation on saying the word "scientific." "You know in my case it didn't work. For three months I was in the clink hovering between life and death, and another month in the hospital, but you got nothing from me."

He paused a moment waiting for the agent to crush the tip of his cigarette firmly into the ashtray, then went on: "There's no reason to think you'd have any better result this time. It would be just the same. So, do what you want."

The investigator made no reply. After several long minutes looking at the prisoner, he got up and went to the window to speak with another agent he found standing there. That agent left, and the investigator returned to his seat at his desk, silently staring at Jerónimo with contempt.

"By the way," Jerónimo suddenly interjected, as if he considered the previous conversation completely closed, "you guys should see to it that you give us food that's edible. The beans today were raw and the soup was pure hogwash."

A glint of evil glistened in the investigator's eyes. "Anything else?" he asked with an affected smile, belied by the sudden apparition of a tremor in one of his cheeks.

"No," Jerónimo answered in the same measured voice as though he hadn't noticed the change in expression on the other's face, nor if the question had been asked in seriousness. "For now, nothing else."

They brought Jerónimo back to prison and didn't call him back for another month. Without pressing him hard, they asked him half a dozen questions, to which he responded denying the accusations.

3

Owing to Túlio's revelations, and to his statement that Party functionaries would generally go there, the Pereira house was raided in an especially dramatic way. While for the arrests of Gaspar, Túlio, Jerónimo and several other Cicol workers just two or three agents would appear in their respective houses, the Pereiras' house was surrounded and the door breached in the middle of the night. From the way they immediately ran through all the rooms, it was clear they believed there could be other people there. They asked in whose care they should hand over the house. Since they mentioned a sister of Pereira who lived nearby, they went to find her right away.

"We need to do a search," the captain of the brigade explained, "but we'll only do it with someone you trust present. We don't want anyone later saying we touched anything."

Saying which, they took Pereira and Conceição with them, the boy clutched in her arms. They had tried to persuade Conceição to leave her son in care of her sister-in-law, but Conceição, whose first move, when she saw the police entering her house, was to rush to her son's cradle and pick him up, refused with every ounce of her energy to leave him behind.

The next morning, the first time they summoned Conceição for interrogation, they gave her a big speech. How they well understood her situation trying to help her legitimate husband—they repeated that expression "legitimate husband" two or three times—and how such an inclination only brought her honor. She could be assured that it was most disagreeable for them to arrest an honest woman, above all one with an infant at her breast. Their hope was to settle this matter promptly and send her peacefully back home. Pereira himself certainly wouldn't be detained very long, they assured her. It all boiled down to the following: They knew that persons from outside the area frequented her house. They wanted to know who they were, how long they had been going there, and when and by what means they would ordinarily come.

"In ten minutes you can say everything you have to say and you'll be released," the investigator finished. "Besides, I'm convinced that neither you nor your legitimate husband had any idea of how important those visitors were. If you did, that wouldn't be a good thing for you. So, the sooner you clear up this case, the sooner you both can go home in peace."

"I don't know what you mean by all this," Conceição said. "I don't understand a word of it."

The agent looked at her a few moments in silence. "You're still rather nervous," he said at last, rising to his feet. "No matter, you'll come back soon enough."

He walked to the door, said something to someone outside, and returned halfway into the office. "If you need anything for the child, don't hesitate, let us know. We're not as terrible as some people say!"

"Yes, I do need something!" Conceição shot back in an irascible, aggressive tone. And opening her shawl, she pointed to her son's chubby, pink legs and his bottom wrapped in a wet, white cloth. "I need to wash his diapers and clothing every day."

"What a cute baby!" said the agent, leaning over the child and smiling at him.

In a lightning flash, like a bird defending her little one from a vulture, Conceição wrapped him up and hid him from view.

"I'll take care of that, rest assured," the investigator said, as though he had not seen Conceição's move. "I'll call you shortly. Meanwhile, think well about it: In ten minutes you can be done with everything and go home."

After lunch they called her again. "Did they give you what you needed?" he asked as he walked in, smiling and trying to give a caress to the baby who, now awake, kept himself close to his mother's breast.

"They did," Conceição responded, once again withdrawing her son from the agent's caress.

In fact, as soon as she had arrived at her cell, they had taken her to the sink where she could wash out the clothes and put them out to dry in the sun in front of a window.

"So?" the investigator asked, crossing his arms with a smile.

He was patently referring to the questions he had asked before and left to Conceição to answer.

"So—" she answered as though she had not understood the intent of his question, and continued in the same animated, aggressive voice as before, "a dark jail is not the place for a woman with an infant of this age."

"Do you wish to send the child home?" the agent asked, smiling all the while.

"No, I want you to put me in a brighter place."

"That won't be necessary," the investigator said after a pause. "What's necessary is for you to be done with all this and go back to your peaceful home." He went quiet and held out a colored pencil to the baby, who grasped it immediately.

"So, Senhora?"

"I don't understand you," Conceição answered.

The agent leaned back in his chair, breathing deeply out of annoyance, and then returned to his smiling, as though asking pardon for his slight sign of impatience.

"You understand. You understand very well. Let's see: When was your friend supposed to be returning?"

"What friend?" Conceição asked, believing she heard in that word an allusion to their "friend," referred to by that name only by her and Pereira. It therefore would be extraordinary were he known as such to the police.

"You're acting naïve," said the agent without knowing the reason nor the meaning of Conceição's excitement, "but the police know everything."

And he kept posing the same questions, always smiling at the baby, always patiently, even in the face of her unfriendly exclamations.

"All right!" he said finally. "Respond to this and I'll order you a bright room where your child can play."

"It's easier to catch a liar than a cripple!" Conceição shouted. "You said over and over again that if I respond to your questions you'll send me back home in peace. And now you say you're sending me from a dark cell to a bright one. So which is it?"

The investigator bit his lips, shrugged his shoulders, stood up and told a colleague to take the prisoner away.

4

Well into the night they summoned her again. As she insisted that no one was going to her house, the agent started toying with a pencil, now tapping the tip on top of the desk, now the blunt end.

"These questionings are for your benefit, not for ours. You believe we need your statements for some reason. We only want to know if we should keep you detained or send you home. If you don't want to answer, it's because you're compromised and so you remain in prison. If you answered, you'd show you had nothing to do with the case, you had no share of responsibility, and you'd leave here in peace. That's the only reason I posed you those questions, because we don't need your statements for anything."

After a pause during which he concentrated his gaze on Conceição, he added, "We know very well that Vaz went to your house and that he was to return this week."

Her heart was pounding in her chest, but she went on denying. "It's not worthwhile putting up such a struggle," the agent said, still speaking in his patient manner. "It's your husband who told us."

"My husband could not invent such things."

When she uttered these words, she heard two agents laugh beside and behind her, and that laughter unsettled her more than anything else that had happened so far.

"Oh, but your husband has quite the gift for invention," the investigator said. "Among other things, he invented that António *and* Vaz went to the house. This is what you'd definitely call a very great inventor."

The agents laughed again. "She's a fool!" one of them said.

The agent signaled them to be quiet, but this first insult, accompanied by the laughter, made Conceição comprehend the gravity of her situation. She pressed her sleeping son closer to her breast.

"I've already said it and I'll repeat it," she insisted. "My husband could not say that things exist that don't exist. I've told you no one went to the house and that's the truth. My husband is incapable of telling lies."

"But he lies!" the agent said. The others laughed again.

"Only hearing it from him would I believe it," Conceição said.

"And you, my dear, will hear," said the agent, standing up as he modified his manner of addressing her from the polite to the familiar.

The investigator and another agent left, and for the nearly two hours that Conceição was there guarded by another agent, they exchanged nary a word. The man constructed and deconstructed a long chain of paperclips and played with it, tirelessly spinning it around his finger.

They surprised her by bringing in Pereira. Conceição jumped up and went straight to him to kiss him. But something about his general expression and posture held her back and repelled her. Not the swollen black and blue bruises that disfigured his face, not the unkempt beard and rumpled hair, not his attire in disarray and his ripped shirt, but something vague and imploring in his eyes, something humiliating and resigned in his bearing, something guilty in the cold glance of his green eyes. He had talked!

"Your wife says you're a liar," the investigator laughed. "That she doesn't know and never saw and never had any Vaz come to the house, nor any other comrade. Tell her. Tell her those lies right here to her face."

"What could I do?" Pereira said, turning to Conceição and shrugging his shoulders, with the look of a beaten dog.

The agents laughed.

"How is it possible?" Conceição asked in a muffled voice. "How is it possible you lowered yourself so far?"

The investigator stepped between them. "No more of that! You are not going to demoralize your husband now. I won't consent to that. Answer the questions and nothing more. Do you insist in stating that Vaz and António did not go to your house?"

"It's a lie!" she exclaimed quickly and excitedly. "I don't know anyone by those names."

The investigator shrugged his shoulders and turned to Pereira.

"Come on, Conceição," Pereira said in that same pleading tone.

"It's a lie!" Conceição shouted as she became more and more excited. "I don't even know what you are. You're not a man, you're nothing!"

"Take her! Take her!" the investigator ordered.

The agents pushed Conceição out of the office. From the door and down the corridor her shouts continued to be heard. "For God's sake, don't talk! Don't talk! Don't talk!"

5

Over the next few days they didn't summon her and went on allowing her to wash her baby's clothes. She prolonged those scarce minutes as long as possible, the only ones in the course of a day that her son could be in a lighted room. The rest of the day was a constant torture so long as the boy was awake. Barely a single ray of light entered her cell, there was no room beyond the bunk bed and, despite the mother's imaginative feats of entertaining and distracting him, despite her offering him her breast at all times—not what she normally did—the boy spent his days crying. Later came the torture of the bedbugs, aggressively hyperactive in the summer heat. Conceição tried not to fall asleep so she could spare her baby from them, forever feeling the folds of his clothes and skin to find the disgusting bugs with her fingers. But sometimes she did fall asleep and when she awoke she couldn't pardon herself for allowing it to happen.

After several days, they summoned her again. The same investigator received her in his office. When she entered, he rose and stood stock still in front of her, staring into her eyes. Every hint of correction and patience had vanished. The only attitude on his face was one of hate and fury. *Holy God, what does this man want of me?* For the first time Conceição felt fear, for herself and for her son. The agent remained in that same stance several moments, and the expression on his face grew ever more hateful and angry. She predicted that this tension would lead to something sudden and violent. All at once, he raised his arm and landed a quick, solid punch directly into her face.

"You whore!" And he struck her again and again until blood was gushing from her lips and nose.

Conceição had not recovered from the shock, the assault and pain before they led her from the office and brought her back to her cell.

Conceição did not understand this incident, neither its cause nor its purpose, and only much, much later would she. The fact is that by the time of the abortive confrontation with his wife, Pereira had not only told them that António and Vaz had come to his house, but had also confirmed Túlio's statements about Gaspar and Jerónimo being members of the Local Committee. After the confrontation, rather than elaborate on his declarations, which the police assumed he certainly would, not only did he not provide any further information about Party activity but, despite repeated beatings, rescinded what he'd said concerning Jerónimo, stating now that they had not properly understood what he said before, for Jerónimo, not even a Party member, could not possibly be on the Local Committee.

The investigator was definitively convinced that Pereira had retreated, when they brought him the news that Ramos had been felled at the door to Pereira's house after he had gone there to meet him. Interrogated and beaten these last days to get him to say if anyone else besides Vaz and António went to his house, Pereira stubbornly refused. Even after Ramos's death, when the investigator cited his name, Pereira refused to talk.

It was at that point that they summoned Conceição to insult and pommel her.

After the confrontation, that night, her son asleep by then, Conceição said her prayers. Among them, the following: *Virgin Mary, Immaculate Lady, free my husband of the temptation to betray his friends and his ideals to spare himself suffering. Give him the courage and strength to accept torture and even death in defense of his honor and the honor of his son.*

Conceição later recounted how her prayer had been heard and attended. The comrade to whom she related this story told her that as she addressed the miracle in Heaven, she, Conceição herself, created a miracle on Earth.

"How can you say such a thing?" Conceição asked, blushing and smiling.

6

Just as Vaz and Ramos had thought, António was arrested when he went to Cesário's house for the first time. Certainly the PIDE were spying in the area and saw him enter. After a few minutes, they broke into the house with weapons in hand. They did a quick search and took Cesário and António away in a van. With an automobile parked at the door, two more agents remained to ransack drawers, suitcases and armoires, taking beds and mattresses apart, emptying the coal from its box, earth from the flowerpots, and sugar from its cone. They gathered up papers and photographs at random without bothering to see what they were about. Cesário's wife, wiping a persistent tear away from time to time, complained, though calmly, and managed to recover only a few receipts having to do with the house and her personal affairs.

Meanwhile, warned by a neighbor, Lisete and her mother arrived. Hearing them at the door, the aroused agents nervously placed more bullets in their pistols and ran to meet them. But when they saw it was the mother and sister of the lady of the house, which they could easily identify by their likeness, they quieted down. It seemed they were even grateful for the presence of more women, especially the young, blond Lisete, with her sweet, shy expression.

They continued combing through the house, now with a better disposition, appreciating with words or gestures what they were seeing or finding, as though such a show before the ladies would be entertaining.

"What do you think of this model?" one agent asked the other, holding up with two fingers, as if dreading contagion, a sock full of holes.

"Russian style," the other replied, laughing, and looking at the women inviting them to join in on the humor.

"Do what you need to do and get out!" Lisete said suddenly, her voice so forceful and ferocious that the mother and sister looked at her in wonder.

Without suspending their operations, the agents glared at the young women condescendingly, as if toward an innocent child assuming grown-up airs.

"Did you see that? So young and so bad!" said one agent slowly stretching his arms into the back of a drawer from which he had just thrown all the clothes onto the floor.

In response, the other one raised his hands and with exaggerated caution unfolded an item of women's lingerie. After looking insolently at Lisete, he blinked at his colleague.

Cesário's wife sat down and started sobbing.

"What are you guys thinking?" Lisete yelled, stomping her foot on the floor, in a voice so sharp and penetrating that neither her mother nor her sister could recognize it. "Is it because there's only women here that you think you can mock us?"

"Hunh!" grunted one of the agents in the same jeering, sickly sweet attitude.

"Keep your 'hunh' and even half a 'hunh!'" Lisete shouted. She went to a window and threw it wide open. "Don't forget to accomplish nothing!"

"Calm down, girl, calm down, someone might think—"

Pacing from one end of the house to the other, Lisete interrupted him, hollering ever more stridently.

"Look! Look!" she bellowed. "Drawers turned inside out, clothes ruined, sugar spilled, and what's this? What *is* this?" she asked, suddenly noticing the pile of papers and photos they had amassed on top of the table to haul off. "My picture here?! What business do you have with my picture?" And in a quick move, she stepped in front of an agent and grasped a handful of papers and photographs.

The agent jumped to grab her arm, twisting her fingers and forcing her to surrender her handful.

"Let go of me!" Lisete shouted desperately. "Don't touch me! Don't touch me! Let me go!" And swinging her arm, she tried once more to grab the papers and photos.

The man gave her a violent shove that threw her off balance and sent her flying to the wall with a hollow thud as she hit her back. Now the man was neither smiling or joking. Livid with rage, everything about him spelled brutality.

At the same time, in deliberate, threatening moves, looking back at the young woman, he placed the papers and photos in his briefcase to avoid further episodes with Lisete—who, hurt as she was, continued screaming and was now joined by her mother. The other agent approached the window and saw the road full of people standing in front of the house.

Turning back inside, he whispered something to his colleague, who also looked through the window and turned to face Lisete. "You may regret this scene, my precious!"

They opened yet another drawer and emptied it on the floor. But right afterward, they shut the briefcase and quickly left the house. They paused for a brief moment in a provocative stance before the gathering, got into the car, and loudly jamming the accelerator to the floor, tore out skidding and squealing, as an exhibition of intrepid arrogance.

Lisete went to the door to watch them depart. Passing her gaze over the crowd, she saw the slender face of Henriques, mingling discreetly behind a group of women. Lisete figured that Henriques was also supposed to meet that evening with her brother-in-law and with the comrade who came from away, and her happiness at that moment seeing him safe (her worry being that not knowing what was going on, he might have knocked on the door) was greater than the pain of knowing her brother-in-law was under arrest.

"Whew!" she sighed as she straightened her bangs and went down into the street to talk with the crowd.

Her blond hair, tied in the back with a ribbon and short in front over her forehead, even further accentuated her excitable, reddened face and her extreme youth, and indeed her whole presence as a modest and peaceable girl.

Inside, in the tender clarity of twilight, Cesário's wife, curved and bent over, surveyed with shock the bed torn apart, the mattress ripped, its stuffing in shreds, the drawers tossed on the floor, the clothing spread all about, the chair overturned, the disorder and disruption of everything, as witness to the misfortune that had befallen the house.

7

That same night, someone went to tell Marques what had happened. Two or three times the carpenter had them repeat the news. Not satisfied, he left and went to the house of Cesário's in-laws. Cesário's wife was there, the mood was heavy, and it seemed to Marques that they looked at him with a strange intentness and spoke to him more guardedly than usual. The news was positively confirmed: Cesário was arrested, not together with Vaz, as Marques assumed, but with a new comrade coming from away. The police raided the house shortly after the new man had arrived.

Marques returned home in a terrible state of mind. *What will my comrades think now?* he asked himself. *I was among the few who knew about the meetings at Cesário's house, to which the comrade at the higher level was directed. I'm sanctioned, they throw me off the Committee and right away this disaster happens. What will they think?*

That night he could barely get to sleep. Not that it occurred to him that they might arrest him too. No, that idea did not come to mind. A clear conscience was all that saved him. *But is that enough?* he wondered. *No, it's not enough,* he answered. *No one should say they are satisfied with a clear conscience. Beyond the clear conscience, we need justice be done to us. If they distrust me, my clear conscience is not going to compensate in any way.*

Later he tried to relax. *The comrades know that I was in prison and I conducted myself well. That I knew many things, and no one was arrested on my account. Besides, Afonso also knew meetings were held there, and Vítor also knew—yes, also Vítor knew.* At that point Marques paused thoughtfully, remembering Vaz's opinions about Vítor. He'd been told a few days before that Vítor was back in the city, but he hadn't seen him yet. And if— *No, I should't even think it. That would be casting on another comrade a suspicion as awful as the one that could fall on myself.*

And then this blinding thought came to him: *As long as I was attending meetings at Cesário's house, nothing happened. I've been sanctioned, I've been removed from the Regional Committee and then this disaster strikes. Considering the opinions people have of me, Vaz's ill will toward me, the complaint and the bad report to the Central Committee, what are they going to think?* And only now did he recapitulate, placing in doubt his own judgment, his own attitudes in relation to the Party orientation, the day laborers' workplace, the mobilization, Vítor, and his conversations with Henriques and other members of his workshop committee. And the fact that he had destroyed the manifestos he had promised to disseminate. *After all this, what will they think? That it was me?*

Morning's light had already begun to filter through the cracks in the window frame, and Marques was still turning from side to side in bed, uselessly attempting to get some sleep.

8

Two days later, on his way to work, Marques ran into Vítor, who walked up to him and held out his hand. "Seems like I came back at a bad time," he said, smiling and looking at Marques intently.

Marques shook his hand and didn't answer.

"When can you and I talk?" Vítor asked. "Is it really true that they arrested Cesário?"

"It appears so," Marques replied in an unintentionally testy tone. "This isn't a great time to have meetings."

Vítor was stunned by his comrade's lack of cordiality. He took out his cigarette case. "Want one?"

Marques shook his head, and Vítor took his time lighting his cigarette, cupping his hands to protect the flame, and all the while keeping a close eye on the carpenter. With his first puff, he grew excited again.

"To me it seems like just the opposite," Vítor rattled off, exhaling smoke at the same time. "It's precisely now that Cesário's been arrested and the organization is going through a difficult situation, that our responsibilities as members of the Regional Committee are even greater—"

Marques interrupted him. "You're not up to date, friend. I'm no longer on the Regional Committee, and I don't believe you are either."

"You're not a member of the Regional Committee!" Vítor blurted, without taking note of Marques's statement that Vitor wasn't either.

"No, I'm not," Marques answered with impatience. "And I do not wish to speak about it any further."

"You want to fool me, but never mind," Vítor commented, trying to overcome his irritation.

He took a few more drags without speaking, and then continued calmly, looking at his companion sidewise and with curiosity. "We have to be prudent and come to some agreement about things. Cesário's been arrested. Who can guarantee we won't be too?"

"Be what?" Marques asked, as though that possibility were absurdly out of the question now that he'd been sanctioned.

In truth, it was the first time since Cesário's arrest that he'd been brought face to face with the idea that he'd be arrested, and to him that idea still seemed unmoored to reality.

"Take it easy," he added ironically, "we won't be."

It was Vítor, however, who got it right. The very next night, the police showed up in the city once again to make arrests. They took Marques, Vítor, a few workers, a peasant from the nearby area, a doctor, a shopowner and a sergeant.

Lisete was arrested too, but they only held her a few days. They accused her of nothing in particular aside from the scandal she created in her brother-in-law's house. A few minutes before she was released, they brought her into an office where a police brigade chief gave her a sermon:

"What you said and did at your sister's house was enough and more for us to keep you here for quite a while. But despite the antics at the Jute Factory, we know you're not a bad girl and we don't wish you ill. You've got a bit of a temper, but who doesn't? We heard your complaint that one of my colleagues slapped you. Believe me, we sincerely regret that, because that is contrary to our procedures and against the orders the boys have. That was excessive, and he will be punished. You, who have a bit of a temper, should be able to excuse a little bit in one of ours, right? So get on your way and be happy."

Lisete exited. An agent who was also in the office came up to the chief, now leafing through some papers, leaned into his ear and murmured a few words.

The brigade chief only replied, "It won't be even a week before they try to get in touch with her."

9

For five days and five nights, Marques was constantly interrogated. Unlike the first time he was arrested, no one beat him. They treated him delicately and frequently showered him with great praise. They just didn't let him sleep. They pushed and pushed and pushed, always obsessively asking the same things, the investigators taking turns with a patience and tenacity that even Marques himself had to admire.

"We don't want you to tell us anything we don't know," the chief investigator told him as he lazily polished his fingernails. "We just want you not to refute us, nor to contradict your comrades. We already have the doctor, and we have the sergeant, so we're quite well aware it was you who controlled them, so why do you insist on denying?"

The police showed they were aware of many things. Still, Marques was surprised by the notions they had about the leadership bodies in the sector.

"Why do you deny that too?" they insisted. "We know perfectly well you're on the Regional Committee, along with Cesário and Vítor. Vítor is remaining silent, but Cesário is friendly with us, and António too. Why do you deny?"

What did this mean? Why did the police have this idea about the composition of the Regional Committee that hadn't been true for quite some time? And if Cesário told them that, to what end? And how could this guy António have said it being new in control? Later, Vítor's arrest brought back memories of his arguments with Vaz. Now he saw who was right. So many doubts about the comrade, and in the end, now that he was under arrest and maybe tortured, he was conducting himself honorably. While Cesário, the fair-haired boy to the Party supervisors—if the investigator was telling the truth—was already singing.

From the second day on, the preferred approach became something else: "I admire men like you, really, I do. But what prize do you get? The best ones, the most dedicated and sincere ones, people like yourself who lead an honest, clean life, you come here and you hold your tongue, and you're regarded poorly and unappreciated by the Party. The adventurers, the kind with no profession who live at your expense, they go on being the great men of the Party, the heroes! There you have it—the justice of the Central Committee. Vaz is out there having a lovely time at the beach, and you're the one suffering."

These words showed Marques that the police knew something about the sanction he'd undergone. With surprise, indignation, anger and despair, he recognized that the police were telling the truth—that while he, who was there firmly defending his comrades, was scorned by the Party and removed from the leadership body, many others whose behavior was dubious at best, are leading, ordering, deciding the politics, the struggles, the cadres. Perhaps the investigator could read in Marques's expression just how much those words matched with his feelings. The fact is that he kept harping on the same themes, recounting incidents severely lowering the prestige of Party leaders, like sordid stories about Ramos's women.

After five days he told him, "You don't care to believe what I'm telling you. Maybe you believe what your comrades are saying. Your ex-comrades," he corrected himself with a faint smile, handing him a carefully folded typewritten piece of paper.

Marques read it. Greedy as he was to take it all in in one gulp, the letters blurred together. Words jumped out without his really seeing them. But overall he got the general meaning. *Considering his attitude...during the mobilization...seeking out comrades and committee members...in order to..contrary to the line of the Party...sabotage the strike...; Considering...charged with distribution...at night...having received...persuaded his comrades...told them it had been canceled because he had not received....; Considering lack of discipline, disunity...sabotage of Party activity...of the working-class struggle...the Secretariat decides to expel from the Party....* Marques reread the last phrase word by word: *Decides to expel from the Party....*

"Clever stunts!" he said, his face gone extremely pale, his eyes glistening behind his glasses. "I'm too old for that."

"You don't believe it?" the investigator asked condescendingly. "You can be sure it's the pure truth. You wouldn't talk, because you think that's what you should do as a member of the Party. But you're not even a member of the Party. They don't want you there; you're too honest for them."

The paper they gave Marques was in fact authentic. The police took it from António, who was carrying it to share at his first meeting with Cesário and Henriques. Although it did not mention Marques by name, it wasn't hard for the police to figure out who it was about. They did not let him read one passage, however, in which Marques's actions in the past were favorably recalled, and which went on to say the doors of the Party were not forever closed to him.

After that interrogation, the investigator redoubled his efforts and, as he'd been informed that Marques was crying in his cell, he made promises to him, sent the doctor to see him, replaced the prison ration with a better diet, and transferred him into a cell with better light. But contrary to expectation, if in the first interrogations Marques responded negatively to the questions or tried to refute the accusations, now he closed down almost completely mute. He grew much thinner over the next days. With his beard grown out, his skin a sickly pallor, his eyes furrowed for the lack of eyeglasses which they had taken away *so he couldn't kill himself with the glass*, he remained obstinately silent in the face of the investigator's questions and subterfuges. Only every once in a while did he shrug his shoulders, irritated and impatient. One day, after another round of futile questioning, the investigator concluded in a tone of contempt that was different from his usual voice. "What does this mean to you, who aren't even a Communist any more? So much bravery, and in the end you're a rat. That's what you are: a rat."

Marques suddenly exploded in rage. "Internal issues in the Party are none of your business," he yelled, out of control. "If I was expelled, that's between the Party and me and no one else. And if you believe you're going to make me talk on account of that, forget about it. It's not titles that make people honest. It's honesty that makes us worthy of the titles."

"Nice speech!" the investigator said, exaggeratedly prolonging his words, his face suddenly seized with a tremor. Then he started screwing the cap of his fountain pen. "As you wish. It's you looking for trouble, not us."

For three days and nights Marques was forced to stand still with his face to the wall. Without any rest, permanently guarded and lifted up by force and beaten when he twice collapsed exhausted to the floor, he no longer felt his body in pain, nor his legs and feet swollen like balloons. On that third day of "statue," when he pissed, he saw drops of blood. Two words came to mind: *Until death!*

10

It was already night when António got to police headquarters. The agent who brought him in led him to a narrow corridor where, seated on a bench, he found three other prisoners. One of them, a young fellow in a denim shirt and pants full of holes, with a long black beard and a face disfigured by beatings, looked at the newcomer with soft eyes, in contrast to his appearance. Another bowed over his knees, supporting his head in his hands and hiding his face. The third, a skinny man in his 70s, with neatly combed sparse white hair and dressed elegantly, sat exaggeratedly upright, visibly out of place with his situation as a prisoner. He made small but constant movements with his head in the direction of the agent guarding them, as if preparing to speak and then quickly reconsidering. Finally the words came out of him, slightly whistling through his dentures.

"You gentlemen have no right… You don't have the right—"

The agent shrugged his shoulders, seeing as how the old man's complaints were coming from behind. At that moment another agent arrived, a rickety young boy with a handsome silk shirt and big suede shoes. He exchanged a few words with his colleague.

"It had to be a false report," the old man went on. "You don't have the right."

The two agents glanced at the old man and exchanged another few words. With a nonchalant air, the boy came to stand in front of the old man and quietly observed him in a stance so alien to his physique that António concluded he must have imitated it from someone of a highly developed athletic constitution. He laughed out loud and, raising his head to the prisoner's nape, ran his hand roughly up his skull, mussing his thin hair all over his scalp. A line of blood ran down the old man's face. Without trying to straighten his hair, he sat up even straighter as though by doing so he would assert all his strength and dignity. The boy let out another howl of laughter and gently grabbed one of the old man's ears. The prisoner with the black beard moved toward the old man, almost placing himself in front of him, evidently trying to call attention to himself from the boy in the silk shirt.

The scene was interrupted by the arrival of the chief of the brigade who had arrested António. He barely looked up and down the corridor before he furiously shouted, "Who was the idiot who put him here with the others?"

The agent on guard responded with something in a low voice, and the boy with the silk shirt stepped away from the old man and joined them. António took another good look at the old man. He stayed in that same position, flushed with anger, rigid, in shock, never attempting to smooth out his white locks now stuck to his scalp, always maintaining his dignified demeanor. The guy with the black beard reached out unseen to the old man's arm and whispered a few words. The agents were talking, but António was so absorbed in watching his companions that he paid no attention to what the agents were saying. Suddenly, a shadow came between him and the other bench and a hand fell heavily on his shoulder.

"Me?" António asked.

"Yeah, you! Are you trying to act stupid?"

António rose. He had hardly taken two steps toward the exit from the corridor when an unexpected violent shove threw him off balance and he hit his face on a doorjamb. He brought his hand to his mouth and his fist was all bloody. *It's begun*, António thought.

11

Indeed, *it had begun*.

"You refuse to say where you live," the head of the brigade said to him seated in his office, "and I want to make things perfectly clear. You have to say. The soft way or the rough way, but you have to say. Now choose: If you want it the soft way, so be it. If you don't want it the soft way, it'll be the rough way."

António stayed quiet, and while he tried to stanch the blood from the open cut on his lip, his eyes, circled by wrinkles and smiling maliciously, stared at the agent. In that moment he envisioned Maria sitting at the table studying. *Don't worry, dear companion*, António thought. *Don't worry*. And his eyes smiled again toward the investigator.

"All right, we won't go for the rough way yet," the agent said, somewhat more calmly. "Have a seat here so we can talk."

You're already backing down, António thought.

He approached the chair. At the precise moment when he was about to sit, someone quickly took it away, and he fell defenseless on the floor, as he heard raucous cackles around him.

Still on the floor, he slowly stood up, looking up from below at each one of them, with his same sly, smiling eyes. *I'm not going to be bothered by so little*, those eyes said. Just as he was almost standing, with the idea of taking a seat in that very chair, he received a brutal punch in the chest and fell down again to a chorus of laughter.

"That's enough picking on the boy," ruled an imperious voice.

Pallid and hurting—his eyes now no longer smiling—looking up in the direction of that voice, António saw a strong and handsome agent who regarded him sympathetically.

"Get up, get up," said the agent, extending his hand.

António grabbed that hand to help him up—he would never forgive himself for doing so—and as soon as he was on his feet, the agent, with his free hand, laid a violent punch in his face. Then the whole crew of them fell on him from all sides with socks, kicks and beatings. Pushed by some, he was held up by the others; set off balance by one blow, he'd be put back on his feet by another. It kept up, kept up, kept up, again and again and again, until the moment came when no beating or body was there to keep him on his feet. He felt empty space before him and fell in a tangle with a thudding collision against the wood of the desk.

"Not like that!" he heard a voice.

After that everything went dark. When he came to, he was sitting in front of the desk. The investigator was playing with a paperweight. Two agents were holding António up. He was drenched—certainly they had emptied the bucket of water on him that he saw next to him on the floor. He felt his face and his whole body swollen and in pain. One especially sharp pain gnawed at one temple. From his nose and bulging lips ran thick ribbons of blood.

"Where do you live?" the agent repeated as soon as António opened his eyes. "Can you hear me? Where do you live?"

António moved his lips, but no sound came out. He struggled to sit up in the chair. Once again he saw the house and Maria, now looking at him with those long-lashed eyes. *Don't worry, my dear companion*, António repeated to himself. *Don't worry.*

"It's best if you say," said a voice behind him almost in his ear.

"Where do you live?" the investigator shouted, putting down the paperweight. "Where do you live? Where do you live?"

António signaled no with a shake of his head. He hadn't even completed the gesture when he felt them covering his head with the bucket down to his shoulders, and they threw him pell-mell together with the chair. They held him by the feet, hit him all over his body, banged on the bucket and rolled him around the floor with more and more strikes. Then they lifted him up and took the bucket off his head. He saw the investigator's fanatical face before him, yelling incomprehensible things, then he was whacked again, and again and again, and the general beating in the middle of the office resumed. Finally they tossed him like a rag on top of a chair placed between the desk and an armoire so he would't fall over. Face and clothing all bloody, swollen and black, eyes lost in a maceration of flesh, mouth deformed full of foam and blood, body tender and disjointed as though they had broken all his bones, his head tossed back, António snorted and moaned. A strong hand grasped him by his hair, flapping his head back and forth with repeated shakes as if it wanted to tear his head off.

"I'm going to kill you, dog!"

And then a quick, heavy fist fell on him, once, twice, over and over, repeatedly, madly across his martyred face. Everything was happening now as if in some unreal world. Whatever weak concentration he had, António focused on marking time, the time that seemed immense, thinking that everything has an end, and that would end too. From time to time, one blow stuck out as particularly painful, and now and then he saw a face, heard questions. "Are you talking or not? Where do you live? Where do you live, you dog?" And shortly it all started up again, that monstrous, dizzying orgy of beating.

At a certain moment, right before his eyes, he saw that sickening face of the boy with the silk shirt, who a few hours before had messed up the old man's hair in the corridor. The boy had a dry little chuckle, and António felt an especially sharp pain on his neck that made him cry out. The pain was neither worse nor better than the others. Just different. He didn't see what caused it, but throughout the beating, it came back several times, on his neck, his hand, his forehead. Only much later he learned that all through that night his skin was the required ashtray for the torturers to put out their burning cigarette stubs.

As day dawned, a beating with the edge of a wooden plank caused him once more to lose his senses. Despite the pails of water they threw on him, he did not come to. The torture stopped there that day.

12

The next night they carried him in by his arms, semiconscious, for another round of interrogation. Still quite addled, he barely perceived they were asking him again where he lived. After a few blows, he lost awareness again. They sent a guy in a white jacket to his cell. He addressed him with good manners, observing him closely, and only asked him off the cuff where he lived. António said nothing, and even if he had wanted to, he couldn't owing to his mouth being so swollen, damaged and lacerated. Over the next days they dressed his wounds. He existed in a constant, strange state of somnolence, in which he saw Maria and his comrades and recalled the moment he'd been arrested with Cesário, and in which he felt a deep sense of satisfaction with himself. In which, also thrown in, were the most disparate images—soccer, landscapes, animals, scenes from his past life, imaginings of the future—without being able to neatly determine if he were awake or dreaming. Most of all, the burns hurt, and his mouth. At a certain point, as if it could alleviate his pain, he stuck a finger in his mouth to find the sore spots. At first, in the swollen, tender and bloody mass, he could not recognize the contours of his own mouth. Only after many long explorations could his finger tell him what had happened. In that shapeless mass of swollen flesh, out of all his teeth there remained only three.

Two or three days later, after a doctor's visit, they took him to a new interrogation and a new torture. As he lay on the floor, almost unconscious, an agent jumped on his chest. Again he lost all of his faculties and only awoke much later, in his cell, with a man in a white coat giving him an injection.

He was interrogated several times more by a new investigator, but they didn't go back to beating him. He did not say where he lived and refused to answer any other questions. The new investigator treated him delicately, as though nothing otherwise had happened, and one day smiled as he said, "You are among the strongest, and I really like your kind. Still, it's hard for me to comprehend how someone prefers to ruin his whole life, staying here and rotting in prison, and all so's not to talk about things which after all the police either already know or can find out without your statements. Word of honor: I find it hard to understand that."

António's face was still distorted by cuts, swellings, black and yellow splotches, two bandages on his scalp and the missing teeth. But his eyes once again smiled perversely amidst a circle of small wrinkles. *Hard to understand*, António thought, *is not that someone doesn't talk. Hard to understand is someone who does talk.*

As a matter of fact, not once during his torture and interrogations did the possibility of not resisting any more—and talking—come to mind. That seemed to António so out of the question that it never even occurred to him as a tragic hypothesis. The agent's observation seemed to him only worthy of sneering at: Say where he was living? The house where his beloved companion lived? The house where his comrades went and where there were documents? Where Ramos would certainly have gone the next day after António's arrest? Name names of comrades? Instigate arrests? Give information of whatever importance to the cruel, pitiless enemy? António felt that in no case whatsoever would he be capable of assuming such an attitude; and that never, never, never would he be capable of accepting the alternatives of torture and betrayal versus death and betrayal. Many, many were the times before his arrest when he argued this question with his comrades. Many times he'd heard opinions saying there were some men stronger than others, some forms of torture more violent than others, and greater or lesser capacity for resistance. *The deciding factor*, António thinks now, *is not the magnitude of the torture. The deciding factor is the magnitude of the character.*

13

Afonso was fired from the cadre of Party workers and, having both refused work in any other region of the country and decided to remove himself from all activity, he returned to his native city days after the arrests. He told his family he wished to make a very circumspect life for himself, not appearing in public, and asked them to get him a job in the shop belonging to an uncle located in the outskirts. His mother, who on Afonso's fleeting visits asked him so many times to return to normal life, received him home enthusiastically. His father received him in a dark mood. First for fear they'd arrest him—then for thinking there was no danger of that happening. In the first two days, he eyed Afonso silently, walked in on whispered conversations between mother and son, witnessed her satisfaction with Afonso's state of mind, and shook his head uneasily. At the end of the second day he exploded.

"I'd rather have seen you arrested like Marques and Cesário than to see you spurned by your own comrades."

These words from his father, along with the jailing of his former comrades, exerted a profound influence on Afonso. Upon learning from Fialho that he'd been expelled from the cadre of Party workers, he had decided to get out of political activity. But now he felt an all-powerful need to know what had happened and to help the local organization. With the arrest of Cesário, Marques and Vítor, he saw the organization completely decapitated, and he knew of many other comrades besides those who'd been arrested. What would happen now? Surely the local comrades would remain dispersed and inactive, disconnected from the Party for months or years, possibly until Cesário and Marques were set free. Afonso feels he cannot passively accept that the situation stay that way.

A few days later, cautiously, at night, he went to Cesário's house. Not knowing that Afonso was living in the city now, and assuming he was still underground, Cesário's wife told him everything that had occurred. But when he told her he was living in the city, she was confused and disconcerted. Nevertheless, Afonso returned several times. The care he showed her seemed so natural, giving her part of his salary without any fanfare, his kind, melancholy face expressing such sincerity that all her reservations about him disappeared. In those days when there was no news of Cesário, for he was strictly incommunicado, Afonso helped the wife of the arrested comrade with his company and moral and material support. Meeting Lisete there, he came away agreeably surprised by the young girl's solid, clear ideas.

Three weeks later, he went to Cesário's house one night and passing through the square he halted suddenly, doubting his own eyes. Standing there, as though waiting for someone, was Vítor, bareheaded and casually smoking. Afonso approached him and it seemed that on recognizing him, Vítor tried to deflect away.

"You here!"

"Shhh!" Vítor warned in a way that did not seem entirely natural. "But it's good I ran into you. I need to talk with you."

He walked Afonso over to an area less well lit, worries upsetting his carefree mood of moments before. He told him quietly and confidentially that he had escaped from prison and needed to contact the Party. Confused and alarmed, Afonso told him that he had withdrawn from everything, and with a spontaneous instinct of self-defense, exaggerated this withdrawal stating he had been expelled from the Party—which was not the case.

"What a shame!" said Vítor, without showing any interest in such serious news as Afonso's expulsion. "I absolutely need the contact. For one thing, because of my own underground situation"—these words, Afonso thought, seemed to be pronounced in a forced manner—"and for another, to report the serious things that are happening."

After a pause, during which he tried to ascertain Afonso's expression in the shadows, he added, "Cesário is a traitor, did you know?"

"A traitor? What do you mean?" Afonso asked, barely audibly.

"A traitor," Vítor repeated, getting more agitated as he spoke. "The arrests are on account of him. He's the one who turned me in, and Marques and other comrades. As much as he knows, he said it," and by this time he was almost shouting.

"Quiet down!" Afonso admonished him.

"It's a shame you lost your contact," Vítor repeated, continuing to ignore Afonso's supposed expulsion and talking in terms with which a leading comrade who's just escaped from prison does not speak to someone expelled from the Party for reasons he doesn't know. "I don't have any money, you know? And in my underground situation"—and once again it seemed to Afonso that Vítor was unnecessarily emphasizing that word—"without money I can't keep going."

"As I said, I don't have any contact because I'm no longer a Party member. And I don't have money. But if a few dozen *escudos* might help, tomorrow I could give them to you."

At that point Vítor's attention was clearly drawn to the other side of the square and he did not follow up or respond to Afonso's words.

"We have to break it up now," Vítor interrupted. "I have to meet a comrade."

Just a couple of minutes ago you needed a contact, Afonso thought. *Now you say you have a meeting with a comrade. What's the meaning of this?*

Ever more confused and wary, Afonso walked away. He hadn't gone fifty meters before he turned back at a quick pace, almost running. Clinging to the shadows on the square, he stuck his neck out looking for something. He clearly found it, suddenly retreating back into the darkness of a doorway.

Alongside the woman from the postoffice, Vítor was parading without a care, not even hiding from the bright lights. Shaking her head and tossing her hair, the woman was laughing out loud hysterically. Afonso distinctly heard Vítor's voice saying, "If you'd like we can go to the movie and leave our plan till later. Or if you wish, we can see the movie tomorrow."

In the dark, Afonso's heart was beating hard.

14

Various things in Vítor's story evidently didn't match up. He said he had escaped, but not only was that extremely difficult from being held incommunicado, but, having escaped, it was not credible that he'd then show up in the city, without any reticence, making dates with a scandalous woman who was friends with legionnaires, and going to the movies where he'd be recognized by all the fascist types in the region. Vítor said he had no money, but Afonso could easily smell the expensive tobacco he was smoking, and sashaying around with that woman, if he wasn't her gigolo, implied some expense. And then there was the unnatural way he talked, and the contrast between his whole satisfied, well-off demeanor and the serious, dangerous situation in which he claimed to have landed. But on top of everything else, the most suspect thing about him, in Afonso's eyes, were the accusations he lobbed against Cesário. Afonso knew the local Party organization well enough to realize that the comrades picked up were known to Marques and Vítor, possibly all of them known to Vítor. There had not been reports of comrades known to Cesário being arrested.

The next afternoon he showed up for the meeting he had arranged with Vítor when they parted. Vítor repeated what he had said the day before, but when Afonso asked him, he provided no further details about his escape. He only said it had occurred during a transfer between prisons. He underscored his need for contact and for money. Afonso told him again he had been expelled from the Party and had no contact at all, and in any case he was not interested in those things now, but out of goodwill and respect for friendship he did bring him a few *escudos* to cover the most urgent necessities. Vítor accepted the money, gazing at his friend ironically. *You are such a jerk*, Afonso read in that look. *You know nothing about life.*

"You need to be careful," said Afonso, whose behavior and words now were entirely guided by his intention to persuade Vítor he was telling the truth. "Watch out they don't nab you again."

"They won't nab me," said Vítor, laughing repulsively and revealing his uneven, damaged teeth.

Afonso left that encounter convinced that Vítor was lying. If so, what was there to conclude except that he was a provocateur? Afonso remembered Vaz's questions and opinions, but the idea that Vítor was a police agent even before the arrests, the idea that he attended committee meetings undercover and participated for so long in Party activity, the idea that he had been the instigator of the disaster, all this required such a sudden effort at adaptation, for someone like Afonso who had worked with him in the Party all that time, that he still balked at accepting it. And if Vítor was a provocateur, who could tell Afonso that it hadn't been at Vítor's orders that they'd been watching his parents' house—he now had no more doubt about that—and had followed him that time he met with Vaz? Such new thoughts, linked to the impact of the arrests, for the first time shaped in Afonso's mind an idea of the gravity of his errors and lapses. He saw himself as so weak and unworthy that the sanction he received now seemed to him too generous.

Talking with Lisete, he told her about the meeting with Vítor and all that had happened with him. At first, Lisete's face reddened visibly and she made no reply. But when Afonso quoted the accusations Vítor made against Cesário, Lisete spoke up indignantly:

"You didn't know this before, but you should know now that I'm also a Party member. I know the comrades that Cesário supervised and I'm in contact with them. Nothing happened to them. Cesário is an honest comrade, he's no Vítor. Time will tell."

Lisete could hardly imagine how soon time would tell.

Lisete's sister went to Lisbon every two weeks to take clean clothes and pick up dirty clothes from the prisoner. They did not allow her to speak with him, and didn't even tell her where he was being held. It was the PIDE headquarters where she went to deliver a package and receive another. A few days after these events, when she arrived at the police building, they handed her the package of dirty clothes, but did not accept her package of clean clothes.

"We have sad news to tell you—" said an agent.

Cesário's wife did not have the courage to go by herself to the address the agent gave her. So the following day, accompanied by Lisete and her mother, she saw her husband once more, in the morgue. Laid out on his back on the cold stone table, he was unrecognizable, his face frighteningly deformed, black and swollen.

"They say he hanged himself," an employee told them. "But the doctors say they killed him."

In the dirty clothes, which somehow escaped inspection by the police, Lisete found a note written on a cigarette paper in a brownish ink, which much later someone said was blood. The note read:

"I've been tortured and I feel sick. Believe me. Help my wife."

When he learned of Cesário's death and way he conducted himself, recalling his long face exuding health and happiness, his brown arms crossed over his chest, his frank and friendly manners, his contented-looking eyes and his smile, Afonso had such a profound reaction that Lisete herself felt obliged to give him a few words of comfort.

Chapter *XVII*

1

When he left António's house, the same night that Ramos left there with Maria, Vaz went looking for Paulo. As decided, he had already given him the contact to José Sagarra. They agreed that Paulo would try to find out from him if anything had happened in the city. Relieved of his most important meetings by Ramos, Vaz would go to arrange for transportation and a safe house and prepare to remove everything from António's house in case his arrest had been confirmed. And then after four days the two of them would meet together with Ramos.

Sagarra had not heard of arrests in the city. By agreement with Paulo, he was to send a comrade there to try and find out anything he could. He later returned with the news that there were definitely a lot of arrests, but couldn't supply any details.

On the assigned date, Paulo went out for his meeting with Vaz and Ramos, set for 10 o'clock in the pine grove the three of them knew well. Having arrived a little ahead of time, ruddy with the heat, he took his jacket off, sat down in the shade and waited.

An intense smell of resin and pine bark hung overall. The cicadas' chirping was so dense it almost made the air vibrate. Paulo looked into the still air as though trying to verify with his eyes what his ears were telling him. At precisely 10 o'clock he stood up and went to the edge of the grove, expecting to see his comrades coming. The road, bathed in sunlight bright enough to hurt his eyes, looked deserted. Accustomed to punctuality, Paulo grew nervous. *They were both arrested* was the first thought that came to mind. He tried to stay calm. *Even the most punctual people could be delayed*, he reflected. *A case of force majeure could happen to anyone*, he repeated to himself. After waiting a quarter of an hour in that spot, he supposed, though for no reason, that maybe the comrades were somewhere else in the grove, and he took a turn through it. Everything was similarly deserted, and the cicadas only heightened the solitude. Paulo returned to his original spot, walked down to the road and under a scalding sun paced a few hundred meters in one direction, another few hundred in the other, and at 10:45 he was back in the pine grove, sitting and anxiously watching the road under the beating sun. He was still there at noon, and still at three in the afternoon. Only then, when he noticed that a peasant had passed by several times looking at him distrustfully, did he decide to leave. Really, he could have left more than four hours earlier, for if Ramos and Vaz hadn't appeared by then, it was because they wouldn't be coming.

From there, having decided to visit Manuel Rato, he took a jitney. He was directed to the Old Factory, that he knew was right in front of the comrade's house, and at nightfall he knocked on the door. The two sisters came to open it, with sewing in their hands, one with her glasses on her forehead, the other with glasses lowered. They looked at him with surprise.

"Who are you?" they asked, not answering whether Manuel Rato lived there or not.

"I'm a fellow countryman of his," Paulo answered. "I'm bearing him news of his wife."

At that moment someone halfway opened a window next to the door, and right away Manuel Rato was standing behind the two owners of the house.

"Come in, come in," he said. "He's a countryman of mine," he confirmed to the sisters.

Reassured, the women stepped aside to let him in, and the two comrades went to Manuel Rato's room. His face drawn, with a deep groove between his eyebrows, Manuel Rato looked at him without inviting him to sit down.

"Do you know already?"

"No, I don't know anything," Paulo responded.

"They killed a comrade," said Manuel Rato. And he related the arrests of Túlio, Pereira, Jerónimo and more than a dozen comrades from Cicol, and mentioned a comrade shot to death right at Pereira's door. "I don't know who that was," he concluded. "Someone who saw him said he was quite a hulk of a man."

It was Ramos, Paulo figured, remembering that Vaz had told him Ramos would go in his place to Pereira's house.

He set another meeting with Manuel Rato and left the area with the intention to find Maria.

Ramos dead, António certainly arrested, Vaz arrested or assassinated, Rosa arrested or in some unknown place. Of the two safe houses in the sector, one had been raided, the other abandoned. The best Local Committee arrested, comrades from the best industrial cell arrested, the city decimated. Paulo imagined he was witnessing the total collapse of the Party, the destruction in less than a week of all the work, the efforts, the sacrifices of numberless comrades over a long period of time. He felt that the unfathomable causative force behind such a disaster was still out there active and threatening; he also felt that force watching him and spying on him from all sides, waiting for him, searching for him. But like that impulsive guy who runs to rescue the victim of a disaster with a high tension wire only to find that he too is caught by it and electrocuted, so Paulo sensed a single thought and only impulse within him: to run in every direction to secure and defend the Party, trying to prevent the disaster from turning into a catastrophe.

2

In the lawyer's office, Paulo told Maria about the latest, most serious events. Maria heard him stolidly.

"Is it certain it was Ramos?" was all she asked, in a hesitant voice that could barely be heard.

"Everything indicates it," Paulo answered.

Maria noticed, to her surprise, that Paulo being generally so sensitive, easily moved by small incidents, showed himself so matter of fact in the face of such terrible news as death, prison and the disappearance of his closest friends. She even picked up a new kind of dry coldness in his words and a new harshness to his expression. Of that Paulo so amiable and attentive toward his friends, and always so tender toward her, the only thing left was the red, freckled hand with short fingers and torn nails that rested on hers.

"You have to help me with two things," Paulo said, as if there were nothing more to be said about all these misfortunes. "First is to go with me to your old house to retrieve whatever's left there. Second is to go to your hometown and try to establish contact with the comrades. Before which, I still have to see if nothing happened there and work out a place to put things. Day after tomorrow is a good time."

They set a date and Paulo rose to his feet, without a word of consolation for António in prison or for Ramos's death. Not a hug, not a loving touch, which Maria in that moment needed so much. Only when he shook her hand as he left, peering at her over the rims of his eyeglasses, did his expression regain his usual compassion for an instant.

"We're going through a very hard time," he said haltingly, in a voice he later brought under control. "All of our efforts and attention need to be focused on defending the Party. All, comrade. We can't take the time to think about ourselves, not even take the time to suffer."

Maria's enormous black long-lashed eyes shone out from her face pale as wax.

"I understand," she said, thinking she wanted to sound firm and resolute.

And in that moment, in a sudden, irrepressible gesture, flying against words and intentions, she desperately embraced her comrade, her head crushed into his shoulder, her hands gripping his arms. Paulo's thick fingers caressed her head through her thick black hair, as with downcast face her tears flowed, heavy and silent.

3

Following Paulo's directions, José Sagarra went to the place where António and Maria had lived. He asked Inácio, of the house with the tile roof overhang, where Senhor Lemos lived, because he had a delivery for him. The man registered no surprise, but told him to ask farther down in the village. He only added that it appeared as if Senhor Lemos and his wife were not there. The grocer later said the same thing. They pointed to the house. Sagarra spoke with another neighbor, who said likewise. He wound up knocking on the door to the empty house, thus confirming that nothing had happened.

Paulo, Sagarra and Maria had agreed to move the things to the Tomé house, and two days later they did so.

All was going smoothly when the landlady appeared with her rude, perturbing manners. As night fell, she entered the house without ceremony and came to the point: She wished to speak with António because it was with him that she had made the contract and they could not go away without paying for three months more and the house had been rented washed and clean and that's how it should be left. Without allowing themselves to be intimidated, and continuing to pack up, Maria and Paulo answered that this business of three months was entirely her invention and that they were leaving her a beautiful cabinet and other objects which would more than compensate the expense she could possibly lay out for the cleaning. But the woman, persistent in her rudeness, insisted on her claim and finally said she'd call her children in to settle the question. If her children came with the same demand, and with the same obstinate arrogance as their mother, it would get extremely complicated, all the more so because even if they wanted to satisfy her claim, the comrades didn't have the money for it. But what disturbed them most was the idea that the woman might call in the authorities, or even that she might already have instructions from the police to do so. At that point José Sagarra lit the oil lamp and handed it to the woman.

"Could you hold this a minute, if you'd be so kind?" he said.

And while the woman, still insisting on her demand, held the oil lamp, the three comrades continued arranging and packing up their things. As darkness fell, the floor and two tables were heaped with useless household stuff, the comrades worked all around her, and the woman couldn't find a way to let go of the lamp. With a sly smile that no one knew he possessed, every now and then José Sagarra said, "Would you be so good as to come over here just for a second... If you please...Thank you...Much obliged...Over here now, be so kind...Thank you so much...So grateful...."

And the woman went on muttering but serving unwillingly in the role of indispensable aide to the three comrades.

After dark, one of the landlady's sons showed up to see what was going on with his mother. He was a tall, slender fellow with a lovely brown face and a curious, ingenuous expression. He didn't look much like his mother. There he stood, silent and reticent in one corner, so as not to be in the way. Then he ran quickly to give Paulo a rope that Paulo was looking for and that he had seen first; and then he ran to help Maria to lift a box too heavy for her alone. And after each of these gestures he quietly returned to his corner. Meanwhile, the mother, the oil lamp in her hand, went on grumbling.

At the end, when all the bags and boxes were ready, José Sagarra wiped the sweat off his forehead and, looking at the boy with his luminously blue eyes, he asked, pointing to his mother with his chin, "Tough to handle, huh?"

The boy smiled and nodded in agreement.

The biggest work began then, given the poor estimate of the total volume of things.

With the books, the remaining printing paper, the metal cylinder of the printing press, the bedclothes and the foodstuffs that Paulo and Maria wanted to leave, but that Sagarra insisted on taking, and all the household items accumulated during the months that António and Maria had lived there, it was a sizable lot. Even leaving behind pottery, the cabinet that António installed and other small things that Sagarra was finally and with difficulty persuaded to abandon, the three comrades left the house so burdened down that they had to rest hundreds of times on the way to the station, where they arrived drenched in sweat and barely able to stand.

Afterward, everything was easy.

At the station at the other end, Tomé was there with an ox-drawn carriage. From that same train on which they continued on to the city, where they would attempt to establish contact, Paulo and Maria could see Sagarra and Tomé in the station's weak oil light, each grasp a grip of a bundle, and carry another package in his other hand, exiting with their burden out the station door.

"It's in good hands," said Paulo.

4

They arrived just before noon at the city limits. Instead of taking the main road into the center, they cut through an isolated sunlit trail and knocked on the door of a little yellow house amongst a row of poor dwellings.

An old woman with brown skin and a black apron opened the door. She looked questioningly at the visitors. Then, in a huge exclamation of surprise, she shouted, "Ay, it's little Mimi! Mimizinha!" Wiping her hands on her apron, she invited her in.

"And Bela?" Maria asked.

The old woman said she would be coming to lunch and they should wait, Maria had a stool and please sit down because surely she was tired, because who knows what had occurred, and she was just going to get a chair for this gentleman, and have a seat and feel at home, and Bela wouldn't be long coming for lunch, and thanks be to God that nothing happened to her, fearful as she had been.

"Ay, Mimizinha," the old woman concluded, "who could have imagined, poor Cesário, such a good man—"

And responding to Maria's questions, she related how they had seized and hanged him for not revealing the names of his companions, and that a very beautiful note came with his clothes written in his own blood, and another whose name she didn't know but he was apparently a carpenter was there too had come close to being hanged too, and that the instigator of all that was some guy Vítor who was arrested just on pretense for a few days so's not to be uncovered, and now he was saying he'd escaped, but only because he wanted to see if he could still do even more damage, and they lay in wait for him one night to teach him a lesson but he managed to get away and run out of the city, and if they had forewarned she would be expecting them—but now she had to add some water to the soup, of course—but clearly many others had been arrested in the city, even a doctor and an officer, and the soup was ready and she had to set the table, and how a commander was arrested along with Cesário at his house and Cesário's wife in all her sorrow got very sick, poor thing, and Lisete whom Mimizinha must remember because she also worked at the Jute, she'd been arrested too but she was only held a few days and that Bela wasn't arrested, but if she had been, and she didn't say this because Bela was her daughter, but she too would be tough—"

"So much sorrow in this world, Mimizinha," the woman concluded, wiping her hands on her black apron. "You know something? It's a pity I'm old and I don't have much strength left. But what pains me more is thinking there are young people who don't even look young."

At that moment voices and laughter were heard coming from the trail, hurried steps, first on the street, then inside the house, and a short woman, a strong brunette, strode into the kitchen. As soon as she saw the visitors, she ran to Maria with loud yelps of joy, kissing her on one cheek, then the other, big, noisy kisses.

"He's a comrade," Maria explained to Bela's inquisitive glance in Paulo's direction.

Shortly after, Bela's nephew appeared, a sensible boy of twelve. As the five of them ate their soup, Maria told them her plans. She needed to talk with Lisete, but didn't want to go to her house because it was in a very central locale and she didn't want to be seen in the city, and because her mother and father were real gossips.

"Does she still work at the Jute?"

Bela said yes, she did, and Maria asked her to bring her to the house in the evening after work.

"You don't mind if we stay here this whole time?"

"Nonsense, Mimizinha!" the old woman replied. "Why would we mind? You and this gentleman can stay here in peace and quiet. If the neighbors ask anything we'll just say they're relatives of Jeremias and that's that. Now don't you go say anything to anyone!" the old woman growled in the direction of her grandson.

"Yeah, I'm an idiot, right?" the boy said, enlarging his voice and shrugging his shoulders.

"One other thing I'd like to ask," Maria said, suddenly blushing. "Remember that fellow who used to wait for me at the Jute?"

"Who? Afonso? Manuel the driver boy?"

"Yes, him. Do you know if he's in the city?"

"He is, yes, he is. Lisete told me," Bela answered with a naughty smile on her round, brown face. "But how come? Still have some feeling for him?"

Maria's cheeks flushed again and she shook her head. "I need to talk with him, but not for what you think."

"Well, it might have been!" Bela excused herself. And she promised to talk with Lisete about it to figure out how best to bring him there.

"But I don't know if it's possible today."

"Manuel the driver's son?" Bela's nephew interrupted, again raising his voice. "I know where he works. If you want, I'll bring him here."

After thinking it over, it was agreed that Bela would bring Lisete and would talk with her about Afonso, and in the meantime Bela's nephew would also try to give Afonso a message, but without telling him who was at the house.

"Now watch you don't let the cat out of the bag," the old woman said. "Let's see if you go on and tell him Mimizinha's here."

"I'm an idiot, right?" the boy repeated, shrugging his shoulders.

Bela got up to return to the factory.

"Listen!" Maria said in a sudden burst of sadness and anxiousness.

Bela turned, looking almost shocked by Maria's tone and expression.

"Have you heard anything about my father?"

"Your father?" The sadness of her friend's face was mirrored on Bela's. "No, I don't know anything," and after a pause she added, "Aren't you going to see him?"

Maria shook her head slowly, her eyes so pleading and unhappy that Bela lowered her gaze away.

5

Afonso showed up before Lisete. Bela's nephew gave him the message, and he asked his uncle, the owner of the shop, to let him off for the afternoon.

"Not even seeing the others burn teaches anything to people like you," the uncle muttered in a bad mood.

The old woman led him into the kitchen. On seeing Maria, Afonso was so shocked that he stood there a few moments not knowing what to say or do. Then he noticed Maria's older, more serious demeanor, her pallor, the loss of that endearing, childlike expressiveness that he had known in her. Maria found Afonso exactly as he had been months before, with that same sad and kindly expression, that same dry ringlet of hair tumbling over his forehead.

"This is the friend who wishes to talk with you," she said right away, as though warding off any thought that Afonso might have of this interview as being the one ha once had requested.

Paulo had told the old woman that he wanted to speak with Afonso privately, so he brought the comrade back to a small interior room and the two of them sat down on the side of a bed.

"You know about the disaster in the city," Paulo began. "But I don't know if you're aware of what's happening in the rest of the sector."

"No, I don't know anything," Afonso mumbled. "You have to know I was—"

"I know. And knowing that you were a Party worker is one of the reasons I sought you out. What's happening can be said in a few words. Ramos was murdered. Vaz, whom you knew also, was either killed or arrested. Another Party worker was also arrested here in the city at Cesário's house. There are yet other arrests. The bottom line is that I'm the only Party worker in this sector and I'm disconnected from the comrades that the others supervised."

Paulo paused, peering at Afonso over his glasses. It was common for those who met Paulo, especially when he looked at them that way, to find him timid and hesitant. Afonso, however, did not see that in this unknown comrade. To the contrary. Despite his soft voice when he spoke, and the overall modesty he projected, he saw in him a tremendous, even commanding energy.

"I know you were expelled from the cadre of Party workers, and I guess by now, after the tragic experiences we've had to go through, you've recognized the seriousness of your mistakes and the correctness of the Party's decision." (Afonso blushed visibly.) "Still, from reports by Ramos and Vaz, I continue to believe you are a sincere comrade, and that's why I wanted to meet you. Comrade Maria also tells me her opinion, that you are a serious friend who can be trusted."

Paulo waited a beat to observe what effect his words would have on the comrade.

"You were the person responsible for distribution throughout the sector, and you had contact with support people controlled by the comrades who were arrested. And it's the contact with those support people that I want you to provide me."

Afonso was happy to do as Paulo asked, and they talked about it in great detail.

After his conversation with Paulo, Afonso returned to the kitchen, looked around indecisively, toward Paulo, toward the old woman and Maria, not knowing if he should leave, or if Maria intended to say anything to him.

"Are you in a rush?" Maria asked

Rush? Afonso thought. *Rush for what, when you're here and the Party's not calling me elsewhere?*

"No," he answered.

"There's one other thing I wanted to say," Maria began. "If I did you any harm, forgive me."

"No." And Afonso blushed again from Maria's words—and that she said them in front of Paulo and the old woman. "There's nothing you have to ask my forgiveness for."

"If I did, forgive me," Maria said again. "It seems we both were mistaken, and today things are clear."

I was mistaken? A brief flash lit up Afonso's eyes. "Yes, they're clear," he responded.

They said goodbye. At the kitchen door, Afonso turned around. "Will you be here for a while?"

Maria looked at Paulo not knowing what to answer.

"Do you want me to find your father and bring you news of him?"

Maria jumped to her feet. "What, dear friend? Would you do that?"

6

Lisete told Paulo that the Jute had not been affected, that she was in contact with Henriques, and that he, for his part, told her that his workshop had not been touched nor had several dispersed comrades. At the Jute, the workers' committee to which Bela belonged continued functioning. As for the committee at Henriques's workplace, she didn't know.

With the arrests of the local leaders and the lack of the Party press, organizational life and the struggles had practically come to a halt. She knew of no meetings being held. The only thing that emerged was a movement to help Cesário's widow, Marques's mother and the families of other comrades. In general, after the arrests and Cesário's death, despite the fact that the number of people was growing who obliquely hinted they were dissatisfied, a notable reluctance to do anything was apparent.

Lisete related all this in her shy fashion, looking toward Maria from time to time as if to ask if she was speaking okay.

Paulo agreed to return in a few days for a meeting together with Lisete and Henriques. The hard part was finding a place to meet.

"It can't be at Henriques's house," Lisete said. "Even when Cesário was alive, I heard him once say that house was too tiny to have friends over."

Bela's mother, who with her daughter had left the kitchen for the little room next to it so as to let them talk freely and not be informed about that which she did not have to know, now entered wiping her hands on the black apron.

"Excuse me, kids, but I have to see if the scissors are here."

With which, she started searching on top of a counter and inside the tableware drawer, with such exaggerated gestures that she plainly meant the others to see. Suddenly, having completely forgotten about the scissors, she turned to the three of them and asked if they weren't comfortable there in the house and how they couldn't be any safer and for her and for Bela it was the greatest pleasure to have them there. Isn't that so, Bela? (she shouted into the next room). How not even Mimizinha knew how happy she'd be to see to her, not to take anything away from Lisete or the gentleman, and the house was always at their disposal for whatever and whenever they needed and oh, she finally remembered she left her scissors in the hutch. The old woman left, it being clear that she and her daughter had heard the whole conversation from the next room.

"It's not out of curiosity nor out of ill will," said Lisete. "The problem is, it's a small house, and we shouldn't have been speaking so loud. It seems to me like we should accept the offer."

They asked Bela and her mother back in, and it was agreed that Paulo could meet there with Henriques and Lisete the next Sunday.

As night fell, Afonso came back with news about Maria's father. The old man was about the same, that is to say, getting worse all the time. Now he was spending most of the day lying down, and the daughter-in-law told him he had started wetting his bed at night. As Afonso was reporting the news, Maria saw her old father before her, with such palpable clarity as though he were right there, tears in his aged eyes, moving his lips without speaking and chewing the white hairs of his mustache. And because she was right there in the city, knowing he was only a few hundred meters away, and she believed she'd probably never see him again, that image of him appeared ever more alive and real.

As Afonso spoke, Maria crouched over, looking at her own hands and distractedly rubbing her fingers together, and silently cried.

"Did you see him?" she asked when Afonso finished.

"Yes, I did, and I asked if he wanted to give you anything. He sent you this."

And he handed her a little glass dove she remembered so well from his house. Pressing it close to her, Maria then broke out in convulsive sobbing. *My little dove* was how her father spoke to her when she was a child.

When Paulo and Maria got ready to leave, Afonso said he wanted to say something more. Bela asked if he wanted the others to go to the next room, but Afonso asked them to stay.

"The words I have to say, I want everyone to hear, and I am only sorry that those who most contributed to their being spoken are not able to hear them." With trembling lips, Afonso stopped for a moment to gather himself. "I want my comrades to know that I acknowledge having made serious mistakes, so serious I don't even know if they're connected to the tragic events of recent weeks. But I also want you to know that you can count on me with everything within my power, everything, absolutely everything, everything, with no limit or exception."

Afonso read surprise in Bela and her mother's expressions, admiring approval from the young boy, confusion in Maria's face, and a certain doubtfulness over such exalted words in Paulo's. Finally, Afonso's gaze found Lisete: straightening out her blond bangs, Lisete was smiling.

7

When he got the news of the disaster, Paulo's first thought was to secure what could be secured, and prevent the disaster from turning into a catastrophe. He saw now this was not only his task. He saw that, despite the severe blows suffered, even if other blows might have hit the organizations from which he had lost contact, the Party was still standing. And not only that. He saw it was not just an obligatory repetition of the well-known concept of the inexhaustible reserves of the proletariat. How well he recalled the carpenter Marques's opinion, that Vaz related, when Maria left the city for underground life. Marques said then that with Maria's departure, the cell and the movement at the Jute would be completely lost. Maria left, and Lisete appeared, proved herself, grew. And if now, for some reason, Lisete had to leave, Paulo saw clearly that the Jute would not be lost, because Bela was there, with her enthusiasm and her brown face saying, no, it won't be lost. That wasn't the only example. Paulo conceived of his job as discovering, beneath the repressive blows, the new cadre in the vanguard of fighters. *They exist*, Paulo thought. *It all depends on us finding them, helping them, and giving them the space to assert and prove themselves.*

Thinking along those lines, he no longer saw the dark horizon that appeared before him in the wake of the first news of the disaster, but instead now he was delighted in discovering new broad possibilities for work. In the place of Cesário and Marques, he now had Henriques and Lisete. In place of Gaspar, Pereira and Jerónimo, he had Manuel Rato and Vicente. Through Sagarra he still could supervise the whole peasant sector. Through Afonso and his old distribution network, Paulo could get to those sectors formerly supervised by António and Vaz. As for those he himself used to supervise, he would space out his meetings with them a little more. Sagarra had already been approved, before the disaster, as a Party worker. Paulo would call upon him as a collaborator in leadership over the whole sector. What they needed now was to install him and Maria the soonest possible in a house, and put a working printer there (Maria had the typewriter from António's house with her), to at least minimally address the lack of printed material—and who could say for how long—owing to the loss of contact with the leadership.

Paulo already could envision the organization reconstituting itself within this simple plan. Now he focused all his attention on devising and firmly deciding for himself the details of his work. He had returned back to his house and was resting on top of his bed pursuing the thread of these thoughts when Rita came in with her bows pinned on and holding hands with her little sister. As if she had something she wanted to ask, she began with an offering.

"Cousin, a *tostão*, take it!" and she handed Paul a coin that she'd found somewhere.

Rita expected to see Paulo get up with his slow, relaxed movements as always, and attend to her. So she was surprised to see him jump up suddenly and slap his forehead with his hand.

The fact is, Rita made him remember an essential problem he had in realizing his plan of work: money! He had on him but a scarce hundred *escudos* or so. Coming from the organizations he supervised, given their poverty, he could not expect significant help. The same could be said of the peasant organizations and those that had just been intensely attacked and had to exert great efforts of solidarity to help the victims of repression. Meanwhile, at the beginning of the month he had to pay Evaristo his rent, he had to give money to Sagarra to sustain him, had to pay for travel, his own, Sagarra's and Afonso's, to do what he had asked him. And to bring his plan to fruition he had the expense of setting up a house, which was no small thing to do, buy a copy machine and ink and paper…. Paulo grasped that the immediate, fundamental problem, without resolving which he couldn't take a single serious step forward, was the problem of money.

"Thank you for the *tostão*," he told the little girl, "everything helps!" And he put the coin in his pocket for good luck.

That night he slept poorly. When he awoke in the morning, he had decided what he had to do.

8

He began with the owner of the very house where he lived. From the conversation overheard at the table, he gathered that business was not going badly. A few weeks back he had even heard that Evaristo had sold premium flour on the pastry shops' black market, using in his fine bread a good amount of second-rate flour instead. Happening to accidentally hear that conversation, Paulo believed it poor judgment for his friend to go down that road, and called his attention to the danger. Evaristo laughed.

"Are you taking pity on the customers for fine bread? Look, it's not the workers who eat it. I can't watch the others moving ahead and me standing still."

His wife vigorously supported her husband's thinking, and Paulo concluded the business must be very profitable. Explaining to Evaristo the current state of the Party, he'd certainly chip in with some decent help.

During lunch he posed exactly that question, but he soon understood they thought it inappropriate.

"If you had spoken up a couple of days ago...," said Evaristo eying his wife. "But now it's a bad time. I'm almost broke, I have to pay my supplier, the customers are not paying, it's hell—"

"And we're poor!" Mariana practically shouted on the verge of anger, suspending the spoon in midair, to the shock of her youngest daughter, with which she was serving the soup.

The three adults were upset, avoiding each other's glances and eating in silence. The children perceived the bad feelings and ate with unusual care and discretion.

"We're almost at the end of the month," Evaristo said at last, again eying his wife as though asking for her opinion. "If you find it hard to pay your monthly rent as usual on the first, and if you fall behind a few days, even a week if need be"—Evaristo looked at his wife—"it's not the end of the world for us—"

"We're poor!" his wife repeated obstinately.

Paulo peered at his comrades above his eyeglasses, and Evaristo looked confused seeing a strange, rare smile on Paulo's lips.

"You have no idea how sorry I am," he added in response to that smile. "Word of honor!"

When Paulo returned to his room, Rita and her sister wanted to follow him. Paulo closed the door and for the first time since he'd been living there, he didn't answer when the children knocked. He was sure that Evaristo was doing quite well, and the couple's attitude, revealing, contrary to his expectation, greed and stinginess, both angered and saddened him. He wished he could leave that house the soonest possible, to avoid the constant intimacy of living with people for whom he felt such a sudden, deep contempt.

Later he calmed down and remembered that it had been several months since they had given him shelter and created the conditions for his work, even though it put their own freedom in jeopardy; and they were risking possible irreparable damage to the little business that was their livelihood; and in the end they were charging him a very favorable rent not even covering expenses; and generally speaking they were in solidarity with him, tolerant and friendly. Paulo recognized it was in that house, in living with that couple and those children, that for the first time since his childhood, he had been afforded a true family life.

We cannot depend on imaginary beings and ideals, Paulo thought. *Of course we have to work to make things better for ourselves and for others. But everyone experiences the influence of the society we live in, and as a result we have, to one degree or another, in one way or another, our flaws, even big flaws. Everyone. We all have them. The best human beings have them. And it's with human beings, after all, that we live, struggle, and succeed.*

9

Paulo remembered two old prison companions of his, both students then, who he knew were living now in substantial comfort. He decided to look for them in L—. According to what they had told him, one received several million *escudos* after the death of his grandfather. With a little good will, without even a minimal adjustment, he could resolve the difficulties. Paulo knew he was removed from and uninterested in any political activity but, trusting in their prison friendship and recollecting the basic spirit of solidarity in his former companion, Paulo was convinced he'd be successful with this attempt.

He found him at home. He was welcomed into a dark, solemn office which in its antique luxuriousness bespoke the comfortable lifestyle of several generations. He hardly recognized his former companion. In place of the skinny, awkward young man dressed in denim and sandals whom he had known in prison, he now had before him a heavyset man of imposing girth and expression, dressed handsomely and expensively.

His old companion also had difficulty recognizing him.

"Ah!" he exclaimed when Paulo refreshed his memory, and without asking him to have a seat, kept on staring at him impatiently.

His manners so arrogantly demonstrated his displeasure with the visit, signaling so clearly that there wasn't nor could there be even a flutter of the old friendship between them, their two lives having separated so widely that there was nothing left in common, that Paulo did not even ask what had brought him there, and to justify his visit limited himself only to asking for news, in which he truly had no interest, about an individual with whom they'd been in prison. The man said he knew nothing, and Paulo left.

He departed that house with such a sad feeling of disappointment that he was tempted not to bother with the other man. *For the most part*, Paulo thought, *the children of the bourgeoisie are like that. When they're young, before they've seized direct control over the means of exploitation, they're sometimes drawn to militant views out of their ideals for social justice. Later, the struggles of their conscience easily make way for the material interests and privileges of their class.* With that in mind, it's only with curiosity that he went to find the other old companion.

He received Paulo in a modern parlor with bright colors and big windows. Similarly changed in physique, he was genuinely surprised and asked Paulo to sit down.

"It's you! You! I never thought—"

"What are you up to?" Paulo asked.

The man cast a glance over the lovely room, a look that said, *What you see is what I'm up to.*

"I'm a medical doctor, I make a living, I'm married, have kids. And you? What's your life like? What do you do?" The doctor's gaze running through Paulo's gray hair and over his modest clothing was glum and caring.

"I haven't changed, except I'm older. What I was is what I am."

The doctor readjusted his position, resting his elbows on the sides of his ample armchair and crossing his long, manicured fingers at his lips. "My life changed," he said after a slight hesitation. "A lot. But inside, I'm still the same as I was."

He paused again and, still with his fingers crossed at his lips, he continued. "My situation is not a comfortable fit for me. On the one hand, I don't have the spirit or the courage to do what I did as a young man. I feel too attached to my wife, to my children, to my profession, to the things I love. On the other hand, I'm suffocating in this protected, egotistical life when my heart is where it always was."

He spoke at length, and posed many questions to Paulo about the Party and the comrades they'd known. Twice the maid came in to summon him, and each time he excused himself for a few moments, returning with evident pleasure in the visit and the conversation. In the end, Paulo said what had brought him there, and the doctor handed him several hundred *escudos*.

"That's all I'm good for," he said as he handed Paulo the money. "But if you can, come by again. I'd like to contribute regularly. That's what I can do."

"And that's something," Paulo agreed.

The two men looked at one another in high esteem. Paulo as much as the doctor felt this was only a beginning.

10

The lawyer in whose house Maria was staying, when Paulo posed the question, handed him a hundred *escudos* and asked, "Is that good?"

"Really good," Paulo said.

And after a long silence, when he had thought more deeply, he added, "Yes, friend, it's good. There are those who give a lot less, though they're capable of much more than you. And of course you have a comrade in your house that represents an additional burden on you and an important assist to the Party. But it's my responsibility to say something more. We're going through an especially difficult time in this sector. Our control was assassinated and we don't have contact with the Party leadership. Of the other two Party workers, one's been arrested and the other either arrested or dead. Of the two safe houses in the sector, one was raided and everything in it's been lost, and from the other they retrieved things, but had to abandon it. Besides myself, there's one comrade who's gone underground and we need to install him in a house where he can live and work and where we can meet. The copier we had was seized and we need a new one. We have to secure contacts with many comrades. We have to keep people on the move and transportation's not cheap. So that just gives you an idea of the situation and the needs."

Paulo paused once again, observing the lawyer above his glasses, as though asking pardon for his words. Perched on the edge of his desk, his face stolid, lined, furrowed and focused, the lawyer drew long draughts on his cigarette.

"Some people say," Paulo went on, "the Party always kills the goose that lays the golden eggs—that when they find a comrade with good intentions, they demand what he can give and what he can't give, and wind up causing him exhaustion, impatience, stepping back, retreat and alienation. Unfortunately we have to recognize this has happened a few times and I hope it doesn't happen now with you."

Having smoked his cigarette halfway down with a half dozen hungry drags, the lawyer slowly crushed it out in the ashtray.

"All right," he said, when Paulo finished. "Wait here a little. I'll talk with my wife."

And after arranging a few papers on his desk and, out of habit, closing the drawers, he added, "I wish you could come to the house, because I know you'd like to see the comrade. But today's a bad day. My sister-in-law is there and she's sharp as a tack and very nosy. If you absolutely needed to speak with your friend, she'd pop in here on some pretext or other. If you could do without it, it would be better."

Paulo agreed with the lawyer, but felt a sadness, that he himself considered exaggerated, about not seeing Maria, having her so nearby.

After three quarters of an hour the lawyer returned.

"I spoke with my companion," he said, smiling and using that word with visible joy that a few months before had seemed almost offensive to him. Beaming, he handed Paulo an envelope. "It's from both of us."

After leaving the lawyer's house, Paulo opened the envelope. The two thousand *escudos* it contained were the highest amount a single comrade had given at any one time up to then in that sector.

11

Manuel Rato now had his wife with him, but he continued to live in the same room in the two sisters' house. As soon as a little house could be found at an affordable price, he would move, and then the Local Committee could meet there. Meanwhile, without a safe house and the means to support it, they met in the countryside.

Paulo met the comrades in a hillside olive grove near the town. From there they could see a factory with a tall chimney, a few houses nestled in the hollow, and part of the massive bullring peeking out from behind a curve in the terrain. Houses, trees, hills, everything in the direction of the silver filament of the river, lengthened with the late afternoon shadows. In the peaceful bright sky flocks of sparrows frolicked in a confusion of chirping. The four comrades' discreet voices seemed to fear disturbing nature.

The Local Committee comprised Manuel Rato, Vicente and Jaime. They reported on the work they'd been doing. Manuel Rato had established contact with cells of comrades formerly connected to Gaspar and Jerónimo and had managed to make contact with those formerly under António's control. Vicente spoke about his factory, where there were important signs of progress: from seven Party members that existed at the time of the strike, they now had almost twenty, of whom five were women. Only Jaime, the heavyset comrade from Cicol, could not give an optimistic overview. He was finding many difficulties. The arrest of Gaspar, who because of his individualist work habits made everything dependent on him personally, and the poor conduct of Túlio with the police, which resulted in the arrest of more than a dozen comrades from the factory, caused a great retraction. Only among the apprentices something different was happening. At the time of the mobilization there was practically no youth organization. Now, thanks to Guilherme's efforts—that young apprentice who, with Jaime, was the only one to walk out on May 18th—an apprentice committee had formed and was now working enthusiastically to create a sports club in the factory. Even in Gaspar's time, Guilherme was a Party member and belonged to the old workers committee. But it was on May 18th and since then that he showed his greater potential.

"This is only an idea," said Jaime, "but it seems to me our work could only gain if we invited that comrade onto the Local Committee."

Shaking his brush of blond hair as though dust had just fallen on his head, Vicente supported the proposal. In his factory too, Party work had developed since the mobilization, above all thanks to the activity of that young woman in the red blouse who stood out so prominently in the strike, the demonstrations, and under arrest. In his opinion it would only be advantageous to have a comrade on the Local Committee solely dedicated to working with youth.

Paulo asked if, before the arrests, there had been any leadership guiding the youth movement in the area, but none of them knew what to answer since none of them belonged to the Local Committee then.

"If there was, it isn't making itself known," said Manuel Rato. "But we can't be held down by ghosts from the past. With Guilherme, with the woman at Vicente's factory, with the seamstress comrade, who has a few others in her circle, and with Renato, the fisherman, whom you know"—he said turning to Paulo—"we could create a leadership committee for all the youth work. Guilherme would work with us."

And thus it was agreed.

The comrades then reported on their efforts to collect funds. Despite having received a serious beating and being burdened with the need to help the families of imprisoned comrades, the organization had responded to the appeal. What impressed the most was not so much the amount obtained (relatively modest) but the alacrity with which the comrades contributed, the high number of donors (more than three hundred), and the overall understanding of the Party's hardships and the need to help overcome them.

Beyond the money handed over as contributions to the Party press, from Manuel Rato, Vicente, Jaime and Guilherme, the woman in the red blouse and several other comrades committed to donate one day's wages. Their names, of course, would not appear in *Avante!* In their place, the slogans they chose would be printed, such as "Long live Lenin!" or "Unity!" Vicente also gave Paulo two objects to be either sold or raffled off in other sectors: a pen and a watch. Paulo didn't know who offered the pen. But the watch, with that same strap of transparent plastic, he had noticed just two weeks earlier on Vicente's wrist when they first met.

12

Paulo spoke to José Sagarra about the need to set himself up immediately. He told him the region where he should look for a house, handed him money, insisted he wear a suit and a pair of António's shoes that he had brought with the other things to Tomé's house—the truth being that Sagarra didn't own either a jacket or shoes—and gave high marks to Maria, with whom Sagarra would be living.

"She's an excellent comrade," Paulo said. "She can help you a lot in everything you do."

Sagarra appeared muddled by the conversation. His eyes lowered and shifting, he held onto the money with awkward hands, and only nodded in the affirmative as a sign of approval.

They then spoke about the peasant organizing, the great work by da Barrosa, a victory with the grain threshing, the comrades' complaints about the lack of printed material; but throughout it all José Sagarra spoke with a worried undercurrent, not hitting on the right position for his arms, and avoiding looking at Paulo straight on. Only after they'd finished dealing with all those things did he look at Paulo directly with his blue eyes and asked, "Is that really so decided?"

"That what?" Paulo asked.

"That part about the house and the friend," Sagarra said.

And before Paulo could respond, he clarified, "It's because I have a girlfriend, you know?"

"What's the problem?"

This response seemed to upset José Sagarra even more, and Paulo, seeing his comrade's confusion, attributing it to the narrow

limitations of his life, to convention, to the absence of experience living in the company of women, felt it necessary to explain to him
how life in a Party house worked, and the fraternal relations possible
between men and women, adding, by way of reinforcement, that the
person with whom he'd be living was also not a free woman.

When he finished his explanation, Paulo was surprised to see José
Sagarra's face light up with a boyish smile, as unexpected as his clear
blue eyes amongst his otherwise troubled facial features.

"That's not the issue, friend," Sagarra said. "The issue is that my
girlfriend is prepared to live with me."

Knowing Sagarra as a bachelor, Paulo was so far removed from
thinking that he could have a woman who would join him in the
underground life that he never even considered such an eventual-
ity. But despite the surprise, this new twist on matters pleased him
exceedingly. The truth was that it actually was hard for him personally to plan and decide on setting up a house with Sagarra and
Maria. More and more impressed with Maria's qualities, he did not
contemplate setting her up with another comrade without a sting
of envy and sadness. After all, why couldn't they set up a house for
himself with Maria? Wasn't it the case that his residence with Evaristo was already getting too prolonged and that for some time now
he recognized he didn't have the best conditions there for his work?
Why did they have to set up houses for the other comrades and not
for him? Wasn't it also true that living with him, Maria could be
more useful and could develop even more?

"All right, friend, all right," said Paulo, happily after talking with
Sagarra about the young woman, a peasant like himself. "It's better
this way. Try to find a house as soon as possible." And saying which,
Paulo envisioned himself looking for a house to live in with Maria.

He finished with the comrade and walked down the road whistling low. Out of tune, of course, because he was out of practice. But
contented, happy, almost impish. If Rita could see him, oh, how
she'd have something to laugh about!

13

Looking at Paulo, no one could imagine the initiative, the activity,
the energy and physical strength which he showed during that time.
Not only did he keep up the old contacts—already enough to keep
him busy—but he picked up and solidified those that originally
belonged to Vaz and António that Afonso, on the one hand, owing to
his old distribution route, and Manuel Rato, on the other, though it's
anyone's guess just how he did it, went out to find and secure. But

Paulo did not restrict himself to maintaining the contacts. He rebuilt the organisms, tried to raise funds, called meetings of activists, handled a variety of issues, trying to imprint on the organization the type of activity from the time of Ramos, Vaz and António. In pursuing all this work he never stopped for an instant, took extensive treks on foot, practically never slept or ate, all the while performing this huge feat with his timorous, low-key affect as usual—and his comrades, to the contrary, stuck to their view of him as a person deliberate in his moves, relaxed and minimally active. They only noticed an appreciable change in the way he spoke, now with greater confidence, more incisively, and sometimes even gruffly. Those who knew him before, although surprised, did not dislike this new attitude, and even smiled gratefully when Paulo dealt with them more bluntly.

Once he was settled in his house, Sagarra handed da Barrosa and other peasants the contacts he had before, so as to pick up others which had been António's province. Soon it became apparent, however, that da Barrosa and the other comrades of the peasant leadership group, having their own jobs to attend to, could move to other areas only every now and again, and so, despite their good intentions, the peasant organization and movement, with Sagarra's removal, weakened visibly. Sagarra picked up a few of his contacts again, but with that Paulo was left considerably overburdened.

There's no other way, Paulo concluded. *To grow the organization in this sector, anything less than three Party workers is too little.* This idea was no great revelation, for the organization, after the breaks in contacts, the hardships and retreats here and there that followed in the wake of the arrests, had fundamentally resumed its previous character. And the places most severely affected, despite the local committees being reconstituted, on one side by Manuel Rato, Vicente and Jaime, and on the other with Henriques, Lisete and Afonso, were conducting even more work than before. Yet Paulo and Sagarra could not possibly do as much as Paulo, Vaz and António did previously, with the help of Ramos and the support of many local cadres now in prison.

Having given much thought to this issue, Paulo met with Manuel Rato to propose that he become a Party worker and set up a house somewhere else in the region. Despite many indications of dedication on Manuel Rato's part, Paulo didn't know how he would embrace such a change in his life. It was one thing for a comrade to become a Party worker when life in the open had become impossible, when he's being followed or is running the risk of arrest, and Paulo knew it was under such circumstances that the greater number of Party workers had been recruited; but it was another thing entirely for a comrade to go cold into the underground with all its privations, sacrifices and dangers.

Manuel Rato heard Paulo out, perfectly composed. "I'd already been thinking about it," he said. "It just didn't seem right for me to propose it myself."

They talked more about what effect it would have on the local organization were Manuel Rato to withdraw. Paulo felt concern, for he couldn't forget how the organization had suffered the recent loss of its whole leadership, comrades with many gifts and much work experience, such as Gaspar, Jerónimo and Pereira, not to mention most of the comrades at the most important factory. Wouldn't Manuel Rato's exit create too many hardships?

"The way I see it, no," Manuel Rato said. "Vicente and Jaime handle their jobs very well. Besides, when the influence of the Party gets to the point the working class in this area has reached, and especially the youth, there's no danger missing some fruits from the tree: For every fruit you harvest, two more are generated."

14

For two and a half months the Central Committee tried unsuccessfully to establish contact with the sector. Ramos didn't appear for his meeting with the comrade from Leadership, nor was he found in the house where he was living. Vaz, who was slated for a meeting with a comrade from the Secretariat to decide on his transfer to another sector, also didn't show up. With extreme caution, a comrade was sent to the region where Vaz was living and once there, learned about the raid on the house and that Vaz and his companion had fled just minutes before. This news only obscured the situation further. Since Vaz had saved himself from the house raid and then failed to appear for meetings with the Leadership, it was concluded that Vaz had been arrested, with Rosa, sometime after leaving the house. The visiting comrade later tried to make contact with a union where it was known that a comrade had been elected president. He learned there that that comrade, Gaspar, had been arrested, that many others from the region had been arrested, and that one comrade from outside had been shot dead. Two weeks after learning this, the Central Committee found out from Ramos's family that it was he who had been the victim, because the police relayed the news to the family to pay for the funeral. Meanwhile, the whole sector continued unconnected; attempts to reach the organization by various routes successively failed.

Paulo being free, and his sector disconnected, it was hoped that Paulo would try to contact the comrades in Lisbon, his longtime friends. The Leadership sought out those comrades, and as Paulo had not contacted them, it concluded that something serious must have happened to Paulo as well. As a last resort, it was decided that Fialho should find Afonso and see what could be learned. That was not so easy, and involved risks, however, because Fialho did not know Afonso's family's house, nor even his full name, and thus he'd be forced to perform tasks and remain for a while in the city, which was dangerous for a comrade with his delicate assignments. For all these reasons, two and a half months had passed since the death of Ramos before Fialho finally succeeded in reaching Afonso.

Afonso introduced Fialho to Lisete, and Lisete, not rushing into anything concerning the contact, agreed that Fialho should return in ten days. Fialho appeared, and Lisete brought him to Bela's house. Shortly after, Paulo arrived. Contact was reestablished.

Fialho limited himself to a quick, very general conversation, for his mission was only to reestablish the contact and set a meeting date.

Paulo told him about António's arrest, Cesário's death, and all the arrests in the sector that the Party Leadership for the most part had not yet heard about. As for Vaz, he corroborated that before the raid he had been able to flee from the house with Rosa. But he missed a meeting with Paulo and never sought him out again, although he knew the house. Paulo figured he had been imprisoned or killed.

The next week, Fialho introduced Paulo to the comrade who had come to lead the sector. Carlos was a man of medium stature, poorly dressed, whose manners and expression were a constant contrast between brusqueness and friendliness.

"Finally, friend," he said, shaking Paulo's hand enthusiastically. "We thought you'd been arrested too. We know now from Fialho about how hard you've been hit. And we know it's been a very difficult time for you. There's only one thing the Central Committee doesn't understand: Why didn't you seek to set up your contact through Lisbon, where you know old comrades and where it would be easy to reestablish it? Seeing you alive—and not under arrest— we don't understand why you didn't do that."

Paulo trembled hearing these words. It's true, he could have and should have done that. The fact is that not even in his dreams did such a simple thing occur to him, which should have occurred to him before anything else. Paulo, who up to that point had felt great personal satisfaction and contentment with his own work throughout those months, now became suddenly conscious that not everything had been positive on his part. All of a sudden he felt a seizure of uncertainty about his other decisions.

"This was a serious mistake of yours," the comrade went on, "which we'll have more to talk about later. But what we're dealing with now is that you keep bearing up the best you can until other comrades can come to help. At that point the sector will be reorganized."

Paulo looked at Carlos above his eyeglasses, and Carlos thought he saw in that look Paulo's embarrassment over the weaknesses in his own work.

"For sure, you did what you could, friend," Carlos said to cheer him up. "No one can produce miracles, and not everyone has the same spirit of initiative. It's already quite something that you've saved yourself in the midst of such a debacle. When the other comrades come, then we'll make up for lost time."

"Are you talking about Party workers?" Paulo asked timidly.

"Yes, Party workers."

"But isn't it you who's coming here to supervise and direct the sector?"

"Yes, I am. But I can't just work with one comrade in the sector. Not just with you. We have to build a whole new leadership body."

Paulo seemed deeply confused by these words. He shuddered once again. Only now did the significance weigh on him of these decisions he made without listening to the Party leadership, particularly when he asked people to go underground and to become Party workers.

"It looks like you're not pleased," said Carlos, surprised by Paulo's reaction.

"No...it's just—" Paulo mumbled.

In the face of the comrade's words he felt at first eaten by doubts about his own work and his own decisions. But as they continued talking, that work, those decisions, the desperate effort he made during those two and a half months, brought greater confidence to his voice, recovering that sober, incisive tone that he had recently gained.

"We still have lots to talk about, comrade," Paulo continued after giving his report on the sector. "Then the Central Committee will decide. But as you see, there's been no debacle. No, we can't speak of debacle and not even of reorganization. Despite the severe beating we got, the organization is not overall weaker than two months ago. In some places there are even some advances to point out. As far as

Party workers go, I want to say that here in the sector a leadership organism is functioning that's made up of Party workers. In three days we're having another meeting, and you can attend it and get an idea."

In Paulo's speech there was no more timidity or indecision. To his own surprise, his words came out clear and commanding.

Chapter *XVIII*

Epilogue

1

It was a little house, corroded by time, dark and isolated, a little set back from a trail on which seldom could be heard the footsteps of people or the heavy, gentle stomp of animals. If anyone had passed by it that misty autumn day, they would have said it was like so many other houses, inhabited by peasants, maybe now abandoned. If someone took a walk through the fields in back, it could be that they'd briefly see a thin, pretty peasant girl with black eyes and a worried-looking face, appear and retrieve a pail of water from the nearby well. But if that someone, that overcast autumn day, were to enter that little house corroded by time, they would certainly be surprised.

Seated on improvised stools around a crude table as dark and rotten as the house, four men were conversing in quiet tones. Each one spoke in turn, simply but with an odd calm. With his short, broad red hands placed motionless on the table, with his gray hair, his eyes peeping from time to time above his eyeglasses, one of them spoke mildly. Supported with all his weight on the table, his face contracted and scorched by sun and wind, his forehead pale and bulging, another interminably sharpened his pencil with a pocket knife. The third, leaning against the wall, his face thin and freckled, looked at the speaker with his eyes of a luminous blue, his gaze constantly moving from the red hands to the gray hair, to one of the arms of the eyeglasses, broken and tied with a colored wire. The fourth kept writing, every once in a while throwing a quick, questioning glance toward the speaker as though to make sure what he was saying.

It was the rented house where Manuel Rato was living, under an assumed name, with his wife. In the meeting were Manuel Rato himself, Sagarra and Paulo, the three constituting the leadership group of the sector. Carlos, the new regional controller, attended.

Seated at the edge of the hearth, her right hand holding her left elbow, and her left hand curled over her mouth, Manuel Rato's wife, without taking her eyes off Paulo, did not waste words. But those shining, passionate black eyes were not seeing what was before them in that moment: They saw Isabel, svelte and adorable, her long, soft white neck, her braids tied in an arch atop the crown of her head, her smile of approval for her comrade's words.

The meeting lasted two days. On balance, given the situation, they saw continuing progress, although many hardships still persisted in the places most affected by the repression. Generally speaking, the organization had grown, and in many places small struggles were taking place over partial demands. The Party press, after a hiatus of months, was circulating again. The Central Committee approved Paulo's activity and the hiring of José Sagarra and Manuel Rato into the ranks of Party workers.

Just as Vaz, António and Paulo had done a year before with Ramos, it was now up to Paulo, Sagarra and Rato, together with Carlos, to parcel out amongst themselves the various organizations and contacts for the most effective guidance and control. Paulo knew almost all of the organizations. He'd stood alongside them at an especially difficult moment. He'd helped to determine their favorable prospects. He was tempted to take control over the most evolved ones. But remembering his own disappointment from a year before, when they distributed the task responsibilities and he was entrusted only with those contacts with the least potential, he proposed an equitable allotment among the three.

At one of the meal breaks, Joana, Manuel Rato's wife, after everyone had eaten their soup, took a piece of salt pork out of the pan, cut it into five small parts, and gave each one a piece with a slice of bread. She did this with visible nervousness, as her thin face suddenly flushed, now and again fidgeting with her hair that insisted on falling over her face. When she gave Paulo his respective portion, she stared at the comrade with such a strange intensity, and Paulo understood that this meal was not prepared haphazardly, and that Joana took pleasure in repeating the same gesture that Paulo had made in that small house in Vale da Égua on a day seemed all too remote because they had lost their beloved daughter.

After the meeting, Carlos and Sagarra left together, and Paulo, sad and ill at ease, remained alone with the couple. To his surprise, like the way he felt when he was given refuge in the little riverside fishing village, Manuel Rato as well as his wife looked truly happy that he was the last to depart. Manuel Rato, much transformed now for having shaved off his mustache, seemed relaxed and rejuvenated. In Joana's thin, anxious face, her black eyes shone with apprehension. Paulo could easily see, from the change in their expressions once Carlos and Sagarra left, by their exchanges of glances and gestures, that they had something to say to him personally, and something nice. In the meantime they both acted indecisively, the wife's black eyes questioning her husband, *So? So?*

"We have some news for you, comrade," Manuel Rato said at last. He paused, and then came to the point: "My wife is pregnant."

A beam of joy lit up her beautifully excited face. The three of them sensed that maybe, in a certain way, this news had come to repair a loss that had seemed irreparable. At that moment they all envisioned Isabel. Not the Isabel who died, but the one who was about to arrive. They all seemed sure that the new child would be a girl and would turn out the equal, the exact equal, of her missing sister.

2

Another surprise, quite an extraordinary one, awaited Paulo at home. Spread out on the bed, but rising upon his entrance, was Vaz! He seemed even thinner than when he had last seen him, but with his closely shaven face, hair combed, sprucely dressed, he didn't show signs of great suffering or fatigue.

"Are you amazed?" Vaz said in his usual calm, serene voice, extending his hand. "You'd have good reason to be."

And in words interrupted by sudden pauses for breath, he related what had happened. When he left Paulo's house nearly three months earlier, with the plan to retrieve António's things from his house, he could hardly remain standing. He managed to get to the home of a sympathizer, where he took refuge with Rosa. But he couldn't leave. Burning with fever, he fell into bed delirious. A doctor was called, who had to treat him for pleurisy accompanied by general exhaustion. For more than a week he was in an almost permanent state of unconsciousness. When he came to, he tried to inform the comrades through Rosa. He even thought of sending Rosa to Paulo's house, but the truth was that although he had gone to that house many times, he'd always taken such circuitous by-ways that he could not explain to anyone else how to get there. Unable to abandon Vaz, it was only two weeks later that Rosa went to the capital to seek contact with comrades she knew. But without success: One had moved, another had vanished. For several weeks, Rosa went back again and again with no result. If Vaz was there with Paulo now, it was the first time he had got out of bed and gone out, against the doctor's express advice. From there he'd go right back and throw himself into bed.

"I escaped the fire," Vaz concluded. "Who knows if I'll escape the ashes?"

Looking at his thin, shaved face, the skin smooth and shiny, Paulo realized that only his very spiffy attire lent him any semblance of good health. Those frequent pauses for breath were hardly a reassuring sign.

In his turn, Paulo spoke of the deaths of Cesário and Ramos, the numerous arrests in the sector and the present situation. Vaz heard all this news with apparent impassibility, but in his emaciated face, the tensing muscles spoke of emotion and effort.

Vaz gave Paulo his address, and it was agreed that he should go there and take Carlos with him, the new regional controller.

In the middle of their talk, two high, meek voices were heard at the door.

Paulo opened it, and Rita and Elsa entered, giving Paulo a kiss. Seeing the other friend, even though they didn't know him, they approached him too to give him a kiss. But Vaz gestured for the children to stand back. And as Paulo registered his surprise, he explained, with a wan smile, pointing to this own chest and tapping on it with his fingertip, "They're small, but they bite."

So Paulo received confirmation of what he suspected. Vaz, that comrade of iron energy, of limitless resistance, that fighter who, as Ramos put it, was not a man but a bull, had tuberculosis.

Paulo seated the two girls at the table, giving them paper and colored pencils to draw with, while the two comrades continued talking. In every word Vaz uttered, in his earnest demeanor, in the fixity of his gaze, he conveyed impatience to take up activity again to whatever new tasks the Party assigned. And Paulo was certain that comrade, with his ravaged health, would go on always and forever with ferocious energy, so long as—not as a literary conceit but in the most literal sense—he had a single breath left in his body.

3

As he headed for the lawyer's town, Paulo couldn't stop thinking about Maria. He truly tried to think about other things, but it didn't work. It made him happy to think that the comrade, after having gone through such difficult sacrifices, was now living for a while in comfort, was sleeping in a good bed, with plenty of good, tasty meals. He knew the lawyer and his wife lavished her with presents:

some beautiful shoes, two almost-new dresses, a purse, a fountain pen. Paulo smiled imagining Maria as the object of such care and attention.

And how was her health? Had she finished reading the books? Had she already typed up the work he had left for her? How would she receive him when he arrived? What expression would her long-lashed eyes reveal? What would her first words to him be?

The jitney bounces down the road, the fields disappear on one side and the other. Paulo really wants to banish all thoughts of Maria but doesn't succeed. Besides, he's finally thinking about setting up a safe house for himself and considers proposing that Maria be the comrade who goes to live with him. He knows she holds him in high regard and that no one more than he thinks so well of her. The solution is already approved.

He was so lost in these ruminations that he didn't even realize he had arrived at his destination: The conductor had to call him and shake him by the arm.

In those few hundred meters between the square and the lawyer's house, Paulo felt an inordinate sense of impatience growing within him. Would there be anything wrong? Would she be in good health? And if she weren't home?

Maria opened the door. With a happy, welcoming expression she brought him into the foyer right away where she usually received him.

"Well, well, dear uncle! I was beginning to think you weren't coming."

Maria soon presented the work she'd typed up, and they conversed as always about the Party situation and activity. But Paulo noticed something off-kilter in her expression—almost imperceptible distractions, quick glances toward the door for no reason, and a certain nervousness in her movements and the way she held her hands.

"Is something going on with the comrades?" he finally asked.

"No, no, nothing," she answered. "Why do you ask that?"

They both went silent and thoughtful. Suddenly, grabbing Paulo's arm and full of emotion, Maria exclaimed, "Take me away from here. Right away, friend. Take me away, take me."

Paulo insisted that Maria say what had happened. Maria insisted that nothing was going on with the comrades, that they continued to treat her attentively and caringly.

In the end, Paulo figured he could guess the reason for Maria's state of mind: it had to be incidents between the lawyer's wife and the maid. Maria's status as friend and guest of the lady of the house certainly made it sadder and more painful to witness the demands, the scolding and the injustices thrown at the young woman in their service. But could that be the cause for such desperation?

"Is it something to do with the comrades?" he repeated once again. Maria did not answer.

"Take me away, dear uncle," she persisted. "Take me with you. Soon, right away. Ask the Party if I can stay with you."

Paulo left the house worried and intrigued. There was some reason, but what? His questions soon gave way to his feelings. He felt moved by the regard Maria had for him, and even more by the tenderness and esteem he felt for her. Something big, something new in his life, profoundly reassuring, took hold of him and gave him pleasure.

When he arrived home, as it was dinner time, he went to his room with his slightly tripping gait to set down his briefcase and wash his hands. On the wall, above the sink, a little mirror hung. Unlike himself, Paulo took hold of the mirror and closely, slowly examined his own face. Then, lowering his head gently, his eyeglasses down, and still looking in the mirror, he ran his thick fingers through his white locks. He found himself ugly, wrinkled and old. *Fool!* he muttered. *Infatuated is what you are.*

When he met with Carlos a few days later, he spoke of the need to extricate Maria from the lawyer's house, and added, "One thing I'd like to ask of the Leadership. They're trying to set up a house for me. I want to ask that I not be set up with Comrade Maria."

4

On a bench in the station, next to a plump, cheerful and perky woman with delicate features, Maria sits with a suitcase, a basket and a bundle at her feet. Maria knows that they will make the trip together, but knows nothing yet about her future assignment. It takes a lot out of her to separate from Paulo. She feels she's leaving behind, in that region, an important part of her life—her family, her joining the Party, her first underground house, António, Ramos—and a generalized sense of discomfort and despondency comes over her. She was happy it was to be a woman, and not a man, with whom she would be connected and living. But then?

"I won't be seeing you after this?" she asked uncertainly.

Prevented from answering by the deafening noise of a baggage cart which passed in front of them at that moment, the comrade looked at her with a smile as her face wrinkled, and put her hands over her ears.

"You're going to be working with me," she answered when the cart stopped.

Maria said something, with a happy, childlike expression, but the comrade didn't understand what she said because just then the cart starting moving again.

Passengers gathered along the platform. A dog with a curled tail was diligently sniffing walls, benches and pieces of hand luggage. From somewhere came the potent odor of fried fish. An old man called out to someone standing by the door, but wasn't heard, and decided not to lose sight of his luggage to go greet him. Two peasant boys pointed to something on the other side of the tracks. A child was crying. The passengers grew in numbers, some quiet and solemn, others excited and observant, some sad and alone, others in noisy groupings, all of them with that mysterious air that waiting for a train in a provincial railway station conveys.

From the comrade's answer, Maria was inclined to believe that she would be going to live with her and help her in the house with her Party work. This thought pleased her to the same extent that it unsettled her to think she'd be living as a support cadre in a new Party house with an unknown male comrade.

"That's so nice that I'll be living with you," Maria said quietly, holding onto the other woman's arm. "You'll see I'll be a great help to you."

The woman smiled again at Maria, who read in that face the kind of comprehensive, caring respect that could only come from someone with a long life experience.

"No, you won't be living with me," the comrade said. "Your new assignment is not in a Party house. You are going to work with me organizing women in the textile industry."

Maria raised her hand to her face.

"Do you like that?" the comrade asked.

How could she ask such a thing? Maria thought.

5

José Sagarra had left the house three days before. In those three days he had trekked across many leagues, eaten little and slept but a few hours. His desiccated face showed no sign of fatigue, however. Only determination. This was the second round he made through the sector he had been assigned. Things were not going badly.

He had met with the always nervous and lively Alfredo, da Barrosa, and the peasant with the sweet high voice whose face disappeared under his big, wide hat. The three now constituted a new Regional Committee that oversaw the peasant organizations in the sector.

Dealing with da Barrosa was still not easy for anyone who didn't already know him. That was not the case with Sagarra. To everything that Sagarra said to him, he invariably answered, "Leave it to me."

Sagarra knew him well, however, and was not content to leave things at that. On every matter, he repeated, underlined, repeated again, and made da Barrosa repeat it back. By the time he left him, he knew he could trust him.

He also met with leaders at the lumber factory, where the Party had grown since the May mobilization. The factory stood in an isolated place. People came to work there from more than a league all around, and thus it was possible, with the comrades, to reach numerous villages.

"We have to be sharp if we want any results," said the comrade with a limp, adjusting his crutch and looking out over one and all, seeking agreement. "If every comrade who was born and raised here can't recruit one other comrade, then what kind of a Communist is he?"

Sagarra left that meeting with the expectation that in short order a broad Party organization would come to fruition.

He also convened that famous Local Committee, whose meetings were sabotaged for a long time by the person responsible, the cobbler. Now the organism was newly reconstituted and, with the imminent opening of a new tannery, new potential for Party work was opening up. The comrade who stood out most for his initiative and dedication was that skinny blacksmith with the drooping lips and the rough tone of voice with whom Paulo had spoken. After the Local Committee meeting, he asked for some time alone with Sagarra. He had obviously just washed his face, but the residue of coal dust remained in his hair, his ears, and in the deepest grooves on his face. Tired eyes edged by that same coal black looked straight at José Sagarra:

"Tell the comrades," the blacksmith said in his bass voice that somehow matched his slender figure, "that my workshop is available for whatever is needed. I'm just a simple artisan, but for whatever you need I'll find a way to do it."

Sagarra spent time over those three days with various other cells and comrades. Everywhere he saw sunny horizons. Even where the comrades indicated little initiative, he was sure of being able to move things forward. Where there are few, expect there will be more. *From small seeds great trees grow*, he thought confidently.

José Sagarra was now on the last lap of meetings for this tour of the sector. Then he could return home, to the underground house where he lives, and where his companion is waiting for him, that modest peasant girl, illiterate and a person of few words, who had left everything to follow the hard, dangerous life of professional revolutionaries.

José Cavalinho was already waiting for him next to the work shed. With his railway worker's cap brashly pulled to the back of his head, and patting down his white mustache, he looked at Sagarra with his keen eyes shining under his thick gray eyebrows.

"The men are here already!" he said with no formal greeting.

And yanking his cap even farther back on his neck with a decidedly challenging gesture, he went to the door of the shed, looked inside and snapped his fingers to summon someone. Appearing right away were a short, dark young man and a tall, extremely thin peasant with a sparse, blond beard and vacant, uncommunicative eyes. According to José Cavalinho, the young man was a fast worker, and the other, as Manuel Rato had confirmed, had played an outstandingly courageous role in the struggle of the smallholders in the pine forest. The young man spoke of the talks he had had in several villages in the area, the formation of groups of sympathizers, and the potential for organizing the struggle. As he spoke, his velvet black eyes exuded intense joy. José Cavalinho looked upon him with an approving, protective air, nodding his head, and with each sentence the young man completed, darted a quick, observant glance toward Sagarra to measure the effect. *How about this fellow?* he seemed to ask. With his enormous arms hanging down the length of his body, the blond peasant responded nervously and indecisively to Sagarra's questions. Sagarra offered to go to Aldeia do Mato to meet with the comrades. To that proposal the blond peasant answered with these unexpected words: "Five aren't enough."

Evidently the guy had not heard anything Sagarra said, not responding to the offer, but following the thread of his own thoughts and expressing something that had been on his mind since they first met.

Sagarra did not immediately understand what the man intended to say, but José Cavalinho certainly did, because he turned his happy youthful eyes toward Sagarra as if to say, *See, didn't I tell you he was a great comrade?* In fact, the five newspapers he had asked for two weeks earlier were no longer sufficient, because in the meantime the peasant with the blond beard had recruited several more readers.

In the end, they agreed that Sagarra would go to Aldeia do Mato in a week's time, he set up another meeting with the young man, and at last Sagarra was alone with José Cavalinho. *So, what do you think? I told you these were great comrades, didn't I?* the railwayman's eyes continued to ask from under the dense gray eyebrows.

"How are things going here?" Sagarra asked.

"Here?" Cavalinho repeated, and coughed a dry, intentional cough. "Here, excellent things are happening, friend. Excellent!" And he initiated a long pause while he watched his comrade, enjoying his eagerness to hear the good news he was going to give him.

Truly, the news was good. At that location, where a year before, the only Party member was José Cavalinho himself—and Manuel Rato was reluctant to give him as a contact even when Vaz insisted on it—now there existed a considerable nucleus of members, three of them fellow railway workers. *How about that, huh?* José Cavalinho's eyes kept asking as he went on talking.

The train would be coming soon. The two men walked the length of the line between the work shed and the station. At their farewell, with his hand already gripping his comrade's, looking kindly at José Sagarra's freckled, chiseled face and his bright blue eyes, José Cavalinho asked, "Are you still working with Manuel Rato?"

"I am," José Sagarra answered, their hands still joined together, and since the railwayman didn't say any more, he added, "Do you have something for him?"

"No, nothing—" José Cavalinho said, letting their hands drop.

Once again his youthful eyes shone slyly behind his gray eyebrows. *You'll never know what I wanted to say to Manuel Rato*, those eyes spoke. *You'll never know. And I won't tell you.*

The cheerful train whistle blew. Sagarra hurried to buy a ticket and José Cavalinho walked onto the platform. The train arrived, Sagarra boarded, and José Cavalinho followed him by sight until he disappeared. He kept staring at the carriage that Sagarra had entered, coughing from time to time as he lightly nodded his head in appreciation for some idea that occurred to him.

About the Author

Manuel Tiago

MANUEL TIAGO was the pen name of Álvaro Cunhal. Edições Avante! in Lisbon published nine titles by Manuel Tiago, all of which now, with the issuance of the present novel, have been released by International Publishers. The separate novella *Lutas e vidas* (Struggle and Life) was published together with *The 3rd Floor*, making eight titles in English.

This book, *Até amanhã, camaradas*, was adapted as a Portuguese television series in 2005, and *Cinco dias, cinco noites* (*Five Days, Five Nights*) was adapted to film in 1996.

Álvaro Cunhal was born in Coimbra, Portugal, on November 9, 1913. He joined the Portuguese Communist Party (Partido Comunista Português, PCP) in 1931. He began his revolutionary activity as a student at the law school (Faculdade de Direito) of Lisbon. He participated in the student movement and was elected in 1934 as the student representative to the University Senate. He was a militant in the Federation of Portuguese Communist Youth (Federação da Juventude Comunista Portuguesa), and was elected its secretary-general in 1935. In that year he went underground and participated in Moscow in the Sixth International Communist Youth Congress.

Arrested in 1937 and 1940, and subjected to torture, he returned to political struggle as soon as he was freed after several months in prison. He participated in the reorganization of the PCP in the early 1940s. Again living clandestinely, he was a member of the party Secretariat from 1942 to 1949.

Arrested anew in 1949 and brought before a fascist court, he delivered a ringing denunciation of the fascist dictatorship and a defense of his party's program. Judged guilty, he remained for 11 years in fascist prisons, almost eight of them in complete isolation. On January 3, 1960, he escaped from the prison fortress at Peniche together with a group of brave Communist militants. Once again called to the Secretariat of the Central Committee, he was elected Secretary General of the PCP in 1961.

Living abroad, in Moscow and Paris, from that time forward he participated in numerous congresses and gatherings with Communist parties and other revolutionary forces in international conferences. He played a critical role in organizing worldwide support, especially within the socialist countries, for the independence movements in the far-flung Portuguese colonies in Africa.

After the downfall of the fascist dictatorship on April 25, 1974, he served as Minister without Portfolio in the first four provisional governments, and was elected as a deputy to the Constituent Assembly in 1975 and to the Assembly for the Republic in 1975, 1979, 1980, 1983, 1985 and 1987. He was a member of the Council of State from 1982 to 1992.

In accordance with the decisions made at the 14th Congress of the PCP in 1992 concerning renewal and a new structure of leadership, he stepped down as Secretary General of the PCP and was elected by the Central Committee as President of the National Council of the party.

In December 1996, the 15th Congress of the PCP eliminated the National Council of the party and its presidency. Cunhal was re-elected as a member of the Central Committee.

He was reelected to the Central Committee at the 16th and 17th party congresses in December 2000 and November 2004 respectively.

Under his own name Cunhal published several books about politics. He was a gifted artist as well: A book of his collected drawings has appeared. In addition, he published an original translation of Shakespeare's *King Lear*.

He died at the age of 91 on June 13, 2005. His funeral in Lisbon was attended by half a million people. He had one daughter, Ana Cunhal. The Portuguese government issued a postage stamp in his memory and later, in 2021, another set of stamps commemorating the centennial of the PCP to which he had devoted his life.

About the Translator

Eric A. Gordon, a Los Angeles resident since 1990, is a native of New Haven, Connecticut. His undergraduate degree is from Yale University, where he majored in Latin American Studies. He studied Spanish five years and Portuguese two years. He also took a summer residency in Portuguese at New York University. He went on to Tulane University, where he continued studying Portuguese and wrote a master's thesis on the opera in Rio de Janeiro in the 19th century, using original sources uncovered in the Arquivo Nacional. He earned a doctorate in history, also from Tulane, with a dissertation about the anarchist movement in Brazil in the pre-World War I era. He also studied Portuguese language and culture under a Gulbenkian Foundation fellowship in Lisbon.

International Publishers initiated its Manuel Tiago series in 2020 with Gordon's translation of *Five Days, Five Nights*. With publication of *Until Tomorrow, Comrades*, the eight-book series (nine works in Portuguese) is now complete, all of them for the first time in English.

Gordon is the author of *Mark the Music: The Life and Work of Marc Blitzstein*, and co-author of *Ballad of an American: The Autobiography of Earl Robinson* (available from International Publishers). A memoir in short story form that he translated from Portuguese, *Waving to the Train and Other Stories*, by Hadasa Cytrynowicz, appeared in 2013 from Blue Thread Press. In 2015 he executive produced the compact disk *City of the Future: Yiddish Songs from the Former Soviet Union*, a collection of songs composed in 1931 by Samuel Polonski to the lyrics of major Soviet Yiddish poets. He is the author of a currently unpublished political autobiography.

From 1995 to 2010, Gordon was the Southern California District Director of the Workers Circle/Arbeter Ring. He previously worked at Social and Public Art Resource Center, helping to produce murals all around the city of Los Angeles, which gave him the experience to commission a mural at the Workers Circle building. He was Southern California Chapter Chair of the National Writers Union for two terms. He has written for dozens of local, national, and international publications, mostly about art, music, culture, and politics. From

2014 onward, he has been a staff writer and editor for *People's World* online newspaper.

From 2006-09 Gordon took coursework toward certification as a Secular Jewish Leader, referred to in Yiddish as a *vegvayzer*. Upon graduation, he became a legal officiant certified to conduct weddings and other ceremonial functions, a role equivalent in law to a minister, priest, or rabbi. He has a similar endorsement as a Humanist celebrant for people of any background. For five years he served as a Deputy Commissioner of Civil Marriage for the County of Los Angeles, where he conducted 1500 marriages.

Eric Gordon can be contacted at ericarthurgo@gmail.com.

Questions to Ponder and Discuss

At the beginning of Chapter XVI, part 9, did you happen to spot the author's mention of "five days and five nights?" That is the title of another book (minus the word "and"), a novella that the author wrote also in prison at the same time he was writing this novel. These two books, completed in the 1950s during the fascist years, were the first two published after the April 1974 Revolution. *Five Days, Five Nights* was the first of the Manuel Tiago series issued by International Publishers in 2020.

You probably noticed that the words providing the title to this novel occur in Chapter XV, part 10, when Ramos says he'll see the almost forgotten couple of elderly comrades the next day. They are such minor figures, Tiago doesn't even give them names. We know what becomes of Ramos, and that couple are never mentioned again. Why did the author choose that particular scene in which to introduce his title phrase?

António announced at a small Party meeting that he and Maria were now a couple. Yet she seemed to avoid him, staying up late studying and denying him the physical company he desired. There's a moving scene of her being comforted in her distress by Paulo. And after she left their house with Ramos, when António failed to return, she almost begged Ramos to get up off the floor and share the pension bed with her. Her central relationship with António is explored in many facets, including her studying and writing at the kitchen table. What was she reading? What was she writing? What do you make of their relationship?

Did you anticipate the cause of Rosa's disturbing bouts of depressive rumination about her past? Why did she reveal it finally at the time she did?

Remember this lighthearted but significant exchange in Chapter X, part 6? "Ramos is going to write a book on fish and the class struggle," António remarked with a smile. "I could do it, old man," Ramos responded. "The existence of class struggle shows itself in everything, even in the most trivial things. Even in the way a mackerel is eaten." Do you agree with this? Everything can be analyzed in terms of class struggle?

The author clearly intends the collective work of the comrades to be the collective protagonists of the novel, not any one individual. But if there were one, in your mind, who would that be?

Did you perhaps think of Paulo, of whom so little was expected, yet who accomplished so much? And if your sympathies were with him, how did you feel when he came under such sharp criticism by the new regional controller? Did the author set him up for a big fall? Did you as a reader earlier entertain that same question about his work?

Were there any characters who appeared in your mind to be without any flaws?

Certain individuals experienced great transformation, such as Paulo, Afonso, the lawyer and his wife, and others. What caused them to change?

Marques was always speaking up in defense of Vítor. Knowing what we know, how do you account for this? How would you describe Marques's character?

Were there characters in the novel whose fate was not resolved by the end and of whom you would have wanted to know more?

We know that the events depicted in this novel took place in the early 1940s, as the Second World War was going on. There is passing reference to the shortage of food because Portugal is sending much of its produce to Nazi Germany. But other references to the specific period are virtually absent. Would you have wanted more to set the time frame more clearly, or do you believe this was intentional on the author's part, as if to say, This story could have taken place at almost any time anywhere?

José Cavalinho seems, when we first meet him, to be an idiosyncratic and unreliable character, but someone who the author leads us to believe will become useful and important, especially as he is within Paulo's circuit of contacts. He largely disappears from most of the story, but in the end were your expectations of him met?

Reading this novel 60-plus years after it was written, and half a century after its first publication, you have to be struck by the obvious sexism and gender inequality. Yet there is also pushback by certain women, and supportive action by men who are conscious enough to want better for them. Though everyone is living at the same time under the same influences, what accounts for the ways different women and men respond to them?

In a couple of his other books, the author has his characters discuss facing future challenges with "certainty" or "confidence." That discussion does not not appear here, but it is relevant. With what attitude should activists do their work—with certainty they will win? Or, certainty never guaranteed, with confidence? What's the difference, and how does that difference affect the work?

The author spins a vast story with the most fully developed characters in all his fictional work. Yet he is also trying to teach the reader some lessons. The novel does have its didactic function. What lessons did you learn from it?

This novel has become the single greatest piece of writing about the fascist period in Portugal. Many Portuguese readers know this book and its characters well. It's a kind of "Genesis" story of the country's long struggle for democracy—that you are now able to read in English. What books have a similar place for you in your understanding of your country's history?